*Keep* 

Larissa  the voice wa  simply existed inside her head. She quickly discovered it didn't matter. She was helpless to disobey, and stranger still, she had no desire to. Together, zombie master and dancer whirled across the empty floor. To Larissa, it seemed as though her feet barely brushed the ground. She began to lose track of where she was, who she was dancing with, even her own identity, and yielded utterly to the sense of power building within her.

It was then that Larissa realized just how cold she was. She still moved swiftly and surely within the iron circle of Misroi's arms, but she could no longer sense her limbs. A slight wisp of fear penetrated her haze of power, and she opened her eyes.

Larissa shrieked, almost stumbling. The hand clasped in Misroi's merciless grip—her hand—was little more than gray, skin-covered bone.

She was turning into a zombie.

Ravenloft is a netherworld of evil, a place of darkness that can be reached from any world—escape is a different matter entirely. The unlucky who stumble into the Dark Domain find themselves trapped in lands filled with vampires, werebeasts, zombies, and worse.

Each novel in the series is a complete story in itself, revealing the chilling tales of the beleaguered heroes and powerful evil lords who populate the Dark domain.

BOOKS

**Vampire of the Mists**
Christie Golden

**Knight of the Black Rose**
James Lowder

**Dance of the Dead**
Christie Golden

**Heart of Midnight**
J. Robert King
*Available in December 1992*

BOOKS

# Dance of the Dead

## Christie Golden

# DANCE OF THE DEAD

Copyright ©1992 TSR, Inc.
All Rights Reserved.

All characters in this book are fictitious. Any resemblance to actual persons, living or dead, is purely coincidental.

This book is protected under the copyright laws of the United States of America. Any reproduction or other unauthorized use of the material or artwork herein is prohibited without the express written permission of TSR, Inc.

Random House and its affiliate companies have worldwide distribution rights in the book trade for English language products of TSR, Inc.

Distributed to the book and hobby trade in the United Kingdom by TSR Ltd.

Distributed to the toy and hobby trade by regional distributors.

Cover art by Clyde Caldwell

RAVENLOFT and the TSR logo are trademarks owned by TSR, Inc.

First Printing: July 1992
Printed in the United States of America
Library of Congress Catalog Card Number: 91-66499

9 8 7 6 5 4 3 2 1

ISBN: 1-56076-352-3

TSR, Inc.
P.O. Box 756
Lake Geneva, WI 53147
U.S.A.

TSR, Ltd.
120 Church End, Cherry Hinton
Cambridge CB1 3LB
United Kingdom

This book is dedicated to my friend Karen Everson, who has always been there for me when I needed her most.

There are many people I wish to thank. First, I extend heartfelt gratitude to Marc Bailey for all his efforts. *Merci, mon ami*.

Thanks to my editor, Jim Lowder, for once again coaxing a better book out of me, and to TSR, for the ultimate compliment.

Finally, I would like to thank the Delta Queen Steamboat Co. for their invaluable help. My *La Demoiselle du Musarde* would still be a shadow but for my experience aboard their *Delta Queen*.

# ONE

"Liza's brilliant tonight, isn't she?" Sardan whispered to Larissa as he watched the star of the show perform.

The white-haired young woman glanced up at Sardan with a happy smile and nodded enthusiastically.

Liza Penelope, the star of *The Pirate's Pleasure*, was alone on the stage of the showboat *La Demoiselle du Musarde*, in the midst of a set created by a mage skilled in illusion. Liza's bare feet were dug into white sand, and swaying palm trees arched over her. There was even the distant lullaby of the waves to be heard, if one cared to ignore Liza's soaring voice. Such attention to detail—and Liza's vocal skill—had made *La Demoiselle* extremely popular with the port cities it visited.

The beautiful soprano flung back her head and sang with full-throated enthusiasm. Her red hair flamed in the glow of an illusionary tropical sun. To Larissa, every note seemed to be even more pure, more powerful than usual.

The young dancer and Sardan, the male lead, were watching Liza from behind the curtains. Larissa's part in the play was finished, but she lingered to listen to this last duet. Handsome Sardan adjusted his costume, brushed distractedly at his blond hair one last time, then strode onstage, arms outstretched to Liza.

*"Nay, fear not, beloved Rose,
Thy love's returned to thee,
By forgiving hand and broken heart
Of the Lady of the Sea."*

"Rose" turned, joy flooding her face as she ran to her beloved "Florian." Their voices, soprano and tenor, twined together.

They kissed passionately, and the audience whooped and applauded its approval. Larissa grinned in the darkness, safely hidden from view by a curtain that appeared to be a palm tree. Here was acting indeed, she thought wryly. She herself was fond of the rakish tenor, but it was well-known that Liza couldn't stand Sardan. As a result, Sardan made it a point to turn every onstage kiss into a passionate one, taking a devilish glee in the fact that Liza had to pretend to enjoy it. Hightempered Liza was always furious afterward.

The stage went dark, and the audience saw the tropical stars appear in the night sky. Then, suddenly, the illusion vanished, and all that could be seen was a bare hull and the smiling performers of *The Pirate's Pleasure*. As Larissa, who portrayed the evil Lady of the Sea, took her bow, her bright blue eyes scanned the audience. She found who she was looking for—Raoul Dumont, captain of *La Demoiselle du Musarde*. He smiled and nodded slightly.

Raoul Dumont was a big man, six foot three and solid with muscle. If his blond hair was starting to gray at the temples and the lines on his sunburned face had deepened over the last forty-three years, he had lost none of his strength and quickness. Many captains grew fat and lazy once they no longer had to do physical labor, content with commanding in name only. Not Dumont.

He was big in more than merely a physical sense. The well-formed frame and booming voice were matched by a domineering personality. With the players—

especially his twenty-year-old ward, Larissa—and with customers, he was smooth and pleasant, and his forcefulness came across as assured competence. The crewmen knew better. Seldom did the captain of *La Demoiselle du Musarde* have to resort to physical violence, however. The flash of his sea-green eyes, the tightening of his sensual mouth, the clenching of the powerful, callused hands—these were warning signals enough for most.

"Uncle Raoul" had reared Larissa since she was twelve and had given her the role of the Lady of the Sea. The young dancer was always anxious to please him with her performance. Larissa was certain that the demanding captain was satisfied with the way things had gone tonight. Still, she tugged on Sardan's sleeve as he passed and whispered, "You think he liked it?"

The tenor looked down at her for a few seconds before replying. Larissa was a true beauty, even more so than Liza; unlike the singer, the young dancer didn't quite realize her gift. Her blue eyes gazed up at him with trust, and her long white hair, braided with seashells, tumbled down her back. She was in excellent shape from years of dancing, and her body curved invitingly under the clinging garb of the Lady of the Sea. A smile tugged at a corner of Sardan's mouth. "As long as you dance, the captain will like the show."

\* \* \* \* \*

A few hours later, Larissa sat at Dumont's side, a guest of the local baron. The revealing costume she wore as the Lady of the Sea had been replaced by a chaste, high-necked dress. The cream hue of the yards of rustling fabric set off Larissa's clear skin to rosy perfection and reinforced the whiteness of her long, thick hair. She had taken the stage name "Snowmane" because of her oddly hued tresses, which were now braided neatly about her head. A cameo was fastened at her throat.

Their port for the next few months was a friendly one, Nevuchar Springs in the land of Darkon. Populated largely by elves, the small port town was as eager for entertainment as other places *La Demoiselle* had sailed and even more gracious in expressing their thanks. Baron Tahlyn Redtree himself had come to the performance tonight. The baron had insisted that the cast and Dumont join him for a late supper at his home.

Larissa, raised on the roughness of the boat, sat fidgeting with her napkin while others carried the conversation. She desperately wished her friend Casilda were here; then she might not feel so out of place.

The hall in which they were dining tonight managed to be both warm and impressive. The mahogany table, draped with the finest linen tablecloth, seated twenty. Carved wooden panels inserted into the marble walls depicted scenes from a nobleman's life—hunting, hawking, and jousting. The fireplace was so huge that Larissa thought she could stand upright in it, and its red glow both illuminated and warmed the large room. Two delicate crystal chandeliers, crowded with candles, provided even more light. The result was that a largely somber-colored room was bright and cheerful.

Baron Tahlyn rose. His long, purple-and sapphire-hued robes swayed slightly with the graceful movement. The light from the chandeliers glinted off his belt and a pendant of silver and crystal. With a gesture that was almost boyish despite his many decades, the elf brushed a wayward lock of black hair out of startlingly violet eyes. Tahlyn's angular face eased into a smile as he lifted his jeweled goblet.

"I should like to propose a toast," the baron began. "To *La Demoiselle*, a great and gallant vessel. To her captain, Raoul Dumont, whose foresight gave birth to the boat's magic and marvels. To my brother elf, Gelaar, whose illusions charm audiences night after night. To the showboat's wonderful cast, which has brought such happiness to my people.

"And finally, if she will permit me—" here Tahlyn turned the power of his deep purple gaze upon a pleased Liza "—to Miss Liza Penelope. My dear, in this bouquet of talent, you are, in truth, the rose." He inclined his head slightly, never breaking eye contact with the soprano, and drank from the golden cup.

Choruses of approval filled the room as the flattered guests drained their own goblets. Larissa hid her smile as she watched her fellow performers' reactions to the toast. Sardan glowered, but drank. Dumont raised one golden eyebrow, but otherwise revealed nothing of what he was thinking. The elven illusionist, Gelaar, seemed flustered by the compliment.

Larissa regarded the illusionist sympathetically for a moment. If *La Demoiselle* was Dumont's creation, from the specially designed paddlewheel to the magical wards the wizard captain had placed on the boat, then the show she was host to belonged to Gelaar. The small elf was directly responsible for the success of *The Pirate's Pleasure*. He conjured the sets, lighting effects, and "monsters" that appeared onstage.

All this, despite the tragedy he had suffered a year ago. Gelaar's daughter, a lovely, sunny-haired girl named Aradnia, had run off with a roguish sell-sword one night. Gelaar had never quite recovered. Now the dark-haired, pale-skinned elf seldom smiled, but his quiet dignity and thinly concealed sorrow engendered immediate, if somber, respect from all who came in contact with him.

Liza, on the other hand, looked like a lioness in the sunlight, a queen at last being paid proper homage. Yet the flame-tressed soprano was gracious in her acceptance, smiling enough to encourage, but not more than was necessary. Larissa couldn't wait to get back to *La*

*Demoiselle* and tell Casilda all about it.

A few moments later, Sardan, who was seated on Larissa's left, leaned over and whispered, "We may have a new patron."

Larissa's delicate white eyebrows drew together in a frown. "What do you mean?" she hissed back.

"Look at those two," the singer continued quietly, inclining his head in the direction of Liza and the baron. "A certain redhead I know is probably going to start wearing some expensive jewelry in the next day or so."

Larissa rolled her eyes. "Sardan, not *everybody* has ulterior motives! Besides, the baron seems very nice."

"My naive little girl, he *is* nice. That's why he'll probably give her the jewelry . . . afterward!"

When Sardan teased her like this aboard the boat, Larissa knew what to do: hit him. Sardan himself had taught her some protective moves against overeager admirers, and Larissa had no compunction about turning them against her tutor. Here, in Baron Tahlyn's fine hall, however, she could only give him a sidelong glare and clench her linen napkin into a crumpled ball.

Dumont noticed the gesture. His shrewd green eyes traveled from the sadly mangled napkin to Larissa's glare to Sardan's grin. The tenor felt the captain's gaze, and his mirth faded.

"Something amuse you, Sardan?" Dumont inquired mildly, tearing off a slice of still-warm bread. "Something about my ward, perhaps?"

"Uh, no, sir, nothing at all," Sardan stammered and hastily turned his attention to the food on his plate.

Dumont kept his gaze on the young man a moment longer, then glanced at Larissa. Gently Dumont rested a big brown hand on her gloved one and squeezed. When she met his gaze, he smiled reassuringly, the gesture emphasizing the crow's-feet around his eyes.

"Don't let Sardan bother you like that," he said, his voice gentle. "You ought to come to me when he does."

"He's just joking, Uncle," Larissa answered. Dumont narrowed his eyes, the smile fading.

"That kind of humor is inappropriate for a young lady," he snapped.

"Aye, sir," Larissa replied, taking care to keep the exasperation from her voice. Her guardian's overprotectiveness occasionally grated, but she always held her tongue. Dumont returned his attention to the baron.

Throughout the rest of the meal, Larissa watched the baron and Liza. Although they were seated at opposite ends of the large table, there was definitely something going on. Their eyes met often; mysterious smiles and gestures were shared. Larissa still clung to her first impression of Tahlyn, though. There was a longing in his violet eyes that spoke of something gentler, steadier, than the kind of carnal craving Sardan had hinted at.

It wasn't until the early hours of the morning that the dinner was finished and the guests returned to the boat. As she and Dumont waited in the courtyard for the carriages to be brought around from the stable, Larissa shivered in the moist, cool air. Fog moved slowly about her knees, hiding the stones from view at times. She had seldom been off the boat at night and wasn't at all sure she liked it. Everything, from the quiet servants to the magnificent building, seemed more sinister to her when draped in darkness.

Dumont wrapped his cape about her. "Thank you, Uncle." She smiled as she gratefully bundled up in its warmth. The carriage, a lovely vehicle with a red-cushioned interior, clattered up. Dumont opened the door, which bore the heraldic red tree of Tahlyn's line, helped Larissa in, then climbed inside himself. Smoothly, the carriage resumed movement down the winding lane that led from Tahlyn's mansion to the wharf.

"The baron seemed to be enjoying himself," Larissa remarked cautiously, waiting for Dumont's reaction.

"Ah, the lovely Liza," mused the captain, with only a

hint of sarcasm. "She and I may not always see eye to eye, but, bless her high-strung little heart, she does bring in the customers."

He settled back on the velvet cushions, folded his brawny arms across his chest, and closed his eyes. A faint rumbling sound issued forth after a moment, and Larissa sighed. When Dumont didn't feel like talking, he curled up wherever he was and went to sleep. It was an effective way of avoiding conversation.

The young dancer surprised herself with a huge yawn. Well, they were in port, so there were no rehearsals. She could sleep in tomorrow, she told herself. Telling Casilda about the evening's affairs could wait.

A few moments later, the carriage halted near the dock. Bracing herself for the cold, Larissa smiled at the coachman as he opened the door and helped her down. She glanced down toward the Vuchar River, and her heart rose as always at the sight of *La Demoiselle*.

The steamboat was a proud and beautiful lady, all right, from the mammoth red paddlewheel at the stern to the carved wooden figure of a golden griffin at the bow. Its wedding-cake frame had four levels, and the stern sported a calliope that blew magical, colored steam when it was played. *La Demoiselle* was large—two hundred feet long and fifty feet wide—but not ostentatious. It glowed whitely in the moonlight, and Larissa could just make out the name written in flowing letters on the starboard side. The paddlewheel was motionless, though it could propel the boat at speeds that no other riverboat could touch.

Dumont had named the boat for the Musarde, the river on which he'd grown up. *La Demoiselle* had not been the only paddleboat on the river, but it had been the best. Twenty-two years had passed since Dumont had begun its construction. He'd given the boat a special theater room and rehearsal halls, made storage areas, and seen to it that most of the cast members had their own cabins—no small feat on so contained a space.

The fog moved slowly about Larissa, hiding and revealing the flickering light of gas lamps, and the moonlight turned the water of the river a silver hue. Larissa forgot the menacing press of the swirling mist and the bone-chilling damp that wafted to her from the river. She saw only the beauty of *La Demoiselle*. Home, she thought to herself.

Dumont had walked down the road a few paces before he realized she was not at his side. "Larissa?" His voice was gentle and concerned. He extended a hand to her.

The dancer smiled wearily, scurrying to catch up to her guardian and taking the proffered hand. "She's just so beautiful in the moonlight."

Dumont squeezed her hand. "Aye, she is," he agreed.

\* \* \* \* \*

As she knew she would, Larissa slept late. It was past noon when she finally woke and, as usual, knocked loudly on Liza's door to awaken her for lunch.

"Larissa!" yelped Casilda, coming up behind the dancer. "I heard that Liza and the baron . . ." She glared meaningfully at her friend.

Larissa went crimson. What if Sardan had been right and Liza had been giving a "special performance" for Tahlyn last night?

Casilda Bannek, a tall, dark-haired young woman who was Liza's understudy, planted her hands on her hips. Then her red lips twisted into a grin and her hazel eyes sparkled. "Well, too late now!"

Giggling, the young women knocked on the door again. There was still no answer. Larissa hesitated, then reached for the knob. Somewhat to her surprise, the door was unlocked. She glanced at Casilda and raised an eyebrow. For her part, Cas was fighting back laughter so hard that her face was quite red.

"One, two, three," whispered Larissa. She and Casilda pushed open the door and yelled "Surprise!"

Casilda screamed and turned her face away, sobbing. Larissa, her eyes huge, clutched her friend's shoulder.

Liza was inside, and alone. Her face was as white as the sheet upon which she lay. She was still in the same formal clothing she had worn to the dinner last night, though her long hair was unbound and spilled about her face in a riot of color. There was a ring of purple and blue about her white throat.

She had been strangled.

\* \* \* \* \*

Ten minutes later, Dumont had called an all-hands emergency meeting. In the theater, deck hands and cast members sat nervously in their seats while Dumont paced before them in the stage area.

Dragoneyes, the golden-eyed half-elf who was Dumont's closest friend, as well as his first mate, leaned against the hull of the boat. Concentrating on whittling a small piece of wood, he appeared totally unconcerned by the goings-on. Soft silver hair fell into his strange-hued eyes as he worked. Larissa knew that Dragoneyes was not ignoring the situation. The half-elf was shrewd and calculating. As much as the young dancer loved her guardian, she had never grown very fond of Dumont's first mate.

"For those of you who haven't yet heard," Dumont began as soon as the crowd had quieted, "Liza Penelope was found strangled in her cabin this morning."

He paused, and many of those assembled gasped with astonishment. A few sobs broke out. Dumont waited for quiet, then continued. "Baron Tahlyn and the local authorities have been notified, and they assure me they'll have this . . . matter solved swiftly. Apparently the constables in this country are not people one would wish to cross."

Dumont smiled thinly, pleased to see a few answering, if halfhearted, smiles in return. Most people, even strangers such as the cast and crew of *La Demoiselle*, had heard chilling tales of the Kargat, Darkon's secret police. They answered only to Azalin, the lord of the land, and were, indeed, not to be crossed.

"Needless to say, we'll be closing down for a while . . . out of respect for poor Miss Penelope's memory. When we do open again, Miss Bannek will be singing the role of Rose. I ask you to give her your full support."

Casilda glanced down and bit her lower lip. A tear crept down her cheek, and Larissa squeezed her friend's hand reassuringly.

"I feel like it's my fault somehow," Casilda whispered. "I wanted the part of Rose so badly . . . but never like this, Larissa, never like . . ." She couldn't go on.

Larissa was miserable but could do nothing to comfort her friend. She remained dry-eyed, not because she didn't care about Liza, but because she never wept. She had cried all her tears long ago.

"Are there any suspects?" asked Sardan.

Dumont shook his head. "I can't think why anyone would want to do this. But," he hastened to add, his gaze sweeping the crowd, "I'm certain that it was someone from the town. We're like family here on *La Demoiselle*. I hope everybody knows that.

"We have been asked to remain on board until the investigation has been completed. I hope that'll only be a few days, but we'll have to wait and see. Representatives of the law will be coming aboard this afternoon and questioning everybody in turn. Please give them your full cooperation. Remember, even in this time of grief and shock, we have a reputation to maintain. People knew the name of *La Demoiselle du Musarde* before Liza came aboard. They'll remember it when this unpleasantness has been forgotten. That's all. Dismissed."

Soberly, silently, people rose and left. Hushed muttering began as they ascended the wide, carpeted staircase. Casilda wiped at her face, muttered, " 'Scuse me, Larissa," and hurried out.

Larissa rose and went to her guardian, wordlessly holding out her arms for a hug. Dragoneyes and the singularly ugly chief pilot, Handsome Jack, respectfully stepped away. Dumont embraced her tightly.

"What do you think, Uncle?" she asked, her face pressed against his crisp white shirt. Beneath her cheek she felt his chest heave with a sigh.

"I think," he said, "that our host, the baron, might not be the kindly figure he wants us to think he is."

Shocked, Larissa pulled away and looked up at the captain. "No! I don't believe it. He seemed—"

"He came to visit Liza last night," Dragoneyes interjected smoothly. "I was on guard duty on the dock. No one else came aboard." Larissa gazed into the half-elf's strangely slitted golden eyes, searching for a hint of truth or lie, then returned her troubled gaze to Dumont's.

"Think about it for a moment," Dumont continued. "You saw how enamored he was of Liza. Maybe he asked her to stay, become his paramour, perhaps even his wife, I don't know." He shrugged and shook his gold head sadly. "She refused. After all, she's got a career. He grew angry, and . . ."

A dull horror began to seep through Larissa. It did make a frightening sense, but she could not shake the memory of the tender look in Tahlyn's eyes when he had gazed at Liza.

Dumont turned his attention to Dragoneyes. "When the authorities come aboard, see if you can't get permission to go into town and purchase some livestock. If we're going to be confined on the boat for a while, I'd just as soon not starve." His voice dripped with resentment, and Larissa could imagine how he chafed under the official restrictions.

Dragoneyes nodded. "Aye, sir. If I may make a suggestion?" The courtesy was for Larissa's sake; Dragoneyes never asked permission to speak frankly when he and Dumont were in private. Dumont nodded. "Take a few moments and visit everyone personally. We're going to start getting the curious coming around to look at the murder boat, and everyone ought to be prepared."

Dumont nodded again. It was a sound idea. He patted Larissa's back and eased her away from him. "You'd best go to your cabin and get ready," he told her. She nodded, and slowly made her way toward the stairs. Dumont's green eyes followed her.

A touch from Dragoneyes brought the captain back to the present, and he banished thoughts of his alluring young ward. There were more urgent matters that needed his attention.

It was a difficult day for everyone aboard *La Demoiselle*. Nerves were strained, and arguments broke out readily. Larissa sat in her cabin, trying not to think about Liza, but failing. She lay on her bed, hands clasped behind her head, and stared at the ceiling.

Her cabin, like all except for Dumont's comparatively lavish quarters, was tiny. There was enough room for a bunk, a small wooden chest of drawers, and a table and chair. She did not have many personal belongings, only a trinket or two that had caught her fancy in some port or other. The dancer retained only one item from her past. Hidden in one of the drawers was a silver locket. It contained a wisp of blond hair, the locks of a child—her own hair before it had turned white.

The room was spartan, but that suited Larissa. It was all that she needed. Her joy lay in her dancing.

A sharp knock on the door broke her reverie, and she opened it to admit a tall human woman in her early forties. The woman's raven hair was streaked with gray and tied back in a ponytail. She was clad in a well-worn leather tunic, underneath which she wore a mail shirt. A bright purple sash at her waist proclaimed her to be in the local militia. She wore a sheathed sword, and her face and gray eyes were as hard as her steel.

"Miss Snowmane, I'm Captain Erina. I've come to question you about the murder of Miss Liza Penelope."

\* \* \* \* \*

Dumont had noticed that Baron Tahlyn had sent high-ranking members of his militia to interview the crew, and he didn't like it one bit. All day he was on edge and busied himself with ordering repairs and such to keep the nervous crew occupied. Erina had agreed to let Dragoneyes and another crewman, Brynn, go ashore and load up with supplies, on the condition that it would be the last time anyone would leave *La Demoiselle* until the case was closed. Dumont agreed. Dragoneyes and Brynn came back with eight sheep, four pigs, two calves, and several chickens, as well as a great deal of fruit, vegetables, and grain. It looked as though they planned for a long stay.

Or a long journey.

That night, Dumont made his way silently to the bow of the main deck. He whistled four clear notes, and a tiny flame appeared on the index finger of his right hand. The blue fire danced without burning the finger, and he brought it to his pipe and lit it, puffing gently.

The crowd of gawkers that had thronged the wharf earlier had gone. Dumont had yet to visit a port city where decent folk willingly ventured out after nightfall, and Nevuchar Springs was no exception. Wait . . . there was a movement over near the road. He narrowed his jade eyes. "Dragoneyes," he called.

"Aye?"

"Come here. Tell me what you see over there."

The half-elf squinted in the direction that Dumont had subtly indicated. "Man. Not elven. Tall. Caped. Pale. He's watching us."

"No sash?"

"No, but he's obviously here on somebody's business."

Dumont swore softly and took a deep pull on his pipe. "Kargat?"

"Could be." The moon cleared a cloud and, for a brief instant, flooded the cobblestone road with milky light. The watching man stepped out of the light quickly, casually, but not before Dragoneyes had noticed something that made him tense.

"Raoul?"

Dumont frowned at the strain in his first mate's usually laconic voice. "Yes?"

"That man casts no shadow."

Dumont went cold inside. Only one being that he knew of failed to cast a shadow in full moonlight, and that creature was something he'd never tangled with before and prayed he never would—a vampire.

"Well," said Dumont after a long moment, "at least the cursed creature can't cross water. Get Gelaar. Both of you meet me in my cabin in five minutes. We've got to get out of this trap. I think perhaps the Kargat have been ordered to detain us for good."

Larissa was asleep when the boat's engines surged to life. Sensitive to changes in *La Demoiselle*'s status, she awoke at once. Her bunk was vibrating, enough so that she realized they were moving at peak speed. She grabbed a robe, struggled into it, and hastened outside.

She was running barefoot along the deck when the night exploded with sounds. The escape attempt had not gone unnoticed by those on shore. Larissa went to the railing and glanced toward the wharf, which was falling to stern with astonishing speed. The militia had piled into the small boats docked near the shore.

Shouting, directly below her, caught Larissa's attention, and she looked down to discover that Dumont hadn't even hauled in the ramp. Six crewmen were straining at the ropes, struggling to free the wooden ramp from the waters and pull it back onto the deck.

"Larissa, what's going on?" came Casilda's cry.

"I think we're trying to escape," Larissa answered, confused. "But I don't know where Uncle thinks he can take us. We're fast, but we're in their country. Look." She pointed at the small boats that were trying to catch up. "We'll have to refuel sometime and—"

"Larissa, we're not going inland," Casilda said in a strangled tone of voice. She was looking toward the bow. Larissa followed her gaze, and her heart sank.

Ahead lay a bank of thick, swirling white fog. Dumont was steering *La Demoiselle du Musarde* directly into it. "He can't be doing this," Larissa murmured, horror slowly filling her beautiful face.

No captain with any sense ever willingly sailed in thick fog. Navigation was impossible. But Dumont was doing even worse—he was taking *La Demoiselle* into the deadly, unnatural mists where few ships had ever traveled.

The dancer could only stare in shocked silence as the whiteness closed about them and Nevuchar Springs disappeared from sight.

# TWO

"Are you mad?"

"You'll kill us all!"

"Captain Dumont, what is going on?"

Questions flooded the theater as the captain entered. He looked tired, his green eyes rimmed with red and the lines around his mouth more prominent than usual. Dragoneyes followed him like a silent shadow.

Brynn, a crewman with red hair and emotionless brown eyes, leaned on the door to the stairs and closed it heavily. The ominous sound caused some of the cast members to look around fearfully; the gesture had quite efficiently silenced them.

"I am not mad," Dumont began, pacing back and forth and keeping his keen eyes on his audience. "I am taking a calculated risk in steering *La Demoiselle* into the mists. Behind us we leave a constabulary that's after my boat and, therefore, your livelihood."

He paused and drew himself up to his full height. "Sardan!" he barked. The tenor's head whipped up, his face pale. "You think they'll want you chasing those pretty elfmaids in Nevuchar Springs? And you, Pakris?" The juggler's fear-filled gaze met Dumont's. "How many jugglers could that small place handle? You want to try wandering around Darkon at night when you're from the murder boat? Hmmm?"

Dumont paused to let his words sink in, then continued. "It is my belief that Baron Tahlyn murdered Liza and tried to shift the blame to someone aboard *La Demoiselle*. It could be any one of us, just as long as someone hangs for it." He shook his head slowly. "I'm not going to let anyone aboard this boat pay that kind of a price. We're family, remember?"

"So you're taking us into the mists instead," one of the chorus girls snapped.

Dumont's eyes went cold, and the impetuous young dancer visibly quailed before that icy green stare. "They won't follow us into the mists. Both Gelaar and I have magical skills, and I have complete faith in my crew. We'll reach land soon—and safely. Then all this unpleasantness will fade into memory."

Or into nightmares, Larissa thought unhappily. No one had ever navigated the dreaded border mists and returned to tell about the adventure.

She felt Dumont's eyes upon her and looked up into his face. A ghost of a smile touched her full lips. Then again, Uncle Raoul had never let her down before.

\* \* \* \* \*

*La Demoiselle* turned its great paddlewheel on the shore—and its dead—then steamed into the mists. The fog closed around the boat and swallowed it up.

Larissa found it disturbing to go out on deck and be able to see nothing but the thick fog. She couldn't even glimpse the water from any deck but the main one, and nowhere could her vision penetrate more than a yard into the shroud of white.

More alarming still were the strange sounds—yowls, shrieks, and groaning noises that rent the air with no warning and abruptly died into silence. It seemed as though unspeakable creatures lurked just beyond sight, that only luck and mutual blindness kept the ship from being assailed by unnamed horrors. People took to speaking in whispers and venturing outside as little as possible. Only necessity took anyone anywhere near the rails. They were too close to whatever was out there.

The least popular job was suddenly that of the leadsman. Drawing that duty now caused even the staunchest of crewmen to blanch. "Sounding" consisted of a crewman sitting alone for four hours on a yawl several feet to either port or starboard, testing the water's depth with a weighted measuring rope. Each depth was marked differently, for ease in identification during dark nights—or thick fog. Four feet was marked by a piece of white flannel woven into the rope; six feet by a piece of leather; nine feet by a piece of red cloth; mark twain, or twelve feet—the ideal depth for a steamboat—by a piece of leather split into two thongs. At mark three, the leather was split into three thongs, and mark four was a single leather strip with a round hole punched into it.

During the entire nerve-wracking trip, each leadsman sang out: "No bottom."

Dumont encouraged rehearsals for the cast and drills for the crew. At first it seemed that the ship was under a spell, perhaps muffled by the terrible fog. The crew hugged the inside decks and the leadsman called his casts in a harsh, croaking parody of his usual bold, musical tones. The players, even within the sheltered rehearsal areas, seemed afraid to raise their voices.

But Dumont had little patience for their fears. Mercilessly he chided the singers back into full voice, urged the dancers and musicians to a more energetic performance. The crew he shamed with his own boldness, spurring them with his contempt and the unspoken threat of his anger.

As the days passed and nothing came from the mist save the same frightening cries and groans, the folk of

La Demoiselle began to return to normal. Everyone threw themselves into their work, eager to take their minds off the unnatural mists and the eerie noises that haunted them.

On the ninth day, Casilda rose early, planning to spend an hour or so before breakfast rehearsing her final solo. She stepped outside of her cabin, frowned at the ever-present, ghostly mist, and continued down the damp deck toward the stairs.

Dragoneyes too was awake and about, sitting on the outer stairs that led up to the next deck. He alone of the crewmen seemed not to be distressed by the eerie mists. Casilda nodded a cool greeting and made as if to pass by.

"Handsome Jack said he'd spotted land," Dragoneyes offered, concentrating on the piece of wood he was whittling. "Off our port side, if you care to take a look and see what you think."

Casilda paused. Larissa would be furious if she didn't wake her up for something as important as sighting land. Sighing, she turned back to Larissa's cabin and pounded on the dancer's door. "Larissa! Wake up!"

A muffled curse sounded from within, then, "What time is it, Cas?"

"A little past dawn. Dragoneyes says there's land ahead. Don't you want to come see?"

Casilda rubbed her own sleep-bleared eyes. There was no further sound from the cabin, and again she banged mercilessly on the door. Larissa swore, a trait she'd picked up through eight years aboard *La Demoiselle du Musarde*, and Casilda laughed outright. "Come on, sleepy!"

A few seconds later the door swung open and Larissa emerged. Her eyes were still half-closed and her clothing—a voluminous red shirt and black trousers— had obviously been thrown on. She stamped her left foot a few times to get the short leather boot completely on and fumbled with a broad black belt that was too big for her trim waist. Larissa's long white hair was a total mess. She clutched a brush in one hand. For a moment Casilda wondered if the dancer was going to hit her with it.

"This better be good," Larissa muttered.

Together the two young women went up to the bow. The promise of land and an end to this horrible journey overcame any lingering dread of what might lurk in the mists, and for the first time the women noticed that the frightful chorus of howls and moans was muffled and distant, less loud than the soft creak of the ship's timbers and the rhythmic chuff-and-gurgle of her great paddlewheel. They leaned against the railing, staring into the grayness, hazel eyes and blue searching for a lightening of the claustrophobic mist.

The early morning air was moist and chilly. Fog clutched wetly at Larissa's long white hair like the fingers of a drowned man. Unconsciously, the girl reached a slim hand to touch her tangled mat, as if to reassure herself that her locks were coated merely with mist and not something more foul. She set to work brushing her hair, her eyes still peering into the fog, a frown of concentration on her face.

"Here, let me. You can't get all those snarls out by yourself," Casilda offered. She held out her hand for the brush. There was no point in both of them straining their eyes peering through the mists.

"Thanks," Larissa said, handing her friend the brush and presenting her tangled white locks. "How's that solo of yours coming along?" she asked. Casilda dragged the brush through the snarls, and Larissa winced under her friend's less than tender ministrations.

Casilda grimaced at Larissa's query. "Not well at all," she confessed. "That last high note always terrifies me. I know it's in my range, but I get nervous and don't trust my voice on it. Now, Liza's voice—" Casilda stopped, her voice going thick, and continued brushing Larissa's hair with unnecessary vigor.

Larissa did not urge her to continue. They stood quietly together, remembering the vivacious soprano. The silence was broken only by the rhythmic cry of the leadsman, calling out "N-o-o-o-o Botto-o-o-m!" A strained note in the clear calls betrayed the crewman's terror of working blindly in the mist.

At last Casilda had finished with Larissa's white hair and stroked its silkiness enviously before starting to tie it up with a ribbon that had been wound around the brush handle. Suddenly Larissa jerked away from Casilda, making the other girl drop brush and ribbon.

"There!" shrieked Larissa, leaning over the railing and pointing excitedly. "It's clearing over there!"

Larissa stepped up on the lowest rung and leaned out, her unbound hair whipping back in the sudden breeze. Casilda bent down and retrieved the dropped brush and ribbon.

Traveling through the unnatural mists had bothered Larissa more than she cared to admit. Even dancing had not completely alleviated her tension as her lively imagination populated the mists with horrors to match each shriek and groan. With land in sight, though, she had to admit that it looked as if Dumont's wild foray into the unknown had been successful.

Perhaps the tales of what lurked in the border mists were just that—tales, legends. It certainly seemed that way, except for the strange sounds. The mist was starting to thin, and Larissa could make out the large, dark shape of hilly terrain up ahead.

Casilda stepped to the rail beside her friend. Without warning, she shuddered violently. It suddenly felt very cold here on deck, and the mist was more clammy than usual. The singer frowned to herself, and glanced out at the spot in the fog where Larissa had glimpsed land.

Larissa had noticed the shudder. "Cas?" she said,

concerned. Casilda ignored her, keeping her eyes on the dark shape ahead.

It still looked like hilly terrain, but with heart-stopping suddenness the whistle in the pilothouse shrilled loudly. The sound was repeated twice more, and Casilda and Larissa looked at one another in horror. Like everyone else aboard *La Demoiselle du Musarde*, they were well aware of what three blasts on the whistle meant—danger ahead.

As they watched, the hill shuddered and began to move in their direction with a steady, awful sense of purpose.

Casilda lurched backward so abruptly that she almost lost her balance and went toppling to the deck floor. She caught herself by grabbing at the railing and clinging to it as if it were a weapon or shield. "Kraken!" she yelled. Her eyes had grown huge and full of animal terror.

The cry was taken up by the crewmen, who sprinted for the spears kept on deck. Casilda, still flooded with fear, began to breathe faster and faster. Larissa grabbed her friend and tried to pull her away from the railing, but Casilda's fingers clung stubbornly.

"Look at it, Larissa, look at it!" Casilda babbled hysterically. "That thing's huge, gigantic, the size of a mountain at least!"

"Casilda, come on!" The dancer seized her friend around her waist and tugged with all her strength, but Casilda remained rooted to the spot, unblinking hazel eyes focused on the mountain of flesh that was drawing near the boat.

The leadsman's musical, steady cry had ceased. Now Larissa and Casilda heard it rise in a shriek. "Pull me in!" the unfortunate crewman screamed. "It's coming! Please, please pull me—"

There was a violent splash, then nothing more.

A pulsating gray tentacle materialized out of the

white mist and groped along the deck. It squirmed like some gargantuan slug, slapping wetly near Larissa's feet. Closing about a chair left on the deck from more pleasant times, it clutched hard enough to shatter the wood and pulled what was left off into the greedy whiteness.

Casilda screamed, a high, piercingly pure sound that reminded Larissa of her friend's singing. The dancer, though, had had enough. She struck Casilda's wrists upward, knocking her hands away from the rail. Cas whimpered and cowered back, and Larissa seized her hand, yanking her away from the danger. "Come on!"

Together they ran toward the stairs and the safety of the theater, deep within the boat. Casilda flew down the stairs, her feet clattering noisily. Larissa started to follow, but the kraken had no desire to lose so tender a morsel.

The white-haired dancer gasped as a slimy limb brushed one of her long, muscled legs. Her heart pounding, she leaped upward before the horrid thing could close on her. The water that dripped from the creature's tentacle made the deck slippery, and the normally sure-footed young woman lost her balance as she landed. One hand shot out and seized the wooden banister before she fell down the stairs.

The rubbery tentacle struck noisily on the deck, groping for her. Larissa scrambled the rest of the way down the water-slick stairs, with the kraken closing in on her. She hit the next deck running and dived for one of the spears. She heaved the heavy weapon at the questing limb with all her might and pinned the gray, pulsating flesh to the deck.

The creature bellowed in pain. With a mammoth wrench, it pulled the harpoon free and retracted its injured member, dragging the weapon along with it. Without thinking, Larissa dived after the rapidly disappearing spear, her hands closing on the shaft. To her distress, it stayed firmly in the grasp of the monster's moist flesh. For a fear-fraught instant she thought the kraken would drag her and the spear with it into the unseen waters below.

Then strong hands closed about her, pulling her back, away from the railing. Larissa stubbornly clung to the spear, managing to tug it free. The tentacle was swallowed up by the fog, but not before Larissa noticed that the spear didn't appear to have harmed it at all. She glanced back to determine who her savior might be and encountered the furious face of her guardian.

Before either could speak, four crewmen ran past, armed with spears, grim determination on their features. They appeared to have recovered from their initial fear and swore with a new earnestness as they battled the creature. Dumont opened the door to the theater lounge, shoved Larissa inside, and pulled the door shut again.

Larissa peered out the door's window, watching the struggle and wishing desperately that she could help. A few yards away, a tentacle closed around a hapless deck hand and lifted the squirming figure into the air. The gray limb tightened, and there was an awful popping sound that Larissa heard even from inside the boat. The sailor's struggles ceased. The corpse was flung to the deck, knocking down two other men.

A small, slight figure hastened to join the battle, and Larissa's white eyebrows rose in astonishment. What could Gelaar hope to do against a kraken? He was just an illusionist! As she watched, the elf began to cast a spell, waving his thin arms and closing his eyes in concentration.

All at once the fearful kraken was gone. A swirling shape of mist, a slightly darker shade of gray than the surrounding fog, appeared in its place. "An illusion," Larissa breathed. "Its form was just an illusion!"

Yet the dark cloud of mist did not dissipate. The kraken form had been an illusion, but only to hide their attacker's true form.

Dumont, pushing Gelaar away from the entity, whistled a few clear, sharp notes that sliced through the cacophony of battle. A huge wave welled up beside *La Demoiselle*. For an instant, Larissa felt sure that the wall of water was going to come crashing down on the riverboat. Instead, it smacked the mist creature with a resounding clap. The creature, startled, dissolved completely into mist and rapidly blended with the eerie but harmless fog. There was a pause, but nothing further happened. The crew, relieved, began to cheer.

Larissa, also relieved, opened the door and stepped onto the deck. She felt a strong grip on her arm and looked up to meet Dumont's fury-darkened face.

"Damn you to the bottom of the Sea of Sorrows, girl!" Dumont spat angrily, fear and apprehension staining his rage. "I've told you what to do if ever this boat was in danger, haven't I? Haven't I?" He jerked on her arm for emphasis, and the girl winced.

"Aye, Uncle, but there wasn't time for me to get below deck, and the spear was right there—"

"Don't talk back." Dumont relaxed his grip and glowered down at his ward. "I saw that you had time to get Casiope out of the way."

"Casilda," she corrected.

Dumont exploded again. "Don't interrupt me!" Larissa lowered her blue eyes, but amusement quirked one corner of her mouth. The crew might all run from his bluster, but Larissa knew that Uncle Raoul would never do a thing to hurt her.

"Now then," Dumont continued, his tone softening. "You might have been hurt, child, and you know I couldn't bear that. So next time, just you get your pretty little self below deck and let the crew handle it, all right?"

"Yes, Captain. Sorry, sir."

He slipped a strong, tanned hand underneath her chin and tilted her face up to him. "And besides," he said jokingly, his handsome features crinkling into a smile, "who would play the Lady of the Sea? No one else has your sea-foam hair."

Larissa smiled, and amusement lit up her face until she glowed.

Dumont inhaled swiftly. Gods, but the child had grown up, hadn't she? Into such a beauty, too. Momentarily lost in his ward's loveliness, the captain found himself staring into her blue eyes.

"Is it gone, Captain?"

The young crewman who had dared interrupt gazed earnestly at his commander. Abruptly Dumont remembered the mist horror, gone for the moment but no doubt reforming itself for a second attack. Without a word he left Larissa and went below deck. A few moments later, *La Demoiselle* surged ahead with a sudden burst of speed.

To Larissa's delight, the true landscape began to take shape in the distance. Dragoneyes had been right about sighting land, and Dumont's gamble had paid off.

Larissa leaned against a pile of rope, conscientiously staying out of the way of the scurrying crew members, and watched the new territory emerge. It seemed to be rather flat country, and as they drew nearer she saw that there was a fairly large town located near the shore. It had a long wharf that was home to several small boats and a few larger vessels. Some of them were out going about their business, closer to the steamboat than to the shore.

Larissa caught glimpses of the sailors and waved at them in a friendly fashion. Normally, the arrival of *La Demoiselle* was a happy occasion, and the cry "Steamboat a-comin'!" preceded the boat's docking. Here, however, no one was expecting the magnificent, magical showboat, and judging by the frightened, suspicious looks on the faces turned toward Larissa, no one welcomed her arrival. Larissa's grin faded as the boats made haste to turn their sails and flee from *La Demoiselle du Musarde*.

Discouraged, the dancer turned her attention back to the approaching town. She could see more of it now, and something about it seemed curiously familiar to her. The dancer frowned and leaned against the railing. Surely she was just confusing the port with another she had seen in her eight years aboard the boat.

Something else caught her eye, drawing her attention away from the dock area. The citizens of this place had only partly succeeded in keeping nature at bay. To the right of the town, a verdant forest dominated the landscape. Yet it was unlike most forests the girl had seen. The trees were huge and grew right up to—and in—the marshy water. Gnarled roots broke the tea-colored surface, looking for all the world like an old man's knees. A strange substance that looked almost like gray-green hair was snarled in the tops of the trees. Plants clotted the water at first, but Larissa could see the river opened up as it wound inland.

Larissa frowned to herself. How could this landscape be so strange and yet so familiar? The dancer did not like to think about the years before she had become Captain Dumont's ward, before she had found her home aboard *La Demoiselle*. Now, however, a memory surged to the forefront.

She shook her head in vain denial, her hands clutching the railings for support as her legs suddenly went weak. She recognized this coastline, knew the name of this island, that town. As Larissa fled to her uncle's cabin, more frightened by the innocent-looking coastline than the horrid monster in the mist, she heard the heartbeat sounds of drums in the distance.

Dumont's cabin was located directly beneath the pilothouse. Larissa pounded on the door with both fists, fully aware that she was behaving like a child, but too terrified to care. "Uncle!" she cried, her voice a sharp cry.

Dumont opened the door at once. His face changed from brusque to concerned when he realized who his visitor was. "Larissa, sweetheart, what is it?"

Larissa merely stared at him, cheeks ashen. "I—I— the island—"

Dumont frowned, extending a hand to gently pull her inside. "Come on in and tell me," he soothed.

Dumont's room was the largest private cabin on the boat and was furnished lavishly. There was an ornate wardrobe that had an expensive mirror mounted on it, two plush chairs, a large, canopied bed, and a carved mahogany table. Wares from over a dozen lands cluttered the room, from tapestries to carvings to strange items that no one who visited even dared to identify.

The captain steered his distraught young ward to the bed and sat her down. "Take a deep breath," he told her in a comforting tone, "and when you're a bit calmer, tell me what has upset you so much."

The dancer obeyed, her breath coming in short gasps. "I know this place," she said thickly.

Dumont quirked an eyebrow. "Indeed?"

She nodded, her tangled white hair falling into her flushed face. "I was here once, long ago, with my father. It's an island called Souragne. My—my hair turned white here. My father said something bad almost happened to me in the swamp." She looked up at Dumont with an imploring gaze that nearly broke his heart. "I'm frightened, Uncle. I know it's silly, but . . ."

Tenderly, Dumont placed an arm about her, drawing her head down to his chest and resting his cheek on her white hair. "There, *ma petite*," he soothed, "I'm taking care of you now, not your father. I won't leave you like he did. You know that, Larissa."

He felt her nod against his chest. "And anything out

there that tries to hurt you is going to have me to deal with."

She laughed, albeit shakily, then drew away. "I know it's foolish of me," she repeated, "but seeing that coastline . . . Uncle, I can't remember a thing, but somehow I recognized the place. And those drums!" She shuddered. "They're eerie."

Dumont frowned. "Drums? I heard nothing."

Larissa went pale. "I thought I heard . . . well, it must have been my imagination, I suppose. I can't hear them now."

Her guardian laughed, a deep, rumbling sound. "What an odd little thing you are! You tackle creatures from the mist without so much as a by-your-leave and yet a marshy little island frightens you. There's nothing here that's going to hurt you, child. I promise. You don't even have to leave the boat if you don't want to."

His voice had changed, taken on the slightest tinge of condescension. Larissa's pride, which had fled before the island's appearance, surged back on a hot wave of embarrassment. It was more important to her that Dumont think well of her than that she be comforted.

"No, Uncle, that won't be necessary," she replied crisply. She rose, steadying herself. "I'm fine now. I'm going to my cabin for a bit. Thank you."

Dumont watched her as she let herself out of his cabin, closing the door firmly behind her. There was grace and an innocent power in her movements. Slowly, a smile twisted the captain's lips. Larissa's frantic visit had given him a marvelous idea.

# THREE

To Handsome Jack, the amazingly ugly chief pilot of *La Demoiselle du Musarde*, the coastline was anything but a nightmare. There was plenty of room for the boat's docking, and already a crowd was gathering on the pier. Because of the attack of the mist monster and the subsequent excitement of sighting the real coastline, he was alone in the pilothouse for the moment.

The pilothouse was larger and more habitable than most. The pilots—Handsome Jack, Tane, and Jahedrin—rotated six-hour shifts. Generally, two pilots, or a pilot and a first or second mate, were in the pilothouse during a shift. The wheel was huge, bigger than any of the men who maneuvered it, and hard to turn. Often a pilot would find himself standing on one of the spokes, using his own weight to help turn the wheel. This physical requirement of piloting eliminated the clever but slender Dragoneyes from the post, though few of the true pilots could navigate quite as well as the sharp-sighted half-elf.

There was a comfortable chaise for those who were in the pilothouse merely to keep the pilot company. The whistle was within easy reach of the wheel, as was the voice tube and ship's telegraph, by which the pilot communicated with the engine room in the stern. Large windows provided a full view of the river directly in front and to port and starboard. Behind the pilot, a narrow stairway led directly to Dumont's cabin.

Jack reached over and pulled the lever on the boat telegraph to "slow." He grinned to himself. The three livid white scars, running the length and breadth of his face from right temple to left ear, wrinkled grotesquely with the gesture.

The tall, beefy Handsome Jack was quite proud of those scars. He bragged that he had gotten them in a hand-to-jaw struggle with a wolf back in Arkandale. When he was drunk, which was often, the tale grew in the telling until his opponent was a werewolf—"An' very highly placed in society he was, too, I tells you. Hoo, I could tell tales of the riverboats in *that* country!" he'd slur.

Those within hearing who were sober enough to worry about such things would exchange glances. Handsome Jack might well be telling the truth, they'd mutter to themselves; gods knew he'd shown up one night on *La Demoiselle*, shaking and begging for a job that would take him out of Arkandale. . . .

*"Ah, she's a pretty maiden, aye,
A pretty maiden she,
But my poor heart's already bound
To the Lady of the Sea!*

*The Lady of the Sea, hey, hey,
Has put her spell on me,
I'm doomed to love no other than
The Lady of the Sea."*

What Handsome Jack's voice lacked in musical quality—and it was a great deal—was more than made up for in enthusiasm and sheer volume. This was his favorite number from *The Pirate's Pleasure*, and, in his own pleasure at finally sighting land after floundering in the fog, he belted out the number with gusto.

"Damn you, Jack, you know you're not supposed to sing on my boat!" exploded Dumont as he climbed up the stairs from his cabin.

Jack cringed like a whipped dog. Every captain had his superstitions, and one of Dumont's was singing on the boat. Only cast members were permitted to sing, and even they had to restrict themselves to songs from the show.

"Sorry, Cap'n, I just forgot, that's all. You know I'm not meanin' no harm, sir."

Dumont's displeasure did not fade. Handsome Jack's statement was true enough, as far as it went. He never did "mean no harm." Not when he was drunk and came perilously close to grounding the boat. Not when he leered at some of the more attractive patrons, causing them to bridle and complain and swear never to set foot on *La Demoiselle* again. Not when he sang contrary to direct orders.

Jack had his uses. When sober, he was the finest pilot aboard the boat. Not even Dragoneyes possessed Jack's instinct for negotiating unknown territory. He'd been loyal and worked hard, almost pathetically grateful for the job Dumont had given him.

"Yes," Dumont sighed at last, "I know you meant no harm, Jacky my lad."

Handsome Jack grinned with relief. "You're a gentleman, sir, through and through, that's what I always said. Here, Cap'n." Stepping aside, he offered the bigger man the wheel. It was Dumont's custom to always bring *La Demoiselle* into port himself, though the rest of the time he left the piloting to Jack or the other pilots.

Dumont took the huge wheel, which was taller even than he. His strong hands closed about it possessively as he gazed at the approaching dock. He reached up after a moment and pulled on the whistle, causing it to shrill loudly.

"Jacky," mused Dumont, his eyes on the dock as he turned the wheel gently to starboard, "did you see the battle with the mist creature?"

"Aye, sir, that I did. What a brilliant move, to use the waves against the—"

"Yes, yes. But did you see Miss Snowmane risking her life down there?"

Jack gulped. It was obvious that Dumont wanted to hear something specific, but the pilot wasn't sure what. "Uh . . . aye, sir, I did." He hazarded a guess. "Mighty brave for a girl, don't you think, sir?"

Dumont turned his hard gaze upon his pilot, and Jack shrank back even farther. "Gods, man, she's my ward *and* my leading dancer. Brave or not, she shouldn't be on deck when there's danger!" He took a deep breath to calm himself. "I need to teach Miss Snowmane a lesson, and I'd like you to help."

Jack's eyes bugged. "Me, sir? 'Course, sir!"

Dumont suppressed a smile. He kept his voice calm and friendly.

"I'm glad you're willing, Jack. We'll be docking in a few moments, and I'll be going ashore to meet with the leader of the town. Then, tomorrow, we'll have our—"

"Parade!" Jack answered happily. "Cap'n, you're goin' to let me see the parade?"

The thought of actually seeing the performances Jack heard each night through the walls of the sailors' quarters thrilled the pilot. It was customary for the riverboat's cast to parade down the main avenue in costume, and then perform a scene or two from the show. Many of the towns they came to were so starved for entertainment that a glimpse of the magic and music they could experience aboard *La Demoiselle* was generally more than enough to ensure a packed house.

Dumont had always been careful to segregate the players and the crew, and he had never permitted crewmen to watch the parade. Apparently, and to Jack's disappointment, this time was to be no different.

"No, Jacky, I'm afraid I can't do that. You know the rules." Jack's face fell, the remorse on his homely features causing him to appear even less attractive. "As I was saying, we'll have the traditional parade. Afterward, when the cast and the townsfolk are milling about, Miss Snowmane will be accosted by a, shall we say, rather shady character." He looked meaningfully at Jack.

Jack's thick brows knotted together ponderously. "Me?"

"You, Jacky lad. Disguised, of course. You shall threaten poor Miss Snowmane, and I'll hurry to her rescue. Then you'll run away into the darkness and back to the boat while I tell Miss Snowmane how dangerous it is to take foolish risks." He intensified his gaze. "I can count on you, can't I, Jack?"

Handsome Jack nodded vigorously.

"I thought so. Why don't you go to the dining room and let Brock cook you up something? Tell him I said it was all right."

"Thank you, sir." Handsome Jack touched his greasy forelock and left, licking his lips at the thought of Brock's fine food.

Dumont watched him go, a sneer of contempt twisting his strong features. He had had enough of Jack and his lapses, and what he had planned after the parade would finally free him of the fool.

The captain returned his attention to the dock. There was a good-sized crowd on the pier now. The boat was close enough for Dumont to see faces that registered understandable suspicion. He'd lay their fears to rest soon enough, he and the dazzling performers of *La Demoiselle*. Reaching up, he pulled a rope and the riverboat's whistle blasted forth again. The captain smiled as some of the people on the dock jumped, startled.

Some of the denizens of this place—what was it Larissa had called it? Souragne, that was the name—were extremely well-dressed. One young, dark-haired dandy sported what appeared to be a silk tunic and fine leather boots. The youth turned to get a better view of the steamboat, and something glinted in the sunlight. Jewelry, Dumont noted with a sharp eye. The dandy's companion, a comely dark-skinned lass, was equally well attired. Earrings dripped from her ears, matching the sparkle of the jewels about her long, slim throat.

Standing right next to the wealthy couple was a thin, tall man in shabby clothes. The pair maneuvered away from him, distaste on their aristocratic features. Here and there were the haunted, grimy faces of street children, peeking out carefully and curiously. The dazzling sight of *La Demoiselle du Musarde* had distracted the urchins from their usual job of picking pockets and had apparently caught the attention of the whole town.

Dumont sounded the whistle once more and pulled the riverboat to the dock with a smoothness born of years of practice. From his vantage point, he could see his crewmen scurrying to place down the ramp. The people on the dock drew back, fear replacing curiosity.

Dumont's mind was not on the activities of his crew, but on the people and place he was about to encounter. The town appeared to promise diversity. Dumont could see stately manors in the distance that contrasted sharply with the shabby buildings that huddled along the dock. It appeared that the agricultural community fared better here than the fishermen did. Probably that soft-looking young dandy hailed from one of those lavish mansions, bred to a life of ease by his great-grandfather's labor, or perhaps the unsavory sweat of slaves. The dock area's run-down appearance spoke of shadier doings and more immediate wealth—and danger.

Such a lovely jumble of things from which to choose, Dumont mused to himself with a slow smile. There would be many new and exciting things here for him to experience—new customs, new ideas, new creatures. Many an attractive woman had wondered why the handsome, wealthy Dumont hadn't settled down in one land—or at least confined himself to one waterway.

But variety called with a siren song that drowned out any other call: variety in people, place, terrain, knowledge, adventures. That keen pleasure forbade Dumont from making any one place his home. The tall, strong captain was too much in love with diversity.

As for business, the dandies and their mansions boded well for the financial success of *The Pirate's Pleasure*, while the seamy underbelly of the town promised evenings rife with less wholesome entertainment.

Dumont's smile widened into a predatory grin. The crewmen secured the boat to the dock, and the captain hastened down the ramp.

The first thing Dumont noticed when he stepped outside the pilothouse was the humidity and heat. It was still early in the day, but already the air was warm and thick. It had been chilly in Darkon, but here summer was well on its way. A thin layer of perspiration began to coat his face before he had even set foot on land.

A small, spidery man, clad in a splendidly embroidered blue tunic that seemed a bit too large for him, moved toward the front of the throng. An ornate silver chain was draped about his scrawny throat. The crowd parted to allow him passage. When he reached Dumont, the man craned his neck to look up at him, hooked his thumbs in his well-tooled leather belt, and cleared his throat.

"My name is Bernard Foquelaine," he said in a thin, high-pitched voice. "I am the mayor of Port d'Elhour, here on the island of Souragne. We do not often have strangers in our land, as you might imagine. What is your purpose in visiting our isle?"

So, Larissa had been right about the place's name,

the captain thought to himself. Dumont put on his best smile, the one that showed off his white teeth to advantage. He stuck out a big hand. Tentatively, Foquelaine took it in his own moist palm.

"Mayor Foquelaine, I am very pleased to visit your lovely town. I am Captain Raoul Dumont, and this is my vessel, *La Demoiselle du Musarde*. She's a showboat, sir, with the finest entertainment available in any land. We come as visitors, friends, and honest performers."

Foquelaine's watery blue eyes brightened a bit, but he remained tense. Behind him, the crowd began murmuring excitedly. "What kind of entertainment?" he queried.

Sensing the shift in attention, Dumont began to address the crowd. "Why, all kinds, ladies and gentlemen. We have a musical, *The Pirate's Pleasure*, that features dancing, singing, and the best in thespian skill. There's always an honest game of cards to be had, and—"

"Ye got any fire-eaters?" called the man who had stood next to the wealthy couple. He was every bit as grubby as Dumont had suspected, and smelled as if he hadn't bathed in far too long.

Without missing a beat or losing his smile, Dumont turned and pointed at the man. "Indeed, sir, we do, and a host of fine magicians who will perform acts that will amaze and astonish you. Mayor Foquelaine, may I have your permission to dock here in your fair port and entertain your populace for the most modest of fees?"

Foquelaine hesitated, blinking rapidly. "Well . . ."

"Let me give you—all of you—an opportunity to experience a taste of what an evening aboard *La Demoiselle* will be like. Tomorrow at twilight, my cast will perform a few scenes from our show. And good sir," Dumont added, turning and addressing the filthy man as if he were royalty, "the fire-eaters and jugglers and illusionists will be out in full force for your entertainment."

"Hmmm," mused Foquelaine, still not completely

convinced. "How much is this going to cost?"

Dumont let himself beam in an avuncular fashion. "Not a copper, Mayor. This is my gift. And if you don't like what you see, my cast and I will just go right back on our boat and steam away. Do we have a deal?"

Mayor Foquelaine was obviously not comfortable with the idea, but he could sense his people's excitement. There was little in their lives as bright or beautiful as the showboat. Few traveled out of the mists to visit Souragne, and most who did were haunted, broken souls or evil, greedy wanderers.

"Very well," Foquelaine yielded. "Your crew may come ashore as well."

Dumont smiled the smile of a hungry tiger. All was going according to plan.

The minute that he returned to *La Demoiselle*, Dumont rounded up seven of his crewmen and took them into his cabin. The men stood at attention as Dumont ushered them inside, glanced around quickly, then closed the door quietly behind him.

"Gentlemen," the captain began, sitting down in one of the large, comfortable chairs and staring up at the standing men, "you know what I want."

The seven men nodded. Only Dragoneyes dared lounge casually against the door. His knife was out, and a shape was beginning to form in the lump of wood he was carving. Wood shavings floated down to form a pile at his feet. Dumont didn't care.

"Dragoneyes, Tane, and Jahedrin, I want you to go into the town. Mix with the populace as much as you can. Go into their bars, their brothels, their homes if you can manage it without arousing suspicion."

The three men grinned, exchanging pleased glances. They'd drawn the soft duty this time.

"But don't get careless," Dumont warned. "I don't want to hear about a mistreated whore or a drunken brawl or even one stolen piece of silver. I'll condemn it publicly and leave you for the folks of Port d'Elhour to handle. They may not be the Kargat, but I'll bet they have some unpleasant ways of punishing criminals nonetheless."

His eyes contained no hint of teasing, and the men knew that he was as good as his word. None of them resented it. Working aboard *La Demoiselle* had an outrageous set of advantages with a balancing chance of danger, and they had long ago agreed to Dumont's terms.

"Astyn, Philippe, Brynn, and Kandrix, you take the yawl and scout out the swamp," Dumont continued, reaching for his pipe and beginning to pack it with a fruity-smelling tobacco. "You all know what I'm looking for. If you see anything I might like, get it."

The men nodded again.

"Excellent. You're a fine bunch of lads. Report back to me before the parade tomorrow night. As always, the first of you who brings back something that strikes my fancy gets a night on the town at my expense." He whistled, then lit his pipe from the blue flame that flickered on the tip of his index finger. "Dismissed."

The men saluted and filed out of the cabin, using the main doorway rather than the small stairs that led up to the pilothouse. Dumont rose, puffing on his fragrant pipe, and gazed out the porthole.

The morning was fast becoming afternoon. The trees were still, and the moss that covered them dripped down unmolested by a cooling breeze. Dumont's green eyes roved the swamp, then traveled back to the dock area and the proud mansions to the south. He began to smile. This was new, unexplored territory for him and his boat. He could hardly wait until tomorrow.

"What do you hold for me?" he whispered to the trees and waters, to the slums and the mansions. "What will I find?"

# FOUR

"Come in," Larissa called, putting the cork back on the small jar of blue paint.

Casilda, clad in her costume of Rose for the parade, entered. Her garb was a stunning example of the fashions of Richemulot, Dumont's homeland. A low-cut pink gown of softly rustling silk clung to her full, shapely figure and revealed it to the best advantage. Her raven hair was up and tied with embroidered bows, and her hazel eyes sparkled underneath the heavy layer of eye coloring. Her mouth and cheeks had been pinkened to the same shade as her garb.

Larissa glanced up at her in the mirror and smiled as she finished applying her own makeup. "Oh, Cas, you always look so lovely in that outfit. Rose suits you."

Casilda rolled her eyes and made a face, and both girls erupted with laughter. In *The Pirate's Pleasure*, Rose was the nauseatingly sweet maiden who won the love of the tormented Florian, freeing him from the grasp of the evil Lady of the Sea—Larissa's role.

Casilda smiled at her friend. "If I didn't move like a cow, I'd rather have your part. It's much more fun."

Larissa laughed. "Yes, but the only reason I got it is because I have all the singing talent of a crow with a sore throat." It was not a modest statement. She squawked when she sang and so did very little of it.

"The Lady of the Sea" rose and finished putting on her costume. Casilda shook her head admiringly. She had seen Larissa in this outfit hundreds of times by now, but the sight never failed to send a shiver down her spine. Larissa was a lovely young woman even in the plainest attire. In her guise as the Lady of the Sea, however, she was breathtakingly beautiful.

Her slim body was covered with a tight-fitting, shimmering blue material that encased her from her neck down, leaving little to the imagination. Wisps of fluttering blue-green, gauzy fabric did little to disguise her slim figure. Tiny seashells were fastened to her garments and braided into her hair. The dancer's uncanny white mane, as Dumont had noted so often, looked like sea-foam. The overall impression was of a powerful woman who appeared slightly unreal, and the audiences never failed to inhale swiftly at her first appearance.

Casilda's thoughts turned suddenly sober. "Are you going to be all right out there? You were pretty upset last night."

Larissa hesitated, then nodded. Her bold words to Dumont after their conversation had been false bravado. As soon as she had left her guardian's cabin, the dancer had spent the rest of the day and all of the night huddled in her bed. Casilda had come to check on her after dinner, and Larissa had explained the situation. Casilda sympathized, of course, but couldn't completely understand. No one could.

After Casilda had left, Larissa had tried to sleep. The distant pounding of the drums had started again, this time refusing to be silenced—even when she put a pillow over her ears. Thankfully, they had stopped some time during the night.

Now Larissa rose, opened one of the drawers, and pulled out the silver locket, gently fingering the downy hair, and remembered Aubrey Helson. As always when she thought of her father, a wave of mingled sorrow and resentment rolled through the young woman. Larissa's father had been a good man, but a weak one, and her last memories of him were tainted with recollections of his drunkenness and penchant for gambling. Eight years ago, he had abandoned Larissa and Raoul Dumont had stepped in to raise her. Eight years ago, Larissa Snowmane had been born.

The whistle blew, interrupting her morose reflections. "Already?" moaned Larissa, grabbing the cloak she wore to disguise her outfit during the parade.

Casilda opened the door and mockingly bowed her friend through.

\* \* \* \* \*

"Well?" queried Dumont. "The parade's about to start, so give me your report quickly."

Dragoneyes shook his head. "Nothing of any interest, Captain. If there's anything worthwhile here at all, they do a damn good job of hiding both it and any knowledge of it."

"They're an awful superstitious lot," Jahedrin volunteered. "There's lots of talk about nature gods, everything from animals to spirits, and things in the swamp. The folks're *really* afraid of that swamp," he emphasized.

Dragoneyes nodded. "They say it's the home of the Lord of the Dead. Most of the time, he leaves well enough alone. If you don't go into the swamp, you're pretty safe. But sometimes, the swamp comes after them."

Dumont frowned. The yawl he had sent into the swamp was overdue. He hoped nothing had gone wrong. "It sounds like the swamp might be where we should concentrate our efforts," he mused.

There was an uncomfortable silence. "There's good beer at the Two Hares Inn," Tane volunteered. Dumont laughed, breaking the tension.

"Well, that *is* important information," he chuckled. "Fine job, lads. Go get your grub." Dumont wasn't angry with the men. If they had found nothing, he knew it was not from the lack of looking.

As the crewmen left, the captain climbed up the stairway to the pilothouse. From this vantage point, Dumont watched with satisfaction as his cast paraded into the town. The crowd was so thick, he wondered if the entire population of the island had turned out for the event.

The jugglers, fire-eaters, and other traditional performers went first, followed by Sardan and his mandolin. Dumont noted with amusement that the fastidious ladies who were unimpressed by the feats of manual dexterity were enchanted by the bard's sweet voice and youthful good looks. Sardan was the swashbuckling Florian, and Dumont suspected that in Port d'Elhour, as always, the boyishly pretty actor would not lack for female companionship.

Next was Gelaar, striding purposefully into the crowd, which parted readily for him. Amazement and not a little fear was on the faces of the townsfolk as they watched him pass. An illusionary griffin, phoenix, and unicorn pranced at his side, eliciting gasps and applause. The paved road under his feet suddenly shimmered and changed into a flower-strewn country road, and the crowd applauded madly.

Whooping and laughing, the tumblers were next, followed by the chorus, clad in garb similar to but not as dramatic as Larissa's. Larissa and Casilda had gone on ahead earlier to prepare for the performance in the town square. They would be performing a scene from the second act, in which the Lady of the Sea imprisons virtuous Rose.

Dumont had turned to descend the stairs when he caught a movement out of the corner of his eye. The yawl, a raft that was little more than a few planks tied together, was returning. Only one man appeared to be on it, using the paddle to propel himself along. It was too far away for the captain to make out which of the crewmen it was.

Dumont swore angrily. The fool! He could hardly have picked a worse time to arrive than during the parade. Dumont looked back anxiously at the crowd lining the road. To his relief, he saw that the parade was leaving the dock area and the throng was happily following.

Dumont went down to the main deck, shielding his eyes from the last rays of the dying sun. The lone crewman on the yawl was Brynn. The red-haired sailor paddled the yawl along steadily, almost mechanically. He was close enough now that Dumont could see that his clothing was torn and stained with blood.

Silent as a shadow, Dragoneyes stepped beside Dumont. Captain and half-elf mate both stared down, startled, at the crewman as the yawl drew alongside *La Demoiselle*.

Brynn was a native of Invidia, a land whose inhabitants were not known for their gentleness or trusting natures. Fear was second-nature to the Invidians. Brynn was the exception, being possessed of an icy calm. He had joined the crew when the showboat had stopped in the port city of Karina. A hard man with more than one murder on his hands, the sailor had gone on many "explorations" for Dumont in the past. The captain knew there was very little that could shake the redhead's cool composure.

Something obviously had done just that. Brynn huddled on the wooden floor of the yawl, his clothing torn and covered with blood from innumerable scratches. He shook uncontrollably, and his normally icy eyes were bloodshot and filled with terror. He made no attempt to secure the yawl to the showboat.

Dragoneyes climbed down and began to tie the wooden raft securely to the larger boat. Brynn didn't even appear to notice him, and Dumont had to call his name twice before he looked up and blinked dazedly.

"Captain?"

"Brynn, what happened to you? Where are the others?"

Brynn didn't answer, only licked dry lips. Dumont and Dragoneyes exchanged glances, then the captain frowned.

"Damn you, I order you to report or I'll throw you to whatever creatures live in that swamp!"

The threat seemed to penetrate Brynn's trance, and his eyes refocused. "They got them, sir," he answered in a frail voice. "Philippe went first, when the—" he shuddered and looked away. "And then Kandrix . . . But he was the one who found them for you, Captain, and he and Astyn caught them and brought them back to the yawl."

Brynn paused, and his brown eyes went vacant again. Dragoneyes shook him roughly. With a start, the sailor continued.

"But in the water, it—it got them, both of them, and it tried to get me, too, but I got in and poled like a madman. So I got 'em for you, sir, right here, I got 'em." To Dumont's consternation, tears welled up in the haunted brown eyes and spilled in rivulets down Brynn's freckled face.

Dumont shook his head, then extended a hand and helped Brynn clamber out of the yawl. Once on the dock, the sailor simply stood there, trembling and blinking stupidly. His captain sighed. There'd be no getting anything useful out of the man for a while.

"Go to the tub room, Brynn," Dumont ordered. "Dragoneyes will draw you a bath, and I'll have Brock send you up something for dinner—including a stiff drink or two. Don't leave that room until I come, though, you understand?" Softly he said to Dragoneyes, "Don't let him out—or anyone but Brock in." Dragoneyes nodded.

"Come on," the half-elf said in an uncharacteristically gentle voice, taking Brynn's arm. "A hot bath will do you a world of good."

As Brynn shuffled off with Dragoneyes, he muttered to himself. "Things like that . . . man to do . . . terrible . . ."

The captain listened, watching the broken man hobbling away, then turned his attention to the box that remained in the bottom of the yawl. Carefully he stepped onto the yawl. He prodded the box gingerly with a booted foot. There was no reaction. The captain reached out a hand to touch the seemingly ordinary box. The wood felt warm, warmer than being in the setting sun would warrant. Dumont frowned to himself, picked the box up, and returned to the deck. He tucked it under his arm and hastened up the nearby stairs to the empty pilothouse and then into the safety of his cabin.

Dumont placed the box on the table and examined it for a moment. It still retained its curious heat. Carefully, he sat down, peering at the box. He closed his eyes and began to sing softly. The incantation would have baffled most listeners, but the tune was from *The Pirate's Pleasure*. Dumont's cabin had been heavily warded many times, as had the ship itself. There was little that could harm him here, but Dumont was in no mood to take a chance. Whatever was in that box had some connection with Brynn's breakdown.

The spell finished, Dumont opened his eyes. The box looked just the same. The captain flexed his hands, then cautiously eased the box open just a crack.

White light spilled out, caressing his hands softly.

The sensation was extremely pleasurable, but Dumont was disconcerted and let the lid drop. The pleasure ceased. His heart starting to beat faster, the captain opened the box again and peered inside.

Dozens of tiny white lights blinked rapidly and milled about inside the box. Their radiance stroked his face. Suddenly Dumont was filled with long-forgotten memories of his childhood, when he and his father would ride through green fields together, when his younger sister Jeanne-Marie was still alive, when the shadows hadn't begun to lengthen on his energetic life.

Unconsciously, filled with the joy of it, he raised the lid higher . . . higher . . .

And slammed it down again when the little lights, having nearly lulled him into carelessness, tried to escape. Dumont began to laugh uproariously. What a find! He had no idea what the tiny creatures were, but he already knew how to harness the pleasurable sensations they caused.

"Well done, Brynn!" he said to himself, thinking that such a prize was well worth the lives of three crewmen and the sanity of a fourth. If Brynn recovered sufficiently, he would find himself treated to a night on the town he would never forget.

Carefully cradling the precious box in his arms, Dumont went to the wardrobe. He placed his treasure on the floor, then closed and magically locked the door. He hesitated. His curiosity about the lights urged him to stay and find out more about them, but the sun was sinking low on the horizon. Dumont would have to hurry if he wished to get to the performance on time.

* * * * *

The market square in Port d'Elhour was unremarkable. It was a literal square, flanked by sad little storefronts and dingy alleys. Uneven stones made for difficult walking, and most people kept to the sides, where the shops were. There was a large basinlike object in the center, used to catch rain, and every roof had gutters and ample rain barrels. Everything seemed functional, but little more.

This shabby scene was what the inhabitants of Souragne had seen for years. Not tonight. Gelaar had given them a little taste of paradise. Gone were the uneven gray stones, replaced by silken white sands. The cypresses were palm trees, the storefronts the open ocean. One woman, clutching her children, wept openly at the beauty.

Florian's apparently dead body lay on the shore. Sardan had taken care to sprawl in a fashion that accentuated his broad chest and strong thighs. Rose wept prettily above his corpse, then launched into her solo, "Alas! My Love Is No More."

Larissa watched the performance, her hand closed firmly about the pendant draped about her neck. An emerald with a small jet stone embedded in it was set in an oval of silver. The overall affect was that of an open eye. When held so that the eye was "covered," the wearer of the pendant was invisible, as Larissa was now.

Dumont had spent years collecting various magical items, using them to further the appeal of *La Demoiselle*. The Eye, as Dumont called it, was one of the most valuable, and also produced an excited reaction when the wearer uncovered it and magically appeared onstage. The dancer listened to Casilda and held her breath as the song drew near its conclusion. *Concentrate, Cas*, Larissa thought. *I know you can hit that note!*

*"Alas, my hopes have faded
Like the light in my love's eyes;
Like a dream at morning,
Like summertime, he dies!"*

Casilda's sweet voice swelled, reached for the high note—and went flat, as she always did. Not badly so, but enough that Larissa knew she'd be consoling her friend after the performance. She shook her head in sympathy, assumed her position, and uncovered the Eye.

The crowd gasped and drew back a little as the beautiful, white-haired Lady of the Sea materialized. She leaped onto the sand, a fey water sprite of beauty and danger. Larissa closed her eyes and surrendered to the music and the role.

From the crowd, Raoul Dumont watched her, a hot light smoldering in his eyes. Watching his star dancer perform always awakened the banked fires that lurked inside of him. This role in particular showcased her young body's beauty and grace, and Dumont grinned a tigerish grin. Tonight, he would have her—provided, of course, that idiot Handsome Jack remembered to play his role properly.

Larissa leaped upward and kicked, arching her back and letting her seashell-braided white mane toss like a wave, then twirled about the prone body of Florian, who magically awoke. Part of the young woman exulted in the fact that she was performing well; this was a good night. She felt the music flowing in her as if it were her lifeblood. The other part of her did not care that she was executing her role well. It just reveled in the movement.

Suddenly, the drums that had haunted Larissa the day before began to beat again. Their deep, ominous rhythm clashed with the music of the dance. Startled by the unexpected sound booming out of the darkness, Larissa stumbled, and her blue eyes flew open in horror at the error.

The dancer recovered quickly, and the audience noticed nothing. Her fellow performers, however, caught the brief misstep, and they were as stunned as she was. Larissa was little short of magical in her dancing—no one had ever known her to make a mistake. Larissa finished, assumed a dramatic pose, and closed her hand about the Eye.

The minute she was safely invisible, Larissa ran to the fringes of the crowd and leaned against one of the big cypress trees, breathing heavily. She was furious with herself. Nothing in the world was as important to her as her dancing. Certainly the drums were a distraction, especially as she knew nothing about their origins, but she was a professional. She shouldn't have let the new rhythm interfere with her performing.

She struck the cypress with her fist in impotent anger. It hurt, and she was even more annoyed with herself.

"The trees don't like that. And I don't think it does much good for your hand, either," came a voice from behind her.

Startled, Larissa whirled around. She came face-to-face with a young man who was looking directly at her and smiling. For an instant she thought she had loosened her grasp on the magical pendant, but her hand was securely closed around it. She gasped in surprise.

"Can you see me?" she asked.

" 'Course I can," the young man replied, his grin widening. "How else would I know that you were hitting a tree?" He leaned up against the cypress and folded his hands, his eyes bright with amusement. He seemed to be enjoying her discomfiture, but there was no sense of malice in his mirth.

Larissa was utterly confused and continued staring at the stranger. Admittedly, he was worth staring at. His clothes were plain but functional: a voluminous white shirt, plain vest, breeches, and short leather boots. The youth was tall, topping six feet, and well-built, though not laden with muscles. Thick, wavy brown hair matched dancing brown eyes. His face was well-chiseled and strong, but there were laugh lines around his eyes and mouth that suggested he didn't take himself too seriously.

Larissa found herself smiling as well. She opened her mouth to ask him how he could see through the magic when she realized the music had stopped. Larissa groaned. For the second time in the same evening, she'd done something wrong. Now she was late for the final bow.

The dancer fled the company of the charming young man and hastened to take her place beside Casilda and Sardan. The applause was tremendous, and the faces above the clapping hands were alight with pleasure. Their people in the audience had clearly had the time of their lives.

Curtsying, Larissa searched about the crowd until she found Dumont, and she felt a sudden chill. He was not smiling, and his green eyes were as hard as jade.

He'd noticed the misstep too, she realized. And the fact that she was late for the final bow. Larissa felt herself shrinking inside. It would seem that it wasn't going to be such a good night after all.

She stole a furtive glance in the direction of the young man, but he had gone. The dancer felt curiously disappointed. The crowd came up to congratulate the players, and idle conversation replaced songs and music.

Wordlessly Dumont held out his hand. Larissa removed the Eye and dropped it into the callused palm. The captain was extremely protective of his treasures.

"What happened to you?" Dumont demanded, putting the pendant safely away in a pouch around his neck.

Larissa lowered her eyes. "I'm sorry, Uncle. The drums distracted me."

Dumont's face was like stone. "What drums? The drums that got you so upset the other day?" he demanded.

Larissa stared up at him, dumfounded. They were still going on, their pounding rhythm weaving through the night sounds of cicadas and human voices. Was it possible he couldn't hear them? "*Those* drums," she said, gesturing in the direction of the swamp.

Dumont's expression didn't soften. "Everyone makes mistakes," he said in a voice that was carefully patient. "But you can't learn from them if you pretend they're not there. Don't blame your bad step on nonexistent drumming! This is the second time you say you've heard them, and I simply cannot. I've had about enough of that particular excuse."

Larissa couldn't believe it. There the drums were, pounding away in a rhythm that pulled at her soul, and the captain claimed he couldn't hear them. She tried to continue the argument, but was abruptly interrupted.

"Ah, Captain Dumont!" exclaimed Foquelaine, striding up to them with a huge smile on his face. "What a performance! What talent you have aboard your showboat!"

"Thank you, Mayor Foquelaine," said Dumont. "Mayor, this is my ward, Larissa Snowmane. Larissa, my dear, may I present Mayor Bernard Foquelaine."

Foquelaine, delighted, took the dancer's hand and planted an unpleasantly moist kiss on it.

"Such a pleasure, mademoiselle," he enthused. "Your Lady of the Sea was stunning! Never have I seen such graceful movement! Captain, you and your marvelous boat must stay for a little while here at Port d'Elhour."

Dumont's smile returned. "It would be an honor to perform for your people. They do seem to have enjoyed themselves."

He looked out on the sea of smiling faces, illuminated by the many torches in the square. The illusion of the island paradise had gone, but its memory lingered. The market square somehow didn't seem as bleak as it had before. The cast and entertainers were mingling;

the folk of Souragne seemed to have forgotten their initial suspicion and were now chatting animatedly.

"There is, of course, the question of cost," said Foquelaine. "The people of this land do not have much money."

Dumont allowed himself a laugh. "I see fine clothes, beautiful jewelry, lovely homes. No money, sir?"

"We barter here. Services, goods, so on. I would think that a copper or two . . ."

Larissa allowed herself to ignore the conversation as it floated off into a bargaining contest. She returned her attention to the drums and looked around. Nobody else seemed to be bothered by the steady pounding. She could understand that perhaps the Souragniens were used to the sound, but what of the cast of *The Pirate's Pleasure*?

Casilda was chatting with a handsome young fellow, and Sardan was the center of a group of giggling young girls. Neither of them seemed the least bit discomfited. To her disappointment, Larissa did not glimpse the handsome face of the strange young man in the happy throng. She allowed herself to remember his broad grin and the laughing light in his eyes. Where could he have gone?

A gentle touch on Larissa's arm brought her back. Foquelaine had departed, and Dumont was now gazing at her intently. "Where were you a moment ago, *cherie*?" he asked, his normally robust voice velvet soft.

She blushed and wasn't sure why. "Nowhere, just going over that bad step," she lied. "What kind of a deal did you strike with the mayor?"

"One silver piece per person, plus all our supplies for the duration of our stay. But you don't care about that. Come, it is too hot a night to be pressed so close to the crowd. Will you join me on a little walk?" He proffered his arm.

Larissa smiled back, relieved to see the more familiar

guardian reappear. She took the arm and squeezed it affectionately as the captain of *La Demoiselle* led her away from the babbling of the market square and down a cobblestone lane.

They walked for a while in silence. The road took them out of the main town and into the countryside, winding past some of the beautiful houses they had glimpsed from the boat. The mansions were located back from the cobblestone road, each having its own pathway, often guarded by fences. Larissa gazed up at one of the rich homes, a dream of luxury made of cypress wood and stone. It was too dark for her to see much detail of the manor itself, but she could tell there were large windows—an expensive luxury in an isolated community. Carved dragons holding flickering torches guarded a wrought-iron gate that blocked the path to the house. The broad road wound on, but Dumont paused and took Larissa's hands in his. She gazed up at him inquiringly.

"I didn't mean to snap at you yesterday," Dumont said sincerely. "You were very, very brave, the way you handled that mist horror. Just understand, I was afraid for your safety."

"I know that, Uncle," Larissa said affectionately, squeezing his hands. "And I promise I—oh!"

A large, hunched shape had suddenly darted out in front of them. The man wore a black hood and gripped a sword, which he swiftly pointed at Larissa's throat. He stood calmly, quite certain of his armed advantage on the dark, deserted road.

"One wrong move, and the girl dies," he hissed menacingly.

# FIVE

Larissa was not about to make one wrong move. In fact, she didn't move a muscle. Sardan's teachings had taught her how to handle drunken, leering men and lovestruck young pups. Ruffians with swords at her neck were another matter indeed, and she held very still while her mind went over various courses of action.

"That's right," said the hooded man. "Now, sir, if you would be so good as to hand over all the money on your person?"

Larissa blinked. There was something familiar about that voice, about the whole situation. She prayed Dumont would cooperate and the thug would retreat, but to her dismay she heard the snick of a sword being unsheathed.

"Get away from her, you pathetic excuse for a man," Dumont growled, his expression switching from surprised to brutal in a heartbeat. "I'm loathe to spill blood in a hosting town, but I will."

"Choose you death, then, you dog? So be it! Have at you!" The hooded man darted away from Larissa, making a clumsy swipe at Dumont that the captain effortlessly parried. Larissa didn't waste a moment. She dived for cover, getting one of the stone dragons between her and the thug.

The man grunted and struck again. Dumont blocked the blow and heaved the man backward. He stumbled but didn't lose his balance. He stood for a moment, panting. Dumont hadn't even broken into a sweat. The captain balanced, ready to block whatever blow his enemy might make.

"A brave, brave fight, yet my sword shall taste your blood ere long. See how it thirsts!" The robber waved the sword in the air before charging Dumont again.

Larissa gasped. Now she knew why this was so familiar. The words the man had been uttering were stolen directly from the third act of *The Pirate's Pleasure*.

"No!" cried Larissa, stepping out from behind the stone dragon. "Uncle, stop it! He's not a killer! Someone's playing a joke on you—" But her words were lost in the singing of steel.

The thug landed a lucky blow, and Dumont gasped with pain. The faint torchlight illuminated a bloody gash across his bicep, making the red liquid seem black. He turned his angry gaze upon the robber, who looked as startled as he.

"The game's over," Dumont growled and began to attack in earnest. The robber didn't stand a chance. Desperately, the man tried to fend off blows that came with staggering speed. He succeeded for a few seconds, but Dumont's skill was by far the superior. With the efficiency of a panther slaying a rabbit, Dumont slid his blade home. The false robber gazed down at his midsection. He stared at the blood that was beginning to turn his shirt front a wet black.

"Scum like you deserve to die," Dumont said coldly.

The man staggered, collapsing to his knees with a grunt. He looked up at Larissa who, frozen with horror, could only return his stare. "Liza . . ." he said, then pitched forward to sprawl on the stone. An inky puddle began to seep out from under his body.

For a moment there was silence, broken only by the

steady rhythm of the distant drums that apparently only Larissa could hear. Slowly the dancer dragged her gaze from the dead man. "Uncle," she said in a steady voice, "what about Liza?"

Dumont had fished out a handkerchief and was fastidiously cleaning the blood off his blade, but he froze at her words. Carefully, he asked, "What do you mean?"

"That man said—"

"He said 'lies,' Larissa dear, not Liza. I called him scum, he claimed my insults were lies. Poor child, this has upset you dreadfully, I can see that." He sheathed his sword and went to the fallen man. "Let's see who you are, my good—Jack!"

Dumont's voice was filled with feigned shock. Larissa turned her head away after she recognized the face of the chief pilot. Pity for the pilot's idiocy surged through her. What had possessed him to play such a trick on Dumont? He should have known how the captain would react. The dead man's eyes were wide open, filled with pained surprise.

"Oh, Jacky lad," Dumont sighed, kneeling beside the corpse. "Why'd you do such a crazy thing?" He bent his head in mock sorrow, then rose. He turned, arms extended, to Larissa. She backed up a step, and he paused. "Larissa!"

The name was infused with genuine pain. Dumont had entertained happy thoughts of Larissa embracing him gratefully after he had slain the wretch on her behalf. He had decided to eliminate Handsome Jack even before he invited the man to participate in the incident. The pilot, stupid though he was, knew enough about Dumont to make him dangerous, and his drinking was getting worse, not better. There was no telling what he'd say if his tongue was loose enough.

But it had been a bad gamble for the captain of *La Demoiselle*. Dumont apparently had lost not only his pilot but also Larissa's trust. "Larissa!" he said again.

The pain in her guardian's voice softened Larissa's mistrust, and she felt ashamed of herself. Even if it was a crewman Dumont had slain, he'd been disguised and he'd been pointing a sword at her throat. Dumont could have done no less than attack him.

"I'm sorry, Uncle, it's just . . ."

"There, there, *ma cherie*," Dumont soothed, stepping to her quickly and embracing her. "You were just frightened, that's all."

She hugged him, nestling her head against his broad chest as she had done so often over the last eight years. Dumont caressed her long white hair and slid an arm about her waist, pressing her against him. Desire began to blend with the excitement of the kill.

"Larissa . . ." His voice was deeper, huskier, and he turned her face up to his.

Larissa had heard that note in men's voices before and had learned to mistrust it. Hearing it from Dumont filled her with shock and a sense of betrayal. She pushed him away and stared up at him, anger, fear, and disbelief mingled in her face. Displeasure darkened his own as he stepped forward.

Larissa panicked and dived for the sword the unfortunate Handsome Jack had dropped. It was far heavier than the prop swords she had handled from time to time, and her wrist hurt as she picked it up. Nevertheless, she grasped it with both hands and grimly aimed its point at Dumont's stomach.

"Keep away," she warned in a voice that shook.

Through his rising rage, Dumont laughed, a harsh, cruel sound. "You haven't the slightest idea how to use that," he reminded her. He was right, of course, and Larissa knew it full well. Still, she kept her grip on the weapon and set her jaw to indicate a confidence she didn't feel.

"Maybe not," she admitted, "but it's still a sword, and I can still swing it."

Dumont had had enough. Everything seemed to be going wrong on this island, from the attack of the mist horror to Brynn's unexpected gibbering to this present disagreeable turn of events. He had no patience left to squander arguing with Larissa. He straightened, and the flickering of the torchlight over his face gave it a demonic cast.

"You are such a child," he snapped. "And I am in no mood to play games. It's time to grow up." Larissa held her position, glaring at him defiantly to mask her fear. Dumont frowned. "You will give me that sword!" He strode toward her, appearing to the confused young woman far more menacing than Handsome Jack had been.

"Take it, then!" she cried, hurling the heavy weapon at him with all her strength. The sword tripped him, cutting with a grating pain across his left shin, and he hit the ground heavily.

Larissa didn't linger to see the results of her efforts. She had turned away the minute the sword left her hands and fled back toward the town as fast as her legs would carry her. The angry bellow behind her told her that Dumont was giving chase.

She hadn't realized just how far away from the center of Port d'Elhour—and the safety of lights and people—they had wandered. As she sped past the stately mansions, she wondered briefly if she should seek sanctuary from their inhabitants. A quick glance up at the menacing gargoyles that guarded the gates made her decide against such action.

She heard Dumont calling her name, then narrowed her eyes in determination. Her legs pumped rapidly and, in her costume, she was unencumbered by long skirts, but she didn't know how long she could keep ahead of the longer-legged captain.

Larissa had never felt so frightened or so alone in her life. The moonlight illuminated her way only enough to emphasize the shadows on the sides of the cobblestone path. Ground fog began to swirl about her ankles, hiding the road, and she nearly fell more than once. The sounds of the drums increased in volume, and she said a silent prayer. The town was near.

"Larissa!"

Her heart, already pounding, leaped painfully. Without breaking stride, the young dancer swerved to the left and climbed like a squirrel over a rusty iron fence. She hit the ground running, smiling grimly at the knowledge that Dumont would not be able to negotiate the fence as easily as she. It would buy her a few precious seconds.

She bolted down a dark alleyway and rounded a corner, realizing that she had nearly made it back to the market square. It was only a few streets away. Larissa didn't stop to think that she was safe now. Her world was in shambles around her. She was a hunted beast and wanted only to escape.

The small wooden building on her right was an inn. Its sign proclaimed it to be the Scolding Jay and depicted a riled bird shrieking away at a meddlesome squirrel. Off-key music and voices drifted to her ears, almost drowned out by the pounding of the drums from the swamp.

Larissa leaped upward without even stopping to think, grabbed onto the sturdy beam from which the sign hung and shinnied up until she was sitting on it. She edged backward onto the shingled roof, bracing her feet against the gutters that ran alongside the inn's roof. Larissa moved cautiously down the other side. She winced as a splinter dug its way into her thigh, but kept utterly silent.

When Dumont rounded the corner, his shin was bleeding and he ran with a limp. The captain's rugged face was contorted with rage, and he looked around angrily, furious that she had apparently vanished. The sign of the Scolding Jay was still swinging, but he didn't seem to notice. He went inside. The door slammed shut behind him, and Larissa heard him talking to the innkeeper. She let her breath out in a quavering sigh and closed her eyes, permitting relief to wash over her. She was safe.

"Well, well, what kind of pretty bird are you, up there on the roof?"

Larissa was so startled she nearly lost her precarious grip. She craned her neck to see who had spoken and recognized the dark-haired youth she had talked to earlier. He was standing directly below her, his arms folded and a grin on his face. The girl put a finger to her lips and shook her head.

Grinning broadly, the young man nodded and disappeared from her view. Larissa's heart sank when she heard him fling open the door and cry, "Milord, I've seen that girl you were chasing!"

"Where?" came Dumont's cold voice.

"She took off down Old Cypress Way. She might try to hide in one of the, uh, houses."

Larissa's head came up in pleased surprise. Her first instinct about this curious youth had been right after all.

Dumont swore, and Larissa heard his heavy stride fade away. She waited a few moments, then cautiously peered over the crest of the roof. The young man was beneath the sign again, still grinning up at her.

"You . . . you didn't give me away," Larissa managed.

" 'Course I didn't. He looked like he might be meaning you harm. Are you coming down, or do I have to climb up there?"

Larissa laughed. "I can manage. You've rescued me once already tonight." She edged down the roof and then dropped to the earth, landing lightly and gracefully. "Might the former damsel in distress inquire as to her savior's name?"

He looked totally surprised, and Larissa raised an eyebrow. "Um . . ." he said, glancing around. "It's . . . it's Willen."

She arched an eyebrow, not believing it for a minute. Larissa suspected that this was a young man not much given to lying, and he had just told a whopper of a falsehood. His manner and the way he averted his eyes reinforced her hunch.

"Well, Willen, I'm Larissa Snowmane, and I am—"

"The Lady of the Sea in *The Pirate's Pleasure*. I was at the performance, remember?" His genuinely friendly smile took any sting out of the teasing. "It's nice to properly meet you, Miss Snowmane. Although," he added, glancing around and dropping his voice, "we may want to continue this conversation elsewhere."

The young woman felt a stab of apprehension mixed with a generous portion of annoyance. She didn't want to spend the entire evening fleeing from unwanted male attention. A quick glance at her surroundings, however, soon set her mind at rest regarding his intentions.

The poorly kept street stank of refuse. A woman wearing altogether too much makeup and too little clothing stumbled out of a nearby building. When she saw Willen, she leered and preened. Two men rounded a corner and paused, also eyeing the young pair.

"You're right," she told her mysterious rescuer, "let's go someplace else."

"Shall I take you back to *La Demoiselle du Musarde*?" Larissa nodded slowly. "Yes, but not right away. Is there a better part of town? I need some time to think."

"Whatever you like," he said, touching her shoulder gently. A thoughtful expression crossed his face. "There's a nice place a few streets down, where you can get something to eat. If you're hungry, that is."

Larissa had just been thinking how nice it would be to

silence the rumbling in her stomach. The dancer inevitably developed a terrible case of stage fright and couldn't keep food down before a performance. Afterward, however, she was ravenous. When one danced as often and as intently as Larissa did, one didn't have to eat lightly.

"I'm hungry enough to eat an entire horse," she told Willen.

He frowned. "I don't think anybody here serves horse meat, but we can ask."

Larissa exploded with laughter, feeling happier than she had since Liza had been murdered. Willen seemed confused for a moment, then grinned. He proffered his arm with exaggerated gallantry. She took it in the same manner, curling her slim fingers over his arm.

They kept to the center of the cobblestone street, avoiding alleyways and dark entrances. Larissa didn't like the area one bit and was relieved when the rundown buildings gave way to private homes and better-tended taverns and shops. At one point, Larissa suddenly became aware that the drums had stopped. She wondered how long it had taken her to notice that they had fallen silent.

As they walked, Larissa asked, "What if Captain Dumont finds us?"

Willen shook his head and tried to suppress a laugh. He failed, and it burst forth, a merry music on the hot summer's night. "He won't. I sent him down Old Cypress Way." At Larissa's blank look, he explained, "That's where all the brothels are."

His dancing brown glances met hers, inviting her to join in on the joke he had played on the captain. Larissa did. By the time they reached the comparatively cozy little inn called the Two Hares, Larissa's stomach hurt, and not just from hunger pangs.

She glanced up and almost started laughing again at the comical sign, which depicted two rabbits with their forelegs on each other's shoulders and goblets of wine in their paws. One still looked sharp and somewhat sober, while the other was so intoxicated even his ears drooped.

Larissa's pleasant mood faded when they entered. The room was dark, with only a few smoky lanterns and a fire for illumination. Conversation stopped, and the three musicians who had been playing halted in a jumble of discordant notes. There were not many patrons at this time of night, but the few lingering over their pints of ale stared openly at the young dancer. Suspicious eyes roamed over her shapely figure, and Larissa became acutely aware that she was still in her revealing costume from the play.

She was about to suggest leaving, but Willen strode forward into the heart of the room, marching directly up to the enormously fat innkeeper behind the bar. The man paused in his task of cleaning glasses and glared at Willen with small, hostile black eyes.

"Jean—it is Jean, isn't it?—you are to be honored tonight!" Willen enthused. "We have one of the leading ladies from the showboat here, and she's hungry for some of your wonderful food. I told her it was the best in Port d'Elhour."

Jean stared at Willen for a long moment, then his black beard parted to reveal stained yellow teeth. "Best in Port d'Elhour?" he scoffed. "The best in all of Souragne! So, my lady, you are from the showboat, eh?"

Larissa was stunned at the change in atmosphere. Almost before Jean had finished speaking, normalcy returned. The musicians began to play again, and the patrons returned to their mugs, taking no further interest in her. "Yes, I am," she answered the innkeeper.

"Ah, yes, now I recall—the Lady of the Sea! By all means, sit, and I shall bring you a glass of our best wine." Moving with more speed than Larissa had thought a man of his girth could manage, he cleaned off a small wooden table near the fire and motioned them to the hard chairs.

"There's a word for men like you," Larissa whispered to her companion as they sat.

Willen looked suddenly suspicious. "What?"

"Charming!" Larissa announced.

Willen smiled, relieved.

"So, what's good to eat here?" she asked.

The young man looked perplexed. "I don't know."

"Willen, you told me this was a good place to eat, and you don't even know what they serve?"

He shrugged. "I said this was a nice little place. I didn't say I ate here."

Jean returned with their wine, fortunately too late to overhear Willen's comment. "Our specialty, per the sign, is rabbit sautéed in a wine sauce, served with stewed *makshee* and *cushaw*."

Larissa recognized the words "rabbit" and "wine" and that was enough for her. "Mmm, that sounds wonderful," she said. The innkeeper bowed and left them alone. The dancer critically surveyed her new friend.

Willen was the strangest person she had ever met. He hadn't yet bothered to explain how it was that he could see her when she was invisible. His reaction when she asked him his name was also peculiar. Why did he want to hide his name? In anybody else, such behavior would have warned her to be on her guard. Willen, however, had already proven himself a friend, someone she could trust.

"Tell me about yourself," she said impulsively.

Willen smiled his easy grin. "There's not all that much to tell. I'm sure your life's been much more interesting than mine."

"I don't know about that. Somebody who can see me when I'm invisible is someone I'd like to know more about," Larissa replied, taking a sip of the wine and trying to hide a grimace. It was not a vintage year, apparently.

Willen looked sheepish at her comment. "Point well taken. Well, let me see." He leaned back in his chair and folded his hands behind his head, screwing his face up in concentration. The contrast between the almost childlike expression and his handsome young man's body was extremely appealing.

"I was born on this island, and I've lived here all my life. My mother was from Port d'Elhour, but she didn't much like city life and the people in town didn't much like her. So, we went into the swamp when I was just a baby."

Larissa went cold inside, though outwardly she remained calm. Willen's mother had taken him into the swamp. She had a fleeting impression of cypress trees dripping airmoss, of misty darkness and strange illumination that didn't come from a torch. Annoyed with herself, she banished the image.

"I can't imagine what it would be like to grow up there," she said, keeping her voice neutral.

Willen shrugged. "I didn't think it was so bad."

"Did you have any playmates?"

He smiled strangely. "Well, yes, but they were . . . very different from the children of the town. The only drawback is, now that I'm here in Port d'Elhour, I sometimes say and do things that seem a little odd to most people."

"But how did you see through the pendant's magic?" Larissa persisted.

Willen started to reply, but fell silent as Jean presented their meal. Larissa sniffed appreciatively. The vegetables served alongside the juicy-looking meat were alien to her, but she attacked them with vigor and found them delicious. Willen watched her for a moment, then picked up his own knife and fork and began to eat.

Larissa closed her eyes, savoring the tender rabbit flavored with wine. Willen had been right after all. "The pendant?" she reminded him, chewing.

The youth countered with a question of his own. "How do you do magic? Or recognize it, or know how to combat it?"

"Well, you study it, I sup—oh." She stared, suddenly comprehending. The townsfolk had driven his mother away. . . . "She used magic—your mother, I—"

"I memorized spells the way some children do stories," he confirmed with a slight smile. "I sometimes forget myself."

"Like tonight."

He nodded with mock ruefulness. "Like tonight."

For a time they were silent, devoting themselves to Jean's good food with the attention it deserved. Larissa felt better about Willen. His upbringing explained most of his strangeness. It did not, however, explain why she felt so comfortable around him.

She glanced up, wondering how to articulate that question, and he met her look straight on. Larissa fell into his bright, clear gaze. That was the only way she could describe it: she simply fell into his eyes. The feelings with which she was inundated gladdened her, excited her, and frightened her to death. He was nothing like the men she had met before—smitten youths who wanted only to get her alone in some dark corner. There was respect and admiration in those brown eyes, and a marvelously compelling sense of . . . play.

"I have to go," she stammered. She automatically reached for the pouch she normally carried when she went ashore, then realized to her chagrin that she was still in costume.

"Willen, do you have any . . ." Larissa's voice trailed off as Willen sheepishly turned his own pockets out. Jean, seeing the gesture, appeared at their table.

"I have money in my cabin," Larissa began. "You can come with me, or come find me tomorrow, or I can come back here—"

Willen turned the power of his radiant smile fully upon the innkeeper. "Yes, Jean, come by the boat tomorrow, and not only will you be paid in full but you'll receive a tour as well. Isn't that right, Miss Snowmane?" Willen almost turned his charismatic eyes upon her, but she kept her attention on the innkeeper and nodded eagerly.

The big man smiled, revealing several missing teeth. "To walk on such a vessel! Yes, dear lady, I will come see you tomorrow—you and the magnificent showboat!"

Larissa smiled, relieved. "Thank you, Jean. I'll be sure to send everyone to the Two Hares when they come ashore."

At that moment, a distant rumbling noise was heard. Larissa tensed, thinking that the drums had begun again, then realized the sound was only thunder. She let her breath out in a quiet sigh of relief. Everyone else, though, put their mugs down, tossed money on the table, and began to hasten out the door. Even Jean turned a little pale and left without a word to start closing his tavern.

Larissa was thoroughly confused. "What's going on?"

The youth looked solemn. "There's a saying in Souragne that Death rides in the rain. Souragniens both long for and fear storms. There are no wells, because the water is tainted. And, of course, you can't drink swamp water. So the rain replenishes the fresh water supply, but . . ." His voice trailed off. "It's just as well that you're leaving now, that's all."

Larissa shivered, though she wasn't sure why. She, too, was glad that they were heading back to the safety and familiarity of the boat. She thought that Willen would question her abrupt decision to leave, but he said nothing about it as they made their way back through the now-deserted market square.

The thunder rumbled again as they walked, and the air smelled sharp and clean. They had almost reached the port when the heavens opened. Rain poured down with a vengeance, drenching the two almost immediately. Larissa gasped, shivering in the sudden, wet cold. Willen put an arm around her and shielded her with his body, ushering them into what little cover a closed storefront could afford.

"Shouldn't take long," Willen said. "These things blow over pretty quick."

His body was warm, and, in spite of everything she'd been taught, Larissa felt it was safe to accept his warmth. His arms were protective and sheltering, nothing more. That only caused the dancer to start violently when Willen tensed.

"What is it?"

"Oh, no," he said in a soft voice. He pulled her back as far as he could, then stepped in front of her. Panic sounded as sharply as *La Demoiselle*'s horn, and Larissa struggled. "Don't look out there," Willen said, fear tingeing his voice.

Larissa ceased struggling, but couldn't help gazing past Willen into the street. She heard through the pounding of the rain and the occasional sullen bouts of thunder another noise: a swift, clopping sound that drew closer and closer.

A black shadow was silhouetted against the gray of the market square. A huge horse, black as a nightmare, galloped past, its hooves devouring the cobblestones. Of its rider Larissa saw nothing, save the swirl of an equally black cape. Then it was gone, the clatter of frantic hooves swallowed by the sounds of the storm. She wasn't sure why, but the young dancer was extremely glad that she had been permitted only a brief look at the sinister, dark rider.

"He's gone," said Willen gently, stepping politely away from her.

"Who . . . what?"

Willen shook his head. "Don't ask," he pleaded in a

low voice. "Just be thankful he did not choose to stop."

Larissa desperately wanted to be back aboard the boat, where it was safe. "I've frightened you, haven't I?" Willen said unexpectedly. "Not just with . . . with the rider, but me. I've frightened you."

The quick, polite denial was on her lips, but Larissa found that she couldn't lie to that open, honest face and those troubled brown eyes.

"Yes," she admitted slowly, "but I honestly can't tell you why. Maybe I'm just jittery tonight. Let's go back."

They left the shelter of the storefront. The rain had died somewhat, and they reached the harbor in just a few moments. Larissa paused. The rain had now faded to a faint drizzle, and she wanted to say something before she left, but words escaped her.

Willen looked at her for a long moment but made no move to touch her, respecting her confusion. Then, as if he had reached a decision, he tugged at a string around his neck and produced a crude-looking necklace of tightly woven threads. The necklace was strung through what appeared to be a root of some sort. Before she could protest, he had slipped it over her head.

"It's for protection," Willen said quickly. "Keep it on you at all times. Please."

One slim hand reached up to finger the curious necklace as Larissa considered Willen's actions. Dumont had always warned her about accepting gifts from strangers. Larissa's full mouth went hard. Tonight, though, it had been Dumont she had feared, not this kind young man. She knew with a sudden inner certainty that, magical or not, the necklace could not harm her if it had come from Willen.

"Thank you," she said simply, flashed a fleeting smile, then scurried up the ramp. She did not glance back.

Larissa went to her cabin, bolted the door, and prepared for sleep. Still sitting up, propped against the down pillows, she pulled the coverlet up to her chin.

The young dancer didn't fall asleep until dawn began to lighten the room. Neither did she remove the necklace the strange young man who called himself Willen had given her.

* * * * *

Marcel cursed to himself as he left the Two Hares. It had looked like rain earlier today, and he should have been prepared. Now, here he was, clear on the wrong side of town when . . .

Angrily the musician wrapped his cloak around himself and his precious flute. The thin fabric of his cloak did little to keep out the oppressive wetness, and he was soon soaked. Marcel hugged the flute case to his chest, shielding it as best he could.

He hurried, glancing about nervously and stepping into ankle-deep puddles. Soon he was partway across the market square. His home, such as it was, was just down the road from the Scolding Jay, and his heart began to lighten as he glimpsed the sign creaking in the sudden whipping breeze. He almost laughed to himself. By Bouki's whiskers, he was going to make it.

It was then that he heard the hoofbeats.

His heart spasmed, and he almost dropped his flute case. Marcel broke into a quick trot, then into a dead run, his cloak flying behind him. He tried unsuccessfully to calm himself. *Other people in the town have horses besides* him . . . *and maybe they're simply hurrying home, just like I am.*

It was a melodious clopping sound now, the sound of a horse in full gallop on a cobblestone street. There was another sound, too, a sort of cracking noise that his mind couldn't place.

The flute case clattered to the shiny wet stones as a big hand reached down and closed on Marcel's throat.

## SIX

It had been a very bad evening for Captain Dumont.

The young man might not have been lying when he said he had seen Larissa run down Old Cypress Way. Still, Dumont had failed to locate his young ward. He spent about an hour going in and out of the brothels that lined the street, asking questions and receiving no information. Some of the young women were attractive enough, but Dumont had no inclination to sample their charms tonight. After assuring himself that the frightened girl hadn't sought shelter in one of the houses, he assumed that Larissa had returned to the safety of the boat.

He strode angrily up the ramp around midnight, thoughts on Larissa, but was distracted by the curious message that Caleb, the crewman standing watch, gave him.

"Someone came to see you, sir. Said his name was Lond and that he had urgent business to discuss."

Dumont fixed the hapless Caleb, a young man barely old enough to shave, with a sharp look.

"Did he say when he'd be back?"

Caleb looked frightened. "He—he didn't leave, Captain. He insisted on waiting for you in your cabin." The boy shuddered. "I didn't like him, sir. All wrapped up, he was, and I never did get a look at his face."

Dumont frowned. "Very well, Caleb. I'll deal with him shortly."

Before he spoke to the stranger waiting for him, Dumont wanted to check on Brynn. He hoped that a hot bath and some of Brock's fine cooking had settled the crewman's wits somewhat. Brynn had information locked up in that terrified brain, and Dumont wanted it.

He hastened up the deck stairs to the tub room and found Dragoneyes leaning against the door, whittling. A twisted shape with batlike wings was starting to emerge from the half-carved wood, and there was a pile of shavings at the mate's feet.

"No problems?" Dumont asked.

"None, sir," Dragoneyes replied. "Brock sent up some dinner a few hours ago, and I took it in. Brynn seemed a little calmer. He asked for some paper and pen and ink."

"That's odd. Brynn's barely literate."

The half-elf's thin lips twisted in a smile. "Well, he seemed pretty insistent, so I got the stuff for him. It's been quiet in there since. I thought he needed some privacy."

"Be just my luck if he fell asleep and drowned in the tub. Well, let's see what we can coax from him now." He rapped on the door. "Brynn, it's Captain Dumont. I've come to see how you're doing, son." There was no answer. Dumont gestured to Dragoneyes. The first mate pocketed his unsettling carving and stepped forward to unlock the door with the master key. The door swung open, and Dumont peered into the darkness.

The tub room was unique to the showboat. While most of the costumes in *The Pirate's Pleasure* were sturdy enough, there were a few delicate items of clothing, mostly belonging to Larissa and Casilda, that needed to be gently washed by hand in pure water. There were two tubs, one for washing and one for rinsing. Other than that, there was no decoration; the room was not even painted. The captain bathed here and occasionally granted similar privileges to the cast. The crew members had to content themselves with swimming in the river.

Costumes drying in the rafters brushed their faces as Dumont and Dragoneyes entered. There were lanterns, but Brynn had apparently not noticed they had guttered out. Dumont whistled a simple series of notes, and the keys Dragoneyes held began to glow brightly, illuminating the bare room. The magical radiance revealed a sight that filled Dumont with angry frustration and faint nausea.

Brynn was still in the tub, but he hadn't drowned. The water in which his fish-white corpse floated was a dark crimson. The knife he had used to open his veins lay on the floor beside the tub. One hand rested on the side, the ragged flesh of the wrist a pale reddish gray.

Dumont strode up to the tub and glared down at the body accusingly, as if his displeasure would be enough to animate the bloodless corpse.

"Here's what he wanted to write so badly," the half-elf mate told his captain, handing Dumont a crumpled piece of paper. Scrawled in Brynn's messy, childish hand was a message: FOR MERCYS SAKE BURN MY BODDY DONT BERY IT. Dumont read Brynn's last message and shook his head. He wondered briefly what had so terrified the rough crewman that he had taken his own life.

"Ah, Brynn, you never could spell worth a damn." Angrily, he crumpled the note. "Why'd you go and cut yourself before you told me what was in that swamp?"

"I know what is in the swamp," came a raspy voice.

Startled, the captain wheeled to encounter a slender, cloaked figure of medium height. The stranger had pulled the hood down so no part of his face could be seen. The cloak was ebony, and matching gloves covered the man's hands.

Dragoneyes had already unsheathed his dagger. He stood tensely, awaiting his captain's command. Dumont recognized the intruder from the crewman's description.

"You are Lond, I assume," he stated coolly. The only hint of his anger was the fire in his jade-green eyes.

The stranger bowed in acknowledgment. "You have a magnificent boat, Captain Dumont. I congratulate you on it."

"You should know. You've trespassed through enough of it tonight."

The dark shape in the doorway shrugged. "It was a long wait." Nonchalantly Lond moved forward, closing the door behind him.

Dumont had been startled by Lond's strange and silent appearance, but he had recovered. He flicked his right wrist and a knife slid into his hand from his sleeve. "I'm extremely protective of my boat," he said conversationally. "Men have died for lesser infractions than trespassing aboard her."

Because of the hood, Dumont was unable to see Lond's reaction, but his slim figure revealed no apprehension. "I have not come to spy or to threaten you, Captain. I have a business proposition for you, which I think you will find most agreeable."

"I'm always willing to talk business," Dumont admitted, "but I like to know my partners first."

Lond's slim shoulders began to shake, and a scratchy, gurgling laugh issued forth from inside the hood. The captain frowned.

"Ah, good Captain Dumont, you wish my credentials, is that it? I am happy to prove myself to you. But perhaps you wish to dismiss your mate?"

Dumont glanced at the half-elf. He had not moved from his position of armed alertness. "Dragoneyes stays."

"What I have to say is for your ears, Captain, not

those of a crewman."

"Dragoneyes is my most trusted man. He stays," Dumont repeated. Dragoneyes quirked an eyebrow, and the captain nodded slightly. Keeping his slit-pupiled eyes on Lond, the half-elf lowered his weapon. Dumont sheathed his own dagger and spread his hands. "So. Let us talk."

"Here?" queried Lond, somewhat surprised.

"Here. Now."

The black figure shrugged. "As you wish. I was at the performance tonight in the market square. You have quite a cadre of talent here—both magical and mundane. It must have taken years to find such talent and to master such magic.

"I am a wizard, like you," the mysterious hooded man continued, moving about the room as he spoke, occasionally reaching out a gloved hand to touch the wooden walls or a dangling costume. "I appreciate such things. However, I may have certain advantages over you, Captain. I have not had to burden myself with the running of a showboat. I know a great deal about Souragne, and that knowledge coupled with my magic could prove very useful to someone like you."

"What do you mean, someone like me?"

"A wizard," repeated Lond, his voice mild and placating. "A connoisseur of the finer things . . . a collector, as it were, of rare and interesting items." Lond paused to let his words sink in.

Dumont kept his face expressionless. "Go on."

"I know where to find the sorts of things you are seeking. I know how to put them to excellent use. I can get you a crew that will work hard and cost little to maintain. I offer you my service, skill, and wisdom."

Dumont let his handsome face crinkle into a sneer. "Of course, you want something in return."

"I want to get out of this watery hole." The voice was cold and flat. "Eventually, you will be leaving Souragne.

I want you to take me with you. I have learned all I can learn here. This place is too trifling for my talents, and I yearn to stretch my skills. Surely, what I offer is worth what I ask."

"I don't know," answered the captain. "I'm not about to take someone on faith—especially not someone who creeps up on me as you do. How do I know you are what you say?"

Again the raspy laugh. "Allow me a chance to prove it to you."

The caped figure brushed past Dumont and Dragoneyes as if they weren't there and stood gazing down at the marble-fleshed form of the dead Brynn. "What did that last note say?"

A bit nonplussed, Dumont replied, "He wanted to be cremated, not buried."

"That will not be possible here. No one is cremated."

"Why not?"

Lond did not reply at once, then said, "It's a local custom. The Souragniens, as you will no doubt discover, are extremely superstitious. They believe burning the dead offends . . . the higher powers that rule this place." He turned toward Dumont, still keeping his face hidden. "I will take care of the body. You will allow me to empty the tub first?"

A bucket, used for filling the tub, rested nearby. Lond grasped it with his gloved hands. He dipped the bucket into the blood-tinted water and partially filled it. For a moment, he swirled it about, gazing into its maroon depths as if scrying. Dragoneyes and Dumont exchanged glances, but did not interrupt the wizard. Then, to the horror of the watching men, Lond lifted the liquid to his hidden mouth and drank a noisy gulp.

As one, Dumont and Dragoneyes tackled the cloaked mage. The bucket went flying, its crimson contents spattering then soaking into the wooden beams of the floor.

"You are the sickest—" began Dumont, but the words turned into a grunt of pain as icy coldness numbed his hands. The chill spread up his arms, as if he had plunged his hands into a snowdrift. He heard Dragoneyes gasp softly and guessed the half-elf was feeling the strange sensation as well. Dumont released his hold and warmth flooded painfully into his icy hands.

Lond scrambled to his feet. "You fools!" he hissed angrily. "This is part of my magic! Your nerves are those of children! Would you see my demonstration, Captain Raoul Dumont, or will your weak stomach not tolerate it?"

Dumont was stung by the insult, and his own anger stirred. "You startled me, nothing more. I have seen—and done—far worse. The dead are the dead. Brynn is yours to do with as you will, now that I know what to expect from your kind of magic."

Lond appeared mollified. "Have your men drain the tub, but keep the water. Then lay out the crewman's body. I will return with proof of my power."

Without another word, Lond dipped up another bucketful of the bloody water and left. Dragoneyes tensed to spring after him, but Dumont laid a warning hand on his friend's arm and shook his head. "Let him go."

"He's carrying a bucket of blood!" the mate protested.

"Young Caleb already knows of Lond. He's not likely to go out of his way to question our guest's departure."

The half-elf narrowed his eyes, and his voice was deep with misgiving. "I think you're making a mistake. There's something about that man . . . I don't trust him, Raoul!"

"Neither do I," Dumont replied. "Not for a moment. But I want to see what he can do that would be so important to me. We'll watch him, old friend." He smiled coldly. "We'll watch him like a pair of wolves in winter."

* * * * *

Caleb shuddered as Lond strode past him, walking briskly down the ramp onto the dock. As Dumont had predicted, the young crewman was too glad to see the sinister figure leaving to question him. Lond's dark shape was soon swallowed up by the surrounding darkness.

The market square was as quiet as a cemetery at this time of night. The torches had been permitted to burn out and would not be relit until the following nightfall. Lond was midway across the square when he heard the drums start up again, an urgent counterpoint to the distant rumble of thunder. He frowned underneath his hood. He knew what creatures dwelt in the swamp of Souragne, and he disliked the interest they were taking in the strangers from the boat.

His rapid stride soon carried him beyond the market square into the less savory portion of town referred to as Past-the-Port. Few walked here even in daylight hours without a weapon and a readiness to use it. After night fell on Past-the-Port, one didn't walk at all, unless one was going about business as foul as that practiced by the other inhabitants. Even murderous intentions were no guarantee against things darker—and deadlier—than a pure soul could conceive. Fear dwelled in the slum of Past-the-Port, along with her companion, Death.

Lond knew Past-the-Port intimately, and his slender, black-cloaked frame was recognized and given a wide berth by most ne'er-do-wells. The cloaked man laughed to himself as he caught the big, burly would-be killers blanching and turning away. He knew that with a few well-spoken words and the right ingredients he could shatter their tiny minds and warp their souls. They knew it, too.

There was only one person in Past-the-Port who welcomed Lond's arrival. Murduc lived in a shabby, gloomy little house with boarded-up windows in the worst part of the slum. He'd have been murdered long ago, his throat slit or his neck broken in some dark side street, had it not been for Lond's protection. Everyone knew that the skinny old madman who played with poisons was somehow in the cloaked man's favor, and thus the pathetic hovel hadn't been torched or ransacked.

The street was dark and deserted. Most of the buildings were abandoned or were homes only to rats. The notable exception was the one across from Murduc's shack. It looked like a tavern, and indeed even had a sign that proclaimed it the Cat and Mouse. Lond, however, knew it to be a meeting place of the most unsavory of a bad group of men. Light crept out of the cracks in the wall and from under the door.

Lond knocked on Murduc's door, feeling the rotting timbers shudder beneath his gloved knuckles. A good wind would collapse the entire building, he thought to himself. He heard scuffling sounds from within.

"Who's there?" came the old man's thin voice.

"Why, who but your master?" answered Lond, smiling to himself. He heard the sound of several bolts being drawn back. Then Murduc peered out cautiously, a lantern clutched in one grimy hand. His toothless mouth widened in a grin, and he opened the door to the only guest who ever visited.

"My laird, my laird!" he enthused in his thin, high voice. "Come in at once! How kin yer humble servant help ye?"

"Good evening, Murduc." Lond's sharp eyes flitted disinterestedly about the place as he entered. Murduc set the lantern on a precarious table, then scurried to bolt the door behind his guest.

The little man did not keep a tidy shop. Herbs were scattered carelessly in piles in the corners, their fragrances both pleasant and noxious. More hung drying from the wooden rafters. Murduc's bed, a pile of filthy rags, occupied one corner. As Lond watched, a rat scurried from under the pile and hastened out through a large hole in the wall.

"I will need large quantities of the usual items—and take care that you don't confuse them like you did last time," the wizard added. The last time he had employed Murduc's services, the senile old fool had accidentally switched an aphrodisiac with a deadly poison. Lond had ended up with a corpse instead of a passionate lover, and had been mightily displeased.

Murduc cringed visibly at the memory. Lond's anger was a terrible thing, and he had no wish to incur it again. "Aye, my laird," he said, ducking his head respectfully. "That'll no happen again, I assure ye."

He scurried about like a scrawny spider, scooping up various herbs and placing them in small pouches. Shelves filled with bottles of potions, some of them thick with dust, lined all four walls. Lond helped himself to several, carefully checking the crudely written labels. Occasionally he would open a bottle to examine and sniff the contents.

At last, Murduc turned to him, grinning. "All collected, sair. Shall I put 'em in a sack for ye?"

"Yes, that would be helpful," Lond answered absently. He took several more jars and bottles from the shelf.

"Oh, sair, ye've practically bought me out!" Murduc exclaimed happily, peering at the bottles in Lond's arms. These, too, were placed in the sack. The wizard fished out ten gold coins from the pouch at his side and handed them to the stunned poisoner.

Murduc's eyes grew enormous. "My laird!" he whispered. "I'll ne'er have to sell another thing!" His hand trembled as his thin fingers closed about the gold.

"True enough, Murduc. True enough. Farewell." He swept out of the room like a shadow, closing the door behind him, then went to the Cat and Mouse Tavern.

He opened the door without a pause. Several men with scarred and angry visages clustered around a table. The dim light threw their unhandsome features into sharp relief as they turned to look at the intruder. They averted their eyes, however, when they saw who it was.

"The little poisoner has ten gold pieces in his hands right now," Lond told them. "Kill him and burn his filthy shop, and the money's yours."

He had scarcely gone five paces when he heard the door burst open behind him. Ten minutes later, the night grew orange, and smoke spiraled up into the overcast skies. Lond smiled to himself. He was leaving Souragne, and had no more use for the little man.

The cloaked man paused a few yards out of the city limits and fished an agate out of his pouch. He pulled down his black hood and, murmuring an incantation, gently rubbed the stone on his eyelids. When he opened them a few moments later, he could see as well as a night creature. Replacing the agate in his pocket, he carefully pulled his hood back on.

The wizard continued on down the main road, called Tristepas, toward a place seldom visited by people during the daylight and avoided after nightfall: the graveyard.

A light mist swirled a few feet off the ground as he left the road, the gravel of a wide but ill-kept path gritting under his feet. Moonlight brightened the scene, flickering amid the branches of live oak and elm and cedar, giving ghostly illumination to the stone sarcophagi. Souragne was too marshy, even this far away from the swamp, for corpses to be buried. Diggers struck water three feet down. As a result, even thieves and murderers rotted in large, elaborate sepulchers instead of moldering in the soil.

Lond walked to the wrought-iron gate, spoke a few abrupt words, and made fluttering gestures with his gloved hands. Like a snake uncoiling, the chain wrapped securely about the iron bars unwound itself and fell with a dull thud to the soft soil. With a slow creak, the doors reluctantly yielded to the wizard's touch and permitted him entrance.

The black-cloaked man strode through the cemetery with absolute familiarity. He headed straight for a certain unadorned tomb far from the main gate, striding briskly past the last resting places of warriors, noblemen, and the base-born rich. The fog swirled damply around his knees, but he paid it no heed. There was nothing in this cemetery that could harm Lond.

He came to the tomb he wanted. "Rogue's Rest" was its nickname, where the nameless dead were carelessly tossed. Again the wizard reached in his pocket, emerging with a small length of leather string. Chanting softly, he tied it into a loop and tossed it onto the tomb's lid. Lond raised his hands, and the enormously heavy stone slab trembled and began to rise. It floated upward until it was six feet over the tomb, then hovered in the air.

A horrible stench wafted from the tomb, but it did not bother Lond. He smiled to himself as he peered inside.

The bones of many dead were piled high in the grave. Atop them was a comparatively fresh corpse. Lond looked closer and began to smile as he recognized the dead man's features.

"Well, good fellow," he said. "You'll do splendidly. You'll impress the good captain no end, I daresay."

He tugged off the glove from his left hand and draped it carefully on the tomb wall. Then he rolled up his black sleeve to the elbow and drew his knife. The finely honed blade glinted in the moonlight as Lond, biting back a cry of painful pleasure, drew the dagger across his own forearm.

# SEVEN

Larissa stood alone on the main deck of *La Demoiselle*. The mists pressed in thickly on three sides, but before her loomed the gray-green swamp and tea-colored water. The young dancer gazed down at the water, and a slow smile spread across her face. She felt strong, and her body began to move to an inner music.

As she danced, reveling in her new confidence, there came a disturbance in the muddy water. It roiled angrily, and slowly, steadily, a serpentine monster rose from the depths. Larissa felt no fear, just as she was no longer worried by either the mists or the swamp. She was surprised but not alarmed when the snake began to speak to her in Willen's friendly voice. She couldn't understand its garbled words, but the tones were so gentle and concerned that she listened anyway.

In the middle of speaking, the creature began to bleed. Wounds spontaneously erupted on its scaly body, spewing crimson streams. Redness spattered Larissa, staining her clothes and white hair.

The dancer's unnatural peace was shattered. She screamed, but the creature kept right on talking. It was then that she realized that it wasn't even alive. It was only the corpse of a snakelike creature, and suddenly the voice wasn't Willen's, but Dumont's. The undead snake-thing began to slither toward her. She tried to flee but her feet wouldn't obey her.

The girl had heard stories of how snakes hypnotized their victims, and Larissa knew that she had been caught. Somehow she knew that if she could move, could dance, she could escape, but it was too late, too late. . . .

A sharp rap on the door caused Larissa to bolt upright, wide awake though completely disoriented. "Y-yes?" she called, her voice cracking.

"Are you going to stay in bed all day?" came Casilda's voice.

It was a welcome intrusion of normalcy after Larissa's dream and the confusing incidents of last night. The dancer hurried to the door to admit her friend.

"Did you *hear* me last night? Oh, gods, I sounded like a calf at slaughtering time, bellowing away—" Casilda stopped abruptly when she saw her friend's pale visage. "What's wrong?"

Larissa shook her head. "Nothing. I just didn't sleep very well." Casilda looked skeptical. Larissa squeezed her friend's arm reassuringly. "Really."

"Poor Larissa. You don't like this place at all, do you?" Casilda gave the dancer an impulsive hug. "Come on. Some breakfast will make you feel better."

Larissa thought quickly. The dining hall at breakfast was a likely place to run into Dumont. The dancer realized that it would be impossible to avoid her guardian for very long on a space as enclosed as *La Demoiselle*, but after last night she wanted to postpone that meeting as long as possible.

"No, I think I'll go practice first." The thought calmed her. Yes, Larissa decided, I need to dance.

Without Gelaar's illusions to enliven the stage, it was a bare, wooden floor. The chairs were pushed back to the far end of the room, thus permitting the actors to rehearse on the stage area while the dancers went over their numbers where the audience would normally be. Larissa, wearing the short, bare-armed cotton chemise that was her practice outfit, smiled to herself as she entered. She began to warm up her sleep-stiff body by doing gentle stretches.

A wolf whistle caused her to look up, hoping it wasn't Dumont. However, it was only Sardan, and she glowered at him.

"If you're going to spy on my dancing, at least you can play for me."

Sardan bowed. "Delighted to be of service to so lovely a lady," he replied gallantly.

Larissa snorted. "Save it for the paying customers," she retorted, but a hint of a smile touched her face. After fleeing from Dumont, Sardan's blatant yet harmless flirting was refreshing.

He plucked on his ever-present mandolin, cocking his head to listen for the pitch, then adjusting the strings. Larissa sighed inwardly. When it came to his music, Sardan was a perfectionist, even when it was just for rehearsal. At last the bard looked up at her and nodded, satisfied with the instrument's tone.

"What song do you want?" he asked, strumming absently.

" 'And So Floweth Love,' " the dancer replied, referring to the Lady of the Sea's final number, where she relinquishes her hold on Florian. Sardan began to play.

Larissa had been growing increasingly dissatisfied with the choreography of this dance. The older she grew and the more she performed, the more demands she made on herself and her art. It was time to experiment with some new steps for this number. She began to move. Her fingers traced patterns in the air, and her feet were as light as foam on the ocean's waves. She half-closed her eyes and allowed her body to sway more freely.

Even though the Lady of the Sea was ostensibly the

villain, you have to pity her a bit, she thought to herself as her fingers mimed tears flowing down her face. All coldness and lack of feeling, until this sailor entered her heart. Larissa's feet brushed lightly, rhythmically, on the boards of the stage. She wrapped her long arms about her body, weaving back and forth with the Lady of the Sea's anguish. And she must let him leave, return to the world of air and sunlight, to the woman he loves.

Larissa's chest contracted with emotion. Her movements became more powerful and yet more graceful. The young woman was no longer aware of the wooden boards beneath her feet, or of the rivulets of sweat beginning to trickle down her flushed face. Her unbound white hair floated freely, and it felt to her as if she were submerged in water. She breathed, but did not notice the air she gasped in; danced, but knew not what movements she made.

She felt herself growing, as if she and her gestures filled every corner of the suddenly confining room. Heat flooded her body. Movement was effortless and undirected, and she leaped and swirled about the stage with utter oblivion, surrendering to that inner heat, to the power that suddenly swelled within her and—

"Larissa!"

There was a painful pressure about her wrists, and her movement, her glorious, wild movement was abruptly halted. Larissa's blue eyes flew open, but she saw nothing as she struggled against her captor. She heard herself cry out, a sharp, high wail. He was not letting her *dance*, and she would die if he did not—

"Larissa, look at me! Stop it and *look at me*!"

It was Sardan's voice, coming as though from a great distance. With an effort that drained her, Larissa focused her eyes and met his frantic gaze.

Sardan was pale and his eyes were enormous with fright. He gripped each of her wrists in a strong hand. The singer waited until he was sure that she was fully aware of her surroundings before he let his grip relax. "Are you all right?"

Larissa discovered that her heart was pounding furiously. She licked dry lips and nodded slowly. She felt very tired all of a sudden. As if he sensed this, Sardan helped her to the back of the room and eased her into a chair. He waited until she had caught her breath before asking slowly, "What happened when you were dancing?"

"Nothing. Just—just going over some new ideas."

Sardan shook his head, his eyes still concerned. "I've watched you dance for the last four years. You've never looked like that. That was—" he floundered for words. "Larissa, your dancing is flawless."

She opened her mouth to protest, but he held up a hand and continued. "No, I mean that. You're perfect. Almost too perfect. A few minutes ago you were *wild*. You looked like—like some kind of monster, or fairy, or something not human." He paused, not meeting her eyes for a moment. When he did, his look was wary. "You really frightened me. It was almost as though you weren't there anymore."

Larissa tried to reassure him. "Really, Sardan, it was just a dance. You're imagining—"

He arched an eyebrow. "You look exhausted, and don't tell me you're not. You try doing something like that every night and you'll be dead inside of a week."

"I'm fine . . . just a little thirsty. Could you get me some water?" she suggested, hoping to buy a few moments of time to collect herself. The young man sprinted off.

Larissa exhaled and rested her head in her hands, willing her heart to slow its erratic beating. She had gotten carried away with the music before, but never like this. For a few moments she had tasted ecstasy, and her body had flamed with energy. It had been a terrifying sensation, yet oddly compelling. If she had been able to use that energy, harness it somehow, what might she have done?

"Here," said Sardan, handing her a goblet of cold water. She drank gratefully.

"I didn't have anything to eat this morning," said Larissa. "Maybe that might have something to do with it."

Sardan looked dubious. "Maybe. Get something to eat and then go back to sleep. You've got a performance tonight." He helped her up, and she gave him a tired smile.

"One might think you actually cared," she joked.

Sardan feigned offense. "I'm only protecting my chances of seducing you."

* * * * *

Larissa had experienced many opening nights with *The Pirate's Pleasure*, but none like this. The entertainment-hungry folk of Port d'Elhour had turned out in force, and the show was sold out.

Safely invisible, Larissa looked at the delighted faces in the audience and grinned. No one had missed a cue. The dancers had performed magnificently. It seemed to her that the tired, clichéd musical suddenly sparkled with, if not exactly wit, then warmth. The love story was a sweet one, and she, the Lady of the Sea, full of beautiful, alluring peril.

Larissa listened to Casilda sing "Alas! My Love Is No More" with anticipation. She hoped the luck of the evening would rub off on her friend. Casilda, too, was caught up in the excitement and joy of performing before so receptive an audience and was doing her finest job yet. But she still couldn't hit that last note.

Larissa was glad the audience appeared oblivious. The applause for each number was deafening, and the cast received a thunderous standing ovation. When they left the stage, the sweaty, elated performers hugged each other and laughed with sheer pleasure. It was nights like this, nights when everything came together almost as magically as one of Gelaar's illusions, that made everything worthwhile.

Still walking on air, Larissa literally danced back to her cabin. Crewman, cast member, or patron alike who crossed her path was treated to a radiant smile. She removed her makeup and changed swiftly, then went to the main deck to meet the patrons as all the cast did after each show. When she arrived, she had another pleasant surprise.

The boat was glowing with dozens of small lights, fastened to the railings at regular intervals. They twinkled softly, like stars that had wandered down from the heavens and decided to stay for a while. They blinked and shimmered, shedding their cool, pleasant light on the laughing cast members, their guests from the town, and the wine-bearing crewmen. As Larissa watched, a young man trying to impress a giggling chorus girl attempted to touch one of the lights. It immediately went dark, but resumed glowing when the man withdrew his hand.

Larissa assumed the effect was another one of Gelaar's illusions. She looked around for the elf and spotted him standing alone down near the paddlewheel. Smiling to herself, she hastened down the deck toward him. He glanced over at her briefly, then returned his attention to the small glowing lights. His slim, long-fingered hand stretched out to one of them, but didn't touch it. It glowed brightly.

"They're beautiful, Gelaar," Larissa said warmly. "One of the nicest illusions I've ever seen. Everyone loves them."

Gelaar looked at her oddly. "I can't take credit for them, Miss Snowmane," he said in a cold voice. "They are something the captain has provided for the ship."

"And a fine job, too," came Dragoneyes' silky voice. Gelaar turned to the first mate, and his expression hardened even further.

Larissa felt a vague stirring of discomfort penetrate her euphoria. The half-elf mate and the elven mage had a tenuous truce at best. Like a wolf and a tiger, they were natural enemies.

"You might want to take better care of yourself, Gelaar," Dragoneyes continued in a mock-concerned tone. "You're seeming pretty tired these days. Looked in a mirror lately?" He laughed harshly, and Larissa cringed from the hate-filled expression on Gelaar's gaunt face.

"Excuse me, Miss Snowmane," the mage said, his voice emotionless. "The night has suddenly grown unpleasant." He nodded courteously, then swept past Dragoneyes with a dignity that would have embarrassed anyone but the half-elf. Dragoneyes merely watched the illusionist leave. He looked over at Larissa, touched his forelock in a casual salute, and left.

Larissa watched him go, discontent stirring within her. She shook her head, trying to forget the unpleasant incident she'd just been witness to, and leaned over the rail so she could get a better look at the twinkling lights.

Their brightness fluctuated, and they sometimes even blinked rapidly. The young dancer watched, fascinated, and, to her pleasure, saw that the colors even changed, going from yellow to green to blue to purple and myriad other shades in between. Like a child, she laughed aloud.

"Aren't they gorgeous?" said Casilda.

Larissa beamed. "More than anything I've ever seen. I feel like—like I've just walked into a fairy tale or something."

The two women stood quietly, watching the display of uncanny, lovely lights that festooned *La Demoiselle*.

"The crowd was so good, I wish I'd been able to hit that damned note," Casilda sighed at last.

Larissa squeezed her arm. "*You* were so good, the crowd didn't even care."

"Mademoiselle Snowmane?" came a tentative voice, and Larissa glanced up to see the innkeeper of the Two Hares gazing sheepishly at her. He removed his hat and played with it nervously, rendering it into a shapeless mass. "I have come for my tour. You remember?"

"Of course!" Larissa smiled, and Jean felt as if he had just seen the sun rise. "Casilda, this is Jean. He owns an inn in Port d'Elhour with the funniest sign I've ever seen." Quickly she described the drunken rabbits, and Casilda chuckled.

"The rabbits are from an old folk story," said Jean. He was delighted to be so well received by two lovely young ladies. "There are two heroes, Longears and Bouki. Longears is the clever one. Poor Bouki, he is always finding a way to get into trouble and Longears must always get him out of it."

"If your sign was any indication, Bouki is going to have one terrible headache in the morning," laughed Casilda. "Larissa, what's this about a tour?"

When Larissa explained, carefully leaving out any mention of Willen, Casilda brightened. "Well," the singer said, "we can't take you everywhere, but we will give you a quick tour of *La Demoiselle*'s decks."

Jean couldn't believe his good fortune. He knew that these were ladies, and that nothing untoward was going to happen. Still, it would make a great taproom tale, of the night when Jean the innkeeper was escorted about a magical boat with a stunning woman on either arm. He laughed, a warm, booming sound that mixed pleasantly with the animated chatter from the other guests.

"Larissa, my dear," came Dumont's voice, "I don't believe you have introduced me to your friend."

The young dancer had been apprehensive about running into her guardian, but the effervescent mood of the evening apparently lingered on. She turned, smiling, to Dumont.

"Uncle Raoul, this is Jean, the innkeeper at the Two Hares. Last night, I had no money with me because I was in costume, and he was good enough to forgive me for it. I promised him a tour."

There was a bit of quiet defiance in her attitude, and she knew it. Larissa's message was clear: she would ignore what had happened last night if Dumont would. The captain's green-eyed gaze met hers evenly.

"Good Jean," he said at last, "you are kind. My ward is right to treat you as hospitably as you have treated her. Enjoy your tour."

The three walked toward the bow of the ship, Larissa chatting enthusiastically about *La Demoiselle*. Dumont watched them with narrowed eyes. Larissa was not angry with him, but neither was she cowed. He deliberately loosened his shoulders and puffed on his pipe, forcing his thoughts to take a happier turn.

The boat had been packed. Both performers and audience had apparently had the time of their lives. The little lights that had cost the lives of four men twinkled gaily. They had the ability to manipulate emotions, for they had made Dumont feel happy when he'd looked at them yesterday. Now he had harnessed their energy, and they were making everyone on the whole damned boat feel happy. This ebullience was a boon to business, but Dumont wondered if his crew would still be as efficient when they were giddy with magically induced pleasure. He'd have to wait and see. Or else, he mused to himself, he'd just pack the glowing creatures away during work times.

The captain leaned up against the railing, his eyes on the shimmer of the lights reflected in the water. A movement on the shore caught his eye, and he drew deeply on his pipe, suddenly alert.

As the newcomers drew closer, Dumont recognized one of them as Lond. The mage's companion was clad in a dark cloak that hid his face completely. The two men came on board. The throng of happy, chattering people parted for them unconsciously, their pleasure not abating a bit. Lond and his comrade walked up the ramp onto the main deck, heading directly for Dumont. As they drew closer, the wind shifted and the captain grimaced. A terrible stench was emanating from the two, borne on the hot, muggy breeze.

"I have completed the first part of my own performance. May we retire to your cabin, Captain?" came Lond's raspy whisper.

Dumont frowned, clenching his pipe between his teeth. He tried to concentrate on its fruity fragrance.

"Who is your friend?" he demanded. The stranger kept his head down and his face turned away.

"You shall meet him momentarily, Captain. Let us go to your room."

"You will not toy with me. If you won't introduce me, you and your stinking friend can leave right now."

Lond sighed. "Very well, Captain. Although there is in truth no need, for you know this man."

Lond stepped in front of the stranger and rearranged the hood so that Dumont could see the newcomer's face clearly. The captain stepped back, eyes wide.

It was Handsome Jack.

The corpse's ugly face was still recognizable, but the first stages of decay had begun to set in on its two-day-dead body. Its skin was a sickly gray, and its milky eyes were unfocused. Dumont's startled gaze dropped to the dead man's stomach, and he pulled aside the cloak enough to see dried blood encrusted on the white shirt.

"No," he whispered. "You're dead!"

"Yes, Captain Dumont, he is," Lond agreed. "Now, may we retire to your cabin?"

# EIGHT

"You're goin' to go *where*?" The man's face grew pale.

"Through the swamp," Dumont repeated with strained patience. "How familiar are you with its waterways?"

The would-be sailor shook his head rapidly. "Sorry, Captain Dumont. I'd love to join you, but I'll not be goin' nowhere near *that* place. There's bad magic in there, there is. Ain't nobody told you? That's the home of the Lord of the Dead!"

It was the fourteenth time this morning Dumont had heard the "advice," and it took every ounce of control he possessed not to stand up and throttle the man.

"I have heard that, yes," the captain replied. "If you do not wish to sign up, you may go."

The man opened his mouth as if to say more, but a good look at the anger in Dumont's eyes apparently changed his mind. He bowed clumsily and hastened back down to the ramp.

Dumont, seated at a small table on the bow of the main deck, frowned to himself. He had thought it would be easy to hire a few new crew members after last night's opening performance had been so well received. Dumont had not bargained on how terrified these people were of the swamp.

"They were turned out thicker than wolves in Arkandale earlier," he growled to Dragoneyes, who was lounging against the railing.

"Not to worry. There'll be a couple willing to face the swamp, I'm sure," the mate replied, concentrating on his whittling. The breeze stirred his silver hair. He seemed to take no interest in the proceedings, though he was discreetly observing everything with his slitted, amber eyes. Only his pose and dress were casual.

Dumont, in sharp contrast, was dressed in full uniform. The sun glinted brightly on the shiny gold buttons and braids of the blue outfit, and his green eyes raked the potential crewmen more obviously than did Dragoneyes. The next applicant stepped up to the table.

Dumont glanced up. There was something familiar about this one. "Do I know you, son?" he inquired politely.

The youth smiled. "No, Captain."

"Name?" Dumont asked briskly.

"Willen."

The captain duly inscribed the youth's name on the parchment. "Present occupation?"

"None."

"Residence?"

"The swamp, until about—oh, three, four days ago."

Dumont glanced up from the parchment. "I must," he drawled sarcastically, "hear the explanation for *this*."

Willen met Dumont's gaze and smiled disarmingly. "Well, Captain, I grew up in the swamp. My mother was a hermit, and she took me with her when I was a baby."

The captain didn't avert his gaze from Willen's, but he noticed that Dragoneyes had stopped whittling. That was a clear sign that the crewman was interested in a candidate. Dumont continued.

"What are your qualifications for working aboard my vessel? Have you ever served on a boat before?"

Willen looked a bit abashed, and his grin turned slightly sheepish. "Well, truth be told, no, sir. Unless you count the canoes we use in the swamp. We call them pirogues, and I know those very well. Even know how to make them out of cypress logs. I know the swamp well, too."

He leaned forward slightly and placed his hands on the table. All hint of shamefacedness was gone, replaced by a quiet competence. Willen continued.

"I know every turn, where the currents flow fast and at what time of year, what's underneath every foot of the water's surface. I know what's dangerous and what isn't, how to avoid trouble and how to treat it when it comes looking for you.

"The rest of the folk around these parts, they're scared of the swamp. They don't know a thing about it except the superstitions, and they don't want to get close enough to it to learn anything more than that. You ask them. They won't want to go. If you've a mind to head on down there, well, you won't find anyone better suited than I am to take you through it."

There was nothing in Willen's manner that bespoke a braggart. Dumont decided that the young man was telling the truth. He narrowed his jade eyes.

Brynn's discovery of the light creatures was the only thing of interest his men had discovered in Souragne thus far. The little port town, though delightfully corrupt in some places, was disappointingly normal. Few here knew any magic at all, apparently. Certainly no one—other than Lond, of course—had any knowledge or item worthy of Dumont's attention.

It would be foolish to traverse the swamp without a guide. Dumont was also in desperate need of another pilot. Handsome Jack was first drunk, then dead, and now a mindless, walking corpse. The enthusiastic youth before him seemed to be a gift from the heavens.

The captain turned his gaze back to the piece of

parchment and circled Willen's name.

"Where can I reach you if I need you, Will?" He deliberately changed the youth's name. If the boy had an ego . . .

"I'm here and there. I won't go far, though. You'll be able to find me easily enough if you want to."

"Well, then, I'll be talking to you more later."

Willen's face split into a big grin. "Thank *you*, Captain Dumont!" He glanced over at the watching Dragoneyes and gave him the same friendly smile, then sauntered down the ramp, whistling.

Dumont turned his attention to his first mate, and to his surprise found the half-elf watching Willen's retreat. There was a slight smile on Dragoneyes' lips. He turned his amber gaze on his captain.

"I like that man, Captain. You could do a lot worse than hire him." He resumed his whittling.

Dragoneyes' attitude was curious. The crewman didn't much like anyone except Dumont, and the captain made a mental note of the half-elf's comment.

\* \* \* \* \*

"What do you mean, you are going through the swamp?" Lond demanded.

The mage and the captain were in Dumont's cabin, a few hours after the last crew candidate had left the ship. *The Pirate's Pleasure* was in performance on the deck below them, and strains of the music floated in occasionally. Its sweet, innocent melodies were a vivid contrast with the scene of darkness and death that was playing itself out around Dumont.

For his part, the captain did not permit himself to become angry. He stood, towering over Lond's slight frame. Even the two dead men who stood at the mage's side didn't worry Dumont.

"I mean exactly what I said. You want to get out of

Souragne? Fine. You have passage aboard my boat, but *La Demoiselle du Musarde* is leaving via the swamp. The only thing of interest in this boring little hole has come from there, and I want to find more. I've told you how my boat works, what—and who—we use to make her what she is. My goal is to make *La Demoiselle* legendary."

"If you travel through that darkness, you *will* pass into legend!" the mage protested.

"Just what is in there that has everybody so terrified?" Dumont stepped closer, and Lond averted his shadowed face. "You said when we first met that you knew what was in the swamp. Tell me."

The black-cloaked figure did not reply at once. Then, he chuckled throatily.

"Death, Captain Dumont. Death dwells in the swamp. But Death dwells aboard your lovely showboat, too . . . death under my control." He walked behind Brynn, stroking the crewman's back almost affectionately as he passed.

Both corpses stared ahead impassively. Brynn, in Dumont's mind, was the real triumph of Lond's obviously powerful magic. The riverboat captain had seen zombies before. One tended to run into many horrible things if one traveled enough, and Dumont had been steaming up and down dark waterways for over twenty years. Handsome Jack's appearance had startled him badly, but had not horrified or surprised him.

Brynn, however, was something else again. He was capable of passing for a living being. Dumont had concocted a story about Brynn having contracted swamp fever, an illness that left the red-haired crewman listless and smelling rather foul. The zombie was lifelike enough that no one had questioned the explanation. Lond had promised more such crewmen—crewmen who never ate or complained and who could work tirelessly.

"I am an ambitious man myself, Captain," Lond resumed. "I appreciate your desires, but a wise man recognizes the value of discretion. You already have the *feu follets*. They are unique to this place. Are they not enough for you?"

"Oh, so that's what the little lights are called. *Feu follets*, you say? Like will-o'-the-wisps, are they?"

Lond's cloaked body radiated tension. "You can't seriously be thinking about navigating this huge boat down those tiny waterways."

Dumont reached for his pipe and leisurely began to pack it. "That is precisely what I'm going to do."

"Handsome Jack is in no condition to pilot a boat."

Dumont glanced at the corpse and uttered a harsh, quick laugh. "That's for certain. I've hired a new pilot today, a young man who grew up in the swamp. He'll get us through safely."

The captain had not, in fact, actually hired Willen. However, Lond's reluctance only whet his appetite to explore the swamp, and it would be foolish not to hire the only man who knew the area—and who was willing to travel through the swamp.

Lond fell silent. "You leave me no choice. I wish to leave this island, and I must travel by the route you choose." He exited without another word. Brynn followed, as did Handsome Jack. Dumont opened the window to let the stench of death escape, lit his pipe, then went to the theater to enjoy the rest of the evening's show.

The performance went beautifully, and Dumont almost wished that he could linger in Port d'Elhour. Almost. After the show, he asked the cast to remain in the theater while the patrons went up to the main deck to partake of refreshments.

Larissa had no idea what Dumont wished to talk with the cast about, but she was mistrustful. Casilda, however, was excited.

"Maybe we'll dock here for a long time. The audiences seem to be enjoying themselves, and I know I am," she gushed.

The dancer shook her head slowly. "I hope so, but I doubt it somehow. Uncle never likes to stay in one place very long."

Their chatter was cut short as Brynn shuffled toward the back of the room, passing them without sparing a glance. Larissa shuddered to herself. She had never much cared for Brynn, with his icy eyes and aura of tightly leashed violence. After he had recovered from the swamp fever, though, she found him even less appealing. He looked paler than usual, as though the brief illness had sapped his vigor, and moved with a deliberateness that he had never before exhibited. It was obvious he hadn't bathed in days, too. He seemed polite enough, though of few words. But it was his gaze that really unsettled the young woman. It was a dull stare, quite unlike his customary, piercing scrutiny, as if there was no life behind the brown orbs.

Casilda, too, felt uncomfortable around him. "He gives me the shudders," she told Larissa in a low voice. Her friend nodded.

Dumont walked onto the stage and faced his cast and crew. "Ladies and gentlemen, I know we've enjoyed our time in Port d'Elhour, but there are too few patrons here to make it worth our while. We'll be in port a few more days, then we'll be leaving."

The jovial mood dissipated somewhat. "Into the mists again," someone muttered.

Dumont heard the comment. "Yes, into the mists. We have traveled them safely before, haven't we? Before we leave Souragne altogether, I'd like to take a look at what's on the other side of the island. We'll be traveling through the swamp to reach the southern parts."

Low murmuring began to ripple through the room. Some had heard rumors about the swamp, and even those who hadn't felt little desire to enter the forbidding, muddy waters.

Larissa grew pale, her eyes wide. *Airmoss dripping from the trees . . . snakes twined around trunks of brooding cypress . . . dark waters, broken only by some hidden creature dwelling in the depths . . . dancing lights that called to her . . .* Angrily, she shook her head to clear the eerie images from her mind.

Dumont ignored the reaction of his cast. "We have someone who'll take us safely through. Will, come up here. I'd like to introduce you to my cast and crew." Beaming paternally, he motioned the young man forward.

Smiling sheepishly, Willen joined Dumont on the stage. His eyes found Larissa's, and the smile widened. He gave her a wink.

"Well, he's quite handsome," Casilda whispered, "even if he is a bit bold. Did you see that wink?"

Larissa nodded, feeling a blush creep to her cheeks.

The dancer hadn't ever really expected to see the strange young man again, and at this moment wasn't sure that it was fortuitous. Handsome? Yes, she supposed he was that, especially with the light catching the glimmer of mirth in his brown eyes. But he aroused in her more than admiration with that smile and those deep eyes, and the feeling was disconcerting. He threatened to thoroughly disrupt the comfortable routine into which Larissa had fallen over the last eight years. Through her doubt and strange attraction, one emotion welled to the surface: she was suddenly quite glad that he was on *La Demoiselle*.

She came back to herself with a start and realized that Dumont had been introducing Willen. Larissa frowned to herself. Dumont never introduced a new crewman to the cast, much less encouraged him to mingle with them, as the young man was now doing. She raised a white eyebrow, watching the youth chatting animatedly with everyone from Gelaar to Sardan.

"Well, I'm going to say hello," announced Casilda, smoothing her raven curls. Larissa grinned, but hung back a bit. She suspected that Dumont wouldn't be nearly as fond of his newest crewman if he guessed that Willen and Larissa had already met—and under what circumstances.

"And this is Dragoneyes," continued Dumont. Willen stuck out a big hand. The half-elf hesitated, then shook it. A slow, tentative smile spread across his sharp features.

"Welcome aboard," he said in tones that sounded like he truly meant the words.

Willen stared openly at the feature that had given Dragoneyes his nickname. "Your pupils are slitted, just like a snake's!" he exclaimed. "How interesting! Why are they like that?"

Larissa shuddered in distaste. The analogy she'd used, when she thought about it, was a cat. Cats were much more pleasant than snakes.

There was a sudden silence. Dumont's righthand man was almost as much feared and avoided as the captain himself. No one had ever dared ask Dragoneyes about his curious eyes before. For a moment, no one moved. Dumont himself waited for the half-elf's reply.

Then Dragoneyes smiled again. "My mother always said my father was a snake. 'Course, there are some that said he was a monster, but never to her face. Glad I got my mother's teeth, though. Kind of hard to chew with fangs."

Out of profound relief, everyone laughed much harder than the joke warranted—everyone except for Willen, who squeezed Dragoneyes' hand one last time and gave him a look of tremendous pity. Only the first mate and the observant Larissa noticed. A shadow of pain brushed across the half-elf's face for a moment, then was replaced by the emotionless mask.

"Dragoneyes, I'm going to take Will downstairs and teach him how to handle the supplies."

Dragoneyes raised an eyebrow. "Are you sure, Captain?"

Dumont frowned. He didn't like his judgment questioned, not even by Dragoneyes, and certainly not in front of the cast and crew.

"Of course I'm sure. And tell Jahedrin that I want Will instructed in piloting. He's big enough to manage the wheel, and he's going to be our guide. He ought to know how to handle the boat. The rest of you," he said, addressing the cast and crew who still pressed about Willen, "on deck. We've patrons waiting."

Larissa turned to leave with the others, but a hand closed on her arm. "Miss Snowmane," said Willen as she turned to face him, "I just wanted to say how nice it is to finally meet you after watching you perform."

His face and voice revealed nothing but courteous sincerity, and a surge of relief at his discretion went through Larissa.

"Thank you," she replied in a like tone. At the last minute, she remembered to use the nickname the captain had given him, not the name he had used to introduce himself. "Welcome aboard *La Demoiselle du Musarde*, Will." She smiled politely at Dumont, then went up to the main deck.

Willen and Dumont watched her go. "Of all the many treasures on my boat, she is the brightest. Do you find her beautiful, Will?"

"Anyone would, sir."

Dumont laughed. "A perfect answer, both complimentary and cautious. I'll tell you what I tell all my men—keep your hands off her and you'll keep your hands. Now, as to our present business." He turned to face the youth, his arms folded across his chest. "*La Demoiselle*'s a showboat. We entertain. And the better we can make our entertainment, the more profit we turn.

Simple enough. You've seen the show. The elf Gelaar is responsible for some of the wonderful effects. But that's not all there is to this boat, not by any means."

He strode to a door at the back of the theater. It was fairly well concealed, painted to blend in with the rest of the wall, but certainly not hidden. Dumont fished out a large ring of keys and located the appropriate one. He inserted it into the lock and whistled a series of notes. The key started to glow faintly, and the door unlocked. Willen raised an inquiring eyebrow.

"It's a key, certainly, but it's also magical," Dumont explained, pulling the door open and descending a small, dark stairway. Willen followed. "There are certain notes you have to whistle, which I'll teach you later. The door can't be opened without both the key and the song."

As they descended into the darkness, Dumont whistled again and the key ring began to glow, illuminating their way with a gentle blue light. Dumont glanced back at Willen.

"I know all this magic must be disconcerting to you, but you'll get used to it. *La Demoiselle* practically teems with magic, and she damn well ought to, after all the years of effort I've put into her."

The stairs ended, and Willen looked around. The large room contained boxes, pieces of equipment, extra chairs, tools, sacks of flour, and other items.

"We often have to travel for long periods of time between towns," Dumont said, "and I don't like to be caught short. This is the main storage area. Back here's where we keep the livestock." Dumont turned to another door and opened it with a magical key, motioning for Willen to enter.

Without warning the young man found himself sprawled facedown on a pile of hay. He heard the door slam behind him and hastened to get up, but Dumont planted a heavy boot on his neck.

"You'll get up slowly, my lad, and take a good look around. If I'm not satisfied with your reaction, you don't leave this room alive."

The captain removed his boot. Hardly breathing, Willen rose, easing himself into a sitting position. Only then did he look around the room.

It was about the same size as the first storage room. The only illumination came from Dumont's keys, though there were a few empty sconces on the walls. The floor was covered with dirty hay, and Willen saw the livestock that Dumont had mentioned—two calves, several chickens, a few sheep, and pigs. They stared back at him without curiosity. It was not the ordinary livestock that stunned the young man, however. The startling thing was the other creatures also kept in the dark, close room.

*La Demoiselle* was obviously a showboat. It was also a slave galley.

A small, slight, dark-haired human woman was shackled to the walls. She might have been pretty once, but now she was emaciated and dirty, and only dull fear burned in her large, unusually round eyes as she regarded Willen. Her clothes hung in tattered rags about her bony frame.

A gigantic fox, the size of one of the calves, lay in one corner. As he glared at Dumont, a low rumble began in his throat. He, too, was securely chained, and a harness of sorts crisscrossed his white breast.

In a golden cage hung from the ceiling a raven huddled. Nearby, a black cat with a leather collar was busy grooming itself. Its chain was just short enough to prevent it attacking the raven. It tried to studiously ignore Dumont and Willen. At one point, though, it paused in its cleaning and fixed the two intruding humans with a gaze that radiated hatred.

As Willen watched, the animal's fur began to change color. A bright blue began at its tail and bled across its body, and the creature hissed, flattening its ears. Willen saw that its incisors were twice as long as those of a normal cat. The sound awakened a reptile that looked like a miniature dragon. Confined to a small, barred cage, the creature raised its red, scaly head and narrowed its gold eyes as it looked at Dumont.

"You see before you my collection," Dumont drawled. "Each of these creatures contributes something of value to the boat or to me personally. I've harvested them from all over. Let me introduce you. This pretty thing," he said, kneeling by the brunette woman, "is an owl maid from Falkovnia. When I permit her, she becomes a night bird and scouts ahead for me. Isn't that right, Yelusa, my sweet?" He reached out and stroked her grimy cheek possessively. She stayed quiet and unresisting, her eyes lowered.

Dumont rose and continued. "The fox is from Richemulot. The fellow has staggering speed. I can tap it for the boat when I need to make a hasty exit. Bushtail, are you hungry? Hmmm?" The fox regarded him with glittering eyes. "We haven't fed him for two days now. He's been uncooperative recently. Bet you'd love one of those chickens right now, wouldn't you?"

Bushtail bared his teeth. "You bastard," he growled. "I would sink my teeth into you, except you are so wicked you would make me sick. Bah!" The fox shook his head as if to get a bad taste from his mouth.

The captain only laughed and went on. "The ravenkin hails from Barovia, and he knows more about the history of every land hereabouts than any other creature I've run across. He knows better than to lie to me, don't you, Skreesha?"

The bird cawed, but no noise issued forth. Dumont chuckled. "The cage keeps him silent. His knowledge is only for me, not his fellow prisoners.

"Colorcats," he continued, "are extremely rare. They're found only in G'Henna. Their fur is invaluable to Gelaar's illusion spells. The pseudodragon, whom I picked up in Mordent, will occasionally cooperate in my spell casting—when he's been hurt enough."

The captain turned his gaze toward his newest crewman. "So, Will, are you impressed with my collection?"

The youth searched Dumont's eyes, then looked around at the prisoners. "Impressed is hardly the word," he said slowly. He stuck out his hand, and Dumont hauled him to his feet. "What you've done is truly amazing, Captain Dumont. And I see that you've already found the *feu follets*."

Dumont's eyes narrowed. "What do you know about them?"

Willen smiled. "A lot. I'm from the swamp, remember? *Feu follets* are related to will-o'-the-wisps, except instead of feeding on pain and unhappiness, they live on good feelings. Perfect for your showboat."

Dumont grinned avariciously. He had made the right choice in hiring this young man. Willen couldn't have reacted better if he had read the captain's mind.

"Are there other creatures in the swamp that you think we could use?"

The youth's smile widened. "Hundreds," he said. "And I can take you right to them."

"Will, you almost make me believe in the gods again."

"There are those in the swamp, too."

Dumont threw back his head and laughed.

\* \* \* \* \*

An hour later, Willen bade good night to his new employer and retired to his cabin. Alone, he closed the door, locked it, then pressed his flushed face up against the cool wood. He let down the barrier he had erected for the evening, and a tidal wave of emotions flooded him, causing him to gasp and then sob with pain. Uncaring, he slid down the door, shaking as tears poured down his face.

During the time he had been in Dumont's livestock area, he had been buffeted with the prisoners' emotions. Some of them had been chained down there for years. He felt their physical pain and emotional anguish, their despair, their hatred. The young man let himself weep until he had regained a finger hold on control, then rose shakily. He poured some water into a basin and splashed his face, forcing himself to calm down.

A few minutes later, Willen left the cabin and went down to the main deck. The guests had returned to their homes on shore, and the cast and crew had retired for the night. Only a watchman or two patrolled a lazy route about the boat. As nonchalantly as possible, Willen strolled up to the railing and leaned over, ostensibly gazing at the waxing moon's reflection in the gently rolling water.

As soon as they felt his presence, the little lights held in magical chains to the boat began to shine more brightly. Their colors changed swiftly, and they crowded as close to Willen as their magical bonds would let them. Again, Willen felt tears sting his eyes and hastily blinked them back. He glanced around. Fortunately, he was alone for the moment.

Willen extended his big hand toward one of the lights. Its radiance increased, and it blinked quickly. An answering light began to glow softly from the ring on the youth's right hand. He accepted the creature's comfort and felt the ice in his chest begin to melt.

"Oh, my brothers, I am so sorry," he whispered.

# NINE

" 'Morning, Miss Snowmane," Willen chirped.

Larissa, hastening up the stairs on her way back from breakfast, smiled briefly at him and stepped aside to let him pass. Instead, Willen appeared to miss a step and bumped into her heavily. She stumbled, barely catching her balance, then felt his boot slide along her ankle. The dancer crashed to the stairs in a graceless heap, staring up at the new crewman with a startled and irritated expression. He had deliberately tripped her!

"Oh, Miss Snowmane!" Willen exclaimed as he grabbed her hands and pulled her to her feet, "I am so sorry! That was very clumsy of me! Are you all right?"

His expression was concerned and chagrined, but not overly so. Something crinkled against Larissa's palm, and her hand closed over a small piece of paper. Suddenly Willen's eyes were not casually polite, but leaping with an intense light.

Larissa found her tongue. "Why, yes, Will, I'm fine. Thank you. If you'll excuse me?" She swept coolly past him, her hand clutching the scrap of paper he had slipped her. Larissa waited until she was safely in her cabin with the door locked before unfolding Willen's note with trembling hands.

*Miss Snowmane,*
  *I have to speak to you on a matter of the utmost importance. My shift ends soon, and I will be waiting for you at the Two Hares in an hour.*
  *Please come.*

Larissa sat on her bed, thinking and chewing her lower lip. She read the message twice, then set the paper in a small dish and touched a candle flame to it. The paper twisted as it burned, smoking and turning black. Larissa watched, but her mind was not on the burning paper.

She knew she ought to just leave well enough alone, that to get any more involved with the handsome young crewman simply meant trouble.

Nevertheless, an hour later she was waiting outside the Two Hares.

Despite the sultriness of the day, she had pulled on a lightweight cloak and tugged the hood low over her head. Her white hair was unmistakable, and she wanted no word of her whereabouts to drift back to Dumont's eager ears.

"I'm so glad you came," said Willen's warm, sweet voice. She turned, a bit startled. She had not heard him approach. He extended a hand and Larissa hesitated, then took it.

"Your hand," she gasped as she felt its roughness on her palm. She glanced down and saw that his palm was crusted with scabs from recent and present blisters. Where the skin was not lacerated it was as soft and pink as her own. Quickly Willen clenched his fist.

"Come," he said softly. "It wouldn't do for any of the captain's men to see me with you."

"Where are we going?"

Willen hesitated, then said, "Someplace where I can be sure we'll be safe."

Larissa narrowed her eyes, slightly suspicious, but

Willen was already walking swiftly away from the inn. Questions tumbled in her mind like an avalanche, but she held her tongue.

They walked in silence for a time, striding down the road. As on the night she and Dumont had left the market square, the business area of the town fell away. However, Willen was not taking them to mansions or plantations, but into a much wilder area.

Larissa began to grow apprehensive. The earth was becoming increasingly soggy. She kept her voice steady when she asked "Willen, are you taking me to the swamp?"

He nodded. "It's safe there. We—"

Larissa stopped, anger flashing in her blue eyes. "I am going nowhere *near* that horrible place." She turned on her heel and marched back along the road, her back rigid and her stride swift.

He was beside her in an instant, his hands warm and strong on her shoulders. "Because of what happened there when you were a child. I'm sorry. I didn't think."

She twisted, pulling free and turning to face him. "Who told you about that?"

He seemed uncomfortable. "No one." She threw him a disgusted look and walked on. "Larissa, wait. You're in danger!"

"Spin me another tale."

He grew agitated, almost frantic. "You have to believe me. You could be killed, or—You have to trust me on this. Did I let you down before?"

Her steps slowed, halted. He was right. He had never given her any cause to doubt him, up to this very moment. She turned to face him, still skeptical.

"Let me prove that you can trust me. Give me your hand."

Slowly, reluctantly, Larissa did so. Swiftly he covered it with his and gazed into her eyes, penetrating, it seemed, to her very soul. She stared back, hardly breathing, transfixed.

"Your hair wasn't always this color. It turned white when you were a child, here in Souragne."

She nodded, and he continued. "You didn't grow up in a real home, because your father was always traveling. When you were twelve, he ran off and left you, and since then, the showboat has been your home. The only thing you've kept from your childhood is a silver locket, with a scrap of your own blond hair in it.

"You hear drums from the swamp at night, but you don't tell anyone about it because no one else seems to hear them." He paused, his hands tightening about hers, his dark eyes gazing into her soul. "*I* hear them, Larissa."

Her mouth went suddenly dry.

"You haven't wept since you were twelve. You're afraid of tears, afraid of being weak, scared to death that weakness will be your downfall."

The dancer gasped. It was her dark, hard, proud secret, that terror of tears. There was no way Willen could have known about this, not unless—

"You said I'm in danger," Larissa whispered. "Go on, then. I'm listening."

\* \* \* \* \*

It was a glorious sunset, and Casilda lingered a few minutes longer than usual to enjoy the spectacle. She propped her elbows up on the railing and rested her slightly round cheek on her hands.

Here in Souragne, it seemed that the sun was closer than it was in some of the other lands that *La Demoiselle* had visited. The island was the warmest place Casilda had ever traveled, certainly, and as the sun neared the horizon it appeared enormous to the young woman. Slowly, in its orange and yellow glory, the orb began to sink below the horizon. The sky's hues cooled, taking on twilight shades. The water turned a darker color, too. Casilda enjoyed the sight, but her thoughts started drifting toward Larissa.

Casilda and Larissa had been the closest of friends for the last two years, ever since the singer had joined *La Demoiselle* in Valachan. Larissa was easy company. She never seemed to have any problems, and Casilda envied her that. She, on the other hand, had wept on the dancer's shoulder many a time, but had never had to return the favor. This morning, when Larissa had left for a stroll in town, she seemed uneasy. She hadn't returned yet, either. Casilda hoped her friend was all right. She probably was; Larissa knew how to take care of herself.

The sun was almost gone. With a sigh, she turned away, ready to go to her cabin and prepare for the evening's performance.

"Hey, Casilda!" came Sardan's voice. "Can you do me a favor?" His cabin door was partially open, and he peered out at her as he fiddled with the ties on his voluminous shirt. "I left my mandolin in the pilothouse. Can you get it for me?"

Sardan often played for the pilots. It kept them awake and alert during what could often be a rather dull shift, and the hardworking crewmen appreciated it.

Casilda frowned. "Sardan, my dear, I have to make the same curtain time as you, and I haven't even started dressing."

His boyish face grew pleading. "Oh, come on. Please? I don't have my trousers on."

"You know cast members aren't allowed in the pilothouse. You're the only exception. The captain will be furious."

"It's an off shift right now. Nobody'll be there. It's right by the—"

"Oh, all right."

"Casilda, beloved, my heart is yours."

"Mine and every other woman's," the singer retorted. She was annoyed, but she hastened to the task and scurried up to the sun deck. She glanced around to make sure there was no one about, then quickly ascended the stairs to the pilothouse.

There, on the chaise, lay Sardan's mandolin, and she picked it up carefully. The curious singer couldn't help glancing around a bit. She was amazed at the size of the wheel. She had never imagined it would be that big.

Suddenly she tensed.

"Be right with you, Caleb," came Jahedrin's voice.

His footsteps were coming up to the pilothouse. Casilda was sure of it. She bit her lip, then saw the stairway that led toward the captain's cabin. She could hurry down there and leave Dumont's cabin through the other door. Casilda had heard the captain was in town, and it was better than getting caught in the pilothouse. As quietly as possible, she descended the narrow stairs and closed the door behind her.

She hadn't been seen. Casilda closed her eyes in relief. Grasping the mandolin firmly, she turned toward the door. She had just reached for the knob when it started to turn.

For a second, fear flooded her. Then she looked frantically around the room, searching for someplace, anyplace, to hide. Her eyes fell on the partially opened wardrobe, and she ducked inside, pulling the troublesome mandolin close to her chest. She left the door open a crack, so that she wouldn't be trapped.

Dumont entered just as she pulled the door nearly closed. He strode over to one of the chairs and eased himself down, apparently waiting for someone or something. A few seconds later, there came a loud knock. Dumont rose and went to the center of the room. He pulled aside the rug and revealed a trap door. He tugged it open while Tane, a big, swarthy man, pushed from below.

"Can you manage?" Dumont asked.

"Aye, sir," Tane replied. He disappeared from view for an instant, than reappeared carrying one end of a box about four feet long. Something appeared to be alive inside of it, for Casilda heard rustling and thumping noises.

Dragoneyes emerged carrying the other end of the box. They heaved it up onto the floor, then sat down for a moment to catch their breath. Dragoneyes rubbed his sore arms and glared at the box.

"Boy, you sure cause a lot of trouble, don't you?" the half-elf said, kicking the box viciously.

A muffled cry came from within. It sounded like a child's voice. From her hiding place, Casilda gasped. Were they kidnapping someone? Who? And why?

Dumont stood staring down at the box. "Well, Dragoneyes," he boomed, "what have you found?"

Tane began to pry off the top of the box with a crowbar while Dragoneyes explained. "Easiest catch yet, Captain. We saw him hopping around and set a trap. Bang, we got him. Had to tie him up. Noisy fellow, but mighty stupid."

Tane had removed the top, and for a moment, nothing happened. Casilda, so curious it was almost painful, held her breath.

Slowly, two long brown ears appeared over the top. A pair of whiskers next to a quivering nose tentatively thrust out, followed by a smooth head and large, liquid, fear-filled brown eyes. It was the biggest rabbit Casilda had ever seen, about the size of a large dog.

Dumont frowned. "Well, gentlemen, it's interesting, I grant you, but I've seen big rabbits before. What can it do for me and my boat?"

Dragoneyes grinned, his gold eyes crinkling with knowing amusement. "Watch this," he said. The half-elf leaned into the box, and the frightened rabbit cringed.

"Hey," barked Dragoneyes. "Say something, rabbit."

"No," replied the rabbit. Its voice was clear and unmistakable, the high treble of a child. "I'm not going to let him know I can—oops." The brown eyes looked very contrite, and the ears lowered in shame.

Dragoneyes laughed aloud. "Like I said, Captain. He's mighty stupid."

Dumont's expression had changed, and he rubbed his hands together happily. "Stupid, yes, but unique! *Très bien*, Dragoneyes! Who did you say found him?"

"I did," said the half-elf, adding loyally, "but Tane was with me."

"You are both relieved of tonight's duties. Visit the purser, tell him I said to give you a week's wages, and enjoy yourselves, boys." The two men grinned happily. "But first, take our new friend down and put him with the others. Oh, wait just one moment." Dumont peered at the rabbit. "What do you eat, little fellow?"

The rabbit remained stubbornly silent, its nose twitching nervously.

Dumont heaved an exaggerated sigh. "Why, then, we won't feed you anything."

"Oh!" gasped the rabbit. "Don't do that!"

"So what do you eat? Grass and carrots like other rabbits?"

The rabbit shuddered in apparent distaste. "No! I can't eat that! I have to have meat."

Dumont raised an eyebrow in surprise. "Meat?"

"Yes, preferably the insides of things. I love livers and kidneys—and hearts. Hearts are my favorite. Do you have a heart I can eat, please? I am a little hungry." It bared its teeth, but judging by the way it cringed, the gesture was meant to be placating. Its teeth were as sharp as any fox's.

Dumont shook his head. "Well, my friend, we'll see what we can do. You'll find things go easier if you cooperate. Tane, give the rabbit a heart or something before you and Dragoneyes leave, will you?"

"Sure thing, Captain," Tane replied, putting the top on the box again and nailing it shut. The rabbit resumed its crying. Tane and Dragoneyes picked up the box and carried it back down the secret passageway. Once they had disappeared from view, Dumont carefully covered the door and left his cabin. At last the door slammed shut, and the room fell silent.

For a long time, Casilda didn't move. She huddled on the floor of the wardrobe, trembling. She had obviously just been witness to something she wasn't supposed to have seen, and it was terrifying. What if Dumont had decided to change clothes for the performance and had caught her spying on him? What might he have done? And the rabbit—dear gods, a flesh-eating *rabbit*—and they were going to put it with the others? What others?

Come on, Cas, she told herself, you got away with it. And that . . . animal . . . is none of your business. She took a deep breath, took a last quick look to make sure there was no one in the room, then pushed open the wardrobe door.

And gasped. Just out of her sight, a shadow moved. The singer recognized it as Lond, the new passenger. He advanced toward her slowly, pulling his hood off. Her eyes widened in terror.

"I think," said Lond menacingly, pouring some powder from a small vial into his gloved right palm, "that your understudy will be performing tonight."

\* \* \* \* \*

"Dumont a slaver?" Larissa echoed incredulously. Her eyes went hard. "Willen, that just isn't possible. I know him. I've grown up on that boat."

Willen looked at her with sympathy, but continued to press his case. "Would the man you know kill one of his own deck hands? Would he chase you through the square after pressing his advances on you?"

Larissa didn't want to remember, but she had to. She recalled Handsome Jack's dying word—"Liza"—and the sinister, unexpected change in Dumont from tender guardian to predator.

She felt a sinking sensation in her stomach as the reality of her guardian's duplicity began to take hold. The creatures Willen had described were sentient beings, not zoo curiosities. Imprisoning them to use their magic for the boat was slavery. She did not doubt for a minute that he had indeed seen the creatures; her faith in her new friend was absolute.

"When I was younger—I think fifteen or so," she began in a low voice, "Uncle Raoul let me travel in town by myself for the first time." She smiled a little in remembrance. "I was so proud of myself—a little bit too proud. I ended up getting the pouch that had all my spending money in it stolen.

"Well, Uncle found out about it and he was livid. He found out who had stolen the money. He even tried to be polite about it at first. 'I don't like to quarrel in a hosting town,' he always says. But, of course, the robbers weren't about to give back the money, big old Captain Dumont or no. So Uncle stormed back up to the boat and put the crew to work. They dragged out this enormous cable and hitched it to the house where the robbers were making their stand. Then Uncle cried out, 'If I don't see my ward's money by the time this cable pulls tight, you and your house'll be bathing in the river!' "

Larissa was laughing at the memory despite the pain of the awful news Willen had imparted, and he was glad of it. She continued. "I never saw anyone move so fast. I got my money back, every last copper. See, folks knew Uncle, and they knew he'd do exactly what he said he would."

Her smile faded, and there was pain in her blue eyes as she lifted them to Willen. "That is the only Raoul Dumont I ever knew. Hearing that he's a slaver . . ."

A thought occurred to her, and the pain on her face deepened. "He wants to use me," she said softly. "He *has* been using me, just as he's using those creatures. I'm a slave, too."

They were sitting by the road, which was not well traveled this far out of town. Larissa unconsciously drew her knees up to her chest and hugged them. Filled with sympathy, Willen reached to brush back a curl of his companion's milk-white hair.

"I'm sorry."

She looked up at him, and there was determination on her face. "Don't be," she said in a voice suddenly strong. "I know the truth now. I can defend myself."

"Don't trust Lond for a moment, either," Willen continued. "He's at least as strong as Dumont, and maybe even more dangerous."

She smiled a hard smile at that. "Don't worry. I would never trust that man. When he first signed on board I wondered why Dumont would tolerate him. We've never taken passengers before, and Lond seems so . . . arrogant and sinister."

"We'd better be getting back," Willen noted sadly. "If you're late for the show, it would make Dumont suspicious. I've got more I need to tell you, but I'm not sure when we'll have time. I don't want to speak to you on the boat, but . . ."

"We'll find someplace," Larissa reassured him. Her own heart was heavy with the bitter information Willen had given her, but she was glad he had spoken. Now she could take precautions against whatever dark forces were at work aboard *La Demoiselle du Musarde*. She slipped her hand in his as they walked back toward Port d'Elhour.

They boarded separately, to arouse no suspicion, and Larissa flew to her cabin. She dressed swiftly, then realized that she still had to get the Eye from Dumont. A shiver of fear rippled through her, but she ruthlessly quelled it. If she behaved normally but kept her wits about her, she should come to no danger.

She went to Dumont's cabin, took a deep breath, and knocked on the door. Silence. Larissa knocked again, then tried the door. It was locked, of course. Well, someone in the pilothouse would know where Dumont was.

"What did you need, my dear?" Dumont purred in her ear.

She jumped, startled. He was smiling, but there was a hardness about his eyes that indicated suspicion.

"Uncle! I . . . didn't see you come up. I need my amulet." Larissa kept her voice even and casual, and held out her hand expectantly. Her heart was thumping wildly.

Dumont frowned, and for a moment Larissa thought he had seen her with Willen. "*Your* amulet?"

Relief swept through her. "Sorry, Uncle. I meant your amulet, of course."

He nodded, satisfied. "Of course. Come in, my dear."

He unlocked the door and ushered her in. She declined his offer of a chair and stood while he retrieved the Eye. Dumont kept his treasures hidden in various parts of the room, not all in one place. The amulet was in a chest he kept in the wardrobe. As he swung the door open, Larissa noticed the mandolin.

"Wait a minute," she said as he started to close the door, "Isn't that Sardan's?" She stepped beside Dumont and bent to pick up the instrument. "What's it doing in here?"

"He often plays in the pilothouse. No doubt Tane or Jahedrin put it here for me to give back to him." The explanation didn't sound convincing, but Larissa nodded as if she believed it.

"I'll take it to him," she volunteered. Dumont hesitated, then handed it and the pendant to her. "See you after the performance, Uncle." She smiled brightly and left, heading for the theater.

The audience was already seated. Larissa slipped the pendant over her neck and held the Eye shut. Invisible, she easily slipped backstage. Sardan was pacing back and forth nervously when she let go of the pendant and appeared with the mandolin.

"Larissa, marry me," he exclaimed, gathering his instrument to him like a long-lost child. "Casilda was supposed to fetch it for me but I guess it slipped her mind."

"That's not like Cas. She's usually—"

At that moment, Dumont stepped in front of the crowd. "Good evening, ladies and gentlemen. I regret to inform you that Casilda Bannek will not be able to play the part of Rose in tonight's performance. Elann Kalidra will be taking up the role, and we hope to have Miss Bannek back with us soon. Thank you."

As the crowd murmured unhappily, Larissa felt a chill creep through her. Sardan had not seen Casilda since he had asked her to fetch the mandolin. Now she was ill, yet she had been fine earlier that morning.

"Do you know what happened?" the dancer asked Sardan, a creeping fear slowly spreading over her heart.

The handsome young actor shrugged. "The captain says it's swamp fever."

# TEN

The prisoners aboard the showboat were located directly beneath the theater, and as Willen unlocked the door he could hear strains of "Alas! My Love Is No More."

His feigned pleasure in the slaves had won Dumont over completely, and the captain had given word to the crew that Willen was now to be in charge of feeding the creatures. The young crewman carried a large sack of meat, freshly butchered. All the prisoners were carnivores.

He whistled the tune Dumont had taught him, and the key turned easily. It was dark inside, but he had brought a torch and reached to insert it in one of the sconces. He yelped suddenly and nearly dropped the torch onto the dry hay as he felt a sharp stinging in his ankle.

He looked down at the hissing pseudodragon. Its long tail, thin enough to stick through the bars of its cage, had a large stinger on the end. Willen assumed this was what the creature had attacked him with.

The animal glared up at him. Although it was still securely confined in its cage, Willen had foolishly stepped within reach. The other creatures were watching him silently, their eyes flickering in the uncertain light.

The young man frowned. He secured the torch,

dropped his sack and knelt near the pseudodragon, though he was careful to stay far enough away to avoid a second attack.

*Little dragon, I mean you no harm. I am here to set you free.*

The pseudodragon's eyes narrowed, then Willen felt it cautiously probing his thoughts. He did not attempt to shield himself from the probe and after a moment reached his fingers through the bars to the reptile. *My sting is dangerous*, it told him, *but I am glad the poison has no affect on you.*

"You have convinced the dragon, but for myself, I trust you not," said the fox.

"Me neither," came a small, sad voice. "I don't trust anybody anymore." Willen looked in the speaker's direction and his eyes widened in horror.

"*Bouki!*" He sprinted over and fell to his knees beside the trembling rabbit. All four of Bouki's feet were bound with shackles. In addition, a thin wire noose was strung about the creature's neck. The bonds forced Bouki to sit upright; if he relaxed, the noose would tighten.

Willen reached to hold the trapped animal, and the rabbit squirmed in his arms. "Who're you?" he demanded, his voice high and frightened.

"Don't you—oh, you wouldn't recognize me like this, would you? The Maiden sent me."

Bouki's eyes widened. "You're here to rescue us!" he exclaimed. The other occupants of the room tensed, daring to allow a sliver of hope to brighten their eyes. "Better hurry," the rabbit said, glancing at the fox. "Bushtail keeps threatening to eat me."

Willen threw the fox a reproving glance. The animal shrugged. "What can one do? I am a fox, he is a rabbit, no?"

"This rabbit could eat you if he wanted to. What kind of creature are you, anyway?"

The fox bridled and sat up straighter. "My name is Bushtail, and I am the *loah* of the foxes."

Willen nodded respectfully. A *loah* was an animal spirit, a magical hero to the creature's people. *Loahs* had a close link with the land in which they dwelt. Taking Bushtail from Richemulot probably weakened the fox's powers and caused him a great deal of pain.

"Then my friend here is your equal. Bouki is also his people's hero."

"That, a hero?" Bushtail's tone dripped contempt.

Willen smiled. "Bouki has strengths, but not of the mind. I thought foxes were clever. How did Dumont manage to trick you, good Bushtail?"

The fox growled, then suddenly chuckled. "*Touché, mon ami.* I am put in my place."

"What is your plan? If, indeed, you really are here to rescue us," interrupted Yelusa. Willen glanced at the owl maid, who was shackled near the ravenkin. Her body was slight and small, almost boyish. Her round face housed sunken eyes, which gazed at him dully, and her tangled, light brown hair fell just to her shoulders.

Willen glanced from her to the noble bird trapped in the cage. He felt a pang of special sympathy for those two. Imprisonment such as this must be twice as torturous for avian creatures. He rose and went to Yelusa, kneeling beside her.

"Lady, I have signed on to the boat to spy. The men, including Dumont, have complete trust in me. I mean them no harm, but I also mean to put an end to this." He gestured to her chains. "I don't have a plan at the moment, but I won't abandon you."

He rose and began to distribute the creatures' food. Every one of them pounced on the raw meat and began to eat hungrily. "How often are you fed?" Willen inquired.

With her mouth full of flesh and a trickle of blood running down her chin, Yelusa answered, "Only once in every three days. Dumont says he doesn't want to pamper us."

Jaws busy with his own meal, the pseudodragon thought an image to Willen, of Dumont being tortured to death in a variety of painful ways. Willen grinned. At least the little dragon's spirit wasn't completely shattered.

He sat back and watched the creatures eat. "Have any of you tried to escape?" he asked.

Bushtail shook his head and swallowed a chunk of meat. "Escape without assistance is not possible. Several times have I tried to call my people, but Dumont somehow prevents it. I believe that these—" he pawed at his harness scornfully "—negate our magic. We are as simple creatures of the woods in this place."

Willen looked to Yelusa. "You say Dumont uses you to scout ahead. Why can't you leave?"

She still regarded him with a trace of mistrust. "He has my cloak of feathers. When I put it on, I become an owl. But Dumont also has plucked one of my feathers, and as long as he has that, I must return to the boat before dawn." Her eyes were haunted. "So, yes, I'm free, but not really. It's almost worse this way."

Willen touched her hand sympathetically, but she jerked it away. He wanted to linger, but could not afford to arouse suspicion. He had already been gone longer than was necessary to simply deliver the creatures' food. He rose reluctantly.

"I'll be back as soon as I can. Bouki, don't give up. I'll get you out of here." He looked around the room, meeting the eyes of every prisoner evenly. "All of you. I promise."

\* \* \* \* \*

Three days passed before Dumont deemed Casilda well enough to see people. When Larissa went to see her friend, Cas was still in bed. She looked up at Larissa with dull hazel eyes.

"How are you feeling?" Larissa asked, sitting at the foot of the bed.

"Fine, thank you," replied Casilda in a monotone. Her skin was pale, and she lay completely motionless.

Seeing the normally lively Casilda so still was unnerving, and Larissa sought to fill the silence with chatter.

"Your slender little understudy did a fine job singing, but she couldn't do justice to your costume," she said jokingly. "Nobody fills out that dress the way you do!"

Casilda did not smile in return, but regarded Larissa steadily. Larissa continued, a bit thrown by the singer's lack of reaction.

"I wish we didn't have to leave tomorrow. I'm not looking forward to traveling through the swamp. There will be far too many insects and snakes for my liking."

There was no response from Casilda.

"Will you be singing tonight?" Larissa's voice was starting to grow taut with tension.

"Yes," replied Casilda in that same awful, dull voice.

"Well, I'd better let you get dressed then."

"Yes."

As she left Casilda's cabin, Larissa took the long way around the sun deck to her own cabin. She passed by the pilothouse and glanced up at it. Jahedrin was instructing Willen in navigation, pointing at things and talking steadily, though Larissa was too far away to hear.

She fixed Willen with an intent gaze, willing him to glance in her direction. When he did, she let concern flash in her eyes. His expression didn't change, but he nodded ever so slightly. Larissa knew he had gotten the message that something was wrong.

On this, their final performance in Port d'Elhour, Casilda performed well, but there was something missing. Larissa watched her intently from backstage, chewing her lower lip nervously. The notes were right on pitch, the lines spoken correctly. Larissa's alarm increased with every scene and reached a new level when it came time for Casilda's solo.

As Rose, Cas knelt by Florian's "dead" body. Her voice was pure, and Larissa tensed as she reached the final line. Unaware of what she was doing, she mouthed the lines along with Casilda.

*"Like a dream at morning,
Like summertime, he dies!"*

Casilda hit the high C perfectly, her voice sweet and pure—and empty. The audience applauded spontaneously.

Nameless terror shuddered through Larissa. She had always known the note was in Casilda's range, but how had the singer conquered her fear of it? Willen, I have to talk with you! she thought desperately to herself. The music changed, and Larissa took a deep breath, took control of her own fear, and leaped on stage as the Lady of the Sea.

After the performance, Larissa changed clothes and went onto the main deck to mix with the audience as usual. Dumont waylaid her before she had a chance to speak with anyone else.

"My dear, you've been avoiding me," he chided in a friendly tone as he gently took her arm and propelled her to the railing.

Larissa smiled tightly. "I'm glad Casilda was able to perform on our last night in Port d'Elhour."

Dumont's eyes narrowed. "Yes, I'm glad she's feeling better. But let us not talk of others."

Larissa's heart sank, and she averted her gaze from his, looking out over the water. It was a clear night, though steamy, as apparently all nights were in the early summer in this land. The moon, which appeared huge, was full and yellow. Larissa felt that she could see every tiny wave on the calm gray surface of the water. Out beyond the harbor, the mists roiled, waiting, eternally patient.

"We used to be so close, you and I," Dumont murmured. Larissa felt Dumont's hand sliding up her back, felt it playing with her long, moon-silvered hair. "We could be close again, my sweet. There are delights you have not yet sampled, and—"

Larissa jerked away and fixed him with an angry stare.

"Uncle, stop. This isn't going to work. Not now, not tomorrow—not ever." Her mind wailed, Slaver! Betrayer! But she kept the pain from showing.

The captain froze. "I would not distress you, my dear, though I wish I still had your trust."

He bowed slightly and left, but Larissa caught a glimpse of black fury on his face before he turned it away from her. Fear began to penetrate her outrage.

Willen had watched the interchange, had caught a few of the words. Now he followed Dumont like a shadow. In those he touched as he passed, Willen planted the thought: forget. They returned to their conversation, and the next morning would have no recollection of the handsome young man making his way through the crowd.

As Willen had feared, the captain went to Lond's cabin. Willen glanced around, but most of the crew was either in town for a final celebration before departure or else tending to the patrons on the main deck. The crewman pressed an ear to the door.

". . . know why my own magic doesn't work, but it doesn't," Dumont was saying. He was raging, and his voice came through quite clearly. "I'm running out—damn it, *have* run out—of patience with the wench. I want her, and I want her now."

Willen had to strain to hear Lond's raspy voice. "Well,

it will not be tonight, Captain. I must tax that faded patience of yours a little longer."

"But soon?"

"Soon."

The youth backed away in horror then hastened down the stairs to the main deck and Larissa's side. Flashing a grin to the mayor, who was chatting with the dancer, he interrupted them graciously. Then he and Larissa stepped away from the throng.

"I've been trying to—" began Larissa.

"I know. I'm sorry. They've been keeping me awfully busy." He took a deep breath and sorted through the thoughts careening around in his brain. "Larissa, you're in danger."

"I know, you told me—"

Willen shook his head. "No. Immediate danger from Dumont. Within the next day or so. You've got to get off the boat once we're safely into the swamp."

Larissa was shocked. "Dumont's going to kill me?"

"He's made some kind of bargain with Lond. Somehow Lond is going to use his magic to make you fall in love with Dumont."

"Can he do that? I mean, I would think that if Uncle—Dumont—wanted that, he'd have tried on his own." Larissa felt horribly alone and trapped.

Willen's face went hard. "Larissa, you don't know Lond. I don't think Dumont even realizes what he's involving himself with."

"Wait a minute. Isn't leaving the boat to go into the swamp like crawling out of a cauldron into a cook-fire?"

Again, Willen shook his head. "The swamp won't hurt you, not if you go on an errand for me. At least, I hope not."

"Very reassuring." Her tone was flippant, but her heart had started to beat rapidly. She had been dreading the voyage into that steamy, dark marsh. The thought of fleeing *La Demoiselle* and wandering around in the swamp—

Willen took her hand, and suddenly she was calm again. She saw the swamp through his eyes: a place of death to the unwary, fraught with dangers and watching eyes. Certainly, darkness and malevolence dwelled in sunless pockets, but it was also a home to many innocent creatures, a place where growth and death were part of a cycle, not in conflict.

"I wish I could go with you," Willen was saying as Larissa came back to herself, "but that's just not possible." Despite the reassuring vision Willen had sent her, Larissa remained hesitant.

"Yes, you do have the courage," he said in answer to her unspoken words. "Your life, perhaps even your soul, hinges on this. And the lives of others. Will you go, Larissa?"

She licked dry lips, then looked into his concerned brown eyes with what she hoped was confidence.

"Yes, I will. Tell me what I have to do."

\* \* \* \* \*

The guests had departed, and the cast members had retired to their cabins. Only Brynn, standing tireless guard duty, saw Dumont emerge from his cabin and go to the bow of the vessel.

The captain unwrapped a scarf from his neck. He shook the white piece of fabric over the side, causing it to snap, then carefully rewound it about his throat.

With a little ripple, a slim, beautiful young woman appeared on the surface of the water. Her golden hair was plastered to her head, and her emerald eyes were shiny with tears. She gazed up at Dumont, rosebud lips trembling as she treaded water.

"Good evening, Flowswift," Dumont addressed the woman. She stayed sulkily silent. "You've been trying to trick me again, haven't you?"

She shook her head. "No, Captain Dumont. I'd not do that."

Dumont's voice was full of patronizing affection. "Oh, you little liar. I saw you with Caleb last night. You were trying to persuade him to steal your shawl back from me. Well, it didn't work."

He gestured, and the boat's youngest crewman approached. The zombie was newly made and easily passed for living. But the nereid saw that there was no light in Caleb's eyes, and she whimpered at having been discovered. Dumont pursed his lips and a series of notes issued forth. Along the bottom edge, the shawl began to burn smokily.

The nereid arched her back in pain, cramming the heels of her hands into her mouth to stifle her scream. Even in her agony, she knew that Dumont would torture her worse if she cried out.

Then the fire was gone. "Now, perhaps, you'll behave for a little while. I wish to go into the swamp. Swim ahead and let me know if there's any problem. You know what I'll do to this if you ground us."

Flowswift winced and nodded. She sank beneath the surface, vanishing at once without a ripple. Dumont smiled and went below. Between the nereid scouting ahead in the water, the owl maid exploring the land from above, and Willen's navigational skills, the trip should be a smooth and uneventful one.

* * * * *

At dawn, they pulled away from the dock. It was a deceptively merry parting. The populace of Port d'Elhour had turned out despite the early hour, and they were determined to give the great boat a proper farewell. Several musicians played, and Mayor Foquelaine gave a speech in honor of the showboat and its cast. Larissa noticed that a few pretty young ladies were struggling to control tears and suspected that, even in this brief time, Sardan had managed to break his share of hearts.

As the boat steamed away, it saluted the port with music of its own from the huge calliope that adorned the stern. Everyone on board was on the main deck, waving farewell to the hosting town. Slowly but surely, the dock fell away.

Larissa always used to enjoy it when the big boat was on the move. The splashing of the paddlewheel, the gentle hum that continually vibrated through the boat—these things had always marked new beginnings for her. Now they heralded only fear. She had only one day left on the elegant vessel; she planned to escape tonight.

The trees seemed to hunch over *La Demoiselle* as the boat steamed its way into the swamp. The sky was soon shut out by the gray-green, mossy canopy of cypress trees. Long streamers of airmoss and strands of creeper actually trailed against the vessel, catching in the railings and leaving *La Demoiselle* festooned as if with dirty, tattered ribbons.

Larissa was on the main deck at the stern, watching the red paddlewheel churn steadily. The backwash from the wheel climbed up the myriad rootlets of the cypress trees and ebbed back out again, rising and falling like miniature tides. As she watched, she could have sworn the trees closed in behind them to seal them off from the harbor area. But surely, she told herself, that's only my imagination. Trees can't move.

"Goodness, what a lovely sight," Sardan drawled sarcastically, stepping up beside her and following her gaze. He crunched an apple and offered her a bite.

An idea occurred to Larissa. She beamed up at the singer.

"Yes," she said flirtatiously, keeping her eyes on his face. "It is a lovely sight." She accepted the proffered apple and took a small bite. If she were constantly in

Sardan's company until the time came to leave, she'd be less likely to be threatened by either Lond or Dumont.

Startled out of his normal insouciance, Sardan stared down at Larissa, pleased with the unexpected attention. He stood a few inches taller, and his already broad chest swelled with self-importance. They chatted for a time, and Sardan pointed out items of interest. Most of the information he had to impart Larissa already knew, but she feigned wide-eyed interest. Once, to show off, Sardan pointed out a gnarled log floating in the water.

"See that?" he said to her. "Looks just like a harmless log, doesn't it? Well, watch this." He tossed the apple core toward it. The water suddenly came to a frothy life as the creature, revealed now as a crocodile, snapped up the morsel greedily.

Larissa gasped, startled. An instant later, though, the waters were frothing again. A tentacle had wrapped around the crocodile with astonishing speed and was dragging the frantically flailing reptile below the surface. Bubbles broke the surface for a few more heartbeats, then the water was calm again.

Larissa glanced over at Sardan. He was deathly pale, and he gripped the railing so hard that his knuckles were white. Aware of her gaze upon him, the actor deliberately pried loose his clenched fingers.

"I think," he said in an admirably calm voice, "that I won't be throwing any more food to the crocodiles."

All too soon for an apprehensive Larissa, the shadows began to lengthen. The swamp banks, forbidding even during the daylight hours, took on a new menace at night. As they had every night since she had arrived, the drums began as soon as darkness had settled upon the water. They were louder, harder to ignore now, as if they came from only a few yards away. Perhaps they did. Still, only the dancer seemed to hear their primal beat.

Larissa forced herself to eat at dinner—who knew when she would have a real meal again—and stayed out as late as she could with the attentive Sardan. Finally, reluctantly, she went to her cabin.

She had seldom removed the root necklace that Willen had given her on the night they met. Last night he had given her more of the magical, protective plant, as well as other herbs and pouches he called "conjure bags." Per his instructions, Larissa had placed them in every corner of her small room. She knew that she was safer in her cabin than anywhere else on the beautiful boat, which was now starting to feel like a prison.

She picked up one of the conjure bags. Kneeling by her closed door, she untied the bag and poured out a thin line of crumbled earth along the wooden floor of the cabin.

"Nothing evil will cross the line, nor any of evil's creatures," Willen had told her. She prayed he was right.

She rose and began to pack a few items in a sack, including the remaining conjure bags. As she was rummaging through her chest of drawers, she came upon the locket. Larissa sat on the bed, looking at it for a long moment. Dumont had proved that his word couldn't be trusted, and his word was all Larissa had regarding her father. What had really happened between her father and Dumont?

She started at a knock on the door. Heart hammering, she called in a voice that shook, "Who is it?"

"It's Casilda," came the answer.

Relief flooded through the dancer, leaving her momentarily so weak that her legs wouldn't support her. She got her limbs under control and went to open the door. Casilda stared at her with that same dull gaze.

"Come on in, Cas," Larissa invited, returning to her bed and sitting down on it wearily. "I don't think—" Larissa broke off, horrified.

Casilda could not cross the threshold. The singer

raised her hands, trying to push them into the room, but she kept hitting some invisible wall. Her expression didn't change, but she continued to try to enter. Willen's earth-magic thwarted her every attempt.

Larissa stared at the ghastly spectacle. Casilda hadn't been ill. Something had been done to her, to her mind. Willen's words came rushing back: *Nothing evil will cross the line, nor any of evil's creatures.*

After about five minutes, Casilda stopped and gazed at Larissa with an unblinking stare. Hardly breathing, Larissa couldn't take her eyes away from that horrible, empty gaze. Then Casilda turned and walked away slowly.

Larissa sprang up and closed the door, leaning against it for a few minutes, then grabbed her sack of clothes. She and Willen had decided to wait until shortly before dawn, but after seeing what Casilda had become, Larissa was not about to waste another moment aboard *La Demoiselle*. All at once, the swamp seemed far more benign than the boat.

As quietly as she could, Larissa opened her door and peered outside. No one was around. She took a deep breath, then slipped outside, smudging the line of protective earth as she did so. Her footsteps seemed terribly loud as she descended the two flights of stairs to the main deck, but no one crossed her path.

Her plan was to take one of the scout yawls. Although she had had no actual practice with manning the small, poled boats, she'd seen it done enough times that she thought she could manage.

*Hurry, hurry,* the dancer told herself as she lowered the sack onto the yawl. Larissa eased herself over the side, feet first. The yawl bobbed a little as her weight unsettled on it, then righted itself. She reached up and began to untie the rope that bound the yawl to the boat. It was securely knotted, and the water the rope had absorbed served only to swell the knot tighter. Her nails tore, and the ends of her fingers felt raw.

Then Larissa heard footsteps on the deck above her. She mouthed a curse, her fingers scrabbling frantically at the knot. It was loosening.

"Come on, come *on*," Larissa whispered. Then it came. The rope was free.

She shrieked as a strong hand closed on her right wrist. Larissa cast a terrified gaze upward to see her guardian, his face contorted in fury. She struggled, but his grip was unbreakable. He began to haul her up, her light frame no challenge to his anger-driven strength. Her feet kicking wildly, Larissa flailed with her left hand, caught the rope of the yawl, and held on tightly.

A sudden blow on her left wrist caused her to cry out and let go of the rope. The current greedily snatched the yawl, speeding it downstream. Larissa's hand was bleeding and throbbed with intense pain. She looked up to see Dragoneyes grinning mirthlessly down at her. He had struck her hand with the end of the harpoon.

An instant later, the half-elf grunted in pained surprise. Dumont had given him a furious blow with one mammoth fist while retaining his grip on Larissa with the other.

"I don't want her harmed!" the captain roared. "Gods, I'm surrounded by fools!"

"Perhaps not, Captain," came a cool voice. Lond had appeared beside the captain and was gazing down at Larissa. All the young dancer could see in the shadow of his cowl were his small, cold, glittering eyes. Slowly, as her face was drawn closer, he brought up his hand. On the gloved palm was a small pile of powder.

Dumont's grip weakened, and with a violent wrench Larissa tugged free. She barely had time to fill her lungs with air before she disappeared into the murky, green-brown depths of the swamp.

# ELEVEN

Dumont jerked Lond's arm away from Larissa's face. "No! Don't make her one of *them*!" the captain cried, his voice filled with anguish. The powder blew off the mage's hand, most of it going into Dragoneyes' face.

The crewman uttered a sharp cry, toppling backward. His hands clawed at his face and eyes. "Raoul!" he managed, fixing Dumont with an agonized look. Tears streamed down his face as the powder burned his slitted, golden eyes. The look of betrayal on the half-elf's face was a terrible thing to behold, and Dumont's own expression registered shocked surprise. Without realizing it, Dumont had loosed his hold on Larissa, turning instinctively to try to do something, anything, to help the only man on board that he called a friend.

Then the coughing increased, and suddenly Dragoneyes couldn't breathe. His hands clutched his throat, and his mouth opened and closed, but no sound issued forth. His body jerked and flailed like a fish on land. At last Dragoneyes convulsed violently and then lay still.

Dumont was stunned. He turned frantically to the mage. "Is there an antidote?"

The hooded figure shook his head. "None," he said. "Do not distress yourself so, Captain Dumont. His services won't be lost to you. But I fear the girl's are."

"No! Larissa . . ." The captain rushed to the side. Sure enough, all trace of the dancer had vanished. Dumont pounded the railings, swearing. He had lost both his beloved and his best crew member.

"Captain?" It was Tane's voice. He had heard the commotion and stood half-naked on deck, blinking sleepily. "What—Dragoneyes!"

"He fainted," Dumont lied swiftly, keeping pain from his voice with an effort. "Came down with swamp fever. I'll take him to his cabin in a moment. Tane, listen to me and listen hard. Larissa's jumped overboard. I want her found. You and Brynn take the other yawl and start after her. Tell everyone else to keep their eyes open. Thirty gold pieces to the man who spots her first, and a hundred to the man who brings her in—*unharmed*," he added, darting an angry glance in Lond's direction.

Tane left to obey his captain's orders, though not without a glance at the still form of his fellow crewman. When Tane had gone, Dumont turned on the mage.

"What were you thinking of, with Larissa?" he demanded. "I wanted her to fall in love with me, damn it, not become some mindless lump of dead flesh!"

Lond's voice was even when he replied. "My zombies are not mindless. They retain much of their intelligence and many physical capabilities. They are not even, technically, dead. I maintain control of their souls. Had I been permitted to complete my spell with Larissa, you would have had a beautiful, intelligent, obedient woman. You would have been pleased with the result of my spell."

Dumont didn't respond to the comment. Instead, he demanded, "What are you going to do to help find her?"

Lond froze, then said carefully, "I offer no guarantees, but I will do what I can. There are powers here in the swamp, Captain Dumont, powers that do not appreciate being spied upon. I doubt they will permit me—or you—to locate her magically. Let us determine why she fled. Perhaps that will give us a clue as to where she might have gone."

Dumont felt suddenly weary, and there was a dull pain in his chest. "I may have pressed my suit a bit too ardently. She might have been afraid."

"That could be reason enough," Lond agreed. "But there might be something more to it than that. May I see her cabin?"

Dumont glanced down at the limp form of Dragoneyes. "Let me get him to his cabin first." He prodded the body with the toe of his boot. "Damn, I wish he hadn't been the one to get a faceful of your magic," he muttered, pain brushing his heart. "Dragoneyes was a good boatman."

"He still is, Captain." There was a hint of a smile in Lond's voice. "He still is."

A search of Larissa's room revealed that she had packed little more than clothing. What few trinkets she had collected over the years she had left behind, including her locket. Dumont picked it up and opened it, recalling the first time he had seen Larissa. She had been only twelve years old, and the simple silver locket that hung about her slim throat seemed to catch the highlights of her white hair. . . .

"Let me see this," said Lond as his black-gloved fingers took the locket away from Dumont. He opened it and examined the soft blond hair inside. "Whose is this?" he asked, one finger stroking the lock of hair.

"Larissa's, when she was a child."

Dumont heard a sharp hissing intake of breath from Lond. "Her hair was not always white?"

The captain frowned. "No. She doesn't remember the incident, but apparently it turned that color some time ago, when she first came to Souragne. Something about the swamp."

"You idiot!" Lond's voice was a shriek. "Why did you not tell me this sooner?"

Dumont's shock over losing Larissa and grief at Dragoneyes' fate ebbed before a rising tide of anger. "Why should I? What difference does it make what color her hair is?"

"It makes every difference in the world!" Lond's slim body was quivering with anger. "I should have known. How could I have failed to see it? I thought it merely an affectation for her role, not . . . Dumont, for both our sakes, pray that Larissa is slain by the creatures in the swamp. If she survives, she could destroy us both."

* * * * *

Larissa was a good swimmer, but she sank like a stone the moment she hit the water. Luckily it wasn't deep, and the dancer wound up briefly touching the slick mud of the bottom. She pushed off from the soft surface and swam blindly for as long as she could. When she could hold her breath no longer, she finally broke the surface, gasping and wiping water out of her eyes. To her chagrin, she wasn't more than a few yards away from *La Demoiselle*.

A woman's golden head broke the surface immediately beside her. "Take my hand, sister," she said in a voice that sounded like water flowing. "I'll take you as far away from that horrid man as I can."

Confused, Larissa opened her mouth to ask a question, but the woman impatiently seized her and pulled her beneath the surface. Muddy water filled her open mouth and she coughed, only to have more water pour down her throat. Panic shuddered through her, and she struggled against this mysterious girl who was obviously trying to drown her.

The girl did not loosen her hold, only pulled the frantic Larissa down deeper. The dancer's heart thudded and her lungs cried out for oxygen. At last her lungs emptied of their own accord, and water surged into them.

To her absolute shock, Larissa found that she could breathe easily. Utterly baffled, she ceased her struggles, inhaling the water as naturally as a fish would. They were moving at an astonishing speed. She turned to face her rescuer, but could see nothing in the liquid darkness beside her.

She could still hear the woman, however. "I am Flowswift," the nereid explained. "Your wicked Dumont has my shawl, and he commands me. I have been his slave for over a year now. I have tried to escape, but always he discovers me. If you are fleeing from him, you are my friend."

They swam in silence for a long time, slicing through the water like dolphins. At last Flowswift angled upward the surface. She became visible again as soon as she hit the air.

"This is as far as I dare go," she told Larissa. "Be careful. This water—it is not overly friendly, not even to me."

"Thank you, Flowswift," Larissa said sincerely. "I don't know how I can repay you."

The nereid's voice went hard. "If you defeat Dumont, you can return my shawl."

"If I can, I will. I promise."

Illumined by moonlight, Flowswift dived beneath the surface and vanished.

Treading water, her sodden skirts still threatening to drag her under, Larissa glanced around. She was pleased beyond words to see that the nereid had brought her directly to her yawl, which had gotten tangled in a clump of muddy vegetation. Her pack was there, safe and dry, waiting for her.

Larissa swam to the bank and slogged onto comparatively dry land. She looked around a bit and waited for her heart to slow. Then, satisfied that she was at least temporarily safe, she sat down near the yawl and removed the ring Willen had given her, turning it over in her hands.

It was a simple thing, merely a band of metal. She had had to place it on her index finger as Willen's hand was much larger than hers. She set it in her palm and placed her other hand over it, then closed her eyes and concentrated on clearing her mind.

"Think about me," Willen had told her. "Let no other thoughts intrude. Help should come to you then."

Larissa's breathing slowed and deepened as she relaxed, letting thoughts of the young crewman fill her mind's eye. The ring began to grow warm in her hand, and, startled, she opened her eyes.

A small light flickered in front of her. Larissa immediately recognized it as one of the lights from the boat.

"Are you the help Willen sent?" she asked.

It did not respond. She sighed, assuming that the creature's form was too far removed from her own to permit communication. Larissa put her hand to her mouth as the realization hit her. If this was a living creature, then the lights on the boat were not simply illusions. They were slaves. A sudden flood of pity and anger filled her.

The creature danced away suddenly, blinking anxiously. It *was* a living thing, Larissa felt certain. She rose and looked at the little ball of light.

"You can't understand me, but I trust you," she said. "I'll follow your lead." The ball of light flushed to a pale blue and pulsed rhythmically, then flew out over the river. It hovered there, blinking, waiting for her to follow. Larissa dutifully freed the yawl from its entanglement and pushed off into the water. As she did so, what looked like a log rolled a lazy eye in her direction. Larissa held her breath for a moment, but the crocodile seemed in no mood to attack. Cautiously, she began to paddle down the swamp.

Her guide danced about, sometimes flitting around

her head, sometimes soaring high above her. Larissa stayed tense, alert, but the night swamp appeared to pose no immediate dangers. She wondered how much of that was due to the presence of her small guardian. It was definitely taking her someplace, for when they came to a fork in the river it chose one path clearly over the other. Marveling at her temerity, she followed it.

The night wore on. The swamp was unsettlingly silent, save for the constant buzz of cicadas in the distance. The only other noise was that made by her own paddle, breaking the surface of the water with a little splashing sound.

After a time, Larissa became aware that, despite the amount of water all around, she was very thirsty.

"Is there a place where I can drink?" she asked the light creature. It ignored her, and she rolled her eyes in exasperation. She glanced down at the river, immediately deciding that it was nowhere near clean enough for her to drink from. Swallowing dryly, she looked around, hoping to spy a spring or a puddle of rainwater from which to steal a handful of potable liquid.

A clump of huge, beautiful plants floated near the shore. Their white blossoms were about five feet across, and they were filled with inviting pools of pure rainwater. Licking her dry lips, Larissa thankfully paddled close, reaching her hands easily in to the plants.

The light guardian dived in front of her face, blinking crazily. Its colors were now strong tones of red and green, and it whizzed past her head. She paused, hands outstretched to the plants, confused by the creature's actions.

There came a terrible roar, like the sound of a tree branch splitting. A huge tentacle erupted from the earth and closed about Larissa's outstretched arms. Chunks of muddy soil flew everywhere. Even as she screamed and tried to pull away, Larissa realized that the tentacle was a root of some sort.

The root's owner came rapidly into view as Larissa was dragged toward an enormous tree. Another root shot out from the soil to encircle her torso, and a third trapped her legs. The roots began to drag her to the tree, and Larissa could make out what appeared to be a hideous parody of a face on the tree's trunk.

"Let me go!" she cried. The light creature had calmed somewhat, though it still blinked rapidly. She struggled furiously, but the roots' grip was like iron, and her strength was not going to be enough to free her. She glanced up and saw that the hole in the trunk was now moving, like some kind of giant mouth.

Trees can't move! Larissa screamed to herself, recalling the foliage that had seemed to close in on the boat's path. But they did, or this one did, and all at once Larissa was filled with a terrible, irrational certainty that she was about to be eaten by a plant.

Then there came a noise that was becoming very familiar to the terrified dancer . . . the beating of drums. She realized, with a shock, that the noise was made by the tree. It raised its serpentine roots and pounded on its own trunk, sending out a deep, resonant booming. The light creature flickered near her face, and Larissa's white brows drew together in outrage.

"You tricked me!" she cried at the creature, kicking impotently against the unbreakable bonds of the knotted roots. "You *led* me to it! You twice-damned, blazing, bleeding whelp . . ." The furious expletives tumbled from her mouth. Something of what she was saying apparently got through to the creature, for it began to blink agitatedly and withdrew to a distance of several feet. At last, her vast store of curses having finally been depleted, Larissa sagged helplessly against her bonds.

A movement caught her eye. It was a doe, moving with slow elegance along the bank. It paused and regarded her with liquid brown eyes for a moment, large ears twitching, debating. Then, judging Larissa harmless, the deer moved toward the large blossoms, lowered its slim head, and began to drink.

With a suddenness that Larissa wouldn't have thought possible, the blossom snapped closed around the doe. The beast was caught up to its hindquarters. Although it thrashed and kicked, it could not extricate itself from the carnivorous plant. The doe emitted muffled bleating sounds, and Larissa, filled with horror, winced and turned away from the frightful spectacle. Soon, the doe ceased to flail. The plant opened and closed, adjusting the carcass until it fit completely in the blossom's heart, then closed completely.

Larissa, shaking, swallowed hard. The little light being had floated closer. Larissa remembered its agitation when she had tried to drink from the plants.

"You and the tree saved my life."

The light creature bobbed up and down, flushing a gentle rose hue. Slowly, with a voice that sounded like the rustling of leaves, the tree spoke. "The *feu follet* told me that *she* wished it so."

Larissa gasped. "You can talk! Who is 'she'?"

"Someone I personally disagree with, but will obey—for the moment," came a voice from the tree's foot.

Larissa glanced down to see an enormous rabbit. She was about to smile at it gratefully when it sat up on its haunches and looked her in the eye. Larissa had thought the creature appealing at first glance, but she now realized that there was nothing cuddly or innocent in that hard gaze. It grinned maliciously, and she saw that its two front teeth were sharp as a wolf's.

"Had you ventured into these parts without the *feu follet*, I would have slain you and eaten your heart."

Larissa went cold. "I have done no harm to you," she protested.

"My cousin Bouki is a prisoner aboard your boat. That is reason enough to slay anyone from the cursed vessel, as far as I am concerned. Yet," the gigantic rabbit said reluctantly, "you are under the protection of the *feu follets* and the Maiden. I will take you to her. My name is Longears."

Larissa remembered where she had heard the names before. The Two Hares Inn had been named after the legendary rabbit heroes, Bouki and Longears.

The rabbit turned to the tree. "Quickwood-Who-Grows-By-The-Deathplants, the Maiden thanks you for your aid. I will take the girl to her now."

The pressure on Larissa's torso eased as the roots loosed their hold. Her limbs numb, she was barely able to stop herself from falling over. Wincing, she rubbed life back into her unfeeling arms and legs.

Something moved by her feet with a slithering motion. Larissa ignored it, thinking it was just another one of the tree's roots. When cool reptilian skin slid silkily along her bare leg, however, she jerked away with a cry. The snake, equally startled, hastened into the water, where it vanished with a little ripple.

Longears fixed her with a gaze of utter contempt. "You come to rescue the creatures from the boat?" he sneered. "You are afraid of a harmless little snake! You do not deserve your white locks."

Shame mixed with anger washed through Larissa. "Snakes are dangerous," she shot back. "Surely even you are afraid of foxes and wolves, Longears. And mists take you, rabbit, what does my hair color have to do with anything?"

Longears drew his split upper lip back from his razor-sharp teeth in a grin. "On the contrary, Whitemane, I *eat* foxes and wolves, not the other way around. As for your hair—" he shrugged "—you will learn about it soon enough. Come with me. The Maiden of the Swamp wishes to see you."

## TWELVE

Longears was not the pleasant traveling companion that the dancing little light—*feu follet*, Larissa reminded herself—had been. The huge rabbit sat at the front of the yawl, ears pricked, gazing ahead alertly. For the first few hours, as they moved languidly along the still waters, the only words the young dancer heard from him were curt directions. Annoyed, she decided to question the creature as the dawn began to lighten the sky.

"The *feu follets*—what are they?"

"They're kin to will-o'-the-wisps," Longears answered, not turning around to face her. "Except *feu follets* feed on positive emotions, not negative."

"Why did one come to me in the swamp?"

Longears threw her an irritated glance over his furry shoulder. "You called it. It came. As I said, you're lucky." He turned around. "Your captain will curse the day he ever came to Souragne. Bouki *will* be freed."

"That's what Willen and I are trying to do," Larissa explained. "He told me to seek out the Maiden, whoever she is, and tell her of the plight of the creatures aboard the boat."

Again Longears craned his neck to look at the girl. She regarded him steadily as she continued to paddle. He twitched his whiskers, considering.

"If you would free my cousin, then you are my ally," he said with obvious reluctance. He laughed. "I never thought I would join forces with a human, but I will take what I can get. Besides," he added, "you are a whitemane, and there may be more to you than there first seems."

Larissa flushed angrily. There was something quite humiliating about being insulted by a rabbit, even a gigantic talking one with teeth as long as her forefingers.

"I trust I won't disappoint you," she said icily.

Longears ignored the sarcasm. "We'll see. First, you have to meet with the Maiden's approval."

Larissa was about to reply when the current picked up unexpectedly. The narrow waterway down which she had been paddling widened and joined with another to create a river of sorts. Larissa was kept busy with paddling and keeping low on the yawl so as not to overturn it. Then Longears cried, "To the right! That island—that is the Maiden's Isle."

The dancer frantically tried to paddle to starboard, but the current enjoyed playing with the little yawl and was reluctant to let it go aground. Longears leaped into the water, catching the yawl's rope in his mighty teeth, and struck out for the bank. Between his powerful swimming and Larissa's determined efforts, they managed to bring the yawl safely ashore.

Larissa dragged the small raft well onto the muddy bank, away from the greedy waters. Longears emerged a few feet away and began to shake himself dry like a dog. The island was a rare patch of dry land in the bog, and Larissa hadn't realized how wonderful it was to feel the solidity of sand and then earth beneath her feet. The night had seemed to last forever, and she was glad of the morning. She sat down and leaned against a tree, suddenly tired and fully feeling the weight of what she had done.

There came a warm chuckle behind her, and Larissa

leaped up, tense and ready to defend herself.

"Have no fear, Larissa Snowmane," came a soft, rustling voice from the trunk of the tree. The voice grew into dulcet tones that were definitely female. "I am the one you have braved the swamp to see."

As Larissa watched, fascinated and more than a little frightened, the tree she had been reclining against shimmered. A cool green light emanated from it, increasing in brilliance until Larissa was forced to shield her eyes. It moved and twisted, reshaping itself into the likeness of a beautiful woman—albeit a woman unlike anyone Larissa had ever seen.

Fully six feet tall, her skin was a pale, translucent green and her large eyes emerald. White-green hair tumbled down her back, and Larissa saw that it was actually airmoss. She was clad in a robe of leaves and vines. As she moved, her feet never appeared to completely leave the earth, and the hand that clasped a tall, rough-looking wooden staff ended in tendrils rather than fingers.

"You have a message for me, I believe," the Maiden continued in the same soothing, whisper-soft voice.

Larissa swallowed hard. The plant-woman's gentle beauty intimidated her.

"Willen sent me," she managed after a moment.

The Maiden nodded her mossy head. "As I sent Willen. What has he learned? What has the riverboat captain done to our people?"

For an instant, Larissa couldn't meet those amazingly emerald eyes. She felt ashamed that she had any ties to Dumont.

"Captain Dumont has enslaved the *feu follets*. He is using their need for positive emotions to generate business for his showboat. He has also trapped Longears's cousin, Bouki. There are others, too, from other lands. Some of them have been trapped for years, and Willen wants you to know he wishes to free them all."

The Maiden's eyes widened slightly. "All? He was sent only to free our people. Can he not determine how to accomplish that by himself?"

"They are bound by powerful magic, Lady," Larissa told her. "And having seen the other prisoners, Willen says that he will not go without all the creatures."

The Maiden sighed and shook her head. "There is great magic aboard that boat, considering where she travels."

"He also said to tell you that Lond is aboard. He wants—" Larissa broke off. The Maiden's face had darkened with a terrible anger tinged with pain.

"Lond?" the Maiden breathed. She reached with her other hand to clasp the staff, drawing it close to her body in a gesture of defense. "Is this true? For what purpose?"

"Willen thinks that Lond wishes to leave Souragne." Larissa's voice was less certain now. The Maiden looked as if she were in terrible anguish. "Lady . . ." Larissa's voice trailed off helplessly. She glanced down at Longears. The rabbit, too, was solemn.

The Maiden turned as if Larissa weren't even there. She moved with the grace of wind in the trees as she bowed her head in pain for a long moment. Larissa and Longears exchanged glances. At last the Maiden straightened and turned composed features to Larissa.

"If you have traveled aboard the boat for as long as I believe you have, then you have seen a great deal of evil in your life, Larissa. Perhaps you have brushed by it unawares. I would like to think that you have not been hurt by it yet. Your escape from *La Demoiselle du Musarde* may have been even more narrow than you thought it to be. Lond is a man of great evil. That he and your Captain Dumont have joined forces is grim news indeed."

She sighed and, for a moment, shimmered so that she looked more like a plant than a woman. Then her features reformed. "I cannot lend the aid of the swamp and her beings to such a venture as Willen wishes. I am sorrier than you can possibly know."

Larissa was stunned. Not for a moment had she entertained the idea that this mysterious woman whom Willen so obviously revered would deny them her aid. Willen had seemed so certain. She opened her mouth, but Longears interrupted her.

"But it is Bouki who is imprisoned, not some beast!" he cried. "He is a *loah*, Maiden. If you will not rescue him—"

"It is not my decision!" cried the Maiden. The pain of her refusal was evident on her beautiful face. Tears welled in her eyes. "Do you not think I feel his fear? We are both the land's creatures, and that is precisely why I am powerless to aid him, or the *feu follets*, or any of those other unfortunates. It is not in my power to say yea or nay, when Lond traffics in the dark magic of the waterways and the slaver has caught the land's *loah*."

She held out one hand to the rabbit. "You, more than most, know my limits. Do not condemn me for what you know I must do."

Longears hesitated, quivering with anger. Then he was gone, leaping into the verdant growth with a white flash of his tail.

Larissa turned toward the Maiden. The strangely beautiful woman met her gaze evenly.

"Willen was counting on you," the dancer said. She knew she was being rash, unwise, in protesting the Maiden's decision, but the words came of their own accord. "He's trapped on that boat now almost as much as the prisoners he's trying to rescue. Can't you see that?"

The Maiden of the Swamp continued to gaze at Larissa steadily. "Ah, child," she breathed softly, and the trees on the island rustled in sympathy, "you are so young and sure of yourself. And there is so very much that you do not and cannot know."

"I know Willen's in trouble because he's trying to save

lives, mine included," Larissa replied, growing angry. "And if you're not going to help him . . ." She floundered helplessly.

The Maiden tensed slightly. "If I do not help him?" she prompted.

Larissa licked dry lips, then burst out, "Then Longears and I are just going to have to find a way all by ourselves!" The thought of Willen dead or in pain hurt her terribly, far more than she thought it would.

To her surprise, the Maiden chuckled. "Perhaps you will, child. You are a whitemane, after all." She paused, and her beautiful face brightened with new hope. Moving closer, she laid her hands on Larissa's shoulders.

"Yes . . . perhaps there is a way, after all. Do you truly mean what you say? Would you fight your guardian, fight Lond and his dark powers, attack that mighty, magical boat all by yourself?"

The dancer felt herself turning red. The Maiden had called her bluff. But deep within her heart, Larissa knew that she would never consign Willen to his fate, not if there was anything she could do to help him. Fleetingly, she wondered if this meant she was in love with him, but she pushed that thought away. She nodded, fear clutching at her heart.

A slow, pleased smile spread across the Maiden's face. She extended a hand to Larissa. "Then, daughter of the swamp, you must come with me and learn."

The young woman hesitated, then took a step toward the Maiden and grasped the outstretched hand. It was cool, like a leaf, and soft. The slim arm folded gently about her, pulling her up against the Maiden's body. The other arm came up to embrace her also, and the staff pressed against Larissa's back.

"Be not afraid," whispered the Maiden gently. Her breath, filled with the fragrances of summer, was soft against Larissa's white hair.

The beach went away. Larissa found herself enveloped by a wall of swirling brown and green. The Maiden's arms suddenly reminded her of the quickwood's binding roots, and Larissa tasted blind panic for an instant. Scents flooded her senses as she inhaled to cry out—loam, honeysuckle, the odd, dusty scent of the trees themselves.

Then it was over, and Larissa stood on the bank of a small pool. They were in the heart of a forest now, and everything was shadowed and cool. The trees stretched skyward. Somehow, they seemed to be only trees now, not the hunkering, malformed monstrosities that hovered over the waterways.

She blinked dazedly and turned to the Maiden questioningly. The Maiden smiled.

"On this island, I go where I will. You have traveled from one tree that bears my essence to another at the heart of the island. You will learn how to travel so yourself, Larissa."

"I'm not sure I want to," Larissa said, still a bit unsteady.

The Maiden laughed. "You must be thirsty. Drink your fill from the pool. It is fresh and clean."

Larissa obeyed, kneeling in the cool, thick grass beside the little pool. The water reflected her face and white hair, and above her a cloud sailed lazily by in an azure sky. The dancer cupped the sparkling liquid in her hands and drank.

She had forgotten how parched she was, and the water tasted delicious, cold and pure. It was after the third handful that her vision began to blur. She blinked and shook her head, but it didn't help. Her reflection was changing, dissolving.

Her head spinning, Larissa sat down heavily, her fingers digging into the earth as if she could hold onto consciousness by sheer strength.

The Maiden's voice sounded distant and as fragile as a summer zephyr. "Be not afraid," she whispered. "Gaze into the pool, Larissa Snowmane, and learn there the secret of who you are."

Stubbornly Larissa refused to cooperate. She clutched her temples, fearful of her powerlessness. She had never been a victim of a spell before, and—

*It is not a spell. I am giving you answers that you already know. Do not fight me, Larissa.*

This time the voice was inside her head. Larissa felt herself shudder, then melt into acceptance. She turned her eyes to the pool and saw there not the blue sky, but a star-crowded nightscape framed by green grass.

She surrendered, and the edges of the pool dissolved.

Larissa stood at the edge of the swamp. From the city came faint, bustling sounds; from the swamp, the hum of cicadas and the musical noise of the river. She whispered forlornly, with the voice of a child, "Papa . . ."

Nothing was familiar. Larissa wept, horribly frightened. She was five years old again, and her soft blond hair hung in a tangle about her tear-streaked face. As she drew closer to the swamp, however, Larissa felt her fear fading to curiosity. She knelt to look at shiny pebbles, touched a frog's wet back and laughed brightly as it leaped away with an insulted croak.

An increase in light caused Larissa to look up, and she gasped happily. Dozens of swirling lights emerged from the shadows of the forest. There were so many of them clustered around the slim form of the girl that she could easily see by their light. The five-year-old sat down on the riverbank, laughing and clapping her hands at the antics of the glowing balls.

Fifteen, perhaps twenty of the ghostly orbs danced about Larissa's head, hovering, bouncing, swirling around her. Now and then her small hand would reach to catch one, but it would quickly dart away.

Larissa's body began to tingle warmly. It was an extremely pleasant sensation, and it coursed through her from her head to her toes. She giggled, then sobered as she realized that the lights were starting to drift away. Anxious not to lose her new friends, Larissa clambered to her feet and followed them as they began to float toward the swamp.

The night's peace was shattered by a sudden cry.

"Larissa!" her father exclaimed, running up from the town. The girl turned to him and frowned. The light creatures seemed to shrink in size, moving away from Larissa at the sound of her father's shrill voice. Some abandoned her altogether, floating off like innocuous fireflies. Others continued to hover near.

"Papa!" Larissa scolded. "You scared them away!"

Her father charged at the glowing globes of light. He waved his arms about frantically, screaming in anger and pent-up terror. The balls of radiance scattered, all save one.

"Oh, gods, Rissa, I thought I'd lost you!" Aubrey gasped as he gathered his wayward daughter into his arms and squeezed her tightly.

Larissa, however, was not taking kindly to being rescued from the pretty lights.

"Papa, bring them back!" she demanded angrily.

Aubrey took a good look at Larissa and gasped. Sometime over the last few moments his child's hair had turned pure white.

Aubrey's tired mouth set in a hard line, and Larissa's own rosebud lips puckered into a determined frown. When her father picked her up, she struggled. Aubrey hurried back toward the warm, reassuring torchlight of the town, clutching his precious burden. The girl faced over her father's shoulder, and she saw that one of the lights had not deserted her. With an anguished, lost wail, Larissa stuck out her hands imploringly toward the floating ball.

"Don't leave me!" the child screamed, tears pouring down her face. The ball of light was obviously troubled. It blinked rapidly, darting about in a crazy zigzag pattern. For a few moments it followed the child and father, its cold light illuminating Larissa's twisted, weeping features. It hung back as Aubrey drew closer to the town. Its light flickered in distress, then dulled to a barely visible glow as it slowly floated away to rejoin its fellows.

*I remember. . . . I remember. . . .*

"The swamp had need of your magic. The *feu follets* called you. Had you been able to answer their call, had your father not taken you away, you would eventually have become as I am—a part of the swamp."

"But I have no magic," Larissa protested. Even as the words left her lips, she knew them to be a lie. Her body still remembered that warm tingling. She recognized the sensation as an early stage of the wild joy she had experienced dancing while Sardan had played for her. The young woman closed her eyes and again felt power surging through her, power almost out of control.

"You had the potential, which was why the swamp chose you. When did you begin to dance?"

Taken aback by the abrupt question, Larissa opened her eyes and said, "When I was about six, I think."

"And were you trained?" The Maiden's voice was cool, as though she already knew the answers. She cupped her hands together, and they began to glow with a soft radiance. Curious, Larissa watched and didn't answer. The Maiden glanced up from her gleaming hands. "Were you trained?" she repeated, more sternly this time.

"Um, no," Larissa answered. Something began to take shape in the Maiden's hands. "I just—danced. It was fun. I enjoyed it and I seemed to be good at it."

The shape in the Maiden's cupped palms solidified, its color turning from pale green to dark blue. With the barest of smiles, the Maiden extended her berry-filled hands to an astonished Larissa.

"Dancing is your gift from the swamp, the gift granted you when you became a whitemane," she said as Larissa began to eat. "We took the hue of your hair and left you the mark of the swamp's favor. We also gave you a way to control and utilize your magical ability.

"Your body has discovered its magic, and your soul knows the secrets, though your mind is as yet unaware. So I say to you now: You have magical skills. If I teach you how to unlock them, will you use your talents to fight the evil aboard *La Demoiselle*?"

Larissa was surprised to find herself grinning. "Yes."

"Then let us begin. Tell me about what you do aboard the boat."

"I'm the Lady of the Sea in the musical *The Pirate's Pleasure*," Larissa said, finishing the last of the wonderfully sweet berries.

The Maiden nodded, her mossy tresses swaying with the movement. "Since you are familiar with that element, we will begin with water."

Larissa snorted. "I hardly think you could compare anything in *The Pirate's Pleasure* with real magic."

"Not necessarily true. Who choreographed the dance?"

"I did."

"Well, then. You should realize that part of it stems from you. Do you see?" Larissa shook her head. The Maiden laughed, a sweet sound like rain on water. "It doesn't matter. Here, dance your part for me now."

Larissa, suddenly nervous, rose and walked awkwardly to a flat patch of ground. She settled herself on her feet and imagined the prone body of Florian and the weeping Rose, trying not to think about Casilda and wonder what had been done to her. Think of the dance, Larissa told herself sternly.

Her performance was rough at first, and Larissa winced as she moved, knowing how stiff it must appear. Then, gradually, she relaxed into the familiar patterns.

The Maiden watched her closely, her eyes on the lithe

body, the leaping feet, the flowing white mane. Oh, yes, the magic was there in that slender frame. How could Larissa not feel it? the Maiden wondered to herself. The girl practically radiated it. Larissa leaped, tossed her hair, and, sweating, executed a final arch and tumble.

She looked up for the Maiden's reaction. The pale green face was impassive.

"You have much to unlearn," the plant-woman told her. "You are stilted, practiced, predictable. You must learn to forget the steps, concentrate only on the rhythms."

"But there's no music," replied Larissa, catching her breath. She was a little vexed that the Maiden seemed so unimpressed.

"Ah, but there is. I will have the quickwoods play for you while you are learning. After that, you must search your soul for the rhythm that grants the power you seek. Here, watch me. I have not your gift for the dance, but I have learned enough of it to teach you." She rose gracefully, lifting a slender hand to indicate that Larissa should have a seat. "Quickwood-With-Burn-Scars," she said to a nearby tree, bowing, "play for me, that I may teach the whitemane."

The huge tree, who did indeed bear the scars of a terrible fire, rustled obligingly. Two massive roots emerged from the soil and began to pound on the trunk.

It was a deep sound. Something buried just as deeply in Larissa's soul leaped to respond. Her breath came in short gasps as she watched the slim figure of the Maiden perform.

The Maiden began to sway back and forth, her green eyes closed to better her concentration. Her hips began to move, fluid as poured water, and her hands rose up like waves. The tendrils that were fingers waved, as though she were trying to force raindrops from them. The rhythm had the ocean's lull, the river's laugh, and

Larissa wanted to rise and dance with the Maiden more than anything.

"Earth," cried the Maiden abruptly. The quickwood obliged, the pounding becoming more muffled and, if possible, even deeper. It was like a heartbeat, the heartbeat of the earth. The dancer's movements changed, became more deliberate, less fluid. She dropped to her knees, then lay on her back, filtering handfuls of earth through her fingers. Again, Larissa longed to join her, but remained seated. She had not been invited. Not yet.

"Air!" demanded the Maiden. Again the rhythm changed, became light, soaring, like a bird on the wing. For the first time since Larissa had known her, the Maiden's feet tore free of the earth, and the sylvan creature leaped lightly about. Her long, mossy hair caught the wind and floated in it. The slim frame seemed airborne itself. Larissa gasped aloud with the sheer, effortless beauty of it all.

"Fire!"

This, Larissa sensed, was the most difficult and dangerous of the elements to call upon. She tensed without quite knowing why. The drumming became sharp, piercing, louder, and the Maiden's movements were like flame and lightning, all power and energy and sudden, sharp movements. Larissa closed her eyes.

Abruptly all was silent. Larissa opened her eyes to see the Maiden standing before her. The young woman rose, shaking badly. All her life, she had unwittingly been striving for what she had just witnessed. Every leap she had ever made seemed earthbound to her now, every move graceless and empty. She could not bear her own ignorance of the Maiden's dance.

"I must know," she said in a quavering voice. "I must know how to dance like you. Teach me."

# THIRTEEN

"First of all, you cannot dance in that," the Maiden stated flatly, indicating Larissa's dress.

The dancer glanced down at herself. Her clothing was typical of the garb she wore aboard the boat: full skirts, a bodice that laced up the front, and a chemise underneath.

"What's wrong with it, apart from it being filthy?"

"It binds you too much. You cannot wear anything that restricts movement."

To Larissa's annoyance, the Maiden made the dancer remove her clothes and tear them into pieces for new garments. Larissa bound her breasts with a halter made of the skirt's material and fashioned a skirt of the lighter-weight chemise. She fastened the skirt about her slender waist and glanced at the Maiden for approval.

"No," the Maiden chided. She tugged the skirt from Larissa's waist and retied it so that it hugged her hips.

"The only time I've ever worn this little is when I was bathing," Larissa muttered, though she accepted the strange costume.

"There is a reason for this. Each part of your body corresponds with an element," the Maiden explained. "Your hair is air. How you toss your head, play with your hair—that is all for air magic. You can command the wind, conjure beings from the element of air, work with the weather."

"All with this?" she grinned, running her fingers through her still-grimy hair. The Maiden, however, remained serious as she nodded.

"Arms are for fire," she said, making fluttery, flamelike motions with her tendriled fingers and slim green arms. Larissa imitated her. "Fire, fire elementals, electricity, light, and heat come from their movements.

"Water," she said, swaying her hips, "is from your center." She began to undulate her stomach, causing it to roll. "This is why your middle must be free to move. Here in the swamp, it is vital that you know how to command water. And earth," she said, pulling her rooted feet from the soil and leaping, "is the feet, where you make contact with the mother of us all. Now, it is time for your first lesson."

Larissa's heart began to beat faster with anticipation.

"Lie down on the ground."

"What?" Larissa was stunned and disappointed.

The Maiden laughed at her impatience. "The dancing comes last," she told the young woman. "A wizard does not begin to work his magic until he knows the danger he faces and how best to attack it. Nor does he cast a spell without gathering the proper ingredients."

"But this is dancing, not spell casting," Larissa protested. The Maiden touched her cheek softly.

"How much you have to learn, child. First, you must learn to root yourself." At Larissa's baffled look, the Maiden explained. "Your strength comes from where your feet touch, be it soil, or water, or the wood of a boat. I will take you on your first trip. Lie down and close your eyes."

Larissa did as the Maiden requested. The soil was damp, but not muddy, and when Larissa permitted herself to relax she found it quite comfortable.

And then she began to sink into the ground.

With a cry, she bolted upright, but the Maiden shook her head. "Trust me," she urged in her leaf-soft voice, gently pressing Larissa back down to the soil again.

This time, it took longer for Larissa to relax. As she did so, she realized that she was not literally sinking into the loam. Only her mind was making the journey. *Trust me*, came the Maiden's cool voice in her mind. *Trust yourself*.

She was deep in the cool, fragrant soil now. Larissa felt the impalpable heartbeat of the earth, steady and perpetual. Unconsciously her hands dug into the brown soil, as if to bring her body to where her mind was. There was not even the slightest breath of fear. Who could be afraid of earth?

*Feel the life, Larissa. Feel it, grasp it, use its power for your own shaping.*

That was the force, the energy. Life. Growth. Yes . . . Larissa could feel it now. She could hear the plants growing, their roots reaching for sustenance from the rich soil. She reached out with her mind and brushed against that force, finding that it welcomed her tentative probing. Then she directed her efforts to gently bending the energy.

"Larissa," came the Maiden's soft voice.

The dancer opened her eyes. Her body felt heavy, and for a moment it was extremely difficult to move. With a deliberate effort, she sat up, stretching.

"Look by your right hand," the Maiden continued, pleasure burning in her green eyes. Larissa did so. There was a tiny patch of violets in the otherwise bare earth. "They were not there when you lay down."

A tremulous joy spread across Larissa's face, and she gently touched the tiny plants with a forefinger. "I *made* them?"

"No," the Maiden corrected her. "I cannot teach you how to conjure something out of nothing. The seeds were there, but not taking root. You did not create the violets, merely found their potential for growth and hastened it along. You worked with the force of life, not against it. Rise, my child."

Larissa got to her feet and waited expectantly.

"Remember the feeling of finding and directing the energy, and remember which part of your body corresponds with earth. Now, child, you may dance."

Tentatively at first, Larissa began to move her bare feet in a circle around the tiny flowers. Her toes traced patterns in the moist earth, then Larissa trod heavily, deeply planting footprints in the soil. She felt the power tingle up her legs and closed her eyes to concentrate better. The rest of her body began to move, swaying gently, and she danced to the rhythm of the earth's heartbeat, faster and faster, taking control, demanding response. . . .

She halted abruptly when she realized there was plant life under her feet instead of bare earth. Larissa opened her eyes to find the entire area now covered with rich purple violets. The fragrance from the bruised flowers wafted up to her nostrils, and she glanced at the Maiden happily.

"Your gift is great, but you must learn to control it and use it wisely."

A sobering thought struck Larissa, damping her enthusiasm. "Maiden . . . how can this—" she gestured to the violets "—help defeat Dumont and Lond?"

The Maiden looked at her, disappointed. "You do not yet see the potential. Ah, well, that will come. In the meantime, do you wish to bathe and refresh yourself?"

"Is the lesson over?" Larissa cried, fearful that her rash question had abruptly halted her tutoring. "Maiden, they're looking for me right now, and the boat could leave the boundaries of—"

"What they seek, they will not find. This is a safe place. As for the boat leaving, well, there is another in the swamp who might have something to say about that. Your lesson is far from over. Every moment you are with me, you will be learning, though you might not recognize it as such." She smiled a little to herself.

"There is a spring at the far end of this island. I will show you how to get there. Do you remember when I took you to the scrying pool, and I said you would learn to travel that way by yourself?"

Larissa nodded, a bit uncomfortable. There had been something frightening about being closed up inside the tree, even if it had lasted only a few seconds.

"Find a tree that you feel comfortable with, and let me know which one."

The dancer rolled her eyes. Find a tree she felt comfortable with? What kind of nonsense—

"*Whitemane!*" cried the Maiden angrily, her voice no longer the murmur of leaves but the sharp crack of a breaking bough. Larissa's head whipped around, fearful at the banked fury in the Maiden's voice.

"*Nothing* I say is idle prattle. *Nothing* I instruct you to do is for simple amusement. You risk much in asking to learn the dance magic, but I risk more in teaching it to you!"

Larissa blushed with shame, unable to meet the blazing green eyes of the plant-woman. "I'm sorry, Maiden. I meant no disrespect."

The Maiden softened somewhat. "I know, child. And your heart is full of care for those you love. But you must learn patience and discipline. Come then, Whitemane, and I will teach you how to walk through trees."

Larissa looked at the trees that formed a circle about the clearing. At last she paused before a thick-trunked cypress. The breeze stirred the airmoss entangled in its branches, and it looked almost as if the tree was nodding in greeting.

"Introduce yourself," the Maiden instructed. "Root, and let the tree know who you are."

Larissa did so, closing her eyes and letting her toes sink into the soil at the tree's roots.

*Welcome, Whitemane. You may travel through me.*

The young dancer's eyes flew open. "It talked to me!" she gasped.

"Of course it did."

"But it's not a quickwood, or—"

"No," the Maiden agreed smoothly, "it is merely an ordinary cypress tree. All things in nature speak to one who has ears for their words. Now, walk through it."

Larissa took a deep breath and stepped up to the cypress, her arms outstretched. They touched rough bark. "I can't."

"Because you do not trust the tree to open for you. That is an insult, Larissa. It has already told you it would. Leap into the tree. Dance into it. Think of it as a partner who catches you."

Larissa looked at the tree. If the Maiden was right, she would come through in another part of the island. If she was wrong, well, Larissa was prepared for a few bruises.

"Be my doorway," she whispered to the tree. She backed away, took a few running steps and leaped, arms spread gracefully behind her and her white hair flying.

She landed securely beside a cascade that fed a deep, clear pool. The Maiden was already there, watching Larissa's look of joyous incredulity. "A little trust, in yourself and what—or who—you work with," she said gently.

The pool looked indescribably beautiful to Larissa, who was very conscious of the mud and sweat caked on her lithe body. As she bathed, she also washed her clothes and spread them on a large rock to dry. The Maiden moved to the edge of the pool and inserted her root-feet in the water, drinking while her student enjoyed her bath. Larissa gave a happy sigh and lay back, floating in the cool liquid.

"Who's she?" came a female voice.

Larissa started, splashing. A pretty young woman about her own age sat on the bank, peering at her curiously. The girl's shiny brown hair was long and thick, and fell around her like a cloak. She was clad only in a blue gossamer gown. Her lively brown eyes sparkled, and her arms hugged her knees as she rocked back and forth.

"You are very rude, Deniri," the Maiden reprimanded. "This is Larissa Snowmane, and she is my student. Larissa, this is Deniri, a friend—when she behaves."

Deniri tossed her rich brown locks and laughed merrily. A sharp, feral smile was on her face.

"I heard a whitemane had returned to the swamp. Hello, Larissa."

"Hello," Larissa managed, feeling a bit self-conscious. But the curious girl was no longer paying attention to the dancer. She stared intently at the pool a few feet away from Larissa, uncurling her body slowly and gracefully. Deniri crept toward the bank, then shot her hand into the water with astonishing speed. She bared her teeth in a victorious grin as she gazed at the struggling frog in her hand. Then, to Larissa's horror, she bit it in two.

As she ate, Deniri noticed Larissa's shocked expression. She shrugged her slim shoulders. "I'm hungry," she explained, taking another bite.

Larissa turned away in revulsion. "Deniri is not human," the Maiden explained. "Deniri, show Larissa your other appearance."

"I'm not done," she protested.

"She will be less frightened of you if she understands," the Maiden continued, ignoring Deniri's statement.

Deniri took another mouthful of frog, tossed to the ground what remained, and slipped into the water. With a transformation that was too fast for Larissa to follow, the young woman became a giant mink. She surfaced, crawled onto the bank, and returned to her meal, holding it down with one paw.

"Deniri is a minx—a creature who can take on the form of either a woman or a mink. Her mate is someone who might be able to help us, when the time comes," said the Maiden. "Deniri, will you tell Kaedrin to come to the island? I wish to see him, if he has no objection."

The giant mink, luxurious fur glistening with moisture, cocked her head and considered. At last, she nodded. A last bite and the frog had been devoured. With a final glance at Larissa, the mink scurried across the dry land and dived into the murky depths of the river. Larissa stared after her.

"She doesn't seem like a very reliable person," the dancer commented after a moment.

"She isn't," the Maiden confirmed. "No minx is. They are clever, selfish, and have a large streak of cruelty in them. But Deniri seems to be in love with Kaedrin, and Kaedrin I trust. He is one of the swamp's hermits."

"Like Willen's mother," said Larissa.

The Maiden looked at her curiously. "Yes," she said slowly, "that's right. Kaedrin once lived in the land of Dorvinia, but he did not call it home. Some thought that he had Vistani blood, he had so great a wanderlust. He studied soldiering, and he was good at his trade, but it was not what his heart yearned for. He was drawn to the forest, and to the wild things that dwell therein. When at last his wanderings brought him here, he turned his back on towns and people. There could be no better mate for Kaedrin than Deniri.

"I respect Kaedrin's desire for solitude," the Maiden continued. "But we may benefit from his tactical skill. Lond and Dumont are canny foes. We must use every scrap of knowledge available to us if we are to defeat them."

The deep sorrow that Larissa had heard in the Maiden's voice returned when she spoke of Lond. Shyly, not wanting to pry, the dancer asked, "What is it that makes Lond so horrible? How do you know of him?"

The Maiden remained silent for a while. Larissa winced inwardly, afraid she had gone too far. At last the Maiden spoke.

"It is a lasting pain to me. Lond was my greatest failure, and many have suffered from his deeds. It is a dark tale, Larissa, and one which I would not have told you quite yet. But you have asked, so you shall know. Come. Dress, and follow me."

Larissa did so and sat quietly at the Maiden's feet while the plant-woman gazed intently into the scrying pool. The reflections of the green-skinned Maiden and the watching young dancer faded, and Larissa was once again seeing the edge of the forest where she had played with the *feu follets*.

It was winter now, and the long grasses were coated with frost. The sun shone brightly on the chilly afternoon. A young man approached from the village.

Larissa thought him breathtakingly handsome. Graceful and slim he was, with jet-black hair that fell past his shoulders and eyes that were so blue they were almost violet. He moved with the grace of a big cat. A beautiful robe, gaily colored, draped his trim frame, and he carried an intricately carved staff. A necklace of feathers, bits of bone, and pieces of roots hung about his throat. The man walked with the air of one used to being obeyed, though he seemed younger than Willen.

"His name is Alondrin," the Maiden explained, "and he is *bocoru* of Port d'Elhour."

"*Bocoru*?"

"Shaman," the Maiden said, "or priest. Every town had one, once. The *bocoru* tends to his people's spiritual needs, and the swamp accepts him."

"I never heard of Port d'Elhour having a bo—a *bocoru*," Larissa murmured, watching the young man.

"He no longer serves his people in that capacity," said the Maiden sorrowfully.

In the scrying pool, the Maiden emerged from the shadows of the cypress trees to greet Alondrin. They kissed eagerly as the scene dissolved.

"Alondrin and I were lovers, at first. He was the brightest among his people, the cleverest, the most inquisitive. He was a perfect *bocoru*."

Larissa watched as the scene reformed. Alondrin, a few years older but still handsome, had exchanged his colorful robe for a somber black cloak. He wore more necklaces about his throat now and had grown a beard. The necklaces were ornamented not with roots and feathers, but with other items that appeared sinister to Larissa. Many bones were on that necklace, and strange-colored stones. The protective roots were gone. Alondrin's staff sported the skull of some small carnivore on its top.

The *bocoru*'s face, too, had changed. The earlier self-confidence had rotted into arrogance, and his once-beautiful face was now dark and twisted with anger.

"What good is power if you never use it?" Alondrin spat. "Why do you persist in thwarting me thus? I only want to learn, to increase my skills. Where is the danger in that?"

The Maiden's leafy green eyes shone with tears. "Oh, my love," she said in a voice that sounded like the wind in the reeds, "there is more danger than you can know. Fruit and flower magic is a gift, to be used for the betterment of others, not for one's own greed. The knowledge I have taught you cannot be twisted to gain the things you desire."

"Then I will learn other magic," retorted Alondrin, growing even angrier, "magic that will obey me."

"No! Beloved, it will not serve you, it will destroy you! Bone and blood lore is exactly that—and it will take from you much more than it can possibly give. Blood demands more blood!"

"I care not, so long as it is I who spill it!" cried Alondrin. In his fury, he swung his staff at her with all his strength. The Maiden was swift, however. Like grass bending before the wind, she avoided the blow with supple grace. The Maiden made a few motions with her hands, and suddenly the rod began to twist in Alondrin's grasp.

The skull fell to the earth, and the astonished *bocoru* discovered that he was looking at a huge snake. With a cry, he dropped the hissing creature. Alondrin fled toward the town, his dark robes fluttering behind him.

The Maiden bent to pick up the serpent and began to weep. She rubbed her cheek against its head, and its tongue flickered gently on her green skin. The Maiden hung the creature about her neck, caressing it. Almost tenderly, the snake wrapped its length about her as she turned and disappeared into the forest.

The scene dissolved. The scrying pool once again showed only the faces of those who gazed into it and the blue skies above them.

"Alondrin turned against the way of the swamp, against all that had gone before to keep the balance. He abandoned his post as *bocoru*, leaving his people to fend for themselves. Many sickened and died. Still others braved the swamp unprepared for its dangers and were destroyed. Alondrin cared not at all. His only desire, the desire that consumed him, was to learn more and more dark magic.

"He learned what the will-o'-the-wisps and *feu follets* know, that emotions are powerful, and he sought to feed on them. But Alondrin is not such a being, and he only succeeded in perverting his own pleasure into others' pain. He trod the path of blood and bone magic, which never gives enough to satisfy but always creates greater and greater cravings."

She paused, turning her gentle, sorrow-filled eyes

upon Larissa. "What I have been teaching you is fruit and flower magic. It works with nature, not against it. Alondrin chose the darker path and now has learned how to command the dead. This is the man to whom your Captain Dumont has given his hospitality, and even now the results of Lond's labor tread the deck of *La Demoiselle du Musarde*."

"Zombies," Larissa whispered. She had heard of such things, and the thought filled her with loathing. Animated corpses, rotting where they stood, unable to think for themselves at all.

"Yes—and no," the Maiden continued, reading Larissa's thoughts. "Alondrin now works over water, and this lends him power. He has learned how to make intelligent zombies. Zombies who can think and speak, yet who remain completely subject to their maker's whims. Zombies," she said sadly, sympathetic eyes on Larissa, "who can even sing."

Larissa's gut clenched in horror. *Casilda*. "No. Oh, gods, no, not Cas . . ."

"Yes, my child," said the Maiden softly. "Alondrin hides his face and body, for the mark of evil is upon him and would reveal his hideous nature. They have struck a fell bargain, the slaver and the zombie-maker. Lond wishes to escape Souragne. In exchange for passage, he has given Dumont a crew that never wearies and never complains."

Larissa forced her pain away and turned hard eyes upon the Maiden. "When will we be ready to attack?"

"When I deem you ready, child, and not before. Even then, there is one last obstacle." The Maiden paused. "But there is time enough for that. There will have to be. You have been through a great deal. Eat now, and sleep. In the morning, we will begin again."

# FOURTEEN

Gelaar's step was rapid and determined as he strode along the deck, and the zombie at his side who served as guard did little to diminish the elf's eagerness.

They hastened purposefully toward Dumont's cabin, which Dragoneyes unlocked with a slow deliberateness. Anxiously Gelaar shouldered Dragoneyes aside and pushed his way into the room. With the same lack of emotion, Dragoneyes closed and bolted the door.

The elf turned his attention to the mirror mounted on the large wardrobe. He stepped up to it hesitantly and husked a few words in a rough melody. His song was not as pure as Sardan's tenor, or even Dumont's deep baritone, but it sufficed.

The surface of the mirror grew dark, the reflection of the opulent room and the watching Dragoneyes fading like twilight into night. Then, as if from a great distance away, Gelaar could glimpse a faint patch of whiteness. It drew closer and revealed itself to be a patch of swirling mists.

Gelaar clenched his fists. Hints of color began to peek through the white fog: blue, gold, flesh tones, and at last the remaining wisps of fog released their grasp on the slender form of Gelaar's daughter Aradnia. Long blond hair hung loosely about her oval face as she gazed at him lovingly from the mirror.

Eagerly the young elfmaid put her hands up to her side of the glass. "Hello, Papa," she whispered, smiling bravely even though her large eyes were filled with crystal tears.

Gelaar's own eyes were wet also. He placed his hands on the mirror, which was as close as he could come to touching Aradnia.

"Hello, child."

For the last year, the girl had been trapped in a certain segment of the mists known only to Dumont. When Dumont or Gelaar wished to see her, the mirror manifested, and vision and communication was possible. Aradnia was not mistreated, only horribly alone and in a constant state of mind-dulling fear.

Selfishly, Gelaar wanted to spend the half-hour Dumont had allotted him merely gazing at his beautiful child. He put his feelings aside. This time was for her, more than for him. "Where to, my dear?"

"A forest, I think," Aradnia said, her voice catching a little with longing. "At twilight. With beautiful creatures."

Before he began, Gelaar glanced once more at Dragoneyes. The half-elf sat quietly in his chair, watching Gelaar with the patience of the dead.

For an instant, something like pity touched Gelaar. Dragoneyes' catlike grace had hardened into wooden efficiency. The slitted amber eyes held no malicious humor anymore, and the sharp-featured face registered no emotions whatsoever. Then Gelaar remembered the years he'd spent enduring the half-elf's taunts.

Gelaar's pity evaporated like mist under a bright noon sun. Whatever had happened to him, Dragoneyes had earned it—unlike some of the other walking dead aboard *La Demoiselle*.

The illusionist spread his arms and began to murmur an incantation.

The yellow light of Dragoneyes' lantern faded into the cool purples and blues of twilight. The faint twittering of birds could be heard, and the barely audible rustle of a playful breeze. A scene began to take shape before Aradnia's eager eyes.

Pine trees appeared, dark green against a lavender sky. The wooden beams of the ceiling faded away, to be replaced by twinkling stars. Directly in front of the mirror was a clearing of soft green grass encircled by a ring of mushrooms. The birdsong died away, and the pure, heart-rending sound of a single flute trembled through the air. Its player, a beautiful young elven woman, entered the circle.

Other beings joined her—faeries, nymphs, sylphs, and a unicorn—and began to dance joyfully in the glade. Other music, performed by unseen musicians, merged with the elfmaid's song.

The mage fluttered his right hand slightly, conjuring an illusionary fire in the center of the faerie ring, and allowed a whooping satyr to join in. Shouts of laughter, unheard by anyone outside the room, rang through the fictitious glade as Gelaar did what pathetically little he could to ease his daughter's pain.

\* \* \* \* \*

The sultry, early summer night closed in about the land, wrapping it in a steamy blanket. The air was cooler than during the day, but still moist and thick. Dumont, standing alone on the starboard side of *La Demoiselle*, did not like the feel of the humid air in his lungs, but he breathed deeply of it anyway, to clear and calm his thoughts. Above him, the wooden griffin hovered perennially in midflight.

The night was eerily silent. Dumont had ordered the boat stopped until the immediate area could be searched for Larissa, and the rhythmic splash of the paddlewheel had not been heard since she disappeared.

"It can't be true," he muttered to himself. "Larissa has no magic. I'd have known, dammit!" Lond's tale about "whitemanes" and "swamp magic" seemed too preposterous for words. On the other hand, the mage had proven himself a force to be reckoned with. The zombies who walked on Dumont's own boat were testimony to that.

Only one thing shone like a beacon through Dumont's haze of confusion: Larissa had to be found.

A glimmer of light on the bank caught his eye, and he motioned to the four zombies on deck to lower the ramp. Willen, Tane, and Jahedrin trudged wearily on deck. They had been gone for nearly a full day.

"Any sign of her?" Dumont asked, his voice taut.

Willen and the others shook their heads. "Nothing," Jahedrin said. Even in the torchlight, Dumont could see that his eyes were strained and his face haggard. "Lot of dangerous things out there, Captain, any one of which—"

"No," snapped Dumont, "she's alive. I know it. Will, get a few hours of sleep. Around midnight, I want you to start taking her downriver."

"Aye, sir," Willen replied.

"At dawn, we'll stop and start looking again. She probably stayed by the river, and if we follow that . . ." His voice trailed off. Abruptly he turned on his heel and stormed away from his men to his cabin.

He sang the command word in a hard voice and shoved the door open. Gelaar stared at him angrily, interrupted in midgesture. Dumont caught a glimpse of the complex illusion Gelaar had created before the images vanished. Behind the mage, Aradnia, trapped in the mists, cowered from the captain's anger.

"Out," he roared, gesturing toward the door. He stepped up to the mirror and shoved his florid face toward Aradnia. Her lower lip quivered, and her eyes pleaded with him.

"Please, Captain, just a few more minutes with my father," she begged, her sweet voice thick and little more than a timid whisper.

Dumont narrowed his green eyes and took a malicious pleasure in singing the four notes. Aradnia's beautiful face vanished into the enveloping mists. Then even the mists were gone, and the mirror placidly reflected the room.

The captain felt Gelaar's angry gaze boring into his back. Slowly he turned around.

"You hate me, don't you?" he purred. The mage did not rise to the bait, but a muscle near his eye twitched. "You'd like nothing better than to see my head on a pike, wouldn't you? Well, elf, you're not the first, and by the rats of Richemulot you won't be the last, either."

Casually, Dumont reached for a small statue on the top of the wardrobe. At first appearances, it was a beautiful wood nymph, but closer inspection revealed that it had long, sharp fangs. Dumont grasped the small but heavy marble object threateningly.

"One blow with this to that mirror, elf, and your darling child is stranded forever in the mists. I don't think you want that. No one gets the better of Raoul Dumont. Now, get out of my sight, both of you."

Dragoneyes grasped Gelaar by the wrist and twisted. The illusionist cried out once, then left, massaging his wrist. Dragoneyes followed, closing the door behind him.

Dumont watched Dragoneyes leave with a twitch of pain in his gut. He doubted he would ever get used to seeing emptiness in his friend's amber eyes. Angry at his emotion, he opened the wardrobe and grabbed a half-full bottle of whiskey. He opened it and took a strong gulp, feeling it burn as it slid down his throat and settled in his belly.

He eased himself down on the canopied bed and took

another swig, wiping his mouth with the back of his hand. It was all Liza's fault, he mused angrily. Everything. If she hadn't meddled, they would still be in Darkon, Dragoneyes would still be alive, and Larissa would be dancing happily for him every night. The memories of that fateful encounter flooded back as Dumont took another long swallow of whiskey. It had all started with a sharp rap at the door....

"Come," Dumont had called absently, his eyes on the account book in front of him. The ship was making a great deal of money in Darkon, so much that Dumont was finding the accounting a chore.

Liza blew in like a hurricane. Her face was pale, but her green eyes blazed and her red hair streamed down her back like flame.

"You bastard," she snapped.

Dumont was surprised, but only a little. Quickly he rose and went to the door, closing it before anyone could hear her. What on earth had he done now? His leading lady had thrown tantrums before, about everything from her costume to the musicians to the food, but this time she seemed to be in earnest.

"Liza, my dear," he began consolingly. Liza would have none of it, however, and thrust her face up to his.

"It's over, Raoul," she said coldly. "All of it. Tonight was my last performance."

"What do you mean?" Dumont's brows drew together as a horrible suspicion began to take shape in his mind.

Liza smirked. Enjoying every moment, she held out one long-fingered hand. On the fourth finger sat one of the biggest diamonds Dumont had ever seen.

"Tahlyn gave it to me tonight. We're to be wed within the week."

"The baron?"

"Exactly."

Dumont clenched his teeth, furious that his guess had been correct. He forced himself to stay calm.

"Congratulations, my dear. Best of luck in your new life." His mind worked swiftly. Liza had an ego the size of Darkon. She'd not give up the stage quite so easily. If there were some way to tempt her into staying on, at least for a while. . . .

The actress's smile grew. "Oh, but that's not all. You're not only losing your leading lady. You're losing your *Demoiselle*—you damned slaver," she hissed.

Dumont went rigid.

"I know what you keep in the storage room. And this mirror here—" she brushed at her hair in front of the wardrobe mirror "—well, Gelaar will be relieved that his daughter didn't run away with that sell-sword in Mordent after all, won't he? I'm sure the good elven folk of Nevuchar Springs will be delighted to apprehend a slave ship."

Fear and anger shot through Dumont. He'd be ruined. Twenty years spent traveling, carefully building the reputation of *La Demoiselle du Musarde*. That was all at risk now, thanks to one petulant soprano.

"I've got you on the run now, haven't I, Raoul? You've slithered away from me like the snake you are before, but, oh, yes, I've got you now!"

He moved toward her, and she carefully placed between them the small table at which he had been studying. Her cheeks were flushed and her green eyes sparkling. Her low-cut dress, the same one she had worn at dinner, revealed the tops of her breasts. She was absolutely stunning in her rage.

"For the last two years, I've watched you eyeing Larissa when you think nobody sees. I don't know why you haven't tried anything on her yet, but you're not going to now. What else have you got in that hold, Raoul?"

Something chilled to ice inside Dumont at the mention of Larissa's name. Even more than Liza's threats to expose him, her accusations of his intentions toward Larissa enraged him. His green eyes, which had been snapping fire, suddenly went cold.

"Oh, many things worth seeing," he said quietly. "A pseudodragon, though it's more trouble than it's worth, and one of those rare colorcats they told us about in G'Henna. I've an owl maid, a nereid, and a host of other magical creatures. It's quite a collection, and it's made my boat the wonder it is."

Slowly he walked around the table toward her, one big hand casually reaching to pick up a white scarf he had draped on the bedpost. Liza's anger evaporated, and she took a half-step backward toward the door.

"This scarf," continued the captain, "belonged to the nereid. It's mine now, and so is she. As for you—well, you're a pretty thing, Liza. Baron Tahlyn has excellent taste. We're going to miss that fabulous voice. You were a treasure, but a bit expensive to maintain."

Liza was frightened now, and when Dumont lunged at her she reacted swiftly. She shoved a chair in Dumont's path, slowing him down but not stopping him, and fled for the door.

"Help!" she cried, unaware that nothing could be heard outside once the door was closed. Dumont cursed as he regained his balance and went after her. He hadn't locked the door, and if she got out—

With a gasp, the terrified singer tugged the door open.

Dragoneyes was there. He seized Liza and clamped a hand across her mouth, leaning back against the door to shut it. Liza struggled vainly, and in a heartbeat Dumont had reached her, wrapping the magical white scarf about the singer's throat and jerking it tight. She fought briefly, but at last she sagged and her falling body tugged the silky material free from his hands.

Panting, Dumont looked at Dragoneyes. The half-elf regarded him evenly. There was no hint of condemnation in those golden orbs.

"She knew about the collection, and that damned

baron proposed to her. She was going to marry him and turn me over to the people of Nevuchar Springs."

"Elf folk'd hang you for sure for slaving," answered Dragoneyes. He glanced down at the limp body. "I'll miss her singing. Her understudy'll be pleased, though. What should we do with the body?"

A cruel smile twisted Dumont's lips. "I have a great idea. . . ."

Yes, Dumont mused to himself now as the alcohol finally began to hit him, he'd had a great idea that had gone more wrong than he could possibly imagine.

"Liza, m'dear," he slurred, "if your cursed ghost haunts my boat, I'll bet you're damn pleased with the way things are working out."

He took another long pull at the almost empty bottle. As he did so, he told himself that the peal of vindictive laughter he heard in his head was only his whiskey-soaked imagination.

\* \* \* \* \*

A loud crash of thunder woke Willen. He blinked sleepily, confused for a moment, then remembered he needed to get up to the pilothouse. The rain was coming down heavily now, and he winced inwardly. The swamp was a bad place to be when it rained. As he had told Larissa, the folk of Port d'Elhour called it "Death's riding weather," and he knew just how right they were.

He yawned and rubbed his eyes with the heel of his hand. Curious thing, sleep, he mused to himself. It had been difficult at first for Willen to understand the human need for sleep, undeniable though it was. How odd that the body would simply stop cooperating, that the mind would refuse to focus, until the human lay down and turned off conscious thought for a few hours. He dressed, splashed some cold water on his face, and stepped out into the downpour.

He had been up in the pilothouse for only a few moments when Sardan knocked on the door.

"I come bearing gifts, O lucky pilot," the tenor said, setting down a tray laden with a pot of tea, two cups, bread, and slices of meat. "And if my lady has stayed where I left her . . . yes, here she is—" he beamed as he withdrew his mandolin from the stairway "—you'll have food for the body and food for the soul." Sardan poured a mugful of steaming tea and handed it to Willen, who took it gratefully.

"I heard the captain tell you to go on duty in this horrible weather, so I thought I'd come up and entertain you," he explained as he poured a cup of tea for himself.

Willen smiled at him, touched. "Thank you, Sardan."

The handsome bard grimaced. "Don't get any rumors started or my reputation will be ruined," he joked.

Willen took a sip of the fragrant tea, savoring its taste, then set it aside and addressed himself to his task.

There were no lights in the pilothouse at night. It was easier to navigate by the moon and starlight outside, though the rain made certain there was little enough of that. Sardan sat in the back, shadowed in darkness, strumming his mandolin. Willen's mind began to wander.

Lond had turned the majority of the crew into undead minions. The only ones spared were the cooking staff and those that piloted the ship—Willen, Tane, and Jahedrin. Willen assumed that Lond recognized that the pilots had to have fast reflexes in order to deal with any problems the capricious river might hurl their way.

With the exception of Casilda, the cast of the play remained untouched. It didn't make sense to Willen. While he rejoiced that they had not fallen victim to Lond's evil, he couldn't understand why they had been spared. The more zombies on the boat, the better, as far as the evil wizard was concerned. So why leave the cast alone? They, and the few living crewmen, sensed that there was something amiss. They seemed to believe the "swamp fever" story, but Willen wondered how long it would take before somebody figured out what was really going on.

Sardan finished one song that Willen recognized from *The Pirate's Pleasure* and started on another one. The pilot gritted his teeth.

"Don't you know anything but the score from the show?" he asked the tenor, annoyed.

"Of course I do," replied Sardan testily. "I used to be a bard, you know. A long time ago, before I gave in to the easy life. Captain won't hear any music aboard *La Demoiselle* other than what's in the score. And nobody but cast members can sing. It's a direct order."

Willen's eyes widened, and he was glad of the darkness in the pilothouse so that Sardan couldn't see his reaction. He remembered visiting the prisoners and hearing strains of Rose's solo. What he'd seen of Dumont's magic was also linked to music.

"Is *The Pirate's Pleasure* a traditional play?" Willen asked, trying not to sound overanxious as his idea began to take shape.

At that, Sardan laughed aloud. "It's a pretty poor show. Anything traditional would have to be a lot better to last more than a week. No, the tragic tale of Florian and Rose is our good captain's own creation. Although, to be fair, it's not bad for an amateur."

Willen's grin was enormous now. He had guessed correctly. If Dumont had written the score, then the songs from the musical were probably laced with magical words and notes. He'd have to tell the Maiden about this, and fast. The cast rehearsed every afternoon, and each time the spell was performed the bonds holding the prisoners would grow stronger.

# FIFTEEN

"It has no form," the Maiden whispered softly as Larissa floated quietly in the pool. "It expands to fill the container. Become the container. Take water into you, Larissa. Feel it inside of you, feel it in your hands, your head, your body. Know that it is part of you, that it cannot hurt you. Now, when you are ready, perform the dance and feel the water in your lungs."

Lying quietly in the spring, keeping her eyes closed, her mind tranquil, Larissa reached up and ran her fingers through her hair. Air, she thought. She contracted her stomach muscles and undulated just enough so that her head was beneath the surface. Water, she thought. Breathe . . .

Larissa flailed, bolting for the surface and coughing desperately.

"I simply don't understand why this is so difficult for you," the Maiden said. "Come out and try again. Don't jerk—*roll* your hips."

Larissa's lungs hurt, but she obediently climbed out of the pool. She tried, but she had been practicing all morning and was so tired that she wasn't even able to come close to emulating her teacher's liquid movements. The Maiden sighed.

"Rest for a while, my dear. We'll try again this afternoon. You must master water. That is the primary element in Souragne."

She held out her hands to Larissa, and the girl eagerly helped herself to the ripe fruit the Maiden offered. As Larissa bit into a peach, the juice running down her chin, the Maiden cocked her head.

"We have visitors," she told her student. Larissa got to her feet, gazing in the direction of the river. A small canoe came into sight, bearing Deniri and a tall, muscular man clad in swamp-soiled rags. They negotiated the strong current expertly, docking easily and pulling the boat well onto the shore.

The man looked to be in his early fifties, but it was hard for Larissa to tell. The shaggy gray beard could have belonged to an old man, but the muscles that swelled beneath the tattered shreds of clothing and the twinkling gray eyes set in the weatherworn face attested to a more youthful age.

"Greetings, Kaedrin, Deniri. Thank you for coming. I disturb you only because of our great necessity," said the Maiden as the pair approached.

Before anyone else had a chance to speak, a weasel stuck its head out of one of the man's pockets. It fixed the Maiden with bright eyes, whiskers twitching, then dived back into the warm comfort of the pocket. As if the weasel's emergence had been a cue, two mice emerged from another pocket and sniffed about cautiously. A harsh caw distracted Larissa's attention in time to see a magnificent raven swoop down from a nearby tree to perch on the man's shoulder.

Kaedrin smiled at the raven and stroked the ebony head gently with a respectful touch. He turned toward Larissa and gazed at the dancer for a moment.

"Greetings, Whitemane Larissa," he said formally. "Kaedrin, son of Mailir, son of Ash-Tari, is at your service."

Larissa opened her mouth to reply, then froze. A

large snake, covered with rust-colored diamond patches, twined its way into the sunlight from the man's shirt. A black tongue flickered, scenting Larissa, and beady eyes fixed her in a cold, reptilian stare.

"Child, what—oh," Kaedrin said, suddenly comprehending. "I know she's poisonous, but we're good friends. She'll not harm you." Completely unafraid, the ranger picked up the slowly twisting serpent and held it out toward Larissa. "Just pat her and—"

"No!" the dancer cried. Fear swelled inside her. "Get it away...."

"She obviously dislikes snakes, Kaedrin," said the Maiden gently. Abashed, the ranger reinserted the snake into his shirt.

"I'm sorry," Larissa apologized. She felt her cheeks flush with embarrassment and hastened to explain. "It's just—"

"No need," said Kaedrin quickly. "When I return, I'll come without some of my friends, eh?" He smiled warmly at her. "We must go. Deniri and I have hunting to do. Larissa, we will bring you back some of our kill. The Maiden can't conjure a good roast rabbit." He turned without another word, and he and the pretty minx walked hand in hand back to their canoe.

"After meeting Longears, I don't know if I can eat roast rabbit," Larissa said to the Maiden.

The Maiden shrugged. "Life and death are a part of the natural cycle. If one of his people may provide sustenance for you, Longears will not be angry. Wasteful killing, where none benefit—that is another matter. That is a violation of the balance."

Larissa finished her meal quietly, lying on her back and gazing at the blue sky. After all too short a time, the Maiden stood over her. "Come, Larissa. Fire, I think, will be your next lesson."

The dancer groaned, but sat up.

\* \* \* \* \* \*

The new scouting party turned up as empty-handed as the one before. Dumont was starting to truly worry about the fate of his ward. Lond was no help. He had closeted himself in his cabin, unable or unwilling to locate Larissa through magic.

Dumont swore to himself and took another pull at the whiskey bottle. He had always been fond of liquor, but now he found that its warm haze took away some of the strange pangs of regret that were beginning to haunt him since Larissa's disappearance.

His mind wandered as he lay sprawled on his bed, one brawny arm behind his head and the other balancing the bottle on his chest. For the first time since he had laid eyes on Larissa, Dumont wondered if the young woman might not have been better off if he had left her with her father.

Her father. Dumont had spotted the man right away that night when he came aboard *La Demoiselle*. . . .

Aubrey Helson had worn the gaunt, haggard look of a man who was harried by his own personal demons. The man was thin to the point of emaciation, his pale face covered with stubble, and his eyes blinked rapidly as he spoke. Helson's clothes had obviously once been fine. Equally as obvious was the fact that the man's fortunes had been spiraling downward for some time now.

It had been no effort at all for Dumont to entice the man into a game of "Lords and Ladies." In the lounge area, surrounded by the beauty of wrought brass, polished wood, and stained-glass windows, they each acquired a drink and a handful of tokens. They played a few rounds, and Dumont swiftly got a feel for his opponent. He threw the first two games, and Helson's pleasure as his pile of tokens grew was most satisfying to the captain.

Still, Helson's hands shook as he held his cards, and

he drained his glass rapidly and often. So, Dumont mused to himself, gambling and liquor are the names of his demons. The captain drew a card, looked at it without changing expression, and inserted it into his hand.

"Papa," Larissa said softly, draping a slim arm about her father's shoulder, "may I dance outside? I'm tired of sitting."

Helson dragged his bloodshot eyes away from the cards and gazed up at his daughter. A smile tugged at his mouth. The gesture took years off his haunted face.

"Well, let's see if that's all right with the captain." He glanced over the table at Dumont, and the furtive look resettled on his features.

"By all means," Dumont beamed. "I'd like to watch you sometime, my dear, if I may. After all, there are worse things to do with your life than become a dancer aboard a showboat."

Larissa's blue eyes lit up, and she smiled. A blush crept across her face. What an uncommonly pretty child, Dumont thought to himself. And that long white hair . . . uncommon indeed. "Thank you, Captain Dumont. I'll try not to disturb anybody," she said politely, and hastened outside.

With a mock sigh, Dumont spread out his hand. "Your win again, my friend. Perhaps that pretty child of yours is Lady Luck in disguise."

Helson glanced after his daughter fondly. "She's been my best luck ever since she was born," he said, his voice soft.

Briskly Dumont reached for the pack of cards and began to shuffle them expertly. "Another round?" he queried nonchalantly.

"Oh, yes!" exclaimed Helson, his eyes too bright. Dumont nodded to himself. Time to make the kill, he thought.

He dealt the cards, keeping up an easy banter that

distracted the gambler from the delicate movements of the captain's fingers. Dumont had magically marked the cards, and each one radiated a different sensation to his knowing fingers. He gathered his own hand and perused the faces.

The goal of "Lords and Ladies" was to collect as many female cards as possible, preferably ones of high rank. Only two women smiled up at him from the cards, none of whom were Ladies of Power.

The captain concentrated, rubbing the cards slightly with his thumb, and the faces shimmered and changed. Now Dumont held the Lady of the Sea, the Star Queen, Earth's Daughter, and the Fire Maiden. He left the comparatively weak card, Hearthkeeper, unchanged and decided to hold onto the handsome River Lord. Helson, the captain knew, had only one Lady of Power—the Dark Lady—and the rest were all common suit cards. He suppressed a smile.

The hour wore on. The cards Helson drew were good, but not good enough to surpass Dumont's cheating magic. Helson grew paler and paler, and when Dumont spread his hand and the gambler laid down his own pathetic set of cards, the color was nearly gone from his face.

Dumont languidly reached over and gathered the loser's mound of tokens to himself. He glanced over it, and raised a golden eyebrow.

"Doesn't look like there's enough here to cover what you owe me," he commented.

"But I don't have any more money with me," the broken man whispered, his head drooping and finally sinking into his trembling hands.

"Well, that is unfortunate," Dumont commented in a maliciously bright tone of voice. "But perhaps you ought to have thought of that before you began to play."

"I'd been on a lucky streak . . ." Aubrey Helson's voice trailed off.

Dumont grinned like a famished tiger. "Looks like your luck just ran out. I'll give you a moment to think about how you might want to settle that debt. If anything occurs to you, just tell my friend Dragoneyes over there."

He nodded in the half-elf's direction. The golden-eyed first mate glanced up at the sound of his name, caught Dumont's expression, and nodded ever so slightly before returning his attention to his whittling.

Light glinted off his knife. Helson cringed visibly.

The night air was clean and cool, and the night sky brimmed with stars. As he stepped out on the deck, however, Dumont discovered that he didn't need to search the heavens for ethereal beauty.

It was quiet on deck. Most of the patrons were either in the theater watching the performance or else gambling in the lounge like Helson. Alone on deck, the white-haired girl was dancing, keeping perfect time to a rhythm only she could hear and performing solely for her own pleasure. Her hair, which had been tied back in a ponytail, was now loose and floated about her like a cloud shot through with moonlight.

The harsh orange-yellow gleam of the night lanterns detracted from the sight, but not greatly. Little Larissa Helson still managed to look fey and wild, swaying and leaping and turning, graceful and unpredictable as a feather caught by a wanton breeze.

Dumont watched her, enraptured. In a few years, men would pay a great deal to see that child perform. With that mane of white, she was a natural for the Lady of the Sea. Once this graceful girl became associated with *La Demoiselle du Musarde*, Dumont's fame would be secure. Thoughtful, he went inside.

Helson's whipped expression had not changed. Dumont eased himself into the chair opposite the wretched gambler and waited patiently until Helson raised his eyes.

"Your daughter has a gift," Dumont stated bluntly. "I would like her to stay on as a chorus girl. I'd be lying if I said I didn't think she'd have a chance at the leading role in a few years. You could consider her your payment. She'd be well-treated and would lack for nothing."

What color lingered in Helson's sallow face vanished. His mouth opened and closed. "No," he managed at last. "She's the only thing I've got left to . . . No."

"You're holding her back," Dumont pressed. "Didn't you see how her face lit up as I mentioned her dancing with us? She was born to be onstage, man. Anyone can see that."

"No." Helson shook his head decisively. "I'll find some way to settle the debt. Just give me a day or two, please, for pity's sake . . ."

Dumont's green eyes searched Helson's pain-filled blue ones. "Very well," he said finally. "But we will keep the girl on board until you return, as surety."

Helson looked as though he would protest, but before he could articulate his feelings Dragoneyes was there. The half-elf laid a hand on the gambler's shoulder. "You heard the captain, friend," he said in an amiable, soft voice. "I think it's time you went home."

Dragoneyes' other hand grasped the knife with which he had been whittling. It was not held to Helson's throat, but the message was clear.

The man slumped for a moment, then raised pain-filled eyes to Dumont. "May I say good-bye to her?"

Dumont leaned backward and leisurely packed his pipe. "No, I can't let you do that. Dragoneyes will escort you to the shore." He nodded, and the mate slipped a hand beneath the gambler's elbow, firmly pulling the man to his feet. Helson looked back at the captain.

"I'll be back tomorrow. I have some things I can sell. Tell Larissa that I'll be back as soon as I can, so she won't worry."

"Oh, certainly," Dumont agreed smoothly. He snapped his fingers, and Helson gasped as the captain's index finger blazed with a small blue flame, and he proceeded to light his pipe with it.

"I will be back," Helson repeated. "Tomorrow morning. Tell her."

Dumont didn't reply, and Helson and Dragoneyes left.

The captain rose once they had gone, and went on deck again to watch the dancing child. The half-elf returned a few moments later.

"He's taken care of," Dragoneyes said in a low voice.

"Excellent," Dumont replied, taking another puff on his pipe.

Dragoneyes' gaze followed his friend's. "New dancer, eh, Raoul?"

"What do you think about training her for the Lady of the Sea?"

The half-elf nodded. "Perfect."

Dumont's eyes never left Larissa. "What did you do with him?"

Dragoneyes grinned coldly. "There are a lot of hungry wolves in Arkandale. I left him near the fringe of the forest. Won't be more than a skeleton by morning."

"Bright boy, Dragoneyes, bright boy," Dumont approved. "Wait half an hour, then get the fox. We'll run his damned legs off. I want to be out of here by dawn."

"Aye, Raoul." Dragoneyes melted away quietly. Dumont went out onto the deck.

"Larissa?" The girl stopped and turned her innocent face up to his.

"Yes, Captain?"

Dumont hesitated, letting a sympathetic expression form on his face. He laid an avuncular hand on her slender shoulder. "My dear, I've got some very bad news."

A sharp knock startled Dumont out of his reverie and back to the present. He rose slowly and weaved his way to the door, opened it, and peered out.

Willen saluted smartly. "Good afternoon, Captain. I was wondering if perhaps you'd give me permission to take the yawl and scout around for Miss Snowmane. I know the swamp well, sir. No offense to the rest of the boys, but . . . they might slow me down."

Dumont tightened his grip on the doorknob for support. He took a deep breath and demanded that his vision clear. It didn't. "Bit dangerous out there for a lone man, isn't it?" His voice, at least, was steady.

Willen grinned. "Not if you grew up here, sir."

"Oh, that's right. Yes, that's a fine idea, Will. How long do you think you'll be gone?"

Willen thought about it, gnawing his lower lip. "I should be back by morning. You can send the boat on ahead and I'll catch up."

"Good. We'll see you in the morning. Oh, Will—"

The youth turned around. "Aye, sir?"

A muscle in Dumont's cheek twitched. "What does the term 'whitemane' mean to you?"

Willen's expression didn't change. "Nothing, sir. Should it?"

Dumont shook his head, wincing at the sudden pain that shot through it at the gesture. "No, no. Just some damned nonsense Lond was spouting, that's all. Go about your business, boy."

"Aye, sir."

Dumont closed the door and leaned against it for a moment while the room swam. Carefully, he made his way back to the bed. No sooner had he lain down than an urgent pounding came on the door.

Dumont swore loudly. "Curse your mother, come in!"

Lond swept into the room, closing the door behind him. Dumont's stomach tightened. He was becoming increasingly uncomfortable around his alleged ally.

"The swamp boy is taking the yawl!" Lond cried. "You must stop him at once!"

"I told him he could. He knows the swamp, and he's going in search of Larissa." Dumont narrowed his eyes. "And as for that trumped-up yarn of yours, Lond, I don't believe a word of it. Will said he'd never even heard of a whitemane, and he ought to know."

Lond's body shook with anger. With an effort, he calmed himself.

"Captain Dumont," he said in deceptively silky tones, "you are the biggest fool it has ever been my misfortune to come across. Of course he would lie about the whitemane! Of course he would want to scout ahead all alone in the middle of a dangerous swamp! He's one of them and he's gone to warn Larissa!"

Unwillingly, Dumont felt his trust in Willen waver. When the boy was around, it was impossible not to like him. But now, alone and with his head hurting from too much alcohol, Dumont began to doubt. If Lond was correct about Larissa's swamp magic, then the wizard might be right about Willen.

Still, Dumont felt obliged to defend the trust he had placed in the boy. "He's been quite loyal so far, and the crew loves him." It sounded lame, even to his own ears. A thought suddenly occurred to him. "Why didn't he shake the scouting party earlier if he's a spy?"

"I've no idea," Lond snapped, pacing back and forth and rubbing his gloved hands together. "Perhaps to prove his trustworthiness, to lull you into a false sense of security. Obviously," he sneered, "it worked. It's too late to stop him now, but perhaps we could follow him."

"No," replied Dumont. "He'd notice anyone on his track and lose them." He paused, lost in thought. "There is someone who can track him," the captain said at last.

Lond smiled grimly in the masking shadow of his hood.

# SIXTEEN

Gradually, Larissa's young, strong body became used to the unusual movements of the dance magic. She even grew to like them. The wild swaying and leaping was much different than the old choreography, and she relished not having to do a certain step at a certain time. True enough, there were movements that meant things—sort of a magical shorthand. For the most part, however, Larissa just enjoyed the freedom to follow the drumbeats as her body saw fit.

The Maiden had instructed her to build a small fire, and now Larissa gazed into it intently. The flames were dancers themselves, hypnotic and compelling. The young woman lost herself in observing the flickering tongues of heat and light.

"Fire burns," came the Maiden's voice, "fire cleanses, destroys, purifies. Out of the ashes comes rebirth, out of the flames, heat that could save a life. I want you to make this tiny fire a bit larger. Dance the flames."

Slowly, keeping her eyes on the fire, Larissa rose and began to move. The dancer swayed, her arms rising of their own accord. Her fingers fluttered, mimicking the licking of the flames.

She began to smile a little to herself. This was easy, so much easier than water, Larissa thought, letting go and tumbling into the sensations. *Fire burns....*

The young woman felt hot, burning up with energy. Her body responded, her arms swirling and fingers fluttering like tongues of flame. *Fire burns....*

A gigantic crack and a sudden flush of heat brought Larissa abruptly out of the trance. She blinked dazedly and then saw what had happened. One of the old cypress trees by the pool had exploded into flame. Ashes flew into Larissa's face, and the fire, snapping and roaring dangerously, threatened to spread to the other trees. Larissa stared, transfixed with horror.

Fortunately, the Maiden reacted swiftly. She hastened to the pool, immersed her slim, strong body, and called the magic herself. A huge wave exploded from the river. Much of the fire was put out, but the tree's right side still burned brightly. A second wave reared up, drenching the tree and finally extinguishing the crackling flames.

The Maiden returned to the bank, digging her root feet into the soil. Dirt erupted from near the dead tree's roots as if thrown by some giant burrowing creature, and the sizzling embers were safely covered with earth.

For a moment, both women stared at the still-smoking, blackened trunk. Larissa realized it was the tree who had first permitted her to travel through it.

The Maiden shook her head sadly. There was no need for her to say anything to Larissa. The girl knew what she had done, and why it had happened.

"I'm so sorry, Maiden," Larissa whispered, her face still frozen in horror. "I'm so sorry."

The Maiden slipped an arm about the girl's waist. "I know. Look well upon what you have done and learn from it. Then, let it be."

They stood in silence, gazing at the dead tree. A few days ago, Larissa would hardly have cared about one burned cypress. But she knew this tree, had traveled through it, and it had trusted and accepted her. Now she realized how the tree fitted into its environment, what creatures had called it home. And she, with a careless slip of her concentration, had destroyed it.

"Come, child," the Maiden said briskly. "It is time for your dinner. Deal with fire in a more mundane fashion, and prepare yourself the rabbit Deniri so graciously caught for you."

Still flushed with guilt, Larissa turned from the skeletal wreckage of the tree. She skinned the rabbit clumsily, for she had never had to prepare meat before, and managed to contrive a spit upon which to roast the animal. Soon, it began to give off a scent that made Larissa's mouth water.

"That smells wonderful. Got enough for two?" came a cheerful voice. Larissa's head whipped around, and to her shocked delight she saw Willen. He was walking toward her, a swarm of *feu follets* dancing around his head.

"Willen!" she cried, scrambling to her feet and running toward him. They collided clumsily, and she embraced him with a fierce pleasure. The *feu follets* blinked rapidly, flitting about and changing colors. "Willen, I'm so glad to see you!"

"So I gathered," the youth joked, though he clasped her as tightly as she did him. "Did the *feu follet* come for you?"

Larissa nodded happily. "Yes, and a quickwood saved me, and Longears brought me to—"

"Whoa, slow down!" chided Willen. "This is a tale best told over supper, and I'm hungry."

"Welcome, Willen," said the Maiden, stepping beside them. "Eat and refresh yourself, and all tales will be told."

They made a circle of light in the darkness as they ate. Willen encouraged Larissa to tell of her adventure in the swamp, and laughed with delight when he heard that Longears had accepted her.

"He doesn't make friends easily," Willen said. "If you

call someone 'as cautious as Longears,' it means they take a long time to trust anyone."

"As you probably planned," the Maiden noted, "Larissa has agreed to learn the dance magic. She is doing quite well."

"I have a good teacher," she said, deflecting the compliment.

"Then . . ." Willen paused, then continued hesitantly. "Then you know who you are? You remember your first trip to Souragne?"

The dancer nodded, licking her slightly burned fingers. Willen's voice held an odd tension, and she wasn't sure why. "I'm not afraid of the swamp anymore, if that's what you're asking."

The young man was clearly relieved. "You don't know how pleased I am to hear that, Larissa." She looked up at him and again was snared by the sweet mystery that lay in the depths of his dark eyes.

"What of the riverboat?" came the Maiden's voice, interrupting the moment. Willen's expression darkened.

"Lond is moving swiftly," he answered. Larissa started to shiver, despite the humid warmth of the early evening. Willen moved closer to her and put a comforting arm around her. She looked up at him.

"How many?"

"Almost all of the crew now," he said. Gently he stroked her white hair. "The cast, except for Casilda, seems pretty much untouched, though soon they're bound to figure out that something's gone very, very wrong. I've discovered that you can hear the music from the show in the prisoner's hold. I think there's some kind of spell in the music, and Lond's smart enough to know that a living throat imparts something to a song that a zombie can't."

"Then why did Casilda become . . ." Larissa couldn't even finish the sentence. Bile rose in her throat, and she swallowed hard.

"She may have seen something they didn't want her to," Willen replied.

"Yes, that's it, I'm sure of it now. I think Dumont's killed . . . inconvenient cast members before. Liza, the woman Cas understudied, was murdered, and they never found out who did it. She probably happened onto his slaves." She shook her head sadly. "What a wretched, foul mess."

"How are the prisoners?" asked the Maiden.

"Enduring. Not abused."

"And Bouki?"

"He and the fox *loah* are best friends now. I think Bushtail would fight his own brother for the little fellow." He grinned impishly. "Longears will have a fit."

"How much more time can you buy us?" the Maiden inquired.

Willen's grin faded. "I don't know. I've taken them on as roundabout a route as I can without Lond growing suspicious. He knows the swamp, remember. I can still claim things about river depth and such, but if I stall too long, he'll catch on."

The Maiden shook her mossy head. "He always was too clever for his own good," she said softly. "What do you say? A week? Two?"

Willen was silent for a moment. His sober brown eyes gazed into the fire, then he looked directly at the Maiden. "A few days at the most."

The Maiden closed her eyes in pain for a moment. "Larissa needs more training."

"We don't have the time."

The Maiden turned abruptly and walked to the edge of the clearing. Beyond the ring of flickering orange firelight Larissa could see her slim shape. The Maiden stood quietly, not moving at all.

The dancer turned her attention back to Willen. "I'm glad you have avoided trouble. I was afraid that you'd be suspected."

Willen smiled. "Not at all. I am universally trusted. It's extremely convenient."

Larissa chuckled slightly. The *feu follets* continued to dance around Willen, as they had since he arrived.

"The *feu follets* like you," she commented. "This is the first time I've seen them since I came to the island."

Willen assumed a wry expression. "They ought to like me, since I am one of them."

The dancer stared at him. "You're . . . you're a *feu follet*?"

He looked puzzled. "You didn't know?"

Larissa continued to stare. "How could I?"

"I thought the Maiden . . . Don't you remember when you became a whitemane?"

Larissa nodded. Willen closed his hand over hers. "I was the *feu follet* who wouldn't leave you, when your father took you away," he explained. "When the Maiden called for a volunteer to be turned into a human, I couldn't agree fast enough. I became human for you, Larissa—for you as well as my people."

Larissa started to edge away. "But you're not human," she whispered. "Not really."

Willen's quiet joy melted like ice in the spring. He started to taste fear. "I'm human enough," he said, aware that his apprehension was creeping into his voice but not caring. "Look! My hands are getting callused. I have to eat, to sleep—"

"And you read minds with a touch," Larissa retorted, folding her arms about her in an unconscious gesture of protection. "What is going on?"

"Larissa!" Willen's eyes were suddenly wet. He had never known such pain. He rose clumsily and went to join the Maiden.

Larissa glanced after him miserably. Not knowing what else to do, she poked distractedly at the fire. Now and then she glanced up at the two shadowy figures talking together quietly. At one point, the Maiden embraced Willen, who laid his head on her breast like a child. Larissa winced and began to ready herself for bed. She curled up on her side on a pile of airmoss, but her eyes remained wide open.

After a time, the Maiden returned. "Do not be angry with Willen. He is what he is for love of you—not quite human, but never again to be a *feu follet*. Yet he is nothing unnatural, Larissa. Be kind to him, if you can be nothing else. Talk to him, before he returns to the showboat and his duty."

She turned, melting easily into the forest, and was lost to Larissa's view.

The dancer sat up at Willen's approach. Her face was warmly lit from the fire's glow, but her hair held the cool radiance of the moon. Wordlessly, he sank down beside her, looking up at the stars. Then he turned his warm eyes upon her, and Larissa cringed from the pain she saw in their depths. Yet she was unable to look away. For a long time, they simply gazed at one another, then Willen spoke, breaking the silence.

"It is a time for truths," he said quietly. "Things should be said now, or else we'll regret not saying them later."

"You're right," she said in a tone equally as soft, keeping her eyes on his face. "I'm sorry for what I said. I just—well, it was unexpected, to say the least. I'm not sure how I feel about it."

Willen shook his brown head. "It's all right. You're afraid. I understand."

"No, it's not all right. I hurt you, and that was cruel of me."

"Forgiven," he said.

"Your turn," said Larissa briskly, trying to lighten the atmosphere. "Who decided what you would look like as a human?"

"The Maiden," the *feu follet* replied. "She tried to think of the perfect river boatman—young, strong, attractive enough to be popular but not so much that I'd be out of the ordinary." He smiled. "So, here I am."

"How old are you?"

"The body's supposed to be in the early twenties. Me, I've been around for—oh, I don't know, a few hundred years in the way you count time. We don't measure time at all. *Feu follets* just are, until we are . . . not."

Larissa blinked, caught by surprise. More questions flooded her. "Is Willen your real name?"

He laughed at that. "No," he confessed. "When you asked me that in the inn, I was somewhat taken aback. I was still pretty new to the human form and didn't know about a lot of your customs. I'd forgotten that I'd need a name that humans could pronounce, so I picked the first thing that came to me." Seeing her incomprehension, he explained further. "It's local slang. To be 'willened' is to be charmed by the will-o'-the-wisps or *feu follets*."

"Do you have a real name?"

"Oh, yes. Everything has a name."

"What is it?"

He was silent. "I can't tell you."

His refusal stung, but she understood. "You don't trust me with it. Well, I guess the way I reacted, I can't blame you."

"No, you don't see," he insisted, squeezing her hand. "My people don't have a verbal language. We communicate with color, intensity of light, things like that. I've no way of translating it for you, that's all."

Suddenly a thought occurred to him, and a smile touched his mouth. "Wait a minute. Maybe I do," he told her, rising and going to the fringes of the woods.

He returned a few moments later, four or five of the *feu follets* following him. "Watch, and they'll tell you my name."

The *feu follets* danced about a bit, then formed a circle and hovered in the air. Their light dimmed, then all at once flared to new life. Colors rippled across them, shimmering, blending, a flurry of scarlet and violet and turquoise and rose. The intensity of the light, too, faded and flashed, and the sizes increased from pinpricks of illumination to glowing balls larger than her head. All at once, the *feu follets* went dark, then began to glow again with their normal radiance.

Larissa's face was aglow. She had been privileged to see many wonders in her brief life, traveling on the showboat as she had, but she had never seen anything to match the loveliness of Willen's name.

He sat down beside her, excitement and pleasure radiating from him. "I've never actually seen it with human eyes before. It's pretty, isn't it? Did you like it?"

She looked up at him with wide eyes, filled with a joy that was almost agonizing in its keenness. He misread her expression in the dim glow of the fire, and his face fell. With a little cry of protest, she seized his hand, knowing he would read her emotions accurately with his touch.

A soft joy spread across his face. "Then . . . you do like it."

Larissa laughed brokenly, almost a sob. "Willen . . . it's . . . I liked it very much."

He gripped her hand harder, so hard it was almost painful, but Larissa didn't want to pull away. She met his intense brown gaze evenly, captivated, trembling.

Willen licked his lips. "Larissa, I . . ." Now it was his turn to grope for words. "I don't quite understand humans yet," he finally said with an awkward laugh. "I'm not sure what I'm feeling."

Larissa knew what he was feeling, for she was sensing it, too. She recalled the merging with fire that had been so disastrous earlier and tasted something of its wild joy now. Her hands, suddenly hot, clutched his.

"Larissa," whispered Willen, tears springing to his eyes, "you are so beautiful."

"As are you," she said, barely able to get the words past her throat. She reached up a trembling hand to touch his face, brushing her fingers against the stubble on his cheek. "Your form, your name, your way of seeing things, your soul . . ." Suddenly her vision blurred, and he swam before her. She blinked frantically at the stinging in her eyes. "Oh, Willen, I'm crying. *I'm crying.*"

He gathered her to him, meaning to comfort, to soothe. But Larissa would not be soothed. Eagerly she sought his mouth with her own, turning the pent-up pain of eight years into a white-hot, healing passion. Willen was startled for an instant, but then his human body followed the lead his *feu follet*'s heart had set. He returned her kiss with equal ardor.

\* \* \* \* \*

Captain Dumont sat in his cabin, trying to still his trembling hands. The dead eyes of the watching zombie conveyed no censure, no approval.

Dumont assumed that it was his downward spiral into despair that made him perversely want the rotting company of Dragoneyes. The dead pilot sat in the chair opposite him, staring wordlessly, as words gushed out of the captain like blood from a wound.

"It was going so well," Dumont mumbled. "Going *so well*. You remember, don't you?" He leaned forward to emphasize his words.

"I had—" he counted on his fingers "—money, renown, influence. And I had my wonderful collection. And Larissa, sweet, sweet child . . . Then I took my beautiful *Demoiselle* into this cesspit of a swamp." Dumont stopped struggling to control his alchohol-induced palsy. "And I've lost my crew. And I've lost Larissa. What in the world am I going to do when I finally get out of here? Huh? Say something, you mute bastard!"

Dragoneyes merely sat and stared. Dumont cursed,

his face flushed with emotion, and hurled an empty glass at the zombie. It bounced off Dragoneyes' skull and fell to the floor, rolling. And still the first mate didn't move.

Dumont took a thirsty pull directly from the whiskey bottle and wiped his sleeve across his streaming lips.

"Oh, my old friend," he whispered, "how did I permit this to happen to you?"

Impulsively he reached over for the zombie's hand. His callused fingers closed on the rotting white flesh, cold and soft and pliant.

There came a tentative knock on the door. Dumont blinked, attempting to compose himself. He took a deep breath, gestured, and Dragoneyes answered the door.

"Captain?" came Yelusa's voice.

Dumont looked up blearily. The owl maid's round face held none of its usual cowed sullenness. She was grinning.

"Report?" slurred Dumont.

Yelusa held out her shackled hands triumphantly. "First, take these off like you promised. I have the information you seek."

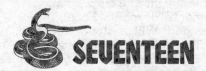

# SEVENTEEN

Willen propped himself up on one elbow and gazed down at Larissa as she slept by his side. Her hair, tousled by their lovemaking, was spread out beneath her head like a wild halo. Her breathing was deep and regular, her lips slightly parted.

Gently, Willen smoothed a lone tendril of moon-white hair from her cheek, following the gesture with a moth-light kiss. More than anything in the world he wanted to stay here with Larissa, drift to sleep with her warmth pressed against his suddenly appreciated human body, but it wasn't possible. He'd been gone too long as it was, and had to be getting back to *La Demoiselle*.

As quietly as he could, the youth eased himself up and began to dress. Then, with a final glance back, he strode off toward the yawl and began the trip back to the boat.

The night seemed to respect the spell that enveloped the young man. All was tranquil, the noises of the swamp harmless and reassuring. Nothing evil could touch him at this moment, Willen thought giddily. He wanted to leap for joy. Larissa loved him, had shared herself with him, and his happiness would not bow to reality—not yet, at least.

He was still smiling to himself when he climbed

aboard *La Demoiselle*. The smile faded when he encountered the staring, slitted gaze of Dragoneyes as he tied up the yawl.

"The master wishes to see you," the half-elf said dully.

Willen went cold inside. "The captain? Why, Dragoneyes? I left last night with his permission."

"Not Dumont. The master. Lond."

For a second, Willen stood stock-still, not even breathing. Then, quicker than a heartbeat, he dived for the railing. Dragoneyes grabbed a fistful of his shirt and hauled him back down to the deck. His expression never changing, Dragoneyes threw back his head and emitted a horrible wail that caused Willen to wince. Four more zombies appeared, moving swiftly and with emotionless purpose.

Fighting the whole time, Willen was dragged to Lond's cabin and hurled inside. He landed heavily on the deck, banging his chin. A terrible scent assaulted his nostrils, and he almost retched. The youth mastered his breathing, then slowly, carefully, eased into a sitting position and raised his brown eyes.

Lond's cabin was like something out of a nightmare. Light that came from nowhere shone a dull yellowish hue to reveal hideous magical artifacts. Gutted corpses of animals—everything from birds to cats to the rotting head of a calf—were strewn about casually. Engorged flies buzzed lazily about the rotting flesh. A row of tiny, delicately made glass bottles lined the wall. They were securely corked and their labels had various runes inscribed on them. The bottles came in an astonishing variety of colors. Feathers, bones, bits of cloth dipped in blood, knives, and pins completed the ghastly decor. There was nothing that did not reek of fear and pain and death.

Lond was seated in a crudely fashioned chair that was entirely constructed of human bones. He sprawled carelessly, a black shape completely at ease here in his own tiny domain of decay. From beneath his cowl, his eyes glittered dimly in the faint illumination.

"Welcome at last, Will," he said in his dry voice. "You've been clever, but not clever enough. There is another here who would like to see you. Dragoneyes—" He gestured with a flick of his gloved hand toward the door. The zombie left obediently.

Lond leaned forward, sniffing at Willen. The *feu follet* drew back, but knew better than to try to run. He was trapped, at least for the moment.

"You have the scent of the swamp about you," Lond growled.

"Not surprising. I've been there all night, scouting ahead for—"

"Shut up." Lond's voice was as cold as ice and brooked no argument. "You've got the scent of *her* on you. And I *don't* mean the little dancing girl, though you might indeed have sampled her charms as well." Lond laughed dryly.

Anger flooded Willen, and, despite his better judgment, the youth lunged for the dark *bocoru*—and slammed up against an invisible wall. He bounced off it and hit the floor hard. The impact sent waves of pain shivering through his body. He curled up into a tight ball.

Lond's laughter increased. "What a shame that you must die. You'd be so amusing to torture. But, alas, there are more practical means of extracting the truth from you."

Dragoneyes and Dumont entered. The captain had been drinking, but was sober for the moment. His face was a combination of fury and betrayal.

"I trusted you, Will," he said in a voice that was low and menacing. "When Lond wanted you followed, I hoped you'd prove my faith in you justified. Larissa liked you. So did Dragoneyes. *I* even liked you, you little bastard. You didn't have an enemy aboard this boat.

Smart, skillful—everything a captain would wish for."

He shook his head slowly, and Willen, with a curious stab of remorse, saw that the pain in his eyes was genuine.

"Damn you to the bottom of the Sea of Sorrows, Will. I hate you for that most of all. Yelusa!" He nodded curtly, and the slim owl maid slipped inside, closing the door behind her.

For a moment Willen didn't understand. Then, dawning comprehension spread across his features.

"You gave me away, didn't you?" he asked, pain filling him at the betrayal.

The owl maid's eyes were shifty, as if she were still wary.

"I trusted you, Yelusa," said Willen. She continued to avoid his gaze. "Do you know what you've done?"

Yelusa looked up, and now her large, round eyes were hard. "Anything's better than slavery, *feu follet*," she spat defensively. "I'd spy on anyone, do anything, to fly freely again."

Willen shook his head sadly. "You'd have been free soon enough. Dumont will never let you go."

Her eyes narrowed. "That's where you're wrong. He's agreed to let me go tonight. Isn't that right, Captain?" She turned to Dumont for confirmation, a smirk on her round face. The captain said nothing, and Yelusa's smile died. "Captain?"

Dumont sighed and rubbed his red eyes. "I burned your feather a long time ago, little owl girl."

Yelusa's brown eyes grew enormous with horror. With the precious item burned, Yelusa would forever have to return to the place where it had been destroyed. Her mouth worked soundlessly, then a terrible cry issued forth. She charged the captain, her fingers going for his eyes. The sight of the tiny girl attacking the burly Dumont would have been comical if the gesture hadn't been so desperately futile.

Dumont seized her wrists, almost as if he were bored. "Lond, tell your lumps of flesh to take the girl below. And gag her first."

Dragoneyes clamped a hand over Yelusa's mouth. She struggled, but her slim frame was no match for his undead strength. Willen saw that the zombie's hand also covered the girl's nose, and her gaze turned from furious to fearful as she realized she couldn't breathe. She kicked and clawed with renewed energy, her eyes rolling crazily.

"She's suffocating!" Willen shrieked. "Dumont, she—"

Dumont saw it too. "Damn it, Lond, can't you get him to—"

There was a horrible crack as Dragoneyes snapped Yelusa's slim neck. The girl's flailing ceased, and Willen winced in sympathetic pain.

"Leave her here," Lond said. "I've never made a zombie out of a nonhuman before. It will be an interesting experiment."

Dragoneyes dropped the body, permitting it to lie where it fell. Dumont was shaken, though he didn't want to admit it. He stared at the girl's corpse. "You are one gods-rotting, cold-hearted son of a bitch, Lond," he said in an almost-conversational tone.

Lond laughed behind his cowl. "Thank you for the compliment."

The mage returned his attention to his living prisoner. "You see, Will, you were watched last night. We know what happened, and what you are. Unfortunately, we are pressed for time, so . . . welcome to my army." He rose and poured some powder from a black bottle into his gloved hand.

Willen's eyes filled with horror. "No!" he cried and bolted for the door. Lond made a quick, zigzag movement with his free hand, and Willen stumbled as though an invisible rope had tripped him. Dragoneyes hauled him up by one arm. The zombie grasped Willen's brown hair and jerked his face up to Lond's.

The wizard blew powder into Willen's face. Frantically the *feu follet* coughed, trying to clear his lungs, and tears filled his eyes as the powder stung them. The grayish powder clung to his throat, choking his lungs, and he doubled over, scrabbling at his face.

The youth's mind was crowded with sensations so intense they were painful. The very air of the room pressed heavily on his face; the wooden floor at his back seemed to hammer at him. Colors pummeled his consciousness with an almost physical intensity, and then his vision faded, the intense hues bleeding to gray and then black. A cold numbness began to seep through his limbs. He was vaguely aware that he had stopped breathing.

Then, suddenly, the numbness was gone. Willen gasped for air, like a newborn devouring its first breath. With an effort, he opened his eyes, his body still twitching as it fought to breathe normally. The *feu follet* cleared his eyes of tears, and met Lond's gaze evenly.

The wizard was frozen with shock. "No," he whispered in his raspy voice. "No . . . it's not possible." Lond swore and, frustrated with his failure, struck Willen heavily across the face.

With an effort, the black-cloaked *bocoru* regained control of his emotions. Lond sank back down in his nightmarish chair, hands clasping and unclasping. Then, quietly, as if to himself alone, he began to laugh. "Dragoneyes, go fetch our little rabbit friend."

A chilling dread began to spread through the *feu follet*.

A few moments later, Dragoneyes returned. Bouki was determined to protest to the last and was literally being dragged by the neck, gasping and choking.

"Oh, Willen! So they got you, too?" he said sadly to his companion.

"Ah, you do know him, Bouki," said Lond. The rabbit glanced up at him and let out a yelp of terror. He hunkered down, shaking, long ears flat against his silky head.

"Yes, I know him," Bouki quavered. "And I know you, too, Alondrin the Betrayer."

"Dragoneyes," Lond ordered calmly, "bind Willen's hand to Bouki's paw."

The zombie did so, and Willen closed his eyes at what he suspected was about to happen.

"You know what wrath you will incur if you hurt a *loah*, Alondrin," he said in a low voice as Dragoneyes wrapped a torn cloth about his wrist. "Not just from the Maiden, either. *Loahs* are tied to the land, and if you hurt the land—"

"Stop prattling to me like I was a novice," Lond reprimanded. "The zombie lord will have to find me first, won't he?"

Dragoneyes tied the knot tight and straightened, awaiting his master's next command. Apparently, however, Lond wanted this pleasure for himself. He extracted a red candle from its place atop a skull. Holding the flame in one black-gloved hand, the wizard crouched down near the terrified rabbit. Because he was touching Bouki, Willen's empathic abilities were multiplied. The *feu follet* was flooded with the *loah*'s fear, though he gritted his teeth so as not to show it. He felt Lond's malevolent gaze on him and kept his own eyes on the floor.

"No, you don't much like fire, do you, poor little Bouki?" Lond murmured.

Bouki by now had edged back so that he was flattened against the door, his left forepaw raised and pressed tightly to Willen's palm. "N-no," he quavered.

Willen thought calming thoughts, but they could not penetrate the thick wall of terror that the fire had aroused in the rabbit's heart.

"Then," Lond continued in that same deceptively soft

voice, "I don't think you'll like *this*!"

Without warning the candle flame erupted, growing from an inch to a full foot high. The flame licked Bouki's face, and the animal shrieked in pain and fear. The scent of charred flesh mingled with the stench of rot in the hellish cabin. The entire side of the creature's face was burned black. Bouki's eye was destroyed, and a thick fluid oozed from the crusted orb, sizzling as it touched the still-hot flesh.

A cry broke from Willen's lips. It was *his* eye blinded, *his* jaw burned and black, and he was so afraid, so horribly *afraid* . . .

The two swamp creatures shivered and whimpered, reaching for one another for comfort. Tears streamed down Willen's face.

"Now, *feu follet*, you will tell me what I wish to know. If not—" Lond shrugged "—I enjoy playing with fire."

* * * * *

Larissa awakened from a beautiful dream to the sounds of tension-filled voices arguing in high-pitched tones.

"What?" she muttered fuzzily, then suddenly realized she was naked. Blushing, she pulled on her discarded clothing, waking up enough to see that the two verbal combatants were Longears and the Maiden.

They were away from the clearing, beside the fast-flowing river. The Maiden was rooted in the muddy soil, and the *loah* sat on his hind legs, gesticulating with his forepaws. Combing her hair with her fingers, Larissa walked over to them.

Longears fell silent at her approach, then without warning exploded with wrath. "You did this!" he shouted, turning on her angrily. "You made him careless. Now who knows what they are going to do to him and my cousin!"

"Longears!" reproved the Maiden, her voice colder than Larissa had ever heard. "She is not to blame. Willen made his own choices and would be angry with you if he heard you now."

Larissa felt the blood drain from her face. "What's happened to Willen?"

The Maiden went to Larissa and gently eased the dancer to the earth, placing her cool lips to the young woman's cheek in a fleeting kiss of reassurance.

"He has been discovered. Longears saw them take him away."

Larissa's gray lips formed Willen's name. She closed her blue eyes, inhaled deeply and deliberately, then spoke in an unnaturally calm voice. "Then we attack *La Demoiselle*," she said.

The Maiden nodded. "I agree. If they discover his true nature, they will be able to torture him in a most hideous fashion. Brave as he is, I doubt he will be able to stand much of that, and they will soon know all our plans. I had hoped for more time to train you, but . . ." Her voice trailed off. She rose, extending a hand to Larissa. "Come. We must make haste."

"To the boat?" Larissa's voice was hard with resolve.

"No, not yet. We must first ask permission to attack Dumont."

"Permission? I thought you ruled here, Maiden. Aren't you the Maiden of the Swamp?"

The Maiden smiled sadly. "I am indeed, but my influence is slight. There is one who is the true lord of all of Souragne. He has permitted Dumont to travel safely through this realm, and it is he who must give us leave to attack his guest.

"If we attack *La Demoiselle* without his leave, then he will attack us. And if he attacks us," she said simply, "we will be destroyed. I tread a delicate line with Misroi. I will not tempt his wrath. This was why I did not wish to become involved with the rescue attempt, as Willen desired. I had hoped that he would be able to free our people on his own."

Larissa remembered the Maiden's initial reluctance. It was only when she had agreed to be the one to lead the fight that the Maiden began teaching her.

"But," the Maiden continued, "for the first time, Misroi and I may be on the same side in this particular battle."

Larissa blinked, thoroughly befuddled. "What?" she managed at last.

The Maiden chuckled sympathetically at her incomprehension. "Hurry up and bathe, my dear. I'm sure you'll understand soon enough." Her smile faded, and her green eyes grew sorrowful. "Sooner than ever I would have wished."

Obediently, Larissa bathed and dressed. She combed her long, wet hair and began to braid it.

"No," said the Maiden, laying a feather-light hand on the young woman's shoulder. "What have I told you about that? Your hair is part of your dancing. Do not bind it."

"Am I going to need to work magic?" The thought alarmed Larissa.

"You may," the Maiden replied grimly.

The Maiden led Larissa to a small boat. It was a hollowed-out cypress trunk that sat low in the water. The Maiden placed her hands on it, and Larissa saw that, for a moment, they grew into the wood. Then the Maiden sighed, and her hands became her own again. She looked tired, the green of her skin and hair even lighter than usual.

"The pirogue will travel where you need to go," she told Larissa, her voice frail. "It will take you to Anton Misroi, then bring you back here safely."

"Maiden, aren't you coming with me?"

"I am unable to leave this island. This is the only place where I may root." She smiled wanly. "Elsewhere, the land is . . . unwholesome for me. It is part of the way my influence is limited. As for Misroi—some call him the Lord of the Dead. He is the master of the zombies. All I can say is that he is dangerous, temperamental—and extremely intelligent. Whatever you expect him to be, he will surprise you. Do not underestimate him, Larissa. And do not fight him. Any battle he enters into, he will win. Child . . ." The Maiden looked at Larissa closely. "You are embarking into danger. It is not too late to turn back. If you go, go of your own free will."

Larissa licked her lips, then pressed them together determinedly. "I love Willen, and he's being held prisoner. How can I not do everything I can to free him?"

The Maiden searched Larissa's blue eyes. "Go, then, brave child. And remember, whatever Anton Misroi may be, you are a whitemane. Let the knowledge give you courage."

She stepped back, and Larissa eased herself into the boat. It was very steady. The Maiden pushed the pirogue into the river, and it slid smoothly through the greenish water.

Larissa forced herself to relax; the pirogue moved as though an invisible sternman were paddling it. She rode the river for a while, then the boat veered sharply to the right and entered into a dark, dank, cypress-shadowed bayou. In the distance was a whirring of insects. Other than that, the only sound was the slight rippling of the water as the pirogue sliced through it.

Larissa closed her eyes, trying to "root" herself as the Maiden had instructed her. She was quite frightened at the thought of meeting someone who was known as the Lord of the Dead. It was bad enough dealing with the zombies aboard *La Demoiselle* when she didn't know their true, horrific nature. Larissa hoped she'd be up to bargaining with the one who was lord of them all.

The wind picked up, grew colder. It stirred up the rank scent of the marsh, and Larissa grimaced. Rain, light at first but becoming increasingly heavy, began to fall.

"I didn't even bring a cloak," Larissa said morosely to herself, hunching over in a futile attempt to avoid being soaked. The fat raindrops pounded carelessly, splashing on the surface of the stagnant water.

Shivering a little, Larissa glanced around, wondering if there wasn't something, anything, she could use to shield herself from the weather. She looked over at the bank and started, gasping.

Four skeletons, clad only in rotting garments, grinned back at her from the limbs of what appeared to be quickwoods. The men must have been trapped by the trees and starved to death, Larissa assumed. The quickwood moved, shifted, and Larissa realized that the "face" of the huge old tree was infinitely more malevolent than any of the quickwoods. A dull fire burned in the hollow areas that served it for eyes, and its mouth was filled with sharp protrusions. As she watched it, the tree lowered its bony ornaments to the grass.

The skeletons rose awkwardly and disappeared into the greenness of the foliage. Larissa's pity for the dead men turned to fear. She knew where they were going—to inform their master, the Lord of the Dead, of her presence. Grimly, Larissa folded her arms tightly about her shivering frame and thought of Willen.

The storm increased in fury, and the little pirogue pitched, but held to its course. At last it headed for a bank and grounded itself. Larissa, half-blinded by the pelting rain, stumbled out, her bare feet sinking to her ankles in the soft, slimy mud. She heaved the pirogue onto the bank, fighting the greedy water for every inch of ground she gained. When she finally got the boat well away from the water, her arms, back, and legs hurt.

She straightened, wincing. Larissa glanced around, hands shielding her eyes from the rain. There was nothing that looked like a house anywhere around.

"Oh, wonderful," Larissa exploded angrily. "Now what happens?"

A sharp neigh was her answer, and Larissa wheeled.

From the concealing draperies of mist and moss, a carriage emerged. There was something wrong with the horses drawing it. They walked oddly, stiffly, with none of a beast's natural grace, and were a curious color. As she drew closer, Larissa's lip curled in disgust. The wind changed, and the scent of the horses—the dead horses—wafted to her. The strange color of the horses was caused by rot, and bits of bone showed through where decomposing flesh had been rubbed off by their harnesses.

The carriage drew closer, and Larissa saw that the driver, too, was a gray-green monstrosity of putrefaction. Larissa was frozen with fear, as rooted to the spot as the Maiden ever had been to her island.

Somehow, Larissa was more terrified of that quiet, patient carriage, drawn by its rotting beasts of burden, than she had been of anything she could remember—not the mist horror, nor the creatures of the swamp, nor even Casilda's horrible transformation. Those were things that had happened, that had been forced upon her. This carriage was here, she knew, because she had chosen to visit the zombie master.

Somehow, she forced her leaden feet to take one step toward the waiting carriage, then another. Confidence returned to her with each step. The zombie coachman climbed slowly down from his perch and silently opened the door for her. The dancer hesitated only an instant, then, with a defiant toss of her white locks, she stepped inside.

# EIGHTEEN

The coachman took his place, slapped the horses' reins, and the carriage lurched forward. Larissa wiped the rain from her face as best she could. As she settled herself in the brown velvet cushions, she noticed that there was a black cape folded neatly on the seat beside her. A faint smile quirked one corner of her mouth. Whoever—whatever—Anton Misroi was, this was a considerate gesture. Gratefully Larissa toweled herself as dry as she could with the soft woolen cloak.

The carriage itself seemed sturdy and wellmade, though it hadn't been cleaned in a while and there were several rips in the cushions and dents in the wood. The dancer wrapped the cloak about her still-shivering frame. The windows of the carriage were fogging up with her breath, and she rubbed a clear patch and peered out.

She felt the carriage jolt and saw that they had left the marsh for a cobblestone road. They traveled for a time, flanked by the swamp, until the carriage halted abruptly.

They had come to a large wrought-iron gate manned by more zombies. As Larissa watched, fingers clenched tightly in the black fabric of Misroi's cloak, the lumbering undead creatures opened the massive gate to permit the carriage to pass through. One of them turned what was left of its face up to her as she passed, and Larissa shuddered. The creature's eyes had rotted away.

Inside the gates, wilderness yielded to civilization. Larissa saw that this was a plantation, similar to the ones near Port d'Elhour. Workers labored in the field despite the downpour—workers who moved with a mechanical, steady rhythm that revealed their true nature. Larissa closed her eyes and took a deep breath to steady herself.

She sat back in the carriage for a time, unwilling to see what new horrors were unfolding as she journeyed toward Misroi. At last, however, the carriage slowed and stopped. The coachman appeared at the window, then opened the door for her to step out.

It was a plantation indeed, a huge, sprawling mansion that was as draped with airmoss and cobwebs as any tree in the swamp. The house proper was elevated about a yard off the ground, supported by wooden poles to keep out the swamp's moisture. Peacocks strutted on the ill-kept lawn, their beautiful plumage drenched by the downpour. The whole image was a grotesque parody of normal plantation life.

Steeling herself, Larissa pulled the cloak's hood over her head and stepped down onto the gravelly drive. She winced a little as her bare feet were bruised by the stones. The dancer made her way slowly and carefully to the house, climbed up the creaking steps to the porch, and lifted the brass knocker carved like a horse's head. She hesitated, just for an instant, then slammed it down hard.

For an agonizingly long moment, there was no answer. Then the door slowly creaked open. Larissa's heart hammered with trepidation.

A zombie, better preserved than the others Larissa had seen on the plantation, stared down at her impassively. His clothing, which was still mostly whole, revealed him to be a highly placed servant. He stank horribly.

"I—" Her voice almost broke. She paused and continued calmly. "I have come to see your master."

The zombie's mouth worked. "Enter," he groaned in a voice that had obviously not been used for some time. He stepped back and opened the door even wider. Larissa went inside, her blue eyes flickering about.

She was in a wide entry hall. Once-fine carpeting, now water-stained and ruined, covered most of the wooden floor and wound up the sweeping spiral staircase that twisted up to the next story. Dust lay thickly on the beautifully carved banisters, disturbed here and there by large handprints. Most of the light was provided by a huge, glittering cut-glass chandelier. A sudden movement off to the side caught her eye, and she turned swiftly, only to meet her own pale reflection in a tarnished mirror.

The zombie servant pointed to a room on her left, then held out his black-nailed hand expectantly. Larissa stared at it for a moment, not understanding. Then she realized what he wanted and handed him her rain-drenched cloak. He bowed and left her alone.

Carefully Larissa stepped into the parlor. Two small, low tables were placed in front of comfortable-looking sofas. A fireplace flanked by two velvet-covered chairs took up a large segment of the wall. Atop the fireplace was a mantlepiece carved from some dark wood upon which a lighted candelabra and what looked like an etching of some sort were placed.

The draperies were opened, pulled back by two brass holders fashioned to look like children's hands. The storm outside, however, dimmed the daylight. Despite the valiant attempts of the candles and the fire, the room remained morosely dark.

The fire snapped, its warmth and crackling sounds incongruously cheerful and welcoming to the soaked dancer. Kneeling in front of the fire, Larissa gratefully spread her hands out to its warmth. She noticed that a poker had been inserted well into the red-hot coals and wondered why.

The storm continued to rage, and Larissa shivered despite the warmth of the fire. Gradually its heat penetrated the damp chill of her clothes, and she began to get warm. She looked around the room again, noticing that the wallpaper was covered by carefully wrought drawings. Curious, she took the candelabra from the mantlepiece and stepped up to the wall.

Handsome couples, clad in full dresses and tailored coats and breeches, waltzed at a party scene. Larissa moved along the wall. Here was a battle, with knights in armor fighting gallantly. And over here was—

A giant flash of lightning illuminated the dim room. By its unforgiving brilliance, Larissa could see what she had not noticed before: all the people in the wallpaper scenes were corpses, painted in various stages of decay.

She stifled a cry and backed away, the hand that held the candelabra trembling and causing its shadows to dance. Thunder roared in a mocking echo of her outburst. She replaced the candelabra on the mantlepiece, taking a second look at the etching as she did so.

It was an illustration of a woman seated, writing, at a desk. The etching was carved onto an extremely thin square of bone, and a burning candle flickered behind it. It gave the etching the appearance of movement, and Larissa, her attention momentarily diverted from the horrors of the wallpaper, watched the young woman, who was busily writing.

Then she noticed the words on the woman's page.
*Help me.*
Larissa blinked, wondering if it was a trick of the unreliable light. The words had changed.
*Set me free.*
Cold horror crept through her and her eyes flickered

from the words to the woman's face. Larissa gasped aloud and stepped backward. The woman was no longer looking at her writing, but directly at Larissa, and a tear crept down her cheek.

Larissa wrapped her arms about herself and shivered. Pity welled within her at the plight of the trapped soul in the etching, but fear drowned out the gentler emotion. Was there a blank sheet of bone waiting for her, someplace in this house of nightmares?

Outside, through the howl of the wind, Larissa thought she heard the shrill neigh of a frightened horse. Her mind flew back to Willen's comment about the superstitious Souragniens. "Death rides in the rain," he had said. Now, she understood. She stepped back toward the fire, unconsciously wanting its warmth at her back as the master of the house approached.

The whitemane heard the doorway to the hall being opened, and a second flash of lightning silhouetted the tall shape of a man. He strode into the parlor where Larissa waited, tossing his cloak carelessly in the direction of the following undead servant. He marched toward her, wiping moisture from his hair, and stepped into the ring of firelight.

The Maiden had been right. Whatever Larissa had expected, it was not this tall, strikingly handsome man. He looked to be in his mid-thirties, and his hair, ravenwing black, curled damply from the ride in the rain. Strong but exquisitely chiseled features radiated a barely subdued excitement. From his thigh-high, black leather boots to the gold buttons glinting on the well-fitted, buff-colored vest, Misroi was every inch the aristocrat. That the boots were streaked with mud and the fine linen shirt had been torn merely emphasized that he was in absolute control. Full lips stretched into a smile as Anton Misroi looked at his guest.

"Well, they didn't tell me you'd be such a lovely creature," he commented, falling gracefully into one of the plush chairs by the fire. His voice matched his face—handsome, masculine, and intense. "Then again, the dead don't notice such subtleties. One of their drawbacks, I've found."

Misroi swung one long leg over the arm of the chair. The mud-spattered boot left brown streaks on the fine velvet, but the zombie master seemed not to notice.

"Wine!" he called impatiently, his long fingers untying the blue silk cravat at his throat. He used it to towel his hair dry, then tossed it to the floor and undid the first two buttons on his shirt.

Larissa continued to stand and stare at the master of Souragne. He raised an eyebrow.

"Sit down," he said. "Don't look so frightened. What, did you think I'd slay you and roast you for dinner upon your immediate arrival?"

The dancer found her tongue. "No, of course not, only you're not . . . you're so . . ." she floundered.

The grin widened. "Alive? Oh, yes." His eyes, a deep blue, flickered over her. "Very much so."

The zombie servant approached, bearing a mug of wine on a silver tray. Misroi took it, went to the fire, and seized the poker that had been lying at the heart of the flames.

Larissa tensed, ready to fight should he turn on her with the heavy iron rod. He noticed the gesture and laughed out loud.

"Dear, dear, Miss Snowmane, I would hope that I'd use something less crude than a poker if I wished to attack you! You haven't sat down yet. Do so."

It was not a request, and Larissa obeyed. Misroi removed the poker and gazed approvingly at its glowing orange tip. He inserted the poker into the mug, and the wine hissed as it heated. Misroi replaced the poker and took a sip of the hot wine. He nodded in approval, then strode over to where Larissa sat.

"Here. Hot spiced wine. A great favorite of mine.

Nothing like it after a hard ride in the rain."

Larissa looked up into those piercing eyes and hesitated. Misroi frowned. "Drink it," he ordered. She closed her hand about the mug and took a cautious sip. It was hot and fragrant with the scents of citrus and spices. Surprised by the pleasant taste, she took a second sip, letting its warmth steal through her chilled body before handing the mug back to the zombie lord.

Misroi seemed satisfied. "Now, you've been properly welcomed to *Maison de la Détresse*." He raised the glass in a silent toast to her, then sat back down and continued to drink while he talked.

"Now, let me see. If my informants are correct, your name is Larissa Snowmane and you are a dancer aboard that lovely boat that's currently steaming down my swamp. Your tender heart is touched by the plight of Dumont's slaves. You've been tutored by that annoying moss creature, the self-styled Maiden of the Swamp, and you'd like to go rescue the creatures. The Maiden, very wisely indeed, refuses to aid you without my cooperation. In a stroke of cowardice, she sent you to ask for it. Tell me, Miss Snowmane," he said, gazing intently into the ruby depths of the wine, "do you really expect to leave here alive?"

The casualness of the question was more chilling than the words themselves. The wine-induced warmth fled Larissa, and her mouth went dry with fear.

"It doesn't matter," she said in a voice that quavered only slightly. "If I can't get your permission to attack *La Demoiselle*, I'd rather die."

"Death is not necessarily an option," the zombie lord reminded her.

Larissa ignored his taunt. "I need your permission to fight Dumont," she repeated. "He's a thief, stealing things that don't belong to him. He's getting fat off the labor of innocent beings. I'm not asking for your aid, only your permission."

Misroi remained impassive. He reminded the trapped dancer of a waiting vulture.

"Don't you understand?" she exploded. "He's trapping creatures from Souragne. From your land, without your permission—without even consulting you!"

Misroi appeared not to have noticed the anger in her voice. He took another long pull at the cooling wine, and rose to reheat it with the poker.

"Lord Misroi—"

He gave her a mock-offended look. "Anton, please, my dear."

"Anton . . . Will you permit us to attack *La Demoiselle*?"

Misroi picked up the poker and warmed up his wine. "I haven't quite made up my mind about that yet."

With the speed of a striking snake, he dashed the mug to the floor and swung the poker at her head. Larissa managed to leap out of the way, turning a handspring and landing on her feet. Using all the Maiden had taught her, she gestured with her left hand and made a movement with her right foot. The poker twisted in Misroi's grasp like a live thing, then went still. The zombie lord stared at the length of vine now in his hand.

Larissa crouched, ready to leap to either side or execute a dance movement. Her blue eyes were alert, waiting for Misroi's next move.

The lord of Souragne looked from the vine to Larissa, surprise on his face. "Very good!" he murmured. "You're better than I thought you would be. This will be enjoyable. Sit down, dear Larissa, if I may call you that. You need have no more fear of me. I have tested your mettle—and you have damaged mine!" He tossed the vine into the fire. "You must have many questions for me. Ask them."

Larissa licked her lips, cautiously sitting back down. "The Maiden says you are the lord of Souragne."

"Quite right. It, and everything in it, belongs to me."

He looked at her with piercing eyes. "That does include you, too, my dear, in case you were wondering."

Larissa was starting to overcome her initial fear. Misroi's arrogance began to annoy her, and she clung to that emotion. "Since you know that Dumont is stealing your creatures, why haven't you stopped him?"

Misroi shrugged. "If he is clever enough to trick creatures and trap them, more power to him. Cleverness and covetousness are not sins in my eyes, Larissa."

"But, he has no right—"

"If he can manage it, that gives him the right. Only the strong and the clever survive. If the animals—or other beings—are stupid enough to let themselves get caught, they deserve whatever happens to them. Harnessing their magic is far from the worst that could befall trapped creatures." He smiled, a cruel, cold smile. "Trapped creatures in my home pray to fare so well."

Larissa's fear had evaporated, leaving her coolly reckless. "Am I a trapped creature?"

Misroi's smile widened. "Everyone is trapped—in one way or another. Some have prettier cages, that's all. No, Dumont's ambition doesn't bother me." He paused thoughtfully. "Alondrin's, however, does."

"Because he makes zombies, like you do?" Larissa wondered the instant the words left her mouth if this had somehow been a breach of etiquette, but Misroi didn't take offense.

"That's hardly the problem. I can control any zombie in this land at a thought. No, Alondrin wants to leave my realm, and I don't wish him to."

He turned his penetrating gaze on the dancer, the smile melting away from his face as if it had never been. "*That's* the problem, Larissa. He's planning to use your showboat to break away from the island."

"But—the Maiden said no one can leave without your permission."

Misroi's handsome face grew cold, and a quiet rage

began to simmer in his blue eyes, causing Larissa to draw back.

"That has always been the case. But Alondrin has taken great care to stack the cards in his favor."

Misroi leaned forward, his eyes snapping like the fire. He began to count on his fingers. "One—he's traveling on water, which strengthens his skill. Two—the boat is warded with Captain Dumont's considerable magic. And three—there are dozens of *feu follets* on the boat, and their presence also enhances magical spells. Alondrin might succeed, which would set a dreadful example. Don't you agree?"

Larissa nodded. "So why haven't you stopped him?"

"Because I'm going to get you and your friends to do it for me," Misroi answered. "Why should I bestir myself when you are all afire to charge to the rescue? But, pretty dancer, I'm going to teach you a few tricks to counter the *bocoru*'s magic." He rose, strode over to her, and pulled her to her feet. Larissa forced herself not to struggle and met his eyes evenly.

One hand reached to smooth back her wet mane of white. Slim, strong fingers slid down her cheek, trailed across her jaw, her throat. Larissa's body tensed, and her eyes narrowed in anger.

"Have no fear for the safety of your person, Larissa," he said, cupping her face in his hands. Wine-scented breath fanned her face. "Who knows better than a zombie lord what pitiful stuff mere flesh is? No, it's your spirit that intrigues me. There's something there that I find . . . fascinating."

He stepped back, taking her hands. A crafty smile spread across his face. "I will give you what you seek, but in my own time and for my own reasons. You are a dancer. Very well, then. I shall teach you a new bransle, my dear. I shall teach you the Dance of the Dead."

# NINETEEN

"Marcel," Anton Misroi called lazily, "show Miss Snowmane to the guest quarters. Draw her a hot bath and—are you hungry, my dear?"

Larissa opened her mouth to say yes then closed it, her face suspicious. Misroi shook his head and clucked his tongue in mock dismay.

"Pretty little dancer, you've already seen that I'm alive. How do you think I stay that way? I assure you, the food is wholesome. You shall join me for an early supper."

She had no choice. Larissa nodded. The zombie master took her cold hand, pressed firm lips to it, then left.

Marcel took the candelabra from the mantlepiece and led Larissa up the wide staircase. She followed, thoughts churning in her head. The dancer had come seeking Misroi's permission, not his aid or his tutelage. How long would he keep her here?

And what would he ask of her in return?

She followed her undead guide as he led her down a large hall. Illumination was provided by brass sconces, fastened to the walls, shaped like arms that clutched flickering candles. Marcel reached the end of the hall, produced a large key ring and unlocked the door. It swung inward with a groan. Larissa wondered how long it had been since this room had had a living occupant.

Marcel motioned her inside. She stepped in tentatively. As with the furniture elsewhere, that within the bedroom was large, old, and dust-covered. The canopied bed was a sprawling, sagging echo of lost grandeur. The wardrobe of intricately carved wood was in sad need of oiling, and the mirror at the little vanity was as tarnished as the one in the hallway. A woman, freshly dead and clad in fairly new clothes, was mechanically pouring buckets of steaming water into a porcelain tub that seemed comparatively clean.

Larissa almost laughed aloud at the macabre absurdity of the scene. She felt hysterical laughter bubble inside her and swiftly quelled it.

The dancer shed her soaked, filthy clothes and stepped into the tub. She felt better at once. The hot, flower-scented water felt wonderful to Larissa's chilled body. As she bathed, the zombie maid opened the wardrobe and began laying out beautiful dresses. Larissa glanced over at her. She wanted no more favors from the zombie lord.

"No," she protested, "I'll wear what I came in."

The maid straightened and fixed Larissa with a fish-eyed stare. She shook her head slowly. "Master said, dress," she told Larissa in a monotone.

Larissa swore and splashed the water impotently. He wasn't even letting her wear her dancing clothing. "A damned fly in a bloody web," she muttered to herself as she reached for a towel.

"Well, don't you tidy up enchantingly," Misroi commented as the dancer descended the stairs an hour later. Larissa glared at him, the expression on her face a contrast with the beautiful gown she had finally decided on. It was dark green with a cloth-of-gold underdress. The upper part of the sleeves were also cloth of gold and puffed out, but her lower arms were encased with more dark green fabric that tied neatly at the wrists. It was shockingly low-cut by Larissa's standards. She had not bound her hair, and it floated about her shoulders like a white cloud.

The lord of the dead met her halfway up the stairs. He, too, had dressed for the occasion. His black hair had been somewhat tamed and was drawn back into a ponytail. Misroi's clothes had obviously been freshly pressed and the colors—dark blue coat, light blue vest, and black breeches—suited him well. Blindingly white silk stockings and shoes with polished gold buckles replaced the mud-spattered riding boots. He offered Larissa his arm, and she cautiously took it.

The dining room was across the hall from the parlor. The table was large and already laid out in preparation for their first course. Misroi pulled out a chair for Larissa, then seated himself at the other end of the table. The rain had stopped, and the sunlight streamed in through the windows at precisely the wrong angle. Misroi squinted.

"Drapes, close," he ordered.

As in the parlor, the drapes were held open by brass hands. At Misroi's command, the clutching metal fingers loosed their hold, and the maroon velvet drapes swung shut.

Two servants emerged from the kitchen area. One moved about diligently lighting several candles. Another entered carrying a large silver soup tureen. Staring emptily, he placed it on the table and began to ladle soup into a bowl for each of the living beings.

"Turtle soup," Misroi said, "delicious, according to my chef. I just acquired him recently. He's a wonder in the kitchen."

Cautiously Larissa spooned up a mouthful of the soup. It was delicious, as thick as stew. The turtle meat had a unique flavor, and there was an undercurrent of something tangy and citrusy.

"Lemon?" she hazarded.

Misroi beamed. "What a discerning palate you have, Mademoiselle Snowmane. Yes, it's lemon."

Misroi proved to be a charming host. Despite herself and the horrors that abounded in the place, Larissa found that she relaxed and occasionally even smiled at some of Misroi's jokes. She had seconds on the soup, devoured a salad made with bitter greens grown near the swamp, and dived cheerfully into a rice dish with seasoned crayfish. Her eyes flew open and she gulped thirstily at the water.

Misroi laughed again. "A bit spicy, I know, but that's typical cuisine for our humble island. Perhaps the next dish will be more to your liking."

Larissa sniffed hungrily as the main course was set before her.

"Rabbit sautéd in wine," Misroi informed her, rubbing his hands together in anticipation. "It's the chef's specialty." He attacked his food with gusto. Larissa's appetite, however, had fled.

"Jean," she said softly, in quiet horror.

Misroi raised a raven brow inquiringly as he lifted his fork to his mouth.

"I beg your pardon?" He took a large bite. Juice ran down his chin, and he wiped absently at it with the back of his hand.

Larissa cleared her throat. "Is your chef named Jean, owner of the Two Hares Inn?" she asked.

"Why, yes, he did run an inn before he got that bone stuck in his throat," Misroi replied with his mouth full. "If you knew him, then you know this is good. Death hasn't interfered with his talent. Eat." He gestured toward her plate with his knife, then sliced off another bite.

Larissa stared mutely across the table at Misroi. He continued to eat with palpable enjoyment, not in the least discomfited by the thought that his meal had been prepared by a corpse. She put her napkin down on the table with a trembling hand and eased her chair back.

"I'm not hungry anymore." She rose and left, heartsick.

She had almost made it to the stairs when her host seized her elbow in a hard grip. "That was rude, my dear. You haven't been excused."

Disgusted by him, Larissa jerked her arm away. He spun her around to face him, and an answering anger smoldered in his blue eyes. "Don't push me, pretty dancer. You keep your life at my whim or lose it that way. Since you refuse to dine with me, perhaps you will dance."

Seizing her hand firmly in his, he pulled her back into the main hallway, shoving open a pair of double doors at the far end. They passed the mirror that had so startled Larissa when she first entered *Maison de la Détresse*, and again her eyes leaped to follow the movement.

Hauling her with him, Misroi entered what remained of a glorious ballroom. The painted walls were dingy and chipped, and the harpsichord that stood like a forgotten toy in the corner looked as though it hadn't felt the touch of a hand in decades.

"Play," Misroi shouted, and at once a tinny melody arose from the instrument. Larissa was jerked tight against the zombie lord's chest. His right hand seized her left in a hard grasp while his other arm snaked around her slim waist. Automatically she reached down with her right hand to lift her skirt out of the way of her feet. Larissa raised her head and met Misroi's approving glance.

"So, you do know how to waltz." His grasp on her relaxed somewhat. "I have not waltzed in a long time. For now, let us enjoy the music and call a temporary truce, hmm?"

The tune was sweet, and Misroi was an excellent dancer. Although Larissa never relaxed her guard, she followed his lead easily and gracefully. After a time, she asked boldly, "Is this the Dance of the Dead you were so anxious to teach me, Lord Misroi?"

The thought amused him tremendously, and he let out a laugh that echoed in the large, empty room. "Anton. No, pretty dancer, this is purely for my own enjoyment. The lessons will come later. Tonight—" he smiled down at her "—we simply dance."

\* \* \* \* \*

The next morning, as she had been instructed, Larissa met Misroi at the stables. She wore the outfit that had been left on her bed the night before—riding breeches, a blouse, boots, and a cloak. The dancer had wondered briefly as she dressed how the zombie master knew her sizes, but decided that she really didn't wish to know.

The earth underneath her boots was wet from yesterday's rain. The sun shone brightly, warming the thick, humid air. The unpleasant scents were stronger in the rainy weather, and Larissa wrinkled her nose as she walked along the gravel path toward the stables.

Like the house, the stables were neglected. The horses, however, seemed to be alert enough. A small roan mare was tethered to a post in the cobblestone courtyard, and a zombie servant was mechanically grooming the beast. Larissa was glad that this one, unlike the ones that had pulled the carriage, was alive.

A clopping sound caused Larissa to turn, and she saw Misroi leading a huge black stallion. The beast looked tired, as if it had recently been ridden hard and put away wet. Its great black head drooped as the beast slowly followed Misroi, the nose almost brushing the ground.

"Good morning, Larissa," the master of *Maison de la Détresse* greeted his guest. "I trust you slept well?"

She managed a wan smile. In truth, she had lain awake for hours, wondering who had last been in the canopied bed and whether she would be safe from midnight intruders—living or dead. Larissa had kept a candle burning beside her bed and had been unpleasantly startled when she woke after a few fitful hours of sleep to discover that the candle had been removed.

The dancer's dreams had been punctured with nightmares, peopled with the dead and the dying. Larissa's drowsing mind had cast herself as the murderer. She had destroyed *La Demoiselle* as she had destroyed the tree in the clearing, only this time, she had thrown back her head and laughed with savage pleasure.

She answered her host's question politely. "As well as could be expected, Lor—Anton."

"I trust you do ride?"

"A little." Very little, she thought to herself.

The beast was saddled and bridled, ready to go, and Misroi mounted the stallion with a smooth, easy movement. He reached down to Larissa and swung her up, onto the saddle in front of him. "Today, my dear, you shall ride more than a little. Come, Incubus!"

Without warning, he whipped the horse smartly with his riding crop, and the weary beast surprised her by leaping into a gallop.

Larissa almost lost her seat but twined her fingers into the horse's coarse mane and hung on grimly. Incubus settled into his stride and tore down the road like the creature he was named for. Abruptly, harshly, Misroi yanked the beast's head to the right, and Incubus leaped off the road into one of the fields. It was fallow, and the horse's hooves sent chunks of wet mud flying.

"Feel his power, Larissa," Misroi hissed in her ear. "All that strength, and it obeys me."

He struck the horse again, and Incubus surged forward even faster. Froth from his jaws spattered Larissa's cheek, and the mane was beginning to grow damp with sweat.

"It's exciting, isn't it, to think of all that power under

your control," Misroi continued, his voice growing tauter. He again whipped the horse with the crop. Incubus tossed his midnight head in pain.

Larissa's breathing came in shallow gasps as she crouched low over the neck of the beast. She smelled the musk of Incubus's sweat. She knew Misroi was pushing the stallion hard, too hard, and that the savage beating was probably drawing blood. Part of her raged at the unnecessary cruelty, but Misroi was right—the wild ride *was* exciting, and her own heart was pounding madly.

She gasped as a felled tree loomed ahead, directly in Incubus's path. With a grunt, the horse gathered himself and sailed easily over the obstacle, touching lightly down and barely breaking stride. Larissa heard herself laughing, and a calm part of her mind noted it as a shrill, cruel sound.

*Crack*, came the sound of the riding crop. *Crack*. *Crack*.

Again Misroi jerked hard on the bit, yanking the steed's head around and sending him off in a new direction. This time, Larissa could see that the foam on Incubus's jaws was pink with blood and the brown eyes were rolling madly. His adrenaline-sparked stride faltered. He had no more to give his master.

Still Misroi pushed, and Larissa hung on, filled with a savage excitement mixed with horror. *Crack*.

Incubus uttered a low, shuddering groan as his heart exploded. The stallion dropped to his front knees, and Misroi grabbed Larissa and pulled them both clear as Incubus rolled over heavily. Larissa was shaking and gasping for breath. Tears filled her eyes and rolled down her cheeks, mixing with rivulets of sweat.

"You killed him!" she shrieked, staring in sick grief at the body of the black stallion. She could see slick patches of dark blood on Incubus's flanks where the crop had struck.

Misroi, on the other hand, seemed exultant. "*We* killed him! You were as intoxicated with the speed and power as I was, Larissa, and you cannot tell me otherwise. Not one word of protest did you raise, nor a hint of condemnation breathe."

Pain wrenched Larissa's heart as guilt flooded her. Misroi was right. He flung himself to his knees beside her in the mud, and there was a feverish fire in his eyes. He grabbed her shoulders.

"You're just like me, Larissa. We're kindred spirits, you and I. I thought so when I first met you, when I realized that I could teach you the Dance of the Dead. Now I'm sure of it. Look at the sort of things we can do!"

Heedless of the mud, Misroi scrambled to where Incubus lay. He seized the horse's huge head in his hands, smoothing the wet mane back from the forehead. He pressed his cheek to the beast's face and closed his eyes.

Incubus twitched. With a rough whinny, he jerked his head from Misroi's grasp. He stumbled a little, but got stiffly to his feet. Misroi turned to Larissa, triumph burning in his eyes.

"You see? Nothing is lost to us! Incubus is dead, but he still runs for me. Your foolish Maiden, insisting on working *with* the forces of nature—bah! That is too little for us. We can *be* the forces of nature, of death—and undeath."

Larissa stared at him. "You're a monster," she whispered.

Misroi smiled, showing white teeth. "We all are, pretty dancer. Deep down inside all of us, there's a monster. Some spend their lives trying to fight it. They fail. Some coexist unhappily with their beast. They are miserable." He dragged her to her feet and grabbed her shoulders. "Larissa," he purred, "you and I *celebrate* it."

Larissa placed her hands on Misroi's chest and tried to push him away. "No, you're wrong! I am nothing like you!"

His eyes searched hers, their fire dimming somewhat. "We shall see, pretty dancer. We shall see."

\* \* \* \* \*

As Larissa descended the stairs, she heard the harpsichord begin to play. Misroi, formally clad as he had been the night before, stepped into the dimly lit hallway, gazing up at her with predatory patience. Wordlessly he extended a hand, flicking the wrist slightly with practiced ease so that the ruffles of the cuff lay flat against the coat sleeve. He was waiting for her, ready to teach her the Dance of the Dead.

*You're just like me.* Her heart lurched in her breast. What if he was right?

Forcing herself to be calm, she continued walking down the stairs with a slow and even step. A smile twitched at one corner of his mouth, and she wondered if, like a wild beast, he could scent her fear.

She placed her hand in his. "No supper before dancing?" she queried in a voice as calm as she could make it.

He shook his head. "First, dancing. Then dinner."

The Dance of the Dead began innocuously enough. It was a waltz, sweeping and grand. Then, almost imperceptibly, the music began to change. It switched gradually from a major to a minor key and grew deeper, more menacing. The tempo increased just as subtly. At one point, Larissa glanced up into Misroi's eyes and found that she could not look away. Fleetingly, she thought of the giant zombie snake in her dream and how it had hypnotized her. She stared into the blue depths of her tutor's eyes, snared.

His fingers dug into her waist, even through the many layers of material. Misroi bent and placed his cheek, flushed and hot as if from a fever, against Larissa's suddenly chilled one.

*Keep dancing.*

Larissa closed her eyes, unsure whether the voice was actually Misroi's or if it simply existed inside her head. It didn't matter. She was helpless to disobey, and, stranger still, she had no desire to. Together, zombie master and dancer whirled across the empty floor. To Larissa, it seemed as though her feet barely even brushed the ground. She began to lose track of where she was, who she was dancing with, even who she was. She yielded utterly to the rising sense of power building within her.

It was then that Larissa realized just how cold she was. She still moved swiftly and surely within the iron circle of Misroi's arms, but she could no longer sense her limbs. A slight wisp of fear penetrated her haze of power, and she opened her eyes.

Larissa shrieked, almost stumbling. The hand clasped in Misroi's merciless grip was little more than gray, skin-covered bone.

She was turning into a zombie.

*Keep dancing!* the voice thundered in her brain. She did so, willing her fear into determination, and she smiled grimly as she watched the desiccated skin of her hand plump out into living human flesh once again. Larissa glanced up at Misroi. A savage snarl twisted her sweet face.

Suddenly Misroi spun her away from him. Startled, she stumbled but recovered swiftly.

"You have passed the first test," he approved, breathing a bit heavily from the exertion. "Now it is time for the second."

He clapped his hands, the sound echoing like the crack of his riding crop in the large room. After a moment, almost a dozen zombies, from servants to field workers, appeared in the ballroom. Larissa stared at them, unsure what Misroi had in mind.

"They are under orders to kill you," he said. "The

Dance of the Dead, if you execute it properly, will keep them confused long enough for me to rescind the order."

Catching her breath, Larissa panted, "But I just learned it! What if I don't do it properly?"

Misroi shrugged. "Then, my dear, they kill you. And I have a new and pretty zombie maidservant. That is, until the rot sets in. I'll set a place for you at dinner . . . in case you survive."

For a moment, Larissa thought that this was merely another one of Misroi's cruel jokes, but he turned and strode out of the ballroom, pulling the door closed behind him with an ominous thud. As if it were a signal, the rotting undead began to move toward Larissa with a slow, terrible purpose.

Trapped! Larissa wailed to herself, momentarily too frightened to move. Like a fly in a web . . . no. This fly is going to fight, the young woman resolved. She was drained from the dance and almost trembled with exhaustion, but she summoned up energy from some hidden reservoir and began to move.

She executed the first steps of the waltz, moving surely to the frantic melody the harpsichord still pounded out. Her slippered feet barely touched the floorboards, and her hands fluttered, making gestures of their own. The young woman let herself dissolve in the growing sensation of power.

Marcel had almost reached her and extended dead arms in an attempt to choke her. As the cold flesh touched her feverish skin, Larissa struck at his arms and her body twisted in protest. The zombie halted, and his arms lowered. He made no further move toward her.

Now the maidservant attempted to halt Larissa, but the white-haired dancer had tasted success and turned with almost vicious glee upon the female walking corpse. This time, the maidservant staggered back from the force of Larissa's mental commands.

Two more of the mindless, undead things were closing in on either side. Larissa leaped, dancing with fiery frenzy and focusing her increasingly powerful will upon the animated corpses. One by one, Misroi's creatures were stopped in their tracks, halted by confusion as to which order they should follow—that of their master, hitherto the only voice they had heard, or the new commands given them by the white-haired, flame-souled woman who danced before them.

When it was done, Larissa staggered to a stop. Her breath came in ragged gasps, and her legs felt rubbery. The harpsichord had ceased playing, and Larissa, suddenly feeling faint, sank to the floor.

When she had caught her breath, she slowly got to her feet. Cool blue eyes raked the frozen forms of the zombies, then Larissa Snowmane went to join the Lord of the Dead for dinner.

# TWENTY

Larissa forced her eyelids open by sheer effort of will, and fear shot through her, almost but not quite dispelling the last dregs of Misroi's drugged wine.

The dancer was alone in the swamp. She had been lying in an awkward position, one arm and leg twisted behind her. They were numb at first and didn't obey her as she tried to sit up. Then the limbs began to feel all too keenly as blood rushed back into them. Larissa ignored the stinging sensation, frantically searching for some familiar landmark in the pressing maze of green and brown.

There was none. No rotting zombie coachman, no pirogue, nothing that she knew. Panic crouched inside of her like a chained beast straining at its tethers. No, Larissa commanded it. I can get out of here. . . . I think.

She was still in her beautiful green gown, and it hampered her movement as she attempted to stand. Her left knee put pressure on something that crinkled. Larissa jerked away at once, startled, then felt relief and surprise as she realized it was merely a folded-up piece of parchment, sealed with a dollop of red wax. Larissa picked it up, examining the seal—a large M.

Swiftly she opened it and began to read.

*My very dear Miss Snowmane,*

*What a dreadful host you must deem me to be. You are correct. I must thank you for your refreshing presence in my home recently. You were a delight to work with.*

*Before you lies your last test. Well, at least the last one I shall be pressing upon you. The riding crop should come in handy. I know you know how to use it. I wish you the very best of luck in finding your way home, pretty dancer, though I doubt you'll need it—you're too much like me. We make our own luck.*

*Perhaps someday we shall dance together again. I will look forward to it.*

—*Anton Misroi*

Larissa crumpled the letter savagely and threw it to the earth. It fluttered gently downward, its sharp, crinkled edges opening slowly like a flower's petals. She saw the riding crop Misroi had mentioned, lying innocuously in the mud, its leather tip encrusted with Incubus's blood. She shuddered, then took a deep breath to calm her frayed nerves.

Root, Larissa told herself. She lay down on the soggy earth, not caring that her gown was getting ruined. Eagerly she plunged her fingers into the wet earth, seeking information and calmness from the soil.

Unlike the sod of the Maiden's island, this earth offered very little comfort. She sensed a sullenness here, a taint, like the underlying flavor of a piece of food just gone bad. Her eyes closed, Larissa frowned. She stretched deeper, not merely asking now, but demanding compliance.

With the reluctance of a spoiled child, the land yielded. There was danger here, she sensed. She was not to trust the ground, the trees, or the creatures. The Maiden's island was approximately a mile to the southeast.

And that, Larissa felt, was all the land was going to tell her. Abruptly, disturbingly, she felt contact break off.

Slowly Larissa came back to herself, pulling her buried hands out of the mud. It let go of her hands with a reluctant, sucking sound. Absently she brushed off the mud on a pile of airmoss.

Her first thought was to travel through one of the trees. She approached a giant live oak, trying to ignore the fact that it looked menacing. It's just a tree, she thought, and the quickwood had been respectful and helpful.

Taking a deep breath, Larissa reached out and placed a hand on the bark. *Greetings. With your permission, I would—*

*No!*

The response exploded in her mind with such ferocity that she winced. The dancer jerked her hand back, but not before an angry branch had seized it. The tree had sprung into frightening life, waving its branches angrily and clamping down on her with menacing strength.

Before it could crush her, Larissa reacted. She didn't have time to think and didn't need to. Even though both wrists were securely held by the dark treant's branches, she was able to move her fingers. Her body twisted, arching. Where the treant's leafy limbs touched her, they exploded into flame. The tree roared in pain, instantly releasing her. It began to beat its fiery branches against its own trunk. The flames leaped for a few frenzied moments, then died.

Larissa was well out of the treant's reach and glared at it defiantly. "I have no wish to hurt anything in the swamp," she cried to the listening foliage. "But I will if you force me to. All I ask is safe passage."

She waited—for what, she wasn't sure. At last the singed treant rumbled in a bass voice, *You may go on your way, Whitemane, but I will not let you pass through me.*

Larissa closed her eyes for an instant in gratitude for the Maiden's teachings. Then the dancer turned back to the treant and planted her hands on her hips.

*I cannot force you to grant me passage to the Maiden's island*, she told it. *But may I have your assurance that you won't throw me down if I climb your branches to see where I am?*

The treant rustled sulkily. Then: *Yes.*

*I can hurt you again*, Larissa warned.

*Understood.*

As Larissa approached, the treant even lowered its branches to aid her climbing. Larissa smothered a self-satisfied grin. It wouldn't do to gloat.

Despite the cumbersome dress, Larissa reached the top fairly easily. The sun shone down cheerily, its careless radiance a sharp contrast with the brooding shadows and gloom that was the world beneath the swamp's mossy canopy.

An ocean of green flowed beneath her. The young woman twisted, grasping onto a branch for support. It curled in her hands, but only to secure a grip on her so that she wouldn't slip. A cold sinking sensation began in Larissa's stomach when she realized that the sheltering trees prevented her from even seeing what part was swamp and what was dry—or fairly dry—land. She craned her neck, her eyes searching, hoping desperately to see—

There it was. Larissa's breath exploded in a sigh of relief. She could see the green glossy surface of the lake catching the sunlight. The Maiden's island looked like a beautiful emerald to the grateful young woman.

"I'm coming, Maiden," she whispered softly. She carefully climbed back down, dropping the last six feet and landing gently in the soft soil.

Her gaze fell upon the riding crop. For a moment she was tempted to just leave it where it lay. It could hurt no one here, lying forgotten in the swamp. But then, without quite knowing why, she bent and picked it up.

It didn't feel strange. It was simply a crop, cool leather lying harmlessly in her palm.

"You meant something by this, Misroi," she said aloud, pulling the length of the crop through her fingers. "What, I don't know, but I'll take it just the same." At least, she added silently, I'll know where it is.

Careful to preserve the niceties, Larissa bowed to the treant. *Thank you*, she said.

For answer, the treant rattled its branches. Larissa was reminded of a dog growling, but declining to attack. If this was another test of Misroi's—and she was sure it was—then she thought she was doing quite well.

One hand grasping Misroi's riding crop, Larissa set off in the direction of the Maiden's island. The earth was soggy, but it held, and her heart began to rise. She mentally went over the layout of the riverboat, wondering what the best way to attack it might be. The attack should come at night, that was for certain. Any creatures that would come to her aid in this place would certainly be able to see in the dark. The humid darkness, together with the gray fog that always seemed to arise in the evening, ought to provide excellent cover.

She wondered how many of the crew members had been turned into zombies and was unable to block out the image of the thing that had been Casilda. For the sake of her friend, if nothing else, Larissa wanted revenge upon Lond.

A warm blink of light flashed behind her. She wheeled, alert for an attack, and smiled in surprised pleasure as she realized it was only a *feu follet*. It drifted about lazily, blinking slowly.

"Well, am I glad to see a friendly . . ." Larissa broke off, laughing. "Face" hardly applied . . .

The glowing ball drew back, then came forward again. It paused, hovering, bathing the dancer with yellow light. A thought struck Larissa.

"Can you take me to the Maiden's island?" she asked, wondering yet again if the creatures understood language as she spoke it.

The *feu follet* paused, pulsating, then began to move slowly over to one side. Larissa frowned. According to what she had seen from the top of the reluctant treant, the most direct route lay straight ahead, but the *feu follets* knew this place far better than she, so she shrugged and followed.

Once it realized that Larissa was following, the little ball of light picked up its pace, sailing ahead with a sense of purpose. Larissa smiled to herself, thinking of Willen. She wondered if he would come with her when she left Souragne. She didn't think he would be hard to convince. That is, if he could leave the island at all. Her smile faded. What if he were somehow linked to the land? What if he—

Larissa's arms flailed as she tried to stop her forward movement, but she tumbled into the quicksand with a little gasp. The mushy substance filled her mouth, and she spat frantically, choking on it. She panicked for a second, thrashing about wildly before she realized that her struggles only caused her to sink deeper.

Almost as if it were a living creature, the quicksand sucked at her limbs, seizing her long hair and pulling her head back and down. Her dress was soaked, and Larissa knew that she had only a few minutes before the ghastly mud closed over her head.

She looked wildly about for the *feu follet*, thinking that somehow it might be able to call for help, but there was no longer only one of the shining orbs. There were four of them now, and they did not express the agitation that the *feu follet* had demonstrated when she had been threatened by the deathplants. Larissa slowly realized that they were enjoying her terror. They pulsed and swelled, growing slightly larger, hovering over the dancer like vultures over a dying beast.

It was then that Larissa knew that they weren't *feu follets* at all. They were the feared will-o'-the-wisps. They had deliberately lured her here to trap her and feast upon her terror.

She tried to think, but no answer came. Breathe water? The quicksand wasn't pure water. It was an in-between substance. Turn it into earth? It would trap her, probably crush her. Then what?

The hovering will-o'-the-wisps drew closer, eager for her horror and fear. At least, Larissa thought grimly, I can deny them that. She forced herself to relax, and to her surprise found that she could float fairly well. The dancer took deep, calming breaths, willing her heart to slow its frantic pace. It was then, when she was composed, that one of her outstretched arms brushed a trailing tree branch.

Slowly Larissa craned her neck, fingers stretching to twine around the slim tendrils. Carefully, so as not to snap the twigs, she closed her hand around them. Hope began to seep through her. The will-o'-the-wisps, thwarted, began to move about agitatedly. She ignored them, keeping her mind as serene as she could and concentrating on the branch.

Larissa began to pull with a slow, steady tug. The branch bent, but held. Now she was close enough to grasp the branch with her other hand. Still moving slowly, she pulled herself toward the bank, hand over hand, until at last she was able to pull herself completely out of the nearly fatal trap.

The dancer crawled out of the muck with a distinct lack of grace. Her limbs were quivering with aftershock, and she sat down heavily. The will-o'-the-wisps drew near, definitely angry with her now. They dived at her with a shrill, humming noise, and Larissa felt fear rise in her as she heard the words they cried in a ghostly, shallow voice: "Whitemane. Die."

Gamely, she tried to force her fear away. They were

only glowing balls of light. What could they possibly—

She found out as one of them swept by her, buzzing angrily. Larissa gasped as a sudden jolt careened through her body, setting every hair on end and knocking the wind out of her. A second one dived at her, but this time she had clambered to her feet. She danced effectively, if awkwardly, and conjured magic housed in the element of fire. A small ball of flame began to take shape between her cupped palms, and she directed it toward the attacking creature.

The creatures whined in annoyance. Then, to the dancer's shock, the ball of flame bounced off the will-o'-the-wisp and ricocheted back toward her. She barely had time to leap clear, and even then the globe of fire singed her side.

Larissa hit the earth hard, wincing at the pain in her burned side. She rolled over, and suddenly saw Misroi's riding crop lying where she had thrown it when the quicksand had claimed her. Eagerly she seized it, then stared at it, wondering what in the world she was supposed to do with it.

The riding crop should come in handy, Misroi's note had said. *I know you know how to use it.*

No, I don't! Larissa's mind wailed, even as another will-o'-the-wisp flew at her with deadly intent. She tried to roll clear, but the being's electrical charge hit home. She gasped again and arched in pain.

Pain. Misroi had beaten the beautiful black stallion, driving the noble creature to its death. Lond used pain, too, but he had taken the path of—how had the Maiden put it?—bone and blood. Blood! That was the answer!

Larissa sat up and struck her left hand sharply with the crop. A red welt appeared, but no blood. She swore, then struck again, harder, forcing herself to ignore the pain. This time, a thin trickle began to meander down her palm, following the lines of her hand.

"Die, Whitemane."

Larissa didn't know if she could survive another attack. She didn't plan to find out, either. As the glowing ball dived again, she was ready. She held the riding crop clenched tightly in her hand, prepared to strike the will-o'-the-wisp with everything she had.

To her astonishment the crop twisted in her hands, the way she herself had caused the poker to writhe in Misroi's grasp at *Maison de la Détresse*. The dancer almost dropped it, but she held on grimly.

Misroi's riding crop grew longer, until its contorting length was over six feet. It filled out until Larissa's small hand could barely close around it, and its color flushed from black to greenish brown. A head took shape at one end, a head that had two slitted golden eyes and fangs—

Larissa screamed, but somehow, despite the terror that flooded her, she kept her grip on the thrashing snake. As she watched, the reptile swung its head toward the glowing balls of light. A black tongue flickered, and then it opened its jaws impossibly wide. As the will-o'-the-wisp dived for the attack, the serpent struck. It gulped down the light creature in one bite. Larissa was reminded of a legend she'd heard once, of how the will-o'-the-wisps were caused by a snake eating the sun.

A shrill sound emanated from the remaining creatures. One flew in a wild, zigzag pattern, its light flickering crazily. A second one hesitated, then attacked Larissa as its fellow had. Again, the snake struck. This time, Larissa raised the serpent in the will-o'-the-wisp's direction, facilitating the reptile's attack.

The last two will-o'-the-wisps had had enough. They sailed off into the hazy green depths of the swamp, and soon their radiance was lost to view.

Larissa's shoulders sagged, and she slackened her grip on the snake. It turned to gaze at her, and she met that slitted, unblinking stare evenly. Its tongue flickered. Then, with the same speed it had demonstrated before, the snake turned back into a simple black riding crop.

A tired smile touched Larissa's lips fleetingly. "Thank you, Anton. But how, by the rats of Richemulot, did you know I loathe snakes?"

She took a few moments to calm herself, then climbed another tree for a second look at the Maiden's island. The treacherous will-o'-the-wisps fortunately had not taken her too far off track.

When Larissa climbed down, she hunted about for a large branch. She would not be caught by quicksand a second time. The dancer continued walking, testing the earth before her with the makeshift pole and avoiding any areas that did not seem completely solid. Larissa kept her ears open for any sign of danger, but there appeared to be nothing hostile—for the moment, at least, she thought grimly.

The heat increased, and so did her hunger and thirst. Her time with the Maiden and, curiously enough, her dinners with Misroi, had given her at least some idea as to what was wholesome to eat in this treacherous place. As for water, since it had rained recently, there was plenty to be found trapped in hollows of stones and trees. The taste was unpleasant, but it slaked the burning of her throat.

Larissa pressed on until nightfall. She made a bed of airmoss, tugged from a nearby live oak, and sank down on it gratefully. Before she went to sleep, however, she danced a protective ring about her bedding. As soon as she hit the earth, her body, weary from the physical exercise and the constant tension, dropped off to sleep.

The young dancer woke a few hours later, thoroughly disoriented. It took her several seconds before she remembered where she was. Something had awakened her, she was sure of that. Careful to remain well within the circle, Larissa rose and looked about cautiously.

The night seemed calm and still, almost peaceful, but Larissa knew better. The trees stayed silent; there was no breeze to bestir their drooping branches, and few of them were anything more hostile than simple trees. No eldritch illumination warned of dangerous will-o'-the-wisps or heralded the more welcome *feu follets*. The hum of distant insects and the occasional splash of a small animal in the water were the only sounds that floated to Larissa's straining ears. All seemed quiet.

What, then, had awakened her? Larissa sat down and hugged her knees to her chest. She didn't relax. She had been through far too much since she entered the swamp to doubt her instincts now. The dancer waited for the sound to come again.

And it did.

"Larissa," sighed the voice.

At once she was on her feet, ready to execute a defensive dance movement if she needed to.

"Who's there?" she snapped, her eyes flickering about. Nothing moved.

"Oh, my child, have you forgotten?" came the same sad, forlorn echo of a voice. Before Larissa's eyes, a translucent shape began to form, solidifying into recognizability. The dancer gasped, feeling as though she had been kicked in the chest.

"Papa," she whispered.

The ghostly figure nodded sadly. Aubrey Helson was dressed just as he had been when last she had seen him. He floated just above the ground, his expression sorrowful. "I have missed you, Larissa."

Tears sprang to Larissa's eyes. "Oh, Papa," she quavered, "I've missed you! What happened? Why didn't you come back for me?"

"I would have, but Dumont murdered me," came the answer. Larissa already knew that to be true in her heart, but hadn't dared examine the thought too closely. "Revenge will be ours soon. Come, my beautiful little daughter. I will take you safely to the Maiden."

Larissa, nearly blinded by tears, swallowed hard and stepped out of the ring.

"No, Larissa! Don't!" came a sharp cry. Willen charged out of nowhere and pulled her back down to the soggy earth. "It's not your father. It's a trap!"

Larissa, her eyes still on the spectral image of the man she had loved, struggled against the *feu follet*. "Willen, no, it's Papa. He wouldn't hurt me—" Willen had wrapped his strong arms around her, pinning Larissa's arms down. She thrashed, trying to reach her father, but her beloved's grip was implacable.

Willen turned his attention to the specter. "Begone!" he cried. "You are nothing at all! I know you for what you are, and you cannot harm her anymore!"

The ghost of Aubrey Helson opened its mouth. A horrible shriek exploded, rending the stillness of the night. It shimmered and changed, until it was nothing more than a shapeless mass of white fog. At last, it vanished altogether.

Larissa abruptly stopped struggling, collapsing limply into Willen's arms. He held her comfortingly. "Willen," she whispered, clinging to the strong arms about her. "Thank you."

"You are very welcome."

Suddenly she turned to look up at him, craning her neck and searching his eyes. "You're free! How did you escape?"

He grinned roguishly. "It took a lot of effort. I'm the only one, though. We've still got to go back and free the others. Come on. Let's get going." He rose and extended an arm to help her up.

"Wait a minute. How did you know that that . . . whatever it was . . . wasn't the ghost of my father?"

"This is my territory, remember? I know what kind of things lurk in the heart of the swamp. That's a creature the locals call a plat-eyes. They generally take a human shape, usually of someone well-known to the victim, but can also appear as a dog, or cat, or any other animal. Always black, though. They keep trying for fresh human bodies. It was hoping to lure you away, just like the will-o'-the-wisps did."

Larissa was still holding onto his hand. She kept her face neutral, but she thought with all her heart, I hate you! I wish you were dead!

Willen grinned down at her. "Come on. The Maiden's waiting."

Larissa jerked her hand away and assumed a defensive position. "What are you?" she demanded.

Willen stared at her. "Larissa, what's the matter?" He took a step toward her.

"Stop right there or I'll hurt you, whatever you are," the dancer warned. "How did you know about the will-o'-the-wisps leading me into the quicksand—and why couldn't you sense my thoughts?"

A slow, terrible grin began to spread over Willen's face. As Larissa watched in horror, the youth's features blurred and changed, reshaping into the visage of an ugly man she had never seen before. Then that face and body changed, too. He grew larger, the grin widening. His teeth, white even now, lengthened and sharpened to suit the reptilian muzzle that suddenly sprouted from the lower half of his face. Hands turned into claws, and a crocodile's tail slid from its lower back.

"Oh, well done indeed, pretty dancer," the monster commended her. It spoke with the voice of Anton Misroi. "You are just full of surprises, aren't you?"

Larissa closed her eyes. She was no longer afraid, just furious. "Anton, you have toyed with me enough. Surely I have provided you with whatever amusement you need. Let me get to the Maiden's island, that I may go about attacking that boat!" Her voice gradually rose until she was almost screaming.

The crocodile-creature laughed merrily. "You do indeed have spirit," he admitted. "Very well. This ugly fellow here is a creature known as a lezard. He will keep you safe and take you to the Maiden's island. After that—" the lezard shrugged "—the rest is up to you. And, by the way, bravo with the crop."

Larissa opened her mouth to reply when the creature's expression changed. The lezard surveyed the dancer with its cold yellow eyes. "I shall serve the whitemane," he said finally. The voice was no longer Misroi's, but a cold growl.

"Take me to the Maiden's Isle," Larissa ordered.

The lezard bowed. It changed yet again, becoming a huge crocodile, and slithered into the swampy waters. There, it waited, and Larissa hesitantly climbed aboard its scaly back.

# TWENTY-ONE

The Maiden of the Swamp had rooted herself in the wet soil as soon as the pirogue bearing Larissa had disappeared from view. She needed periodic, undisturbed rooting from time to time to keep her energy high, and she knew that shortly she would be needing every bit of strength she could muster.

She dug her root-feet deeper, feeling the nutrients being absorbed and moving slowly throughout her body. She closed her green eyes, took a deep breath, let it out, then allowed her head to droop. Soon, she had stopped breathing. Her graceful features blurred and changed, until they were only ridges and hollows in the bark of a tree. Rest . . . rest . . .

"Maiden?"

The Maiden stirred in her deep trance. She did not wish to separate herself from the embrace of the soil just yet and tried to ignore the voice.

"Maiden?" Yes, it was what she was called, and she must answer. Slowly, as if she were swimming upward through a thick layer of mud, the Maiden became aware of her surroundings, became a thinking creature again.

Larissa stood before her, dreadfully pale. Beside her stood an enormous lezard in half-human form, regarding the Maiden coldly. "I have brought the whitemane," he said. "She has told me of the need."

"We will need the help of your people," the Maiden said. "May we rely on you?"

The creature revealed deadly teeth. "It sounds like a feast indeed. We will come when you ask us." Without another word, he dived into the river, assumed full crocodile form, and slowly swam off.

The Maiden returned her attention to the girl. She had clearly been through a terrible ordeal, but there was a hardness to her face, a determination that had not been there before. Fully awake now, the Maiden went to Larissa and caught the girl gently by the shoulders.

"Tell me what happened."

Larissa licked her lips. "He will let us attack," she murmured. "He taught . . . he taught me the Dance of the Dead."

The Maiden gasped in horror. "What have I done?" she whispered. "No . . . oh, Larissa, no . . . You must never use such magic, do you understand? It is contrary to all I have taught you!"

"I know," Larissa answered calmly. "He wants me to use it. That's why he's letting us attack. But I know it for what it is."

"Do you know the danger? Did he tell you what risks you run when you perform such a dance?"

The dancer looked grim. "He didn't tell me, but I found out." There was no way, not if she lived forever, that she would forget the zombie hand on the end of her arm. To lose control of the dance was to become undead herself. But she had beaten the danger and had mastered the dance. It had not mastered her.

The Maiden of the Swamp embraced the weary dancer, placing a pale green hand on Larissa's temple. "I am sorry you underwent such a terrible ordeal, but you are indeed the stronger for it. You are weary, child, and ought to rest before we do anything else. Will you let me send you to sleep?"

Larissa nodded. The one night at *Maison de la Détresse* had been far from restful, and she had been able to snatch only a few hours of sleep in the swamp. The dancer knew the dreams that the Maiden would send would be healing. She closed her eyes as a gentle fog clouded her senses. Gently, the Maiden lowered the sleeping Larissa to the earth, then resumed her meditative state.

Through her contact with the soil, the Maiden was dimly aware of everything transpiring on her island and the waters that touched it. She sensed the slow, silent growth of the mammoth cypresses and felt the flow of the muddy water as it eased sluggishly along. She sensed the vibrations of the creatures, small and benign, large and predatory, as they went about their business. She permitted herself to feed from the land for an hour, and then began to call.

Her range was not large—it was limited only to her island—but others would take the message elsewhere. The lezard was already telling his people. Almost as soon as she began to call, the few quickwoods on the island began to drum a message to their brothers elsewhere in the swamp.

Other sentient plants heard the rhythm of the quickwoods and stirred. Their branches waved, their flowers nodded, and their roots twisted in the soil. Slowly, almost painfully, the trees began to move, the rustling of their leaves a sigh of resignation.

Longears heard the Maiden's call as well, and sat up on his haunches, listening. The loah nodded to himself and began pounding on the earth with a powerful hind leg, beating away in a code his people instinctively knew. One by one, the rabbits in the swamp heard their hero's message and passed it along to other waiting ears.

Less ordinary creatures also heard the summons. Trees rooted near *Maison de la Détresse* stirred to wakefulness, their deep-set eyes burning with hatred and a desire for blood. Slowly, the evil treants moved like their gentler cousins to answer the summons. Creatures that dwelt in the bottom of the swamp came to the surface, filtered sunlight glinting against scaly, or slimy, or rock-hard skin.

A little over a mile downstream, Deniri and Kaedrin were busy building rafts for the attack. Kaedrin had been cutting logs from fallen trees. He raised and lowered the axe tirelessly, sweat pouring off him in the humid warmth. Deniri, with an obvious lack of interest, was securing the logs together with vines. Suddenly, she paused in her task. She tensed, listening.

"There it is," she told her mate in a low voice.

He looked over at her curiously, not understanding. "The signal? I don't hear it."

She wrinkled her pert nose in mock disgust. "After all this time in the swamp, you can't hear it? It's coming through the ground!"

Kaedrin glanced at Sleek, the weasel. The creature was tense and alert. The wolf that had been with him for five years, who had followed him from Arkandale, was stiff and silent, her amber eyes focused on something Kaedrin could not see. Even the squirrel in his pocket poked his head out, curious.

Kaedrin dropped to all fours, digging his strong fingers into the mud for better contact. He listened for a while to the inaudible call, then rose and went to pull his floating house to shore. He entered through the open door and began to rummage in one corner. Deniri followed, silently watching.

Leather armor, stiff from disuse, emerged from a sack. There was also a rusted sword that he would have to grind back into usable shape, and a shield whose device had long since faded into unrecognizability.

As Kaedrin worked, a curious river otter pulled itself up onto the floating house. It ambled over to the ranger and poked its wet black nose into the sack, then glanced up at him with liquid brown eyes. Kaedrin stroked the silky wet fur.

"You're really going to do this, aren't you?" Deniri asked at last. Her voice was strained.

"I swore long ago I'd not use these again, not for love of man or woman. Still true—I touch these cursed relics of war for you, Deniri. You and every other creature here I have come to love and value."

Deniri's temper rose. "You don't have to do this. You're only one man. How much can they expect—"

"I am the only human, besides Larissa, who will fight," Kaedrin retorted. "They need me. And they could use your help, too."

Deniri hissed, her face lengthening into a pointed snout as hair rippled over her elongating body. Fully mink now, she slipped into the water and disappeared. Kaedrin grinned ruefully. She would be back.

Slowly, as the message was passed from tree to tree, beast to beast, various beings converged on the island. Reluctantly, the fox did not attack the hare, nor the deer flee the monstrous crocodiles. Their Maiden had called them, and they had answered.

\* \* \* \* \*

Bouki was unharmed. Unless one slew a *loah*, and that was difficult, they healed rapidly. The large rabbit bore no signs of the atrocities that had been inflicted upon him. Bushtail, straining against his harness, had managed to edge close enough to the rabbit so that Bouki could rest his weight on the fox's back. The wire noose around Bouki's neck was thus loosened, and the rabbit could relax for the first time since he was captured. Now he slept deeply, safe with Bushtail, though he occasionally whimpered and kicked at his manacles.

Ah, Bouki, my friend, thought Willen wryly, looking

at the odd sight of the fox and rabbit. You ought to have been a cat *loah*. You always land on your feet.

Willen, too, was unhurt physically, but his body remembered the pain all too well. Already, it tensed in anticipation of the next horror.

Lond was a master of agony. In that area, at least, his dark path had granted him success. There was indeed power to be found in pain and in the pleasure taken from inflicting pain, but Willen knew it to be a treacherous power and a false pleasure. Sooner or later, it would turn on the wizard. With his own misdeeds of the past, Lond would be undone. Willen hoped only that he could hold out until that time.

The door opened, and three zombies, one of them Dragoneyes, entered. One walked over to Bouki and unlocked the magical shackles. Another reached up to pull out the end of the wire noose.

"No," begged the rabbit. "Please . . ."

Without warning and in predatory silence, Bushtail leaped to his feet and ripped the zombie's throat out. As the body toppled to the floor, Bouki leaped on the corpse. Sharp front claws and even sharper teeth dug into the zombie's chest. The ravenous rabbit *loah* rooted around in the decaying flesh for a moment, then Bouki's face emerged. The rotting, pulpy flesh smeared across his face turned the animal's visage into a grisly mask. In his teeth was the zombie's heart. He devoured it at once.

Dragoneyes reached for the noose and jerked on it, and the *loah* gasped soundlessly. His bloody tongue lolled, and he hastened to keep up with the departing Dragoneyes so that the noose would cease to strangle him.

The other zombie came toward Willen, who didn't even struggle. Protest was useless on these wrecks of humans, and fighting them only wore down what little energy he already possessed.

The zombies took the two swamp beings up into Lond's chamber, and Willen gritted his teeth for another punishing round of pain. Lond, however, sat gazing at them quietly for a while. Near the door, Dumont, green eyes rimmed with red, also looked on.

"You are strong, *feu follet*," the mage acknowledged. "Bouki's pain has been severe, yet you are able to tolerate it. It is time for another tactic."

Willen kept his face expressionless, but his heart sank. What had Lond's warped mind come up with now? His first thought was of Bouki. Longears might have understood why he was being tortured and rationalized the pain. For Bouki, however, it was all senseless agony. The loah huddled as close to the floor as possible, trembling, his nose twitching.

Lond clapped his gloved hands. Brynn entered, carrying a sack in which an unseen creature struggled and kicked. Bouki started violently. He sat up on his haunches, nose twitching as he sniffed, and his eyes grew wide with dawning awareness and horror.

"No," he whispered.

Lond did not answer. He opened the sack and withdrew a frantically twisting rabbit, holding the terrified animal by its ears. "Poor little fellow," the wizard said in a tone that dripped sarcasm. With his free hand, he reached for a knife on the table. "He doesn't understand what's going on, does he? But you do."

Coolly, as if he were carving a piece of wood, Lond drew the razor-sharp blade across the animal's flank. The rabbit screamed shrilly as bright red blood flowed through brown fur.

The utter cruelty of Lond's systematically torturing one of Bouki's people drove the *loah* too far. With a cry of utter despair, he leaped up, kicking and flailing frantically. It took two zombies to hold him down. Willen, tethered to the *loah*, felt himself losing his already tenuous grip on his own sanity. He forced himself to focus on Larissa, envisioning her long white hair and her laughing blue eyes, but the image swam before the red haze of sympathetic terror that exploded from the rabbit.

"I'll stop if you tell me what I want to know," Lond promised.

"Anything!" the hysterical *loah* cried. Unfortunately for Lond, the rabbit possessed little real information, and his sobbing confession only underscored what Lond already knew: that the Maiden was still alive and strong, that Willen served her, that a rescue of sorts was being planned. Bouki knew nothing else.

The wizard turned his dark gaze upon the *feu follet*. "Your friend suffers greatly. A handful of words from you would ease his pain. And," he added for the loah's benefit, "that of his protected."

Bouki turned to the *feu follet*. "Willen, you must make him stop hurting one of my people! He's not using them for sustenance. Make him stop!"

Willen's heart swelled with sympathy for the creature, but there was no way he would betray Larissa and the Maiden. His silence was the only chance of freedom the trapped creatures aboard *La Demoiselle* had left. He could not answer, and, instead, looked at the floor.

Lond's rabbit still struggled, its hindquarters now saturated with scarlet. The wizard rose and went to the table. The large basin in the center was crusted with brown stains. "You can stop this, Willen," he said as he positioned the knife at the panicked rabbit's throat.

Willen shook his head mutely, closed his eyes, and steeled himself for the wave of shattering panic that would soon envelope him. Bouki's wail pierced Willen's soul, and he had little defense to set against the red haze of madness that the rabbit *loah* sent crashing down on him.

Willen stared stupidly at Lond, the *feu follet*'s intellect temporarily numbed by Bouki's terror. He could no longer think or understand words. He could see that the wizard wanted something, but somehow Lond's speech degenerated into angry rumblings and nonsensical shrieks. Willen and Bouki could only stare at him and whimper helplessly.

Lond snarled in disgust and ordered the two prisoners back down to the prison.

Once the physical contact had been broken, Willen slowly came back to his senses. On his second night aboard *La Demoiselle*, Tane and Jahedrin had gotten him thoroughly drunk. Willen didn't recall much of the evening, but he had a perfect recollection of the throbbing headache, heightened senses, and listlessness of the following morning. The *feu follet* felt like that now.

Bouki shuddered and wept alone in one corner. Since the earlier attack, the zombies had separated rabbit and fox. Now, the loah looked over at Willen with huge, fright-filled eyes.

"Tell him," he whispered. "I don't know anything about any attack. He'll stop hurting my people if you tell him."

"Bouki, I can't!" exclaimed Willen. "Our chance for escape will be ruined. Can't you see that?"

The colorcat glared at Willen. The beast was intelligent, Willen had discovered, though it was unable to speak and had no telepathic skills. The look with which it fixed Willen, however, left little doubt in the *feu follet*'s mind that the now-purple cat felt there was no escape being planned at all.

"Willen . . ." Bushtail's voice was strained. "We must stop Bouki from harming himself."

Wearily the *feu follet* looked at the rabbit loah and saw a sight that filled him with horror. Bouki simply could not take any more. He was slowly, deliberately, gnawing on his foreleg to free it from the manacles.

"Bouki!"

The rabbit paused and glanced over at Willen. His

own blood stained his mouth and whiskers, and there was the wildness of the mute beast in his liquid brown eyes.

"Bouki, don't. It won't work!"

The *loah* ignored him and resumed his grisly, single-minded task.

"Little friend, listen to me!" urged Bushtail, straining on his own manacles. He was tense and worried, and his voice lacked its usual nonchalant tone. "Suppose you chew all four of your legs off. It will be difficult to move, yes? How will you run away when you cannot hop? And you will still be bound by the metal noose!"

Bouki ignored all of their efforts to dissuade him. Willen, infused with grief and guilt, turned his face away. The rabbit's actions were all the more painful for their futility—the gnawed-off limb would grow back within a few hours. Even Bouki's desperate gesture therefore counted for nothing.

"This is my fault," he moaned. "All my fault." He began to cry in harsh, racking sobs. He glanced up when Dragoneyes entered. Catching his breath, Willen summoned anger to replace the grief. "What do you want now?"

"Willen, can you hear me?"

The *feu follet* gasped. Dragoneyes' mouth had moved, but the voice that issued forth had been Larissa's! He almost shouted for joy, then grew suspicious. "Is this a trick? Pretty clever, Lond, but it won't work."

"It's really me, Beloved. Remember when you shared your name with me?"

"Yes, I told you," he said, still cautious.

Dragoneyes shook his head. "Your fellow *feu follets* showed me."

"How can you speak through the dead? Larissa, what's happened? Are you—"

"Love, I'm fine. Listen to me. I can't keep this up much longer. We'll be coming soon, and I need to know everything you can tell me about Lond and Dumont. What's happening there now? I can't see you, I can only hear you."

"I'm in the slave hold. Can you get Dragoneyes to release us?"

"No. He'll say what I say, but he'll only do what he's used to doing. If I force him to free you, I'll lose all contact."

"Well, at least you can hear me. They've been torturing Bouki and me for information. We're both all right, though," he lied. He glanced over at the rabbit, winced, and looked away. Bouki had started on his other forepaw and was sitting in a scarlet puddle of his own blood.

"We're located past the storage area, in the livestock hold," the *feu follet* continued. "Dumont keeps a key in his room. You can get here either by going through the theater, or else there's a trap door in the floor of Dumont's cabin. Lond's well prepared. The Maiden will know what I mean by that. He has all kinds of bottles and candles and—"

"How are you imprisoned?"

"Just shackles for me. The rest of us are in cages or harnesses, some magical, some not."

"Courage, Beloved. It will not be too much longer now." Dragoneyes fell silent, then turned slowly and left, locking the door behind him. Willen felt disappointment and fear stab through him at the thought of the dancer's power to manipulate the dead.

"Oh, Larissa," he whispered to himself. "What kind of bargain have you struck?"

# TWENTY-TWO

"I hate moss," Jahedrin muttered as he peered at the dark, swampy water through the spokes of the wheel.

The pilot did indeed hate the gray-green airmoss that draped itself like a shroud across the trees. He hated the twisted, hunching cypress trees, too, and the tea-colored water that seemed to be more mud than liquid. The pilot hated the shallowness of the waterway—seldom did the depth exceed "mark one," or six feet—and the sickly sweet smell of the place.

More than anything else, though, Jahedrin hated what the fetid air of Souragne had done to his fellow crewmen. All but the pilots and the kitchen staff walked around with empty eyes and mechanical movements. "Seems like that swamp fever sucked the souls right out of 'em," Tane had said just yesterday. "D'you remember the story that pilot back in Invidia told us?"

"Yes," Jahedrin had replied. "About the man who walked in his sleep and still navigated the boat better than anybody else aboard."

Tane nodded. "Except that Invidian fellow said he wasn't asleep. Said he was dead." He looked at his friend archly. "Kinda makes you wonder, don't it?"

The idea had so disturbed Jahedrin that he had to pummel his fellow pilot until the fear had gone.

Now Jahedrin rolled his head back and forth, trying to loosen his tense neck and shoulders. Another thing the pilot hated was the night shift aboard *La Demoiselle*. It hadn't been so bad when Handsome Jack, and then Willen, had been rotated in and out. Now that Handsome Jack had been killed back in Port d'Elhour and Willen had disappeared, it was up to Jahedrin and Tane. Jahedrin rubbed his bleary eyes and peered ahead into the green, gray, and black shadows that were the swamp.

The pilot's hands lay lightly on the huge steering wheel of *La Demoiselle*, and a slight gesture was all that was needed to keep the boat on course.

"Thanks, Sardan," he said aloud to the bard who kept him company. "I think I'd fall asleep up here if you didn't come and play for me."

The blond singer strummed idly on his mandolin. "No problem. Since Larissa . . . well, the cast is pretty boring these days. They really hate this swamp."

The pilot snorted and eased the wheel starboard. "They ain't the only ones. I'll be mighty glad to see the last of this muddy pit. It's a minor miracle we ain't lodged on a sandbar yet." He yawned again. "Captain's friend Lond says we'll be clear of this place within a day or so."

Sardan rose and stood by his friend. "The captain won't leave without Larissa."

"He may have to. Trying to find her in this place . . . Well, I miss the pretty little thing, but I think it's a fool's errand."

"The captain doesn't."

Jahedrin was silent for a moment. Then he said in a low voice, "Think he'll find her?"

Sardan shrugged, feigning nonchalance. "Hope so."

The thick, marshy river twined ahead, vanishing into the darkness. The full moonlight caught its sparkle, but only made the night landscape seem more sinister. Sardan shook his head. It was hard to believe that Larissa was somewhere out in that malevolent darkness. He hoped she was safe.

"Here," he said to the weary Jahedrin as he carefully laid down his mandolin, "why don't you let me take the wheel for a while? You look pretty tired."

Jahedrin hesitated. "If the captain found out . . ."

"Oh, come on. I did it for Tane half his shift the other night."

Jahedrin's bushy eyebrows reached skyward, and he scowled. "Really? The lucky bastard. Damn, if he gets to sleep through half his shift, I should get at least an hour or so."

"If there's a problem, I'll wake you. Go ahead, take a quick nap. I won't let you sleep too long, I promise."

The pilot glanced back down at the river. The silence was broken only by the steady splashing of the paddlewheel. It didn't look as though they were in a particularly difficult part of the swamp.

Jahedrin closed his eyes for a second, then nodded. "All right, but you wake me the minute something don't look right to you, understand?"

Sardan nodded with seeming casualness. In reality, he was extremely excited about finally getting to pilot *La Demoiselle*. He'd lied about Tane, of course. Willen had talked a lot about the theory of piloting and had even let Sardan man the wheel for a few moments here and there, but Jahedrin was trusting him with the task unsupervised. It filled the bard with elation.

With a groan of pleasure, Jahedrin eased himself down on the divan. "Oh, damn, that feels good," he mumbled. The next sound Sardan heard from him was deep, regular snoring. The tenor smiled to himself as he caressed the wheel like a lover.

*La Demoiselle* was protected by magic, Sardan knew, and that magic was regulated by Captain Dumont, but there was a power in the simple act of steering the boat that thrilled the singer. Oh, you pretty thing, he thought to the boat, no wonder you're referred to as a lady.

It was an uneventful trip for the next hour or so, and Sardan's mercurial mind began to grow bored. He started to hum to himself, then sing softly, letting his mind drift. When he next glanced ahead and really noticed what he saw, his heart leaped into his mouth. There was something large moving in the water a few yards down the river. Sardan blanched.

"Jahedrin!"

The pilot bolted awake. "What is it, Sardan?"

The tenor pointed a trembling finger. Stumbling a bit, the still-drowsy pilot peered ahead, and he, too, went pale.

The lush vegetation that flourished on the banks and below the surface of the river was moving. Purposefully but slowly, vines were reaching to clasp one another across the waterway. Trees slid from their rooted places to form a dam. River weeds sprouted, waving in the night air. The way ahead would soon be completely blocked.

Jahedrin acted swiftly. He pulled on the whistle three times, hard, sending harsh cries to shatter the quiet of the night. Then, shouldering Sardan aside, he seized the boat telegraph, turning the handle to "reverse." He grabbed the speaking tube and blew into it, sending a piercing whistle to the crew in the engine room. "Full reverse!" he cried. "*Now!*"

Before Jahedrin realized it Dumont was there, coming up behind the pilot. He gazed out the window, his eyes narrowing speculatively. Mist was rising from the stagnant brown water like steam from a kettle—little, ghostlike wisps of fog that nonetheless were beginning to do a fine job of obscuring vision. Through gaps in the rapidly rising curtain, the captain could just glimpse the barrier of vegetation. As he watched, he could see the plants moving.

The boat slowed, stopped, then shuddered back to life again, this time backing away from the lump of encroaching plants.

"Stop reverse," he told the pilot, brushing past Sardan as if the blond singer wasn't even there.

"Captain?" Jahedrin was thoroughly confused.

"Stop reverse until further orders," Dumont growled. He had a hunch, and over the last twenty years he'd learned to listen to his hunches. Dumont clattered down the stairs back to his cabin and grabbed the Eye and his sword. He then hastened to the stern of the boat, running along the sun deck.

The giant paddlewheel was still. In the quiet, Dumont could hear the water dripping from the red spokes into the river. He held the pendant up to his eye, and he was able to see through the darkness and the rising mists. As he had feared, a similar blockage was being formed behind them as well. Something—or someone—was trying to trap them.

The captain slowly scanned the water from one side to the other, but nothing more was revealed to him. He slipped the pendant around his neck and let it drop. There was no sound at first, and then he heard it—a deep, heartbeat rhythm that sounded like distant drums.

Hadn't Larissa heard drums, that first night in Souragne?

Rage filled him, and he pounded his fist impotently on the railing. One of the trapped *feu follets* close to him flickered wildly for an instant before its light faded with a terrible finality.

Dumont didn't even notice. "Battle stations!" he boomed, running swiftly back toward the pilothouse and banging on every door he passed. He took the stairs down to the next deck, two at a time, and began waking up the cast members. "Get to the stage!" he demanded as they peered out sleepily at him. "Hurry!" The cast members muttered, but complied.

"Captain Dumont, what is it, that you disturb my men at this hour?" came Lond's cold voice from the deck above. The door to Lond's cabin was slightly ajar, revealing a dull, red gleam from within. The mage stood looking down at the captain of *La Demoiselle du Musarde*, his slim, cowled black form almost invisible in the darkness. Where his gloved hands clutched the railing, the *feu follets* went dark.

Dumont frowned. "Take a glance fore and aft and you'll see why I need my men on the main deck. I'm going to need your help in defending the boat."

He didn't wait for Lond's reaction, but hastened to the theater. The cast, in various stages of undress, sat sullenly in the chairs. "On stage," he barked.

Dumont faced his cast. His face was florid as he addressed them. "Now, you coddled bastards are going to sing for me."

The actors glanced at each other, confused. One of the chorus members, a spoiled young man who was Sardan's understudy, snapped irritably, "Captain, are you mad? Do you have any idea what time it is?"

Dumont leaped onto the stage, drawing his sword and running the unfortunate actor through with the bright blade. The youth's eyes bulged, and he collapsed to the stage. Someone screamed. Dumont whipped around, sword dripping crimson and jade eyes scanning the crowd for the miscreant. "Anyone else want to question my orders?"

There was utter silence. They stared at him with terror-filled faces.

"Fine. Now, damn you, sing!"

Elann, the elf who had understudied Cas's role, spoke up hesitantly. "What would you like to hear, sir?"

"The opening number, then 'She Waits For Him,' then 'Water Cold.' After that, just keep singing until I tell you to stop!" He tore out of the room as the cast hesitantly began the opening number. He paused only to magically lock the door before continuing to Lond's room.

* * * * *

Willen tensed, listening. Yes, it was singing all right. "Listen!" he cried. "They're singing in the theater. We've got to counteract it if we can. Anyone know any songs?"

Bushtail glanced at him, narrowing his eyes and cocking his head. "Yes, but I do not understand."

"The songs are spells," Willen explained quickly. "The fact that they're singing now, at this hour, means that my friends are boarding the boat. If we set up a counter-rhythm—"

"Say no more, mon ami!" The fox threw back his russet head and began to croon a song in his native tongue. Bushtail's voice was an astoundingly clear baritone.

Skreesha, the ravenkin, was still bound by the spell that enveloped his cage, and the colorcat had no idea what was going on and so remained elegantly silent. But the pseudodragon keened away, his voice a piercing yowl, and Bouki looked up.

His paws had all regenerated, but the legs were still covered with crusted blood. The noose still closed tightly about his thick, furry neck. "I can thump *and* sing," he announced proudly.

Willen's heart swelled, and unexpected tears stung his eyes. "Sometimes, Bouki, I think you're smarter than Longears."

The rabbit *loah* began to sing a piece of doggerel about how he always made the gumbo, but Longears ate it first. His enormous hind leg kept a pounding rhythm. For his part, Willen gave voice to a song of hunting that Deniri had once sung.

It was a riot of sounds within the hold, but Willen was

certain he'd never heard sweeter music. His heart rose with every note.

\* \* \* \* \*

When the boat had halted and then shifted into reverse without warning, many of Lond's magical vials had been knocked from their shelves. Some lay shattered on the floor, their gruesome contents forming sticky puddles on the wood. Others the evil wizard had managed to catch before any damage was done. The disturbance below had distracted him momentarily, but after speaking with Dumont he had returned to his room. Now, he was carefully placing all intact items in a box to guard against further jostling.

When someone began pounding on his door, Lond did not immediately respond. Finally, he waved a hand absently, unlocking the door. He knew who it was—Dumont. No one else aboard *La Demoiselle* would dare disturb him.

The captain stuck his head in. "You're needed on deck," he growled. "We're under attack."

Lond did not even glance up from his task of carefully packing the crates. "I shall be with you later, Captain," he said mildly.

Dumont was already halfway out the door, assuming that Lond would comply at once. He paused, turning a gaze of anger mixed with incredulity back to the wizard. "You'll come with me now, curse you. This is my boat, Lond, and when I give an order, it's followed!"

Lond glanced up from his task, and Dumont could see the glitter of his cold eyes in the dark shadows of the cowl. "You have apparently been oblivious as to what has been transpiring aboard this boat you hold so dear, Captain Dumont," he said icily. "Your crew now obeys me. With a handful of powder and the right word, I could take your soul just as easily. You are captain by my kindness, not your bluster. Have no fear—the safety of my person, such as it is, depends upon the safety of the boat. I'll defend it, certainly, but you shall not tell me when or how.

"For the moment, you must fend for yourself. That is, if you're sober enough to do so. It can be rather amusing to watch a drunken wizard try to cast spells. There are often interesting results." Lond laughed softly to himself.

Dumont flushed with shame and anger. Lond was right—the boat was no longer his. Swallowing his pride, he said, "Then at least surrender control of your zombies to me. I need them to help me maneuver the boat and to fight if—"

Irritated, the dark wizard waved a black-gloved hand in the captain's direction. "They will obey you until I have need of them. Go and defend your boat, Captain. I weary of this conversation."

Shame fled Dumont. Only hatred and rage remained. He stormed out of the room, slamming the door shut behind him. Once out of the stifling place, he breathed deeply of the humid air and examined his options.

He had a zombie crew, assembling stiffly even now on the main deck. He had two pilots who were still human, a terrified cast, and a handful of prisoners who were no doubt only too eager to turn against him. Then, suddenly, Dumont smiled.

He also had Gelaar.

He hastened toward the elven mage's cabin, but Gelaar was already awake and on deck. Dumont's heavy hand clamped down hard on his shoulder. The illusionist spun around quickly, but remembered to hood the hatred in his eyes before Dumont noticed.

"What is your will, Captain?"

Dumont scanned the river. The fog had increased, its damp fingers limned by the moon's glow. The banks, not all that far away, were completely obscured. Even

Dumont's clairvoyance yielded little, save to confirm that there was something out there hidden by magic.

"If I can't see them, they can't see me," he muttered to himself. To Gelaar he said, "Noise. Men's voices. An active crew preparing for battle. Stay up on this level unless I put you somewhere else. You'll be safer here than on the main deck."

Gelaar nodded and fished in his pouch until he found a small ball of wax. Quickly he worked the material in his hands until it was pliant, then nipped off a small piece and molded it into his ear. He pushed the sleeves of his heavy robe back from his lower arms, and began to cast the spell.

Almost at once, voices arose. Gelaar was an extremely powerful illusionist, and Dumont allowed himself the briefest of grins as he recognized the voices of individual crewmen spewing typical comments.

"Here y'are, Captain. We're ready for them. No way they'd attack when we've got this," came Dragoneyes' voice. Dumont's grin faded. My friend, he thought to himself, what I would not give to hear that hint of cold laughter in your voice again.

He shook himself. It would not save *La Demoiselle* for him to grow maudlin at a time like this. "Have the men talk about the powerful wards on the boat, and then make her glow."

Gelaar obeyed. The illusionary men jabbered excitedly about Dumont's new spells, and suddenly the boat began to radiate a cool blue light, studded here and there with the multicolored sparkles of the *feu follets*. There were indeed wards on the boat, wards conjured and reinforced by the music of *The Pirate's Pleasure*. They had already been put into operation when the cast began singing. The radiance conjured by Gelaar was purely cosmetic, but anyone who attempted to hostilely board the showboat when the wards were at full strength would have to fight for every inch.

Bathed in the illusory glow, Dumont went to the pilothouse. Tane and Jahedrin were both there, tense, fully dressed and carrying weapons.

"What's going on, Captain?" Tane asked, his eyes flickering about as he tried vainly to see through the almost solid wall of fog. "And what are those drums?"

"Not sure," Dumont confessed. "There's something out there and I think it or they mean to board us."

"I found one I think I can handle and—oh." Sardan, who was running up the stairs with a sword in his hand, stopped when he saw Dumont.

The captain glowered at his leading man. "What are you doing on deck, boy? Why aren't you down in the theater, singing with the rest of the bloody cast?"

Sardan flushed, but remained resolute. "I can fight," he said stubbornly.

Dumont was about to protest, then gave up. "Maybe you can at that. You'll die at least as well as the rest of us, at any rate. Let's get down to the main deck. No need to stay in the pilothouse when we're not going anywhere." The four men stepped outside and began to move toward the main deck.

There was only the faintest increase of wind to herald the onslaught of bats. Thousands of the winged creatures descended upon *La Demoiselle*, crawling on the glowing blue deck, flapping their leathery wings about the crewmen's heads, searching for toeholds in their clothing. Sharp teeth gnawed at the flesh of the men's faces, searching hungrily for the eyes. Instantly the men threw up their hands to protect themselves.

Dumont sang a few sharp, shrill notes, and the bats still on the wing veered off and disappeared into the roiling white mists. Those who were on the deck or clinging to the men's clothing, however, continued to crawl about. "Ignore them," Dumont cried. "We've got worse things to worry about."

Jahedrin's arms were covered with small, bleeding

bites, and both Tane and Sardan had wounds on their faces. Their vision, however, was intact. Dumont glanced downward at the zombies on the main deck and saw that they had not fared so well. Several of them patted dully at their faces, bumping into one another or the railings. They had not reacted swiftly enough to avoid being blinded.

The captain caught his breath and listened, motioning the men to continue down toward the main deck. The drumbeat had increased its tempo. Dumont knew that some people used the sounds to carry messages, and he wondered what kind of generals were giving orders in this miserable place.

Out of the corner of his eye, he saw Gelaar standing with his eyes closed. The elf's slender hands moved gently, and his lips mouthed a spell. Dumont wasn't sure what he was doing, but it was a reassuring sight nonetheless.

Another, more sinister sight brought the captain's attention down to the water. Because of the mist and the darkness, he couldn't see far beyond *La Demoiselle*, but right near the edge of the boat he saw movement in the water. Dumont ran to the railing, bringing the eye pendant up and peering through it.

At first, it looked as though crocodiles were approaching the boat. Then Dumont saw a human male in the water. There would hardly be humans swimming in crocodile-infested waters. A glance revealed that all sides of the boat were now coming under attack, and Dumont gritted his teeth and charged down the stairs, sword drawn.

Some of the men had already boarded from the river, and Dumont was pleased to see that the zombies were holding their own. He threaded his way through the combat, fighting the whole time, and slew two of the big, ugly men. A splashing sound to his right told him that someone else was trying to board, and Dumont wheeled to face the intruder. He grasped the railing and gazed down onto the brass ladder that connected the boat with the yawls.

Dumont found himself looking into the eyes of his beautiful young ward. She had only just reached out to climb the ladder and was still in the water. Her white hair was loose and floated behind her. It blended with the spiraling wisps of mist and the blue light of the boat to create an eerie, otherworldly halo. The black water lapped under her chin, and the rest of her body was lost to his sight.

Larissa's blue eyes stared up at him, and in them was a wildness that it would have been impossible for Dumont to conceive a few weeks ago, before they had traveled to this cursed island. For that brief instant, she did not look quite human to him, though her beauty seemed to have increased with her savageness.

"Larissa!" Dumont cried hoarsely, suddenly seeing a brown, scaly shape with yellow eyes swimming rapidly toward the girl. He dropped his sword and started to descend the ladder, one arm reaching out to pull her to safety. His outburst shattered the moment, and she vanished with scarcely a ripple beneath the inky surface, merging with the dark waters as if she had been made of them. The last glimpse Dumont had of the dancer was her pale hair disappearing into the depths.

White-hot agony shot through his arm, then Dumont was dimly aware of a loud splash as water slapped him. He stared down at the bleeding stump of his arm, ragged just below the elbow. The crocodile that had bitten off his right hand mouthed the severed limb, using its needle-sharp teeth to maneuver it for easier swallowing, then gulped it down whole.

Dumont stumbled back from the railing, his left hand clutching the slippery raw flesh of the wound in a futile attempt to staunch the pumping blood. The water below him was filled with noise, and the deep bellow of one of the giant reptiles rumbled through the clammy night air.

Lond, Dumont thought fuzzily as he stumbled back in an attempt to get clear of the fighting. Perhaps Lond could heal the maimed limb. Jahedrin came up to him, ripping up his own shirt for use as a tourniquet as he ran. Dumont extended his arm while his crewman tied the material about the pumping wound.

"Lond," he rasped. Jahedrin helped Dumont climb the stairs. He caught the captain once, when the bigger man nearly fainted.

Lond fell silent as Dumont entered his cabin. Jahedrin, seeing the horrifying room for the first time, swore softly and made an ancient gesture to protect himself from evil. Lond looked impassively at the bloody limb.

"You've got to heal me. My boat and I are the only chance you've got left," Dumont managed. He blinked rapidly as Lond's black shape swam before him. The wizard laughed humorlessly.

"As usual, Captain Dumont, you have it backward. I'm the only chance *you've* got left. But," he added, "I do not think you truly wish my help in healing. You might not like the results."

Dumont had spent his life as an active, healthy man. The thought of living without a limb—his right hand—made him reckless. "Do whatever you want, just so long as I'm healed."

Lond shrugged. "As you will." He began to rummage through his grisly collection and casually selected a long, sharp knife. He brushed past Dumont and Jahedrin, who instinctively drew back, and went onto the deck.

"Captain," said Jahedrin in a faint voice, glancing about at the ghoulish room, "what have you gotten us involved with?"

Dumont did not answer for a moment, the pain from his arm choking his words. At last he said, "The world of nightmares. And I don't know that I can get us back out."

Lond returned, Brynn and Dragoneyes in tow. He was carrying something in his cloak. Before Dumont truly realized what was happening, the two dead crewmen had him in a viselike grip. Lond approached. It was then that Dumont saw what the black-cloaked mage was carrying—the desiccated arm of a zombie.

"No!" the captain cried, but his protests were in vain. He heard Lond chanting. A sudden cold replaced the pulsing hot agony in his severed arm, a cold that burned instead of numbed and crept up his arm to his shoulder. Violent pain slashed through him as the dead arm was joined to his pulped flesh. Dumont opened his mouth and wailed, a long, high sound that seemed to go on forever. When Dumont next became aware of himself he was on all fours on the deck. Lond's door was closed, and the zombies had disappeared.

Jahedrin crouched by his side. "Captain?"

Dumont's left arm was brawny and strong, the fingers thick and clever. His right arm was little more than strings of flesh that barely hid the bone. He moved his arm, and like some nightmarish mirror, the dead flesh unnaturally attached to his own living body moved in response.

\* \* \* \* \*

Larissa didn't witness Dumont's mutilation. She had slipped beneath the water, breathing it easily. Dumont's wards had negated her invisibility when she touched the boat's hull.

She swam beneath the flat-bottomed showboat, accompanied by two lezards. The lezards were similar to minxes, creatures that could assume either animal or human form at will and with astonishing speed. They were formidable allies indeed, and Larissa was glad to have them on her side. Some had chosen one form, some the other; hence Dumont's confusion when he saw crocodiles and men swimming together.

The three surfaced on the other side, and Larissa looked around to see how the second wave of attack was doing. Kaedrin, paddling aboard a large raft, had arrived and was preparing to board. With him on the raft was Longears, who was aflame with the desire for revenge, and a sleek gray wolf that was only a little larger than the rabbit *loah*.

Larissa had thought the former ranger an impressive-looking man when she had first met him. Now, he was truly intimidating. There was no playfulness in that muscular build, only a taut sense of readiness. His armor was ancient, but it would serve, and his old weapons had been newly honed and cleaned.

He and the lezards who had chosen human form had collected a large number of cast-off buck antlers, which Larissa and the Maiden had magically strengthened. The warriors had then tied thick, sturdy ropes to the horns.

Larissa swam over to the ranger and nodded. Kaedrin nodded back, then fastened his piercing gaze upon the railings, swung one of the ropes with the attached antlers a few times to build up momentum, then let the makeshift grappling hook fly. It caught on the railing of the cabin deck, with a tinny, clanking sound. The others followed suit, each aiming for various levels, and began to shinny up ropes. Now the zombies would be spread over various levels as they fought the intruders.

Larissa let herself start to sink, relaxing and merging with the water. Then she snapped her body like a mermaid and pushed against the water with arms, shooting back up toward the surface. The river obeyed her. It gently lifted her, as on a giant's hand, until she could reach out for the railings and clamber onto the deck.

A quick glance down showed her that the vanguard of

the swamp's army had made it safely aboard as well and were apparently holding their own. Even as she watched, a tall man with a wicked grin and sharp yellow eyes ducked a skillful sword stroke. The lezard abandoned his pretense, and the grin widened. A thick, scaly tail lashed out, ripping the lezard's now-unnecessary trousers. The flailing limb knocked one zombie to the deck, where Kaedrin's wolf leaped for its throat. Half-human, half-reptile, the lezard lunged at his prey. The sword with which the unfortunate zombie hacked at the beast inflicted only minor damage against the suddenly hard, scaly skin, whereas the mammoth jaws crunched the dead man's head in a single snap.

Larissa shuddered and looked away. A short time ago, she would never have dreamed that she would ally with such violent creatures. But, she told herself, the beings she fought against were far worse. As she hastened to the empty pilothouse, she looked about for Lond. She knew his cabin was on this level, but the mage was nowhere to be seen. The dancer did catch a glimpse of Gelaar, though, standing alone on the sun deck and casting a spell. He didn't appear to have noticed her, fortunately.

She slipped inside the pilothouse and headed down the stairs to Dumont's cabin. Larissa knew where he kept the keys—dangling from the horned skull over his bed. Her luck seemed to be holding, for the large, gold key ring with its many keys was still in place.

She reached for it eagerly—and her fingers closed on empty air. Shocked, Larissa tried again. There were no keys there. It was just an illusion! She let out a sharp cry of panic.

"Looking for these?" came a voice behind her.

# TWENTY-THREE

Larissa spun around.

Gelaar stood behind her, twirling the key ring almost playfully in his thin hand. "I just arrived here myself," he explained. "I ducked into the wardrobe—I was afraid you were Dumont. Do not worry, Larissa, I want to help the prisoners, too. Dumont has my daughter trapped, and I hope perhaps one of the prisoners knows a way to free her."

Larissa blinked, totally confused. "But I just saw you on deck."

Gelaar gave her a quick, conspiratorial smile. "I am an illusionist." He gestured with the key ring. "On deck right now, I am also an illusion. Dumont still thinks I'm there casting spells."

Larissa smiled hesitantly, then laughed. For the first time, she actually believed that the daring attack just might succeed. "There's a trap door—"

"Here," Gelaar finished, pulling back the carpet. Together, they tugged the heavy door open. Larissa appropriated one of the small oil lamps and descended the narrow stairs first.

"Who's in charge of your side?" Gelaar asked as he carefully lowered himself hand over hand.

Larissa had to smile to herself. "I am."

"What?"

"A lot has happened, Gelaar. If we get through this, I'll tell you, but right now I'm the only one who knows enough magic to free the prisoners. That's why I'm here instead of behaving like a good general and sitting safely behind the lines."

She reached the bottom and looked around. The oil lamp's light revealed boxes, tools, sacks of flour, and other items. "We're in the storage room. The livestock area should be—" she paused, hearing the prisoners' singing, and pointed wordlessly to the door. Gelaar began to sort for the keys.

"Wait," Larissa said. She approached the door, laid a gentle hand on it, and closed her eyes. Politely, she asked the wood if it would be safe for her to enter.

What life was left in the wooden door flickered faintly. *Not safe*.

"The door's trapped," she told Gelaar. Larissa closed her eyes again, and began to move her feet gently on the wooden floor. She swayed back and forth, then placed her hands on the wood in a silent command. The door began to radiate a soft blue light. The chorus inside fell silent. Larissa stepped back and nodded to Gelaar, who opened the door.

Larissa rushed in. "Willen!" she cried, falling to her knees on the dirty straw behind him and embracing him tightly.

He returned the embrace as best his manacles would permit him, whispering her name over and over and kissing her desperately when her lips found his. Tears were in both pairs of eyes when she pulled away and looked at his manacles. She almost lost her composure at the sight, but quickly redirected her pain into cold anger at Dumont and Lond.

She rose and began to dance. The manacles began to glow with an orange light. The *feu follet* felt the metal grow warm, but just when it reached the point of being painfully hot the iron bracelets snapped open and fell off his wrists and ankles.

Gelaar, meanwhile, had unlocked the pseudodragon's cage and was now freeing Skreesha. Larissa turned to the fox loah, and his harness, too, began to radiate orange light. Willen quickly freed Bushtail.

"What's going on up there?" the *feu follet* asked Larissa.

Larissa turned her attention to Bouki, who was still singing his song about gumbo. Bushtail sped to his friend, leaped up, and pulled the end of the noose from the ceiling with his teeth. Larissa eased it off Bouki's head, wincing at the thin line of dried blood crusted on the animal's neck. The fox licked Bouki's face furiously. The rabbit loah blinked, his large brown eyes focusing on his friend. Puzzled, he raised a forepaw to his throat and patted it gently. "Look, Bushtail!" he exclaimed brightly, "I'm free!"

"The zombies and what's left of Dumont's crew are being kept busy by lezards," Larissa answered. "I think the rats and other small animals should be aboard by now." She straightened, and looked over at Willen. "I'm going after Lond."

"Larissa, no, he's—"

She raised a hand to silence her lover's protest. "I have to. As long as he can control the zombies, we don't stand a chance. Now that you're free," she continued, turning to include all the prisoners, "you can either leave or fight with us."

Bushtail glanced up, and there was hatred in his eyes. "For myself, I will fight."

"Me, too," said Bouki. All the creatures were nodding. The ravenkin was perched on Gelaar's shoulder, and the mage had tears in his eyes.

"Skreesha knows how to free Aradnia," he said thickly. "I must tend to her, first, before—"

"Of course," Larissa agreed. "The rest of you—on

deck."

They emerged into the theater, to the astonishment of the still-singing cast members. The performers fell silent, staring at Larissa as if they had seen a ghost.

"Larissa!" one of the chorus girls cried, looking at the menagerie that followed the white-haired dancer. "What—"

"No time to explain. The boat is under attack from my friends. They won't hurt you. Stop singing and stay in here. You should be safe."

Before they parted, Larissa to Lond's room and Willen to the battle, they held one another tightly.

"Be careful," Willen warned, knowing how foolish it sounded.

She clutched his hands. "You, too."

He kissed her once, lightly, tenderly, then he and the former prisoners slipped outside. She waited a moment, then followed suit, keeping as much to the shadows as possible as she hastened up two flights of stairs.

* * * * *

Kaedrin staggered back, grateful for an instant's lull in the fighting. He surveyed the situation grimly.

Zombies, most of them with huge chunks of dry flesh missing, were still battling with the lezards, but there were many corpses cluttering the decks. The smaller creatures had now arrived, and the decks crawled with rats, foxes, and other nimble mammals who tripped the zombies and then tore at their flesh when they went down.

To Kaedrin's pleasure, he suddenly saw Longears hasten across the deck and leap, hind legs first, at a zombie. The *loah*'s powerful hind legs kicked the undead creature's face in.

"Tired already?" came a teasing voice, shot through

with strain. Kaedrin whirled, joy and fear mixing in his heart as he saw Deniri clamber on board. She looked at him, love on her sharp face. "Couldn't let you have all the fun, could I?"

"Deniri, it's too dangerous—"

"If you can fight, so can I. You think I'd let you die without getting a chance to kill a few myself?" Without another word, she shimmered and twisted into her mink form and scurried across the deck. He saw her launch herself at a zombie's throat and begin chewing the dry flesh, then she was lost to his view.

"Kaedrin, look out!"

The voice was Willen's, and the ranger reflexively brought his shield up and raised his sword as he turned. A cutlass thwacked heavily on the rounded shield as a zombie with slitted golden eyes swung at him. Kaedrin parried, slowly but in time. He managed to get a clear blow at the silver-haired corpse, but another zombie saw an opening in Kaedrin's defense and struck. The blow bounced off the ranger's armor, but the breath was knocked out of him for an instant.

There was a brown blur, and then he realized that the second zombie had a huge mink at his throat. The beast's teeth ripped furiously, and the zombie's head was severed from the body. The mink nudged it overboard, but the headless body continued to move. Kaedrin returned his attention to the golden-eyed zombie, but saw to his horror that the walking undead had ceased taking an interest in him and instead turned his blade upon the mink. With a quick chopping motion, he stabbed the animal.

Deniri squealed as she died, impaled upon Dragoneyes' sword. Even in her death throes, she bared her teeth and futilely gnawed on the metal blade, her sharp claws shredding anything they came in contact with, even her own flesh. Her blood stained the floorboards.

As Dragoneyes stepped on the furry corpse, holding

it down so he could tug his sword free, Kaedrin's sword ran him through. With a lost wail, the hermit of the swamp hurled himself into the thickest part of the fray, hacking wildly at anything, friend or foe, that came within the bite of his weapon. Willen, seizing a sword from the dead hand of a lezard, tried to go after the grief-crazed hermit, but saw him go down under a press of undead bodies a few moments later.

"Kaedrin!" Willen screamed. All at once he felt large, dead hands clamp about his throat. Slowly the zombie squeezed. Willen twisted, his hands flying up to pry the unbelievably strong fingers from his neck.

The pressure eased and something warm and wet spattered the back of Willen's head. He stumbled away, turning to see who had attacked him. Brynn now had no head. As if the zombie were confused, his hands went to pat the stump of a neck, turning crimson with the flood that still spouted from the shoulders.

With a grunt, Willen grasped Brynn's body and, pushing and tugging, heaved it overboard. It fell with a loud splash, and the *feu follet* turned to see who his savior might be.

Sardan gazed at him with a rather shocked expression. He, too, had droplets of red sprinkled on his face. The singer glanced down at the sword in his hand. "That sword move was from the third act," he muttered. "Damn, it worked. Where the bloody blazes have you been, Will?"

"Imprisoned," Willen managed. Speech was still difficult, and he rubbed his throat. "Are you with me or against me?"

Sardan made a terrible attempt at nonchalance. "I just saved your life, so I don't think I'll try to kill you now."

"Then start attacking the zombies."

Sardan's eyes flew wide. Willen didn't have the time to be gentle. "Yes, they're all dead, Sardan. The things from the swamp are alive, and they're my friends. Come on."

He turned, directing his sword against another of the animated corpses. Still rather stunned at his actions, Sardan nodded, glanced down at the crimson sword, then hurried to join his friend.

* * * * *

Lond watched the battle with the remote interest of a vulture watching two animals battle to the death. Most of the fighting was occurring on the lower three decks. The few foolish lezards who had attempted to attack the dark mage had gotten facefuls of powder for their pains. Already, a few of them were starting to rise, lumbering down to the lower levels to attack their erstwhile allies who stared in shock as they were slain by a friend.

He had enjoyed the little trick he had played on Dumont. For all its callousness, Lond's decision to attach the zombie limb had probably saved the captain's life. He was off somewhere, no doubt, lamenting his fortune.

The swamp creatures were slowly being outnumbered by undead crewmen and their own zombie kin. Lond smiled beneath his cowl. He'd be out of Souragne within the next day or so, free to unleash his skills on a new land.

He realized that he had emptied his vials of powder, and turned to go back to his cabin for more. It was then that he saw the flash of white disappearing into his cabin.

Larissa, curse her white hair. Lond hastened to catch up with her, but she already had a head start of a good minute or two.

The young dancer was appalled at what she found in Lond's cabin, and she lost a few precious seconds simply staring in horror and fighting back nausea from the stench. What was it Willen had said? The frighteningly decorated bottles were important to him. Some of the bottles contained nothing worse than ingredients for his spells; others, Larissa knew, contained something far more horrifying. The Maiden had explained that, not only did the former bocoru animate corpses, he also kept their souls.

Larissa's mouth set in a grim line. She ran to the first box within reach and began hurling its contents to the floor. The vials broke, their contents spilling in sluggish pools of liquid or piles of various powders. She began on the second box.

The first warning she had of Lond's presence was his growling voice chanting an incantation. She moved more swiftly, whipping her white hair back and forth, up and down, and visualized the bottles shattering in the third box.

A sudden wind came out of nowhere, whirling about Lond and snatching away the words of power even as he uttered them. The magical wind conjured by Larissa had found the box and lifted it up to the ceiling. Larissa made a sharp move with her hand, and the box upended. Every one of the glass vials in the box fell to the floor, breaking with high-pitched sounds.

What happened next took only an instant, but it seemed like an eternity to the shocked and horrified young dancer. That unpleasant but very ordinary noise was suddenly joined by others. A low groaning, as of several voices, began to swell from the broken shards of glass. All at once clouds of light shot upward, whirling crazily about the room. Then, as if by an unheard signal, they merged into a cloud and went straight for Lond.

The mage cried out and backed away. Larissa seized her opportunity and bolted for the door. She had only run a few yards down the deck before she collided into an unseen wall and hit the wooden deck hard. Rolling over, she saw that Lond was unhurt. The cloud of trapped souls had been unable to harm him and had vanished. His dark form advanced on her malevolently.

"You've lost me my zombies, Whitemane, but there are more where they came from. As you taste death, know that you have failed everyone who counted on you." He raised his hands.

Larissa tried to think of something, but her mind went absolutely blank. In desperation, she rooted herself, hoping that somehow something would spring to mind.

At that moment, a deep bellow went up behind Lond. "Run, Larissa!" came Dumont's haggard voice. "Leave this bastard to me!"

Startled, Lond wheeled just in time to deflect the captain's sword stroke. It still bit deeply into his right shoulder, and Lond roared in outrage at the insult that Dumont would dare attack him. He wiped the blood up with his left hand, then smeared it together with his right.

Dumont had begun whistling a spell when Lond raised his right hand and squeezed it tightly. Blood dripped down onto the deck. It hissed like a snake as it made contact with the wood.

The captain froze. His face grew gray, and the sword fell from his suddenly numb left hand. His right hand, the zombie limb, crept up to his chest and began to claw frantically. It ripped easily through his shirt, through the flesh of his chest, only to be thwarted by the breastbone. Undaunted, the zombie limb curled into a fist and smashed its way into Dumont's chest cavity. The undead hand groped about, then emerged with what it had been seeking.

Dumont's heart.

It still beat and blood spurted crazily. The hand tightened, and then the heart was only so much pulpy flesh. The captain's eyes rolled back in his head, and he collapsed to the deck. The zombie arm continued to scrabble with a life of its own.

Larissa stared, sickened and full of horror. Her mind was numb for a terrifying instant. She had once loved Dumont like a father and, despite his betrayal, still cared for him. "Uncle," she whispered.

"Meddler," Lond snarled angrily. "Now, Whitemane, it's your turn."

Larissa's eyes blazed with fury. This time, the young woman was ready for him. The few seconds she had rooted herself had given her an idea. She pressed her body to the wooden floor, sending a message to whatever life still lingered there. Her command shivered through the wooden planks until it reached the fanciful carving of a griffin that adorned the pilothouse.

Jeweled eyes blinked. Gold-leafed wings opened, and with a sound like a spar breaking in a storm, the animated carving tore itself free from the confines of the pilothouse. It hovered for a fraction of an instant, then, with the determination of an eagle bearing down on its prey, it flew straight for Lond.

The wizard, however, had ample warning. As the wooden beast bore down on him, beak open and claws outstretched, Lond uttered a spell. The griffin collided with the invisible wall Lond erected, and splintered with a horrible cracking sound. It fell to the deck behind Lond, sticks of wood now and nothing more.

Larissa tasted bitter frustration. She had expended a great deal of energy tonight, and the griffin had taken almost all of what remained. Lond turned slowly around to face her. Panting, Larissa couldn't even summon enough strength to rise. She waited defiantly for the killing blow, her face radiating her loathing.

But Lond did nothing. He surveyed her critically for a moment, not even moving when Larissa haltingly got to her feet to face him.

"Did you really think to stop me with a wooden toy?" he asked her. "Fruit and flower magic is nothing, nothing at all. There's only so much you can do by following all the rules. When you make new rules for yourself, only then can there be no limits to your power."

He stepped closer to her, and she backed away, one slim hand reaching out to the railing for support. "You have a great deal of ability," Lond continued silkily. "No wonder the Maiden was so eager to enlist your aid. But you see how quickly fruit and flower magic fails you. Blood and bone—there lies true power. And I can teach you, Larissa Snowmane. I can guide you along the path."

Larissa kept her eyes on her enemy, but inwardly she was calculating how long it would take her to reach the pilothouse and from there the open space of the roof. If she could escape down the other side—

"Why make something grow greener when you can twist it to your whim? Why encourage life, when death is so much more predictable and manageable? Why be like the *feu follets* when the will-o'-the-wisps are what the people fear and respect?"

He tore at his long sleeves, ripping the black fabric. A knife appeared in his hand, long and sharp, and he touched it to the flesh of his lower arm, then sliced. The waning moon cleared a cloud, and Larissa had a perfect view of that arm.

It was the size and shape of an ordinary man's arm, but the incalculable crisscross of scars made it horrific. Blood magic was bought, not given, and Lond had bought the dark knowledge with his own crimson fluid. Again and again he had cut open his flesh, sometimes removing entire chunks of meat, until there was no spot on the arm that was not scar tissue. The light glistened on the lumpy, shiny flesh.

Red liquid dribbled down, dropping onto the deck with an ominous hiss. Clawing hands tore off the black cloak. The evil mage wore only a tunic beneath his concealing robes, and every bit of visible flesh was a scar.

His face was the most monstrous of all. In his diabolic bartering, he had bargained away most of the flesh of his cheeks. White bone gleamed through like an emerging death's head. Only the eyes, it seemed, had been spared the blade. They gleamed evilly, coldly, out of a mass of raised puckers.

The pool of blood glittered blackly in the moonlight, then began to ooze slowly in Larissa's direction.

Now, thought the dancer. She made a dash for the pilothouse stairs and from them leaped gracefully onto the boat's roof. She ran across the flat surface and was about to slip down the other side when she came face-to-face with a zombie climbing up to meet her.

It was Dumont. His eyes were empty as they fastened on her, and his blood-covered zombie arm reached out and closed around her ankle. Larissa stifled a cry, wrenching her ankle free, and moved farther down. This time, an undead lezard clambered onto the roof with slow and determined movements.

Larissa glanced wildly around. They were closing in on her from all sides now, and even as she watched, Lond appeared on the roof. He was gently levitated as if by an unseen hand, and he landed with a quietness that mocked Larissa's panic.

Abruptly, terror fled Larissa. Her back was against the wall now, and there was no room for fear. She straightened and regarded Lond coolly.

"I am familiar with your path, Alondrin the Betrayer," she said in icy tones as the zombies moved ever closer. "Your dead men do not frighten me. I have dined with the Lord of the Dead, been a welcome guest in *Maison de la Détresse*. I am aboard this boat as emissary of Anton Misroi, someone I believe you know well. Did you really think that he would have let me gather what power I wield on my own?" She laughed, and there was no mirth in the sound.

With poised elegance, she raised her arms and settled herself on her feet. "Misroi was my tutor. He instructed me in the Dance of the Dead. Permit me to demonstrate."

Larissa withdrew the riding crop Misroi had given her and struck her left hand smartly. The blow stung terribly and blood appeared, but she paid it no mind.

The crop lengthened, twisted, transformed into the snake Larissa had worked with earlier in the swamp. It did not bother Larissa at all now. She had conquered that particular fear and was in absolute control of her magic. She was a whitemane, a dancer, and if she shrank from this task, all would be lost.

Without the slightest shudder, she placed the serpent about her neck and shoulders. Swiftly the creature twined itself about her arms. Its weight was cool and comforting, dry and smooth, and Larissa felt new confidence surging through her.

The snake draped about her like a living shawl, Larissa began to dance. Without a second thought, she forsook all the spells she had hitherto learned under the tutelage of the Maiden, and launched into the terrifying Dance of the Dead.

# TWENTY-FOUR

Willen's attention had been briefly diverted when the griffin masthead had cracked to its new life and began to fly. He could pay it little heed, however, because he was fighting with Yelusa, Lond's first nonhuman zombie.

She fought with a sword that Willen wildly thought must be heavier than she was, swinging the weapon with little accuracy but great force. He parried, the impact jarring his arm painfully. Yelusa had one distinct advantage over the *feu follet*: she could fight forever, and Willen was already starting to grow tired.

He decapitated the owl maid, to his own surprise, after she suddenly paused, sword arm raised with a blow that never fell. Gasping, Willen dared a quick look around. All of the zombies had ceased fighting. As one, they turned and started up the stairs to the uppermost level of the boat.

Sardan hurried up to him. The grim expression on his face was far different than the bard's usual insouciant, slightly bored grin. Willen doubted if the handsome blond tenor would ever be the same. "What's happening?" he panted, wiping sweat from his brow with a bloodstained hand.

"I don't know," Willen replied, "but I don't like it. Why

would Lond pull all his zombies out of the fi—Larissa!"

Sardan blanched. "She's here? You're letting her fight? She doesn't know—"

"Sardan, she's our leader. And she's up there, I know it. Come on!"

Willen ran up the stairs with a speed he had not realized his human body possessed. A terrible fear coursed through him. Larissa, powerful though she might be, could never stand alone against the entirety of Lond and his undead army. The *feu follet* had no idea what he might do to save her—his magic was mainly defensive—but he knew he had to try.

He arrived on the rooftop, lungs heaving. Sardan followed. The *feu follet* was behind the crowd of zombies and so couldn't see what was going on.

Larissa's voice floated to him on the sultry night air. "Misroi was my tutor. He instructed me in the Dance of the Dead. Permit me to demonstrate."

Horror flooded through Willen at the words, a horror so great it incapacitated him for a moment. He staggered with the weight of the information. Sardan appeared behind him and placed a steadying hand on his friend's elbow. The *feu follet* summoned his strength and spun around. "Forgive me," he panted, then punched Sardan in the jaw. The tenor went reeling, almost more stunned by the gesture than its consequences.

"What the—?"

Sardan's question was never completed. Willen landed another punch, wincing at the pain in his hand, and Sardan's eyes rolled back in his head. He collapsed to the deck.

Willen knew Sardan would be safe now. He wondered for an instant if there was still time to stop Larissa, but even as his mind pondered the question his feet were taking him toward the bow of the boat, where Larissa had begun to dance in infernal ecstasy.

He shoved his way past the frozen zombies, and then, unexpectedly, Larissa danced into his field of vision.

Willen gasped. He had hoped to tackle her blindly, make the beautiful young woman stop the dance that would surely destroy her and any living human who saw her perform. He had seen her, though. Now he was incapable of tearing his gaze away from her lithe, graceful form.

He was caught, fatally caught, and he felt a deathly cold seep through him. Willen had resisted Lond's evil magic, but he was a creature of Souragne, more so than any natural human could have been. There was no way the *feu follet* could fail to succumb to the magic of the lord of the land, the magic Misroi himself had taught to the dancer. His arms ceased to have feeling, and the numbness crept through his thighs and legs. He could feel his body dying, surrendering control, limb by limb, joint by joint.

The last thing that abandoned him, drifting away gently, reluctantly, was his mind. He thought of Larissa, and tears spilled down his face, tears for all the lost opportunities, for the joys and sorrows that would now never be his to experience.

The last conscious thought Willen had before the dark magic of the Dance of the Dead claimed him forever was how beautiful Larissa was when she danced.

\* \* \* \* \*

Larissa knew she had nothing more to fear from Lond. She was dancing with death now, and the wizard's magic was a paltry song compared to the wild music Larissa heard in her mind. The dancer leaped, and the snake moved with her, twining about her like a lover's hand.

She felt the cold begin from deep within her. It was the cold of death and worse, and it began to seep outward. Fear brushed her, a hint of what she had experienced at *Maison de la Détresse*. As she had discovered, for a living, breathing creature to perform the Dance of the Dead, even with the permission of the lord of the land, was to risk turning into a zombie oneself.

The dance became wilder, and Larissa began to perspire despite the terrible chill that was rampaging through her body. She no longer knew where or who she was; she had become the dance. With a final gasp that almost drained her, she flung up her hands and commanded the zombies: Stop Lond!

For a moment, nothing happened. She had dropped to her knees on the deck. Panting, Larissa brushed her mop of white hair out of her face and glanced up.

Defeat washed over her like acid. The zombies stood frozen in their places; they made no move to attack her enemy.

Lond knew what the Dance of the Dead could do, and he had been unable to do anything save shield his eyes and wait until it was completed. Now he lowered his hands and stared first at Larissa, then at the still-immobile corpses. Shocked and pleased, he began to laugh.

"What a lovely show!" he shrieked. "You have halted my zombies, but you cannot control them. You are safe from them now, perhaps, but, oh, child, you are not safe from me!"

As he began to mutter an incantation, the swamp began to boil. Larissa gasped and got to her feet, staring down at the dark river. Shapes began to break the surface, and as she realized what they were, she began to laugh hysterically.

Some of them were little better than skeletons. Others still had recognizable features. Water had bloated the bodies, rendering the flesh swollen to the point of bursting. They were vomited up from the river's bottom by the dozens—dead men, women, children and animals, whose sole purpose was to destroy Larissa's enemies for her. She knew she had called them, that they were her allies, just as Misroi had assured her.

A giant wave arose, carrying dozens of the zombies, and crashed aboard the roof. Larissa was knocked down by the force, and gasped for breath as the wave drenched her. Methodically, implacably, Larissa's zombies rose to their feet and, dripping water and ichor, turned on their frozen brethren.

A battle between dead men is a horrific thing to witness. The zombies concentrated on tearing one another into pieces too small to fight. Lond retaliated as best he could, and many of Larissa's zombies were destroyed, but even he could not halt so great a tide, and finally several corpses managed to catch hold of him. He shrieked continuously as they dragged him to the side, then vanished over the edge.

Larissa felt a twinge of something akin to remorse. She had ordered the zombies to stop Lond, but they were bent on destroying him. Or could they somehow make him a zombie as well?

The water roiled again, and a new horror emerged. Foot by foot, yard by impossible yard, a gigantic zombie serpent raised itself from the water until it towered over the boat.

Larissa's throat went dry. She had seen this horrible being before, in one of the nightmares she had had when they had first arrived in Sourange. Then, the monstrous undead snake had spoken with Willen's voice. Now, it undulated back and forth, its huge, slitted, dead eyes fastened on the dancer.

Misroi's voice boomed from the zombie snake's mouth. "Well done, pretty dancer. You survived after all. I'm impressed, I must say. And I do thank you for all the new zombies. They'll be leaving shortly."

With an odd grace, the serpent lowered its massive head until it was just a few feet away from her. She did not cringe away. Bending close, it flicked a rotting tongue as thick as her body. "All, that is, except one, I think. Since you were so very fond of the little meddler, you may keep Willen."

Larissa's heart lurched, and she almost fell. "No," she moaned, soft and low. "Not Willen!" She shrieked his name, glancing around frantically.

The zombie that had been Willen stepped forward woodenly. Larissa gasped, her hands to her mouth, and stared in incredulous horror.

Willen stared back at her impassively. There was no laughter in his eyes anymore, no hint of a smile playing about his lips. All was still and cold. Tentatively, Larissa reached and touched his cheek. The flesh was cool to her touch. She drew back her hand and clenched her fist.

Filled with resolve, Larissa wheeled on the zombie snake. "Anton, I have fought your enemies and prevented Lond from escaping. I have learned your dance and done you honor as a teacher. I ask one great favor from you: restore Willen."

The snake shook its gigantic head. "Poor little dancer," it said in a mockingly remorseful tone. "You don't see it yet, do you? I was right. We are kindred spirits, Larissa. You *are* just like me. If it had been Lond's doing, why, I might indeed have been able to restore life to the body. But the Dance of the Dead is much more powerful than Lond's dabbling. I cannot counteract my own magic."

Larissa's eyes widened with a new horror, the truth shattering her soul. She had been the one who had done this to Willen, not Lond, not even Misroi. Now, too late, she recalled the Maiden asking if Larissa knew the dangers connected with the Dance of the Dead.

"I thought she meant me," Larissa whispered. "I thought she meant it would just hurt *me*. . . ." White hot fury flooded her. She seized the riding crop and hurled it into the water. The dancer screamed at Misroi, "*Why didn't you tell me?*"

The undead snake opened its terrible mouth, and a deep, rumbling laugh issued from it. "Ah, pretty dancer, why should I have bothered? You would have used the magic anyway, since it was the only way for you to stop Alondrin."

The riding crop reappeared suddenly in the dancer's hand. Her keening shriek of rage and sorrow could be heard even by the cast huddling in the theater.

* * * * *

The first rays of dawn broke through the mists and laid gentle fingers upon the sleeping dancer. She had found a brief respite from the horrors thrust upon her and had wept herself into blissful unconsciousness. But the reprieve had ended. Day was dawning, hot and steamy and laden with the promise of an existence of pain.

Dimly, she felt someone draping a blanket around her.

Looking up, she saw that it was Sardan. He glanced swiftly away. "I'm glad you're all right, Larissa," he said softly.

"I'm glad *you're* all right," she returned, her voice raspy from crying. She forced herself to sit up, then rose with Sardan's strong arm around her. As they walked toward the pilothouse, Larissa caught a glimpse of Willen and her knees buckled.

She cursed, angry at herself. "I'm weak as a damned kitten."

"With all you've been through, I'm not surprised."

For the first time, she noticed Sardan's bruised face. Frowning, she touched it gently. Even her tender fingers were too much, and he winced. "What happened to you? Are you hurt?"

Sardan couldn't meet her eyes. "Will did that to me. Knocked me out so I—well, so that I couldn't accidentally watch you—"

Larissa refused to give in to tears. "He always thought of others first," she said thickly. She had thought herself cried out, but her store of tears was apparently endless. "What's happened to the bodies?" she asked as Sardan guided her carefully down from the roof.

He hesitated, and when he answered did not meet her eyes. "They're . . . gone, Larissa. I'm not sure just what's been going on, but the snake—they all left to follow him. Disappeared into the river. Even my poor understudy who had the misfortune to make Dumont angry." He paused. "All except Will."

"Well, at least that's one thing we won't have to take care of ourselves." Larissa heard the words coming out of her own mouth and hardly believed it was she who was speaking them. She sounded callous, cruel—but it was the truth. She could not mourn the dead, not yet. She was the only one who knew the scope of what had happened, and the living needed her right now. Larissa knew she had to be strong for their sake, if not her own. For herself, she almost wished that she had died along with her beloved, but apparently it was not to be that easy.

Larissa ordered an all-hands meeting in the theater. As she entered unsteadily, carrying a steaming mug of strong tea, blanket still wrapped around her, everyone rose. Then, slowly, a few people began to applaud. More joined in, until Larissa received the most heartfelt standing ovation she had ever had in her life. She smiled awkwardly and waved everyone back to their seats as she went onstage. Sardan pulled up a chair for her, and she eased into it thankfully, smiling up at him fleetingly.

It was Jahedrin who first voiced the question everyone wanted to ask.

"Miss Snowmane, are you to be our captain now?"

Larissa glanced sharply at the pilot. "Jahedrin, I don't know the first thing about captaining a boat."

"You're the best qualified to lead us, if maybe not tend to the actual running of *La Demoiselle*. Everyone'd follow you without question. And you could learn."

Surprised, Larissa glanced around at the expectant faces of the remaining cast and crew. They all nodded in agreement. Larissa accepted, then spent the next hour in explanation. Her crew would have to trust her to follow her, and she revealed all of Dumont's secrets—the wards on the boat, the prisoners, Liza's murder. She had expected to be bombarded with questions and interruptions, but everyone hung on her words, eyes wide, slightly unbelieving. Clearly, she was in charge now.

"I love this boat," she told them sincerely. "I would like to keep the show going. There's no reason why we can't continue to provide fine entertainment at a fair price. As for the former prisoners, they are to be treated as honored guests. Anyone who wishes to may leave at any time—that goes for cast and crew as well. Those who would like to stay on and add their magic to *La Demoi*—" She paused suddenly, and the ghost of a smile touched her worn face. "Anyone who wishes to stay aboard *River Dancer* will be hired on fairly."

Gelaar smiled, his arm around his daughter. "Aradnia and I have already decided to stay on," he informed Larissa and the crew. "It was not the boat we hated, it was the captain and his greed."

"Could mademoiselle take me home to Richemulot?" said Bushtail hesitantly. "I know it is a great deal to ask—"

"I don't know when we'll get there, but I'm sure we will. And when we do, Bushtail, you are free to go."

Bushtail bowed his head in gracious acknowledgment. "Until that day, Mademoiselle, I am yours to command."

Skreesha had taken a liking to Gelaar, and the pseudodragon ambled about happily. He had decided that Larissa was to be its new adopted friend and seldom left her side. The colorcat, as usual, didn't seem to care too much about anything. But no one, it seemed, was willing to abandon *River Dancer*.

A few hours later, Larissa got up the courage to attend to her most sorrowful task. First, she went to Dumont's cabin, spying a white scarf almost as soon as she entered. Gently she picked it up and wrapped it about her own slim neck. Larissa took a deep breath to steady herself, then went out onto the bow of the main deck.

Leaning over and peering into the green water, she called in a loud voice, "Flowswift!"

Almost at once, the surface of the water rippled and a beautiful, golden-haired maiden emerged. Her face was alight with joy. "You remembered!" she cried, raising her arms toward Larissa.

Larissa smiled wanly. "Yes, I did. I have a last favor to ask of you." She gestured toward the yawl, tied up to the boat and bobbing placidly. "I'm going to cut this yawl loose in a moment. Please see to it that it doesn't ground or snag on any debris."

The nereid pouted a bit, splashing sullenly. "Don't have forever to do your bidding," she said in a whiny voice. "How long must I guide it?"

Grief clenched at Larissa's throat, but she answered calmly, "You'll know when to stop. Here. And thank you." She dropped the shawl, and the nereid seized it and hugged it tightly, her eyes sparkling with tears. Then she wrapped her shawl about her shoulders and vanished.

Larissa rose slowly, tiredly, and glanced up at the roof of the boat. She cleared her throat. "Willen," she called.

The zombie walked slowly toward the edge of the roof and waited for further orders. "Come down to the main deck," she instructed. Her blue eyes followed him, contrasting his wooden, deliberate movements with the living, supple enthusiasm and grace of the man she had loved. Her heart swelled with pain. Still, she knew she was doing the right thing, that what she was about to do was what Willen would have wanted.

The thing that animated Willen's body—she found it easier to think of it that way—stood before her impassively. "Climb down onto the yawl and sit down," she said. The undead being did so.

Larissa walked over to the small raft and cut it free, dropping the rope into the water. An unseen hand seized the trailing line. Slowly, the yawl with the handsome young zombie began to drift downstream.

She watched him go, her heart full of pain.

"Mademoiselle?"

Larissa wiped at the tears that blurred her vision, and smiled shakily down at Bushtail, who had crept up unnoticed.

"It is hard to lose a friend. You have my sympathy."

Larissa remembered the strange friendship that had sprung up between the fox and rabbit *loahs*. "You miss Bouki, huh?"

"*Oui*. I gave him a last gift when we said our goodbyes. I promised him that his people will be safe from mine for a fortnight in this land."

"That's . . . that's quite a sacrifice for your people, isn't it?"

The fox shrugged his massive shoulders. "*Comme ci, comme ça*. Please remember, though, there are not very many foxes in Souragne." He grinned, showing sharp teeth. "And there are always chickens, no?"

Suddenly, to her own surprise, Larissa laughed. She felt as though, after a long struggle with a thunderstorm, the sun was beginning to rise again in her soul. Impulsively, she reached and threw her arms about the fox. The animal started at first, then chuckled warmly and gave her cheek a quick lick. Larissa got to her feet, took a deep breath, and began to dance.

Her movements took her down the deck, all the way to the stern. At the paddlewheel, she paused. For the last time, she gazed at Willen, still sitting stiffly on the bobbing raft.

"You were never made for this, my love," she said softly. "You were a creature of light. Binding you to earthly matter was wrong, and this kind of existence is monstrous." She raised her arms, closed her eyes, and thought of fire. "Be of light once again."

Willen's body exploded into a blazing fireball. Flowswift, true to her word, continued to pull the yawl on a straight path, and Larissa knew the nereid would continue to do so until the flesh had been consumed. The young captain of *River Dancer* watched sparks swirling and vanishing into the air, hoping against hope that she would see a more beautiful spark than the rest leap freely into the sky . . . but she did not.

There had been enough of death. Now, it was time to mend, to heal. Larissa again began to dance. To her contrition, she felt the *feu follets*, still imprisoned on the boat, and with a thought and a graceful movement set them free. As one, they flew to the burning pyre, dipping and swirling about their lost comrade. She watched them, drinking in their beauty, and then realized with a lurch in her heart that they were "speaking" Willen's name. Brilliant colors radiated from them as they bade their own farewells.

"Forgive me," she whispered, though she knew they already had. "I loved him, too."

Then, to prevent another onslaught of tears, she concentrated on the wood beneath her bare feet. She rooted and spread her consciousness carefully through the boat, making note of *River Dancer*'s "wounds." Her feet began to move, and she focused her thought on the areas that needed repair.

Those who had come to watch her farewell to Willen looked around, shocked, as the boat began to mend itself. Shards of brightly painted paddlewheel spokes moved, met and merged, completely whole, if in need of another coat of red paint. The splinters that had once been the magnificent griffin figurehead rolled together and repaired themselves. Then the great creature flew to its former perch and froze in place.

The metal of the boat—damaged door hinges, bent railings, and the like—would need a smith's touch. Larissa's fruit and flower magic could only mend things that had once been alive. Still, the boat was now as secure as it could be, ready to venture once again into the mists and whatever terrors or new adventures they hid from view.

Those infamous, perilous mists loomed just ahead, but Larissa, for this instant, did not care. She had temporarily found a place of solace, and was lost in bittersweet joy, dancing to keep her heart from breaking.

Sardan, enraptured, leaned against the railing and watched her. Jahedrin came up behind him.

"I thought she was just a girl," the pilot said in a low tone.

"She is," Sardan replied, his heart filled with affectionate admiration. "She's a girl, and a dancer, and a wizard, and a woman who's probably tougher than the rest of the crew combined. But you know what else she is?"

When Jahedrin shook his head, Sardan glanced at him. "She's our captain."

novels

## Vampire of the Mists
Christie Golden

Jander Sunstar, an elven vampire, is pulled into the newly formed dark domain of Barovia and forms an alliance with the land's most powerful inhabitant, Count Strahd Von Zarovich, unaware that Strahd is the very enemy he seeks. Available now.

## Knight of the Black Rose
James Lowder

The cruel death knight Soth finds his way into Ravenloft and discovers that it is far easier to get in than to get out--even with the aid of the powerful vampire lord, Strahd. Available now.

## Heart of Midnight
J. Robert King

Casimir, who inherited his father's lycanthropic curse, fled from both his home and his heritage. Now the young werewolf must embrace his dark powers to prevent his own death and to gain revenge on his monstrous father. Available November 1992.

RAVENLOFT is a trademark owned by TSR, Inc. ©1992 TSR, Inc. All Rights Reserved.

# RAVENLOFT™
### ADVENTURES

# YOUR NEW GUIDE TO VAMPIRES

*"I found her voice thrilling. So seductive her words, I gladly bared my neck. I gasped as she touched my flesh. Then an instant of pleasure so piercing, it was like pain. My heartbeat raced with hers. I was one with the creature."*

The most feared characters in Ravenloft are back: VAMPIRES! The new **Van Richten's Guide to Vampires** is the ultimate Gothic horror vampire guide.

This 96-page treasure is a comprehensive collection of Baron Van Richten's findings on these dark lords. It details how vampires live, think, and act; and what their strengths and weaknesses are, it also includes new rules for running vampires in your game.

Find it at book and hobby stores everywhere before it's too late.

AD&D and ADVANCED DUNGEONS & DRAGONS are registered trademarks owned by TSR, Inc. RAVENLOFT and the TSR logo are trademarks owned by TSR, Inc. ©1992 TSR, Inc. All Rights Reserved.

**BOOKS**

# The Cloakmaster Cycle

### *Beyond the Moons* — David Cook
When a spelljamming ship crashes into Teldin Moore's home on Krynn, a dying alien gives him a mysterious cloak that makes him the target of killers and cutthroats. On sale now.

### *Into the Void* — Nigel Findley
Teldin is plunged into a sea of alien faces when his ship is attacked by space pirates. The mind flayer who rescues him offers to help him learn how to use the powers of the cloak--but for whose gain? On sale now.

### *The Maelstrom's Eye* — Roger E. Moore
Teldin allies with a gypsy kender and is reunited with an old friend, but they must fight to find a genius slug to learn more about the cloak. Both scro forces and the elven Imperial Fleet are in hot pursuit. On sale May 1992.

### *The Radiant Dragon* — Elaine Cunningham
A radiant dragon who also possesses a key to control of the *Spelljammer* joins Teldin in his search for the legendary ship, but the quest is interrupted by the coming of the second Unhuman War. On sale November 1992.

SPELLJAMMER is a trademark owned by TSR, Inc. ©1992 TSR, Inc. All Rights Reserved.

# Invaders of Charon Series
## A New Dimension in Outer Space Adventure!

### *The Genesis Web* Book One
C. M. Brennan

Follow the adventures of Black Barney, from his birth in a RAM laboratory to his daring escape from his evil creators and beyond, into a world of danger and intrigue. On sale April 1992.

### *Nomads of the Sky* Book Two
William H. Keith, Jr.

The mysterious, dreaded Space Nomads take Vincent Perelli prisoner, forcing him to fight a ritual battle for survival before he can seek the Device, a missing RAM artifact that may save the life of Buck Rogers. On sale November 1992.

XXVc is a trademark used under license from The Dille Family Trust.
The TSR logo is a trademark owned by TSR, Inc. ®1992 The Dille Family Trust. All Rights Reserved.